THEY ALL WANTED A PIECE OF ERIN CONNOLLY

Her millionaire husband, ANTHONY WELLING-TON—He called her bluff and called in a seven-figure debt.

The brilliant young director, GARTH WERNER —He taught her about love, and learned about betrayal.

Hollywood's hottest columnist, LYNN POWERS —She had a score to settle with the bitch who stole her man.

The "New Brando," DEREK MARSTON—He taught her everything he knew about decadence, line by line.

The lawyer with "connections," ARNOLD SCORSI—He wouldn't take money, but he did take everything else.

WINNERS AND LOSERS

WINNERS
AND
LOSERS

BY
JODIE RHODES

A JOVE BOOK

A Jove Book/published by arrangement with
the author

PRINTING HISTORY
Jove edition/July 1982

ISBN: 0-515-06420-3

Jove books are published by Jove Publications, Inc., 200 Madison
Avenue, New York, N. Y. 10016. The words "A JOVE BOOK" and the
"J" with sunburst are trademarks belonging to Jove Publications, Inc.

PRINTED IN THE UNITED STATES OF AMERICA

FOR BARRY

The best friend a writer could ever have

with gratitude and affection

Jodie

Prologue

"WILL you *please* stop telling me you're just his answering service?" Erin screamed. Her hands trembled as she shook a cigarette out of the pack. She lit it with the solid gold Dunhill lighter that had her name engraved on it in an elegant script. "Now look," she continued, dropping her voice to the warm, low contralto that had successfully charmed a number of people into doing things they didn't want to, "I, of all people, understand Keith Ramsey's need for privacy. As the most exciting and sought-after actor in the industry today, I know he's constantly besieged by people who want to grab a piece of his glory. But I am *not* one of those people. I am Erin Connolly, and I assure you that Keith will be not merely upset but infuriated if he learns that you have refused to put me in touch with him."

"Erin Connolly?" the girl from the service repeated uncertainly. "Are you a personal friend? I don't see your name on this list he gave me."

So he had left a number where he could be reached! Erin slumped back in the specially designed Eames chair and breathed a sigh of relief. You never knew about that independent bastard. He'd been known to disappear for months at a time with no one knowing his whereabouts.

"My dear," Erin said softly, "I am a little more than a personal friend. I am his *career*. You see, I produce his pictures," she lied smoothly. "And he has been waiting for word on a major script that I've been negotiating for. Well, I've got it for him, and I need to talk to him immediately!"

"Oh!" The girl sounded slightly awed. "In that case, I'll certainly pass your message on to him right away. Could you give me your number?"

"There's no need for that," Erin said quickly. "Just tell me how to contact him, and I'll call him myself."

"I can't do that," the girl said firmly. "Mr. Ramsey specifically instructed me to do nothing but pass on messages."

"I think you're making a major mistake, young lady," Erin said threateningly. "Mr. Ramsey could lose the most important role of his career due to your obstruction. Would you give me your name and the name of your supervisor?"

"My . . . my name is Susan Laskey, and my supervisor is Mrs. Morganstern, but you won't be able to reach her until tomorrow." The girl started to cry. "I'm sorry, Miss Connolly, but I have to do what I'm told."

Jesus Christ, Erin muttered to herself. Have I sunk so low I'm now down to intimidating dumb kids from an answering service?

"It's all right, Susan," she said. "You're doing the right thing. Just make sure that Keith calls me as soon as possible. I'll give you two numbers."

"Thank you very much, Miss Connolly." The girl sniffled as she wrote down Erin's business and home phone.

The minute Erin hung up the receiver, her intercom button flashed red. She punched it down and picked up the phone.

"Yes, Nancy, what is it *now*?" she asked.

"Sheldon Avery is on line two. He's been waiting almost five minutes, and he's really steamed."

"Oh God." Erin groaned. "That's all I need right now." She picked up the cigarette which had burned down to the filter, then angrily stubbed it out. "All right, I'll take him."

"Hi, Shel. Really sorry to keep you waiting, but the damn phones have been screwed up all afternoon. Would you believe that I placed a call to Marty Jessup at CBS in New York and ended up talking with a housewife in Crestline, Ohio? I mean, honestly . . ."

"Just cut out the shit, will you?" Sheldon said furiously. "I want to know *now* if Keith Ramsey has signed a contract for the part."

"Shel, luv, what in the *world* has got you so upset?" Erin's voice oozed worried concern.

"You know damn well what! I've been stalling my agent for two weeks now because I was nuts enough to believe you when you said you could deliver Ramsey. You got any idea what it's like to stall Irving?"

Erin laughed. "Darling, I most certainly do. It's like trying to stall a bulldozer that's headed straight at you with its throttle open full."

"It's not funny, Erin. Irving told me today that Columbia's dropping the option on my book unless they get a definite commitment in the next forty-eight hours. That's a million dollars we're talking about, *darling*," he added viciously. "So it's put-up or shut-up time for you."

"I don't much care for your tone of voice," Erin said evenly. She lit another cigarette and inhaled deeply, trying to control the tremors that were beginning to make her body shake like a rag doll's. God, how I need a line, she thought frantically. With a tremendous act of will power, she fought off the need and concentrated on Sheldon Avery.

"Now I *do* understand the kind of pressures you've been under," she murmured, "so I think I can excuse that last remark. But I would appreciate it if you'd remember that you're not talking to some cheap, one-shot producer or money-hungry agent. You're talking to Erin Connolly who, among other things, won both the Oscar and the Cannes Film Festival award for *Street Scene*."

"That Oscar was four years ago," Sheldon snapped. "What have you won lately?"

For one terrifying second Erin went completely blind as the white rage generated by Sheldon's remarks blazed inside her. She groped for the smoldering cigarette and gave a trembling sigh of relief when she was finally able to see the small, glowing red ember. A few seconds later the room came back into focus and she looked up gratefully at the late afternoon sun streaming through the sheer curtains and reflecting off the brilliant paintings hung on her walls.

"Hello? Hello? For Christ's sake, is anyone there?"

"Sorry, Shel," Erin said calmly. "Must be those damn phone lines acting up again. Anyway, to get back to what we were talking about, I'd like you to answer one question for me. And I want you to think about it very carefully before you answer." She paused for a beat and when she did speak again there was an almost solemn tone to her voice.

"Do you really believe wholeheartedly and without reservations, as I do, that Keith Ramsey is the only actor alive today who can be totally trusted to portray the most important character you've ever created without compromising the artistic integrity you wrote your guts out to give him?"

"Well yes, of course I do," Sheldon said, momentarily distracted by the thought of his artistic integrity being compromised. "But . . ."

"No buts," Erin said firmly. "That's the answer I was looking for, and you gave it to me. Now, can Columbia guarantee you Keith Ramsey?"

"You know damn well they can't. There isn't a studio in town who can, because nobody knows how to reach him." Sheldon's suspicions flared up again. "And I think that includes you."

"Really?" she replied coolly. "Then it must have been my overactive imagination that spent a full sixty minutes earlier today talking to that very same Keith Ramsey. He absolutely loved your script, by the way."

There was a stunned silence on the other end of the line. When Sheldon finally managed to speak, he was so excited his voice cracked.

"He did? I mean, he really *said* that?"

"Among other things. Like it was one of the few scripts he's ever read that was worthy of the book that inspired it. He told me something else I think you might be interested in hearing. 'Erin,' he said in that marvelous, deep resonant voice of his. 'When I finished this, I knew I was holding an Academy Award picture in my hands.' "

"My God. Oh my God, I can't tell you what that means to me," Sheldon babbled. "I am so *thrilled*! Did you know Keith Ramsey has always been an idol of mine? My whole life I've dreamed of having him play one of my characters."

"Of course."

"Well, this is such wonderful news I hardly know what to say. Listen, Erin, please accept my apologies for the way I talked earlier. I was just so *uptight* with this deadline hanging over my head that I didn't know what I was saying." He gave a small, embarrassed laugh. "I know this probably sounds a little crazy, but do you think there's any chance you could set up a luncheon or something where I could meet him in person now that he's signed the contract?" Sheldon paused. "He *did* sign the contract, didn't he?"

"Luv, can you imagine that he wouldn't after the way he turned on to the script?"

"Erin, that's not an answer." There was a sudden ominous note in Sheldon's voice. "Now, either he did or he didn't. Which is it?"

"Honestly, Shel, sometimes I wonder why I put up with you." Erin sighed. "I give you everything you've ever asked for and in return I get hit with your paranoid fears. No!" she said sharply as he started to protest. "You listen to *me*! Now I told you I just finished talking with Keith. The operative word is *talking*. As your own wonderful agent along with all those super powerful studios reported to you," she said sarcastically, "no one could get Ramsey for your picture because no one could reach him. Well, *I* reached Keith Ramsey and sent him your script. And he called *me* to say he wanted to do it. But he's two thousand miles away in one of his hideouts. So we're just going to have to wait till he gets back for the actual signing."

"I can't wait, Erin."

"Then you want to lose the whole thing?"

"Look," Sheldon said desperately. "You know I don't want to lose him, and I'd never ask him to come back here just to sign a contract. But I *have* to have that contract. Now you know where he is, so why can't you fly up to wherever that is and have him sign it there?"

"You really ask a lot, Shel."

"I'll pay you for it," Sheldon said frantically. "The plane tickets, your time, whatever you want to charge. I don't have any other choice. Do you understand that? Forty-eight hours. That's all I've got."

"I understand," Erin said slowly. "Okay, Shel, I'll get back to you."

A faint sheen of perspiration covered her face as she hung up the phone. She twisted the slim gold charm bracelet that circled her left wrist, her fingers closing on the miniature snuff box dangling from it. A rapid pulse beat in her throat as she released the catch and gazed hungrily at the fine white powder inside.

Don't do it, an inner voice warned her. You promised yourself you'd never use it in the office, because you know once you start, you won't be able to stop.

She forced her fingers to close the lid and swallowed hard as a wave of nausea flooded her mouth with the bitter taste of bile.

There was a hesitant tap at the door. "Excuse me, Erin." Nancy peeked in. "I just wanted to check and see if there was anything else you wanted me to do before I left for the night."

Erin gazed at her blankly for a moment then blinked. "Is it five already?"

"Five-thirty, actually."

"It *is*?" Erin looked at her watch, a faintly startled expression on her face. "The day seems to have gotten away from me," she said vaguely. "I'm sorry to have kept you overtime."

"Oh for heaven's sake, you didn't keep me overtime!" Nancy burst out impulsively. "Why, I remember when we worked straight through till ten o'clock every night and . . ." She stopped abruptly.

"It's all right," Erin said gently as she watched Nancy flush crimson. "I remember too. But don't worry," she announced with sudden grim determination. "We're going to get those days back!"

"You betcha," Nancy grinned. "We'll show 'em all! Right?"

"Right," Erin smiled. The smile faded as she thought of the forty-eight-hour deadline facing her. Sheldon Avery's script was her last, her only chance to make a comeback. But she was going to lose it unless she got Keith Ramsey. And at the moment she couldn't think of a single way to do that.

"Are you okay?" Nancy asked anxiously.

"What?" Erin's fingers had gone back to the charm bracelet, caressing the tiny, gold snuff box. She let go of it quickly and reached for a cigarette.

"Of course I'm okay," she said, forcing the smile back on her face. "Now run along, Nancy, and enjoy your evening."

"You're sure?"

"I'm sure. Now scat!" she said firmly.

"Well, all right then." Nancy started for the door, stopped abruptly, and whirled around.

"Oh wow, I almost forgot! David called and asked me to remind you that he was picking you up for dinner at seven." She grinned and gave a cheerful wave as she headed back for the door.

"Have a nice evening," she called over her shoulder. "You deserve it."

The traffic was unusually heavy as Erin headed west on Wilshire Boulevard toward the elegant high-rise apartment building that dominated the skyline of the expensive Westwood Village area.

She whipped her white Porsche around the big Cadillacs and Lincoln Continentals that moved with maddening slowness in front of her, switching from one lane to another, accelerating rapidly as she came up to each intersection, trying to beat the light.

She pulled up to the iron gates that guarded the entrance to the underground garage of her apartment building and inserted her plastic card into the electronic lock.

"Shit!" she said angrily as she looked at her watch. Despite all her frenetic maneuverings to get home quickly, it was six-twenty. She raced the car through the opened gates and slotted it into her parking space.

Erin had been counting on at least an hour to relax and pull herself together before David arrived. Now she'd barely have thirty minutes by the time she got up to her apartment. That was hardly enough time to bathe and dress, and certainly left no time for the relaxation she so desperately needed.

And if David was in one of his sullen, depressed moods . . . which was about the only mood he'd been in for the past month, she thought irritably . . . then she was going to have to deal with that along with everything else that had gone wrong on this rotten, miserable day. It was just too fucking much!

Well, the hell with it. There's no law that says I have to meet his damn seven o'clock timetable. He made the date, not me. So I'll do what I need for me, and he can wait till I'm ready!

Erin stepped off the elevator on the lobby floor to check her mailbox. It was stuffed with envelopes: bills from Saks, Bonwit Teller's, Gucci's, Giorgio's, Jorgensens, and Vendome Liquors. There was also a small white envelope, unstamped, from the manager of her building reminding her that the rent on her apartment was now five days overdue. "Welcome home," she announced with a grim smile. "It sure is good to get all these loving letters from family and friends." She shoved the envelopes into her bag and walked back across the lobby to the elevator, stepping inside as it opened with a faint hissing sound. She pressed the button for the penthouse apartment.

The six-foot grandfather clock bonged one slow, solemn note as she walked into her apartment. Erin had discovered it in an antique shop in a small Connecticut town four years ago and had paid for refinishing and shipping to California at ten times its original cost.

"I know," she muttered to it as she switched on the light. "It's six-thirty." She shivered as a cold blast from the air conditioner hit her. "Goddamnit." *Why* couldn't she remember to turn the damn thing off when she left in the morning? That's going to be another hundred-dollar electric bill, she thought unhappily.

She walked quickly into the living room and clicked off the switch, then pulled back the drapes and opened the sliding glass doors to the balcony that looked out on the distant Santa Monica mountains.

Erin stepped out on the balcony, taking a deep breath and

throwing back her head as she looked up at the brilliant stars dotting the sky, their presence revealed by the Santa Ana winds that had swept down from the mountains, blowing the ugly smog out to sea. She shivered, but this time it had nothing to do with the temperature of the apartment. This was an inner chill that only one thing could help.

She turned and almost ran to the bathroom, pulling open the narrow drawer recessed under the handsome marble vanity counter. Taking out the round tin and short plastic tube that lay next to it, she knelt down, carefully lifted the lid off the tin container and positioned the tube over the white powder inside it. She inhaled quick and hard into the right nostril, waited a second, then switched the tube to her left nostril. It was an instant high. She smiled in pleasure as she leaned back against the tub and let the plastic tube fall on the bathroom rug, her hand rubbing absently across her stomach. Slowly she slid down the zipper on her hand-tailored suede skirt and tossed the skirt on top of the counter, then began pulling off her pantyhose. The sheer material caught on her thigh and she reached inside to free it. The soft, searching touch of her fingers, so close to the sensitive lips inside the moist pubic hair, sent her into an immediate orgasm.

Her body spasmed ecstatically, but it was over almost before she'd had a chance to realize what had happened. "Too quick," she mourned. "Not fair." She turned around and smiled at the tub. "I've got an idea," she told it. Giggling, she turned the faucets on full and reached for the bottle of Vitabath Pink, pouring the thick gelée into the water until the tub foamed with bubbles. She stripped off the rest of her clothes, picked up the plastic tube and held it over the tin for one more quick snort, then plunged into the bathtub, splashing water and bubbles all over the bathroom.

For a brief second, all the stars in the sky appeared in front of her as the second hit of cocaine whirled her senses around. "Beautiful," she murmured, "absolutely beautiful." She let herself slide down into the tub until nothing was supporting her except her feet braced against the faucets, the back of her head now barely above water level and her hair soaked with the rich, pink bubbles. Her hand slid down between her legs, moving with long, smooth strokes back and forth across her clitoris. Easy now, she warned herself. You want it to last and last and last.

"Oh God, oh God, that's so good," she moaned as orgasm after orgasm flooded her. She kept her finger on her clitoris, pressing down hard now and moving it faster and faster until her entire body exploded into a climactic spasm so intense she almost passed out. When the frantic pounding of her heart finally subsided, she felt a delicious languor enveloping her as though she were floating on clouds. Faintly, she heard chimes. They stopped for a moment and then sounded again.

"Jesus Christ!" she exclaimed, sitting up abruptly. It was the doorbell. It was David! She scrambled out of the tub, grabbing a robe and wrapping it around her as she ran to the door, her bare feet leaving damp imprints on the thick pile carpet.

"Well, aren't we bright-eyed tonight," David said dryly as he stepped inside.

Erin flushed. "Really, David your attitude toward coke is positively archaic! Absolutely *everyone* uses it these days, and nobody thinks a thing about it."

"Must be my age," he said with a cold smile. "All us old men grew up on liquor."

"Good heavens, I'm forgetting my manners," she said quickly, eager to change the subject. "Let me fix you a drink."

"Why don't I fix my own and let you get dressed?"

"You're a dear." She blew him a kiss and pattered down the hall to her bedroom. She stood in front of the closet that took up one whole wall, trying to decide what to wear. She finally settled on the red velvet pantsuit that had set her back five hundred dollars.

But it was worth every penny, she thought happily as she admired her image in the mirror. The pants, which she wore without any underwear, clearly outlined her small waist, flat tummy, slim hips, and firm, tight ass. The short velvet jacket was cut to reveal the low-necked white silk blouse with its crisp ruffled front. The contrast of the sheer white blouse against the rich red velvet jacket set off to perfection the small, triangular face with its flawless ivory complexion, brilliant jade-green eyes and lustrous short cap of dark hair.

"Not bad for a thirty-year-old broad," she announced thoughtfully to the mirror. Then she laughed. "Hell, it's damn good for a *twenty*-year-old broad." She did a quick pirouette, lost her balance, and fell against the bed. Ooops. Shouldn't have taken that second snort. She turned the charm bracelet around, checking the supply in the miniature snuff box. Enough for a quick one after dinner. Better make that her limit for today.

"Well, I'm ready," Erin announced brightly as she appeared in the entranceway of the living room. "Now that didn't take too long, did it?" Then her eyes widened in shock as she saw the oversized double old-fashioned glass in David's hand which was filled to the brim with a dark amber liquid.

"My God, David, is that all *Scotch* in there?"

"You don't mind, do you?" He raised the glass and gulped down a third of its contents.

"No, of course not," she said uncertainly. "It's just that I . . . well, I've never seen you drink like that."

He gave her a twisted grin. "I'm celebrating," he announced. "An anniversary."

"Anniversary?" She looked at him blankly. "What anniversary?"

He took another large swallow. "I guess it was foolish of me to think you'd remember. You see, it was exactly a year ago tonight that I left my wife and family for you."

Erin's eyes narrowed in anger. "Is this going to be one of those blame-Erin-for-everything-that's-gone-wrong evenings? Because if it is, I'm going to cancel it right now before it starts."

"Oh no, my love, you're not going to cancel this evening," he said softly. "This is very definitely a noncancelable evening."

He stood up and walked over to her, his hand cupping her chin and tilting it up to him as he kissed her lightly on the lips. "You're looking unusually beautiful and desirable tonight," he murmured in the deep, warm voice that had turned her on so totally when she first met him.

Unexpectedly, tears stung her eyes as she looked at the husky, broad-shouldered man with the dark, intense eyes and remembered how things had been then. They'd been so much in love, so ecstatically, wondrously in love that the whole world had glowed. And he'd been everything to her. Friend, lover, the father she'd always longed for. Why had it gone wrong? Why had she lost it?

"I still love you, David," she said tremulously.

"Do you?" He looked at her intently. "But you're not *in* love with me anymore, are you?"

"I don't know." She gave a helpless shrug. "If only . . ."

"If only you still wanted to go to bed with me," he interjected harshly. "That happens to be one hell of an if, doesn't it?"

"I can't help it," she said unhappily. "It's not something I can force."

"But you're not the kind of woman who can go too long without a man," he said broodingly. His eyes clouded. "Soon, very soon, you'll find someone who turns you on," he murmured half to himself. "And that's the one thing I cannot stand to see."

"David, you *promised* it wasn't going to be one of those evenings. I told you, I just can't take it tonight."

"That's right. You did, didn't you?" He smiled suddenly, an engaging smile that lit up his face. "Well, as a man who keeps his promises, I now declare a moratorium on the subject. It shall never be mentioned again." He offered her his arm. "Shall we leave for dinner, my lady?"

"Oh Christ, I almost forgot!" she groaned. "David, I've got to call my answering service and tell them where I'll be this evening. Where are we having dinner?"

He frowned. "You're not planning to meet anyone later tonight, are you?"

"Don't be silly. Of course I'm not." She patted his cheek. "It's just a business thing."

"What kind of a business thing?" he asked suspiciously.

"It's a long story." She smiled. "No, that's not true. It's a very short story. About forty-six hours short, now. I'll tell you about it at dinner. Which is going to be? . . ."

He hesitated. "I made reservations at Chianti's," he said finally.

Erin lifted her eyebrows, wondering just what was going on in that complex head of David's. The small, elegant restaurant with its crisp old world formality had been "their place" for every special occasion in their lives. It was where they'd first admitted they were in love with each other. It was the place where David told her he was getting a divorce and wanted to marry her. It was where they first talked about having a child. Her eyes closed in sudden pain at the last memory.

"I hope you don't mind," David said quickly. "I was just hungry for their food, that's all."

"No, I don't mind." She forced a smile. "Now that I think about it, I'm a little hungry for their food myself."

He looked relieved. "Good. You go ahead and call your answering service, then, while I finish my drink."

The maître d' broke into a delighted smile as Erin and David walked into the restaurant, and rushed toward them.

"Miss Connolly, Mr. Bernstein, what a *pleasure* to see you again. It has been so long!" He looked at them reproachfully. "Why do you stay away for such a time? It is not right for friends to behave so."

"You're absolutely right, Henry," David agreed solemnly. "But you see Miss Connolly's business has been most demanding lately. And how could I come here without her?"

"Ah." Henry nodded. "In that case, you are forgiven." Then he shook a reproving finger at Erin. "But you must not let business deprive you of the joys of life. Work less and enjoy more," he commanded her as he led them briskly to their booth where a waiter stood at attention. "The lobster Fra Diavolo is superb tonight."

"Henry never changes, does he?" Erin laughed as David gave their drink orders and the waiter scurried away to fill them. "He's been making that same speech for as long as I can remember."

"Henry is one of the few things in life that remains constant," David said somberly.

"Hey," she warned. "You promised no gloom tonight."

The waiter appeared at that moment with their drinks. "Would you like to see a menu now, sir?"

"No, we want to relax for a few minutes first." David picked up his double Scotch on the rocks and leaned toward Erin as though he were about to propose a toast. Then his eyes, which had been fixed on her, suddenly grew distant. He brought the glass to his lips and drank deeply, staring into space.

Erin shifted uncomfortably as the brief pause in their conversation grew into a lengthy silence. She had already lost the fine edge of her cocaine high, and the gentle euphoria that usually followed it was quickly dissipating under David's erratic mood shifts. She sipped quickly at her martini, trying to bring back the glow, but the continuing silence was rapidly fraying her nerves.

"How are things in politics these days?" she asked with determined brightness.

"So so," David replied briefly. "How are things in the silver-screen business?"

"Worse than so so," she said with a grimace, taking a cigarette out of her purse and inhaling sharply as David lit it for her. "Christ, I don't know what I'm going to do if I lose this picture!" She began telling him in detail about the conversation with Sheldon Avery, then trailed off as she saw the amused glint in his eyes.

"And just what the hell do you find so funny about all this?"

"Your attitude." He smiled. "To hear you tell it, you're the innocent victim of a cruel and malicious fate. While the truth is it's your own sweet, charming, lying, cheating, conniving, manipulating self that put you in this box."

"Why you supercilious son of a bitch!" she spat, white with rage. "Who the shit do you think you are to talk to me that way?!"

"The person who knows you better than anyone else in the world," he said, the faint smile still on his face.

"Don't flatter yourself," she said contemptuously. "After all, you're just one in a long line of men who felt the same way."

David's fists clenched involuntarily as rage blazed out of his eyes. With a visible effort, he regained his composure.

"Well, that tender loving moment in your apartment didn't last long, did it?"

"None of them do." Erin was furious. "Because you spoil them all. We should have ended this whole relationship two months ago like I wanted to. It's become destructive for both of us, and I have enough problems without having you drag me down too."

"Poor Erin. You do suffer terribly, don't you?" he mocked.

"There was a time you cared about my problems. Now all you care about is your own sick self!"

"That's certainly sick," he agreed coldly. "After all, what could be more important than the meteoric rise and fall of Hollywood's most important producer? Especially when her fall is almost as meteoric as her rise."

"You have two choices. We can order, or you can take me home now. And frankly I don't much care which you choose as long as I don't have to talk to you. Because I am really, finally, finished with you. I just hate to hurt Henry's feelings."

"By all means let us spare Henry's feelings." David signaled the waiter, who appeared immediately at his elbow.

"Henry wanted us to have the lobster Fra Diavolo, shall we go along with that too, for Henry?"

"Just order it and let's get this travesty over with," she hissed.

"The lobster Fra Diavolo for two," David told the waiter. "And a bottle of Pouilly Fuissé." He glanced at Erin. "Unless the lady wants another drink?"

"No, just the wine." She looked up at the waiter. "And could you bring it now?"

"Of course, madame." He bowed politely before leaving.

"You sound a little desperate," David observed. "Lost your high, didn't you? Want to go into the ladies room and powder your nose?"

"Very funny." The unpleasant truth was that he'd read her all too accurately, as usual. She was coming down faster and harder than she could ever remember. But she was damned if she'd let the bastard see how badly she needed the cocaine. Just hold on for a little while longer, she told herself through gritted teeth. Then you can really relax and enjoy it once you get home and David's gone.

The waiter arrived with the Pouilly Fuissé, presented it for

David's approval, then filled Erin's glass. To Erin's horror, her hand shook so badly as she lifted it to her lips that the wine spilled over the edge, making an ugly stain on the tablecloth. Her eyes fiercely dared David to say a word. To her relief, he said nothing as the waiter quickly mopped up and left to bring the entrée.

"Miss Connolly?" Henry appeared suddenly in front of them, a frown on his face. "There's a telephone call for you. Do you wish to take it?"

Erin's face lit up. "Indeed I do, Henry!" She looked triumphantly at David. "I told you I'd get through to Ramsey," she gloated as Henry brought the phone to the table.

"Hello, this is Erin Connolly," she announced with a vibrant warmth.

"It's Susan Laskey," the worried young voice answered. "I'm terribly sorry to disturb you at dinner, but you did say how important it was to call you. The thing is . . . well, I haven't been able to reach Mr. Ramsey. His housekeeper at the lodge told me he's backpacking in the mountains and isn't expected for at least another day."

"For Christ's sake, don't they have forest rangers or something that can reach him in an emergency?" Erin's voice rose in frustrated rage.

"I . . . I really don't know anything about that. Is it really an emergency?"

"His whole career is hanging in the balance and you ask me if it's an emergency?" Erin took a deep breath and lowered her voice. "Susan, maybe I didn't explain it fully. If Keith doesn't get back to me in the next twenty-four hours he's going to lose it all. The script, the picture, the Academy Award. Now do you understand?"

"I didn't realize all that, Miss Connolly. Let me try to reach him again."

"Mr. Ramsey and I would both appreciate that, Susan. Just make sure you succeed this time." She hung up the phone with a crash.

"Bravo!" David smiled sardonically. "A virtuoso performance."

"Oh just shut up." Erin dug in her purse for another cigarette and lit it herself, blowing the smoke across the table as her mind raced furiously. If this kid from the answering service did reach Ramsey, would he call her? Yes, she decided, he would. Not because her dramatic messages would arouse his curiosity. He was too smart and savvy to fall for that. No, the reason he'd call her would be to give her hell for scaring that little Susan Laskey half to death. Which was just fine with her. All she needed was that vital personal contact with him. Once she got that, somehow she'd figure out a way to persuade him to read the script, even if she did have to end up doing what Sheldon had begged her and fly up to that godforsaken wilderness where Ramsey was camped out. But the timing is so goddamn fuckin' tight, she thought desperately. What if he doesn't come back to his crappy rustic lodge before the forty-eight-hour deadline is up? Well he's going to, she told herself. I am *willing* him to come back, and it's going to happen.

"Pardon me, madame."

Erin looked up, startled, as the waiter stood patiently beside her, holding the steaming plate of lobster Fra Diavolo. "Sorry," she murmured automatically, leaning back to allow him to set it down in front of her. Her eyes focused on David, who was staring at her with a peculiarly intent expression.

"Are you all right?" she asked apprehensively.

"Couldn't be better." He continued to stare at her with the strange glitter in his eyes. "And how are you?"

"Tired." She eyed him carefully. "I'm really very tired, David. I'd appreciate your taking me home as soon as we finish dinner."

"That's too bad," he frowned. "I'd planned for us to go to the Polo Lounge."

"The Polo Lounge?" she said incredulously. "David, what *is* it with you this evening? Considering how things are between us now, this nostalgia thing with dinner here tonight was a bit much. But going to the Polo Lounge is *really* too much. That's absolutely wallowing in sentimentality. No," she said emphatically. "We're not going to the Polo Lounge. You can take me home, or I'll call a cab."

"Don't get upset," he said softly. "I'll take you home. But I have to make a phone call first." He stood up abruptly and walked away, leaving Erin to gaze after him bewildered.

An elderly man carrying a miniature poodle under his arm was coming out of Erin's building as she and David walked up to the entrance. He smiled and held the door open for them, bidding them a pleasant good evening as he set the dog down and headed off down the block.

"Some swell maximum-security building," Erin grumbled as they crossed the lobby to the elevator. "Might as well send out engraved invitations to every burglar in West L.A. and be done with it."

"Um," David murmured noncommitally.

Erin shrugged irritably and gave up all attempts at polite conversation as they rode in silence to her floor. The headache which had started in the restaurant was now pounding steadily at her temples, and her hand rubbed nervously at the charm bracelet on her wrist. Soon, she told herself. Very soon.

One of the hall lights had burned out, and Erin stumbled as she stepped out of the elevator, cursing under her breath as she fumbled in her purse for the key to her apartment.

"It's all right, I've got it," David said as he opened the door.

She glared at him in outrage as he reached inside and switched on the light in the foyer. "Goddamnit, David, what are you doing with a key to my place?"

"Don't get so excited. It's an extra one I just discovered after I gave you back the others."

"Just discovered? Don't give me that shit! I know damn well you've kept it all this time. What the fuck were you planning to do with it? Catch me with someone else? Well, maybe that's what you deserve. But it's not going to happen that way. So give it back to me right now," she demanded.

"I was planning to," he smiled. "We'll have a nightcap, and I'll turn over all the keys of your kingdom to you."

"No nightcap," she said grimly. "Just the key."

"Well, then just the key." He looked down at her, his body blocking the doorway. "But I do have to bring you your gift."

"Oh Christ, David, no more gifts!" she exclaimed. "You're

always bringing me gifts, like you think they're going to solve all our problems. Just give me the key."

"No, this time you're wrong. You want this," he insisted. "It will only take me a minute to bring it up from the car."

"David, *please*. Just leave me in peace tonight. I am totally wiped, and I need to be alone. Can't you understand that?"

"Of course I understand that," he said gravely. "That's why you need this."

"All right," she said resignedly. "Bring me the gift. But do me a favor, okay? Bring it into the bedroom where I am going immediately to collapse. You can leave it there along with the key."

Erin padded down the hallway to her bedroom without waiting for David's response, kicking off her shoes and unbuttoning the white silk blouse.

"What a waste," she muttered as she walked into the bedroom and stared into the mirror. "Five hundred dollars worth of clothes for a two-bit evening." Angrily, she ripped off the pants and jacket, threw off the blouse, then crawled into bed, pulling the covers up to her chin and closing her eyes.

She didn't hear the soft opening and closing of the door when David returned, and the thick-pile carpet muffled the sound of his footsteps as he walked down the hall and into the bedroom. The first intimation she had of his presence was when the bed moved under his weight as he sat down at the foot of it.

Her eyes opened lazily and she turned her head to the pillow next to her, David's favorite place for putting the beautiful, expensive presents he loved to get her. But there was nothing there. Puzzled, she turned away and looked down the length of the bed. She gave a short, choked gasp as she saw the gun in David's hand. He held it loosely, its long black barrel pointed at her.

"What kind of filthy, sick joke is this?" she demanded hoarsely.

"It's not a joke, Erin."

"Stop it, David! Stop it this minute!" She sat up in the bed, clutching the covers to her. "This cheap melodramatic trick is beneath you. Now take that ugly thing out of here *right now*!"

His fingers played with the gun, turning it over so that it lay flat in his palm for a moment. He gazed at it idly, then brought it upright again, the snout directed at Erin.

"I am warning you, David, I will not put up with this! You take that thing out of here or I'm calling the police."

"Are you afraid?" He smiled at her, amused. "That would certainly be something to see. I thought Erin Connolly was never afraid of anything."

"I am not afraid," she said evenly. "I am disgusted. Now do you take it away or do I call the police? You may not care about yourself or me anymore, but I don't think you'll want your kids reading about something like this."

"Oh, they'll understand," he said quietly. "They know what it's been like for me lately." He looked at her quizzically. "I thought you realized that. Didn't you know I was calling them when I left you there for a moment in the restaurant?"

And then for the first time Erin was afraid. It was impossible, of course. This whole scene was impossible. David couldn't do a thing like that, she told herself. She swallowed hard as she looked at the man who'd given her so much love. The man she'd loved at one time almost as much as she needed him. No, this couldn't be real. It was just another Hollywood scenario. He would beg her forgiveness when it was over, and she'd make him pay long and hard before she gave it to him. But eventually she'd forgive him. Despite everything, they were still too close to stay away from each other for very long.

"I'm calling your bluff," she announced with narrowed eyes. "Right now!" As she reached for the phone, the shockingly loud report of the gun echoed throughout the room, making her ears ring.

David leaned forward on the bed, his arms outstretched as though he were reaching for her, and Erin dropped the phone as she flung aside the covers and held out her hands toward him. But she was too far away and he slid off the bed to the floor, dragging the bedspread with him. She scrambled frantically over the rumpled bed to where he had fallen.

"David? David, what did you do?" she whispered.

His eyes were open, looking at her, and tears of relief streamed down her cheeks. "Oh, David, you fool, you goddamn fool," she cried. "How could you do a stupid thing like this?"

He refused to answer her, and rage mixed with her tears of relief. She grabbed his shoulders, shaking him savagely. "Tell me," she commanded. "Tell me how you could try such a thing!"

His head fell against her breast. It was terribly, terribly heavy. And then she knew he wasn't going to answer her. Ever.

One

THE nurse was young, and her soft brown eyes were filled with empathetic pain as she watched the woman writhe under the constricting straps that held her to the operating table.

"Don't be embarrassed to cry out," she whispered as she gently wiped away the beads of perspiration from the woman's forehead. "It's a perfectly natural reaction, and it will make you feel better too. Let you relax some of those tense muscles."

Sheila Connolly glared at the nurse, the cords in her throat prominent. "Thank you just the same," she managed to say through gritted teeth, "but I'll do it my way." Then her body spasmed again, and her small white even teeth involuntarily closed on her full lower lip, blood spurting from the sharp bite.

"Good! That was very good!" Aaron Goldman announced enthusiastically. The chubby, balding gynecologist was perspiring almost as much as his patient, for the labor had been going on for almost fourteen hours now and he had been seriously considering performing a cesarean section for the past four. Now it looked like he'd been right to wait, and he gave silent thanks to whatever gods had come to his aid. Cesareans were tricky at best.

"One more big push like that, and I think we'll be there," he said encouragingly. "Come on now, Mrs. Connolly."

Doggedly, Sheila tried to obey. But she was so tired, so goddamn tired. Then nature took over for her, and she felt a convulsive thrust so powerful that for a terrified moment she feared her body was exploding.

The sharp furious cry of the infant echoed for a second in the operating room, then was drowned out by wild yells, screaming, and what sounded like a salvo of gunfire.

"Jesus Christ, what's going on?" Aaron Goldman shouted, his hands clutching at the small slippery body in an instinctive gesture of protection.

A terrified intern sprinted across the operating room and gingerly opened one door, trembling visibly as he peered out. Then his expression changed quickly from one of fear to delight. Grinning from ear to ear, he threw both doors open wide so everyone in the room could see what the commotion was all about.

"The war is over!" ecstatic members of the hospital's staff cried as they danced down the halls. They brandished paper cups filled with fruit juice that had been liberally spiked with two-hundred-proof alcohol from the labs. "The Japs surrendered! The war is over!"

Beaming with pleasure, Aaron Goldman carefully placed the baby in Sheila's arms. "Well congratulations, Mrs. Connolly! It looks like you just delivered a victory girl."

And at first it did indeed seem that Erin Connolly was one of those favored few destined from birth to be a winner. Born on V-J Day, September 2, 1945, her very arrival into the world was infused with the flush of triumph which swept over an exultant country that had just won World War II. And as the first child of parents who were both only children, she immediately became the center of the universe for two sets of adoring grandparents as well as the focus of loving attention from her beautiful, patrician mother and handsome, charming Irish father. Then shortly before her third birthday, her mother gave birth to another baby—a boy—and Erin's small empire crashed.

She fought desperately to regain her lost kingdom in the only way she knew; by proving her superiority to the interloper who had usurped her position. But it was a hopeless endeavor, doomed from the beginning, for not only did no one expect little baby Dennis to compete with his exceptionally bright, inordinately precocious, and now alarmingly aggressive older sister, he refused to even try. It was the final indignity for Erin that her hated brother was totally devoted to her, trotting around after her with wide worshiping eyes and screaming in misery when he was separated from her.

Sheila and Patrick Connolly understood perfectly well why their daughter was acting the way she was. They even knew the sophisticated term for it—sibling rivalry. What they tragically failed to understand was how to handle the problem. Instead of reassuring Erin that she was still loved, cherished, and important to them, they deliberately withheld praise for her accomplishments, often even ridiculing them in the misguided belief that they were teaching her a valuable lesson. As her father succinctly summed it up, "The kid better learn early that nobody likes a show-off."

Of course neither parent ever considered explaining to Erin why they refused to recognize her considerable achievements. After all, that would have destroyed the whole purpose of the lesson. And so the child doubled and tripled her efforts in the hope that the next time, surely the next time, she would finally prove her worth to them. That time never came.

Frustrated to the point of tears by her failure to win the love and approval of her parents, but too proud to show it, she became starved for some sign of recognition and turned in desperation to the only available source—her peers.

It was a choice that initially brought her almost as much grief as her failed attempts to woo her parents, because Erin was not looking for friends; she was looking for subjects. And in the upper-middle-class Detroit suburb where her parents had recently moved, there was already a reigning king, a cocky, good-looking boy named Tommy Fallon who viewed her efforts to take over his territory with amused derision.

With the easy cruelty of a child, he managed to make her the object of snickering ridicule as both an outsider and that most worthless of all human beings to the nine-year-old male mentality, a girl. But Tommy Fallon wasn't laughing three months later when he showed up for his regular Saturday afternoon clubhouse meeting and discovered only two of his members there, the rest, along with everybody else in the neighborhood, at Erin Connolly's home.

Sheila Connolly was more than a little stunned when her daughter told her what she wanted for her eighth birthday party.

"Good heavens, child, you can't be serious!" she exclaimed. "Why, we couldn't possibly afford it! Besides," she added, shaking her head and frowning, "it's really too much. Your playmates will be just as happy with a nice little party where they can have hot dogs and hamburgers and all the cake and ice cream they can eat."

"No they won't!" Erin said with passionate intensity. "They won't even come if that's all I have."

"Now, honey, that's just plain silly," Sheila began.

"*Please*, Mother!" Erin burst in. "It's the only thing in the world I want. I'll give up all my birthday and Christmas presents for the next five years to pay for it. I'll do the dishes every day. I'll . . ." She broke off, trying hard to keep from crying.

It was the first time that Erin had ever openly begged for anything, and Sheila couldn't help but respond to the naked entreaty in her eyes. But it was the realization that her daughter was having problems in being accepted by the children in the neighborhood that finally pushed her into giving Erin what she wanted. Because nothing, in Sheila Connolly's judgment, could be worse than not being accepted.

So Erin celebrated her eighth birthday with an extravagant affair that included, in addition to all the hot dogs, hamburgers, cake, and ice cream anyone could eat, a real live pony who gave free rides to all the kids, and fireworks that lit up the sky just before the cake was cut.

Erin became an overnight sensation with the kids in her neighborhood, who were frankly awed by her birthday party. They'd never seen anything like it in their entire lives; and, as they all agreed, it sure beat those draggy meetings with

Tommy Fallon in his stuffy little clubhouse where all he did was give orders and collect fifteen cents from everyone for membership dues. Which, they muttered rebelliously, didn't even include the Cokes and potato chips. He made them pay extra for that. So they cautiously drew back from Tommy Fallon and waited with curious interest to see what Erin Connolly would come up with next.

What she came up with was a theater, created out of the unused third of the Connolly's three-car garage. Erin's father put up plasterboard walls to enclose the area, and her mother, who was currently in the process of redecorating the den in their home, donated the old furniture originally headed for Good Will Industries. A slightly battered studio couch, two rattan chairs, and a worn nine-by-twelve carpet transformed bare cement into a believable stage; discarded drapes served beautifully as a curtain; and bridge-table chairs provided audience seating.

Production on the first play started immediately, with an open casting session that allowed everyone in the neighborhood to try out. The response was so overwhelming, there was barely enough room in the small theater to hold all the aspiring actors and actresses who surged inside at the appointed hour, pushing and shoving at each other as they fought their way to the stage when Erin called their names and gave them the lines to read.

The lure that drew them in such numbers was not the ego excitement of acting, although it played a small part in the overall mass hysteria. The lure was the astounding news that they'd be paid for their acting, just like real Hollywood stars.

Erin's theater gave six performances a week; one every afternoon after school Monday through Friday, and a matinee on Saturday. Sundays were devoted to casting and rehearsals for the next week's production. Tickets for the weekday performances cost a dime. Saturday matinees, always a big house with parents substantially swelling the audience, went for a quarter.

The enterprise was a financial success from the beginning, tickets sold out for every performance and extra chairs brought in for the blockbuster Saturday afternoon crowd. The raison d'être behind this rather extraordinary achievement rested on the simplest and most basic economic law of supply and demand. Everyone hungered for the privilege of appearing in one of Erin's plays, and Erin never allowed anyone, after the original casting session, to even read for a part until they had proved themselves genuine lovers of the theater by first attending the performances as paying fans.

The most dedicated lover of the theater in the neighborhood was Jeannie Fallon, who longed with all her heart to be in one of Erin's plays and faithfully showed up for every performance, obediently handing over her money to the ticket taker, clapping enthusiastically at the end of every act, and then wistfully hanging around backstage after the final curtain in hopes that someone would take notice of her.

But all her dedication and devotion was in vain, for not only didn't she get a part, she never even got invited to audition for one. So Jeannie finally went bawling to her mother that Erin Connolly had taken all her allowance under false pretenses, since it was now obvious that Erin had never planned to let her be in one of the plays.

Mrs. Fallon marched over to talk with Sheila Connolly, who subsequently informed Erin that Jeannie was going to be in the very next play that was produced.

"No!" Erin screamed in outrage. "She's fat and dumb, and besides, she can't act." What Erin didn't add was that Jeannie also happened to be the sister of the hated Tommy Fallon, and Erin was getting her revenge. She just stared at her mother and announced through clenched teeth, "I *won't* put her in my play!"

"Oh yes you will," Sheila Connolly replied ominously. "And you'll give her a major part, too." Erin's mother rarely used that tone of voice. When she did, no one argued with her.

The news of Mrs. Fallon's visit to Erin's mother was all over the neighborhood in less than five minutes after it occurred, and the theater was jammed when the new play opened. Spectators leaned back in their chairs and watched with open-mouthed fascination as Tommy Fallon swaggered in and took a seat in the front row. It was the first time he'd ever appeared in the theater. Then their heads swiveled around as the curtain slowly parted.

Jeannie Fallon was in the play. And she most certainly had a major part, being onstage and in full view of the audience for the entire performance. It was not a very demanding role, however, as she played the part of a wealthy widow who had been killed by an unknown murderer before the play began, and spent her entire time on stage lying sprawled out on the floor, a speechless, silent corpse.

By the time Erin was thirteen, she was the acknowledged leader of the neighborhood. Tommy Fallon and his family had moved away three years earlier, when his father was transferred by his company to Pittsburgh, and the new family that moved into their house had three kids who immediately recognized Erin's power and eagerly sought out her favors. Not that it would have made any difference if Tommy had stayed in the neighborhood. He'd lost all status after Erin made a laughingstock of his sister, and he was forgotten long before he actually left. The only one who missed him, curiously enough, was Erin. She knew that she'd never really conquered him. He'd been beaten by circumstances beyond his control. And for a brief time, she experienced a strangely disquieting sense of emptiness and regret, marked by disturbing dreams in which she challenged him directly and then found herself running after him, screaming in rage, as he laughed at her and told her she wasn't worth fighting. But the dreams and the disquieting feelings didn't last very long, because Erin suddenly found herself facing a new challenge.

The school system in the Detroit suburb where Erin lived found itself unable to cope with the flood of students (the result of World War II's baby boom) that was pouring into the already overcrowded and antiquated high school. In desperation, they set up a junior high school in a large housing area some five miles north of the suburb. So Erin and her friends would now be shuttled across town to an intermediary school for two years before they entered the high school as sophomores. And no one was more aware than Erin that they'd be going into the intermediary school as outsiders, facing a group of kids who'd grown up in that particular area, gone to elementary school together, and formed their own cliques and power groups. Nevertheless, she was fully determined to rule over the new territory.

It was a lot easier this time, for Erin had learned a great deal since the days of her famous birthday party and the garage theater. And one of the most important things she had learned was that she was different from most people. They liked to talk about being rich and famous and powerful, but they never really did anything to make it happen. In fact, she finally realized with contempt, they were actually afraid to try. They were more than happy to settle for being accepted by the rich, famous, and powerful; which, at that time in their lives, translated into being part of the "in" crowd.

Armed with that useful knowledge, Erin took two weeks to look over the new school and then created the first fraternity and sorority in its history. She did it very cleverly, too. Delta Phi Delta, the fraternity, came into being first, organized by Erin's steady boyfriend, Danny Farentino, an outstanding athlete. He was welcomed eagerly by the student body, since they saw in him a chance to win divisional championships in every major sport. Carefully programmed by Erin, whom he adored to distraction but never felt sure of, he quickly recruited the top football and basketball players for the new fraternity. After they were safely in the fold, he proceeded to bring in the president of the class, the editor of the school newspaper, and the advertising manager of the yearbook. Chi Omicron, the sister sorority, sprang into existence immediately afterward. And when the girls in school learned what a sister sorority meant—that every member of Delta Phi Delta was pledged to seek out only Chi Omicron girls for parties and dates—there was such a rush to join that even Erin found herself a bit overwhelmed.

When Erin was fifteen, she fell in love for the first time. His name was Kirk Abbott, and he was a senior at the high school Erin had just entered. He was also captain of the football team, president of the student council, extraordinarily handsome, a top honor student, and the owner of a brand new gleaming white Thunderbird with red leather upholstery. And he belonged to someone else.

It took Erin a month to make him notice her, and another three months to take him away from the coolly aloof, exquisitely beautiful blond princess who made the fatal mistake of dismissing Erin as just another insignificant sophomore with an amusing crush on her man. But Erin finally won him, and then the happiest time of her life followed. He was the king, she the queen; and they ruled their world in sunny harmony as equals. Not that Erin stopped being competitive. It was too ingrained in her nature by then. But she went about it differently this time, without the fierce cutthroat intensity she used to display. This was partly because she was in love, but mostly because Kirk was a very secure young man who enjoyed her achievements as much as his own and praised her generously.

Of course Erin still continued to bring her accomplishments home to her parents, handing them over as trophies and waiting hopefully for the pleased smile, the look of pride, the compliment that never appeared. But even this perplexing failure no longer devastated her the way it once had. She even began to question if the failure was really her fault. For, after all, hadn't practically everyone else in the world found her to be bright, charming, talented, and desirable . . . even if she was a girl?

The following year Kirk graduated to go on to college, and with distance and time the romance gradually faded. But its beneficial effects on Erin remained; for Kirk had given her more than love, he'd given her a sense of her own worth and taught her how to enjoy the things she won.

At that moment, the future looked very bright for Erin. She was coming of age in a time of economic and emotional liberation for women, and she had all the attributes for becoming a success in that exciting new world. Gifted with the rare combination of a brilliant mind and a quick, intuitive intelligence, she was developing into a strikingly attractive woman who exuded a sensual magnetism that made conventionally beautiful women fade into the background when she was present. She also had guts and a driving ambition nothing could deflect.

If she had directed that ambition toward the newly liberated fields of fashion design, publishing, advertising, medicine, or science, she would not only have risen quickly to the top but probably found personal self-fulfillment as well.

Instead, she went to Hollywood, the last feudal bastion of male supremacy. There she would find herself transported back to the nightmare battles of her childhood, fighting desperately for recognition in a world that laughed with frank amusement at the antics of a ridiculous upstart who was not only an outsider but that most worthless of all human beings to the Hollywood power structure, a female.

It all happened because of James Lee Norton. Of course he wasn't James Lee Norton when Erin met him. He was, as he would have been the first to admit, nobody.

TWO

"IT's a boy, Sarah! A beautiful, perfect baby boy!" Amos Norton was so excited and proud, tears sprang to his eyes. Embarrassed, he surreptitiously wiped them away with his sleeve. They left small dark spots on the fabric, but for once he was oblivious of the blemish on the gray postman's uniform he spent so much time in keeping crisp and immaculately clean.

Beaming, he now extended the hand he'd been hiding behind his back and presented his wife with a bouquet of two dozen red hothouse roses that were bursting into bloom with such vitality they almost leaped out of the wax paper wrapping them.

"Oh. Oh my," Sarah breathed, shaking her head in disbelief. "Amos, have you gone mad? These must have cost a fortune!"

"Hush, now." He leaned over and kissed her. "How many times does a man have a chance to celebrate having his first son?"

She smiled. "Nothing too good for Amos Junior, is that it?" she teased him.

He cleared his throat. "Well, actually I've changed my mind about calling him that." Seeing the look of surprise on her face, he ducked his head self-consciously. "I thought . . . I thought I'd like to name him Jimmy, after your brother."

A long silent moment passed as Sarah bowed her head, trying to control her emotions. Jimmy had been more than her brother. He'd been her adored idol, her protector, and her best friend. The news of his death had come two days before she went into the hospital to have the baby. It was a senseless death. The war had officially ended a month earlier, and her brother had been scheduled to be rotated back to the U.S. three months before that. But he had a very low priority. Soldiers with the right connections constantly preempted his well-earned place on the list, scrambling out of the Pacific theater with desperate haste once they heard a peace settlement was imminent. Jimmy died in a fetid jungle atoll, the victim of a Japanese sniper who was stolidly committed to losing his life along with the war.

"I thank you for that, Amos," Sarah said finally in a low, husky voice. She looked up. "And we'll do right by this Jimmy, won't we? We'll give him the chance my brother never had. We'll work every day of our lives to make a new world for him, one where he'll be respected and important!"

"We'll certainly try," Amos said gently.

"No!" Sarah pulled herself upright in the hospital bed and stared fiercely into her husband's eyes. "Trying isn't good enough. We are going to succeed!"

Jimmy Norton had an exceptionally happy childhood, filled with warmth and love and almost more toys than he knew what to do with. Sometimes he found himself wishing that his mama would leave the toy buying up to his daddy, but he would have cut out his tongue before ever letting her know how he felt. Because it was obvious to him even as a baby that she was as excited about the toys she bought him as though she'd gotten them for herself, and she really needed him to like them; while his daddy, on the other hand, was as easygoing as could be, telling him if he didn't like something they could always exchange it.

So Jimmy tried very hard to like the building blocks, the puzzles and books and erector sets just as much as the cuddly stuffed animals, the rocking horse, the bright red fire engine, and the cowboy outfit his daddy gave him. And when his mama managed to find time away from her shopping and cleaning and sewing and cooking, from her church activities and part-time job at the library, to sit down and play with him; then he really did like her toys just as much. Because the one thing Jimmy Norton missed a lot was having a playmate. In the quiet, respectable middle-class neighborhood where his family lived, he was the only child. The other homeowners on the block were all in their forties and fifties, their children grown up and gone.

When Jimmy was four and his parents asked him what he wanted for Christmas, he answered with passionate intensity, "A brother and sister!"

"You mean a brother *or* sister," Sarah corrected him with a smile.

"No, Mama, I want both!" He never understood what was so funny about that, but his parents were laughing so hard he found himself laughing along with them. The only thing was, he never got either.

Jimmy was truly upset when he crept out of bed that Christmas Eve night and sneaked downstairs to peek under the branches of the majestically beautiful tree that almost filled the small living room. For there were no babies waiting there for him. And the huge pile of presents crowding the area where his babies should have been meant that Santa had already been there and left, forgetting the most important gift of all.

Heartbroken, he trudged back upstairs and crawled into bed, muffling the sound of his crying so his mama wouldn't hear. Somehow his mama seemed to hear everything, no matter how much anyone tried to hide it, and he didn't want her to know that he'd discovered Santa Claus was a failure. She got so upset when anybody failed.

Christmas morning Jimmy made a big fuss over all his presents, assuring his parents that Santa Claus had given him the best Christmas ever.

Sarah watched with increasing concern as her son carefully opened each present, smoothing out the paper and folding it neatly before looking up with a big smile to tell them how wonderful it was and just exactly what he'd wanted. Normally, Jimmy tore through the wrappings in an ecstacy of excitement, hardly able to contain himself in finding out what was inside, because he knew one of them held the really big, special gift he'd been waiting for all year.

It was a family tradition to hide the most important gift in a deceptive box. When he was three and had just learned how to count, he wanted a watch more than anything else in the world. They'd disguised it in a series of little boxes inside succeedingly bigger boxes until the final gaily wrapped package was the size of a carton of groceries. The whole family exploded into delighted laughter when Jimmy finally uncovered the coveted treasure.

This year the special gift was a bicycle. Amos had sweated for weeks dismantling it and then figuring out how to put it back together. It now lay under the tree, wrapped in nine different, intriguingly shaped packages. Jimmy picked up the first clue, a small, oblong package in the shape of a shoebox. Inside, nestled in soft white tissue paper, were two gleaming silver bicycle bells. Jimmy smiled brightly, polished them to show how they glowed, then absently put them back into the box and reached for another package whose shape clearly revealed it was a book. It was too much for Sarah.

"Jimmy, you come over here right now and tell me what's wrong," she commanded.

"Nothing's wrong, Mama," he protested, unable to look at her.

"Seems to me that just about everything's wrong," she said grimly. "You keep holding up all these presents and telling us how much you like them, but then you just put them down and shuffle them around, not even playing with a single one. I get the feeling you don't like any of them."

At this point Sarah was close to tears, for she had spent months searching out just the right things to delight her beloved son and she couldn't understand what had gone wrong. But she resolutely blinked them away as she reached out and drew Jimmy to her, keeping her voice calm and quiet as she spoke.

"Now, son, I can plainly see that something's disappointed you. But we can't help if you won't tell us what it is."

Jimmy had done his best to hide the terrible truth but he was, after all, only four years old. And there was no way he could look his mama straight in the eye and lie to her.

"Santa Claus forgot!" he blurted out, his lower lip trembling uncontrollably. "I told you way, way back even before Thanksgiving, that all I wanted for Christmas was a brother and sister, because I wanted Santa to have plenty of time to get them. And then . . ." Jimmy could no longer control his grief. Burying his head in the comforting lap, he sobbed disconsolately, "And then he forgot all about me, Mama. He gave them to somebody else."

"Oh, Jimmy. Oh, my little baby. I didn't know!" Sarah scooped her son up into her lap, rocking him back and forth as she gazed in despair at her husband. For she had never imagined for a moment that Jimmy had really been serious. And since he'd never brought up the subject since that time, she'd quite frankly forgotten all about it.

Now she realized that in his usual trusting way Jimmy had assumed they'd taken care of his request, because in all these years, Santa had never failed to come through for Jimmy except on those rare occasions when his parents gravely took him aside to inform him they'd received a special letter from the North Pole in which Santa explained that certain things were in short supply that season.

Sarah looked down at her son and for once in her life found herself unable to think of the right thing to say. The silence stretched out painfully.

"It wasn't Santa's fault," Amos finally announced in his slow, deep voice. "He didn't know you wanted a brother and sister."

"You didn't tell him?" Jimmy stared at his daddy in disbelieving shock.

"Well." Amos coughed uncomfortably. "You see, son, the thing is that Santa Claus only gives toys and presents. He doesn't give babies. Only God can do that."

"Then why didn't you tell God?" Jimmy demanded accusingly.

Amos smiled ruefully. "You don't *tell* God anything, Jimmy. The best you can do is ask. Then He does what He thinks is right." A troubled frown crossed his face. "I see now we should have explained that to you, but we just didn't realize how important this was to you."

He leaned forward in his chair and studied his son's unhappy face in puzzlement. "Why *is* it that important to you, Jimmy? I thought we had such a happy family, the three of us. Why do you want a brother and sister so much?"

"Because I'm lonely, Daddy," Jimmy wailed. "Because I don't have anybody to play with!"

Amos was so stunned that for a moment he couldn't speak. The last thing in the world he'd ever imagined was that his son could be lonely. For Amos had been one of eight children in a family that lived on the edge of poverty, and his entire young life had been filled with a fierce longing to get away from his rapacious brothers and sisters who stole all his toys and clothes and beat up on him when the urge struck them. His dream of happiness had been to find a quiet place where he could curl up with his few possessions and enjoy them in blissful solitude.

Sarah had grown up in the same kind of environment. Only the intervention of her big brother Jimmy had allowed her to keep her one prized possession, a Raggedy Ann doll that required constant stitching to keep its stuffing from leaking out. Jimmy stole the necessary pins, needles, and thread from his mother's sewing box to keep the bright button eyes and smiling doll's mouth together.

When Amos and Sarah got married, they made a solemn vow to each other that their children would never have to go through what they had. And so they decided to limit their family to two children. As it turned out, Sarah was only able to have one. But when the doctor sadly informed them of that fact, he was considerably startled to see them turn and smile at each other. Of course he had no way of knowing they had already found out how expensive it was to have just one child.

"It's God's will," Sarah said confidently as they walked out of the doctor's office. "He knows we have only so much to give, and He's letting us have it all for our Jimmy."

But now, inexplicably, the whole thing had gone wrong. Their son who was to have everything, who was to be the happiest baby that had ever been born, was miserable.

It suddenly occurred to Amos he was acting like a damn

fool, brooding about the past this way. His son wasn't miserable because he didn't have brothers and sisters. He was miserable because he didn't have playmates. And that problem was going to resolve itself naturally in just about no time at all.

Smiling, he got up and went over to his son, squatting down beside him and rubbing his head affectionately. "Jimmy, I got some good news for you. Something even better than a brother and sister."

He chuckled as Jimmy's eyes widened in astonishment. "Yes, indeed," he grinned. "Because you see, Jimmy, brothers and sisters all have to start out as babies, and babies are no fun to play with at all. No sir! It takes them at least two years before they even learn how to talk and walk around. So what you need are grown-up playmates like yourself. And you're going to get lots of them real soon. Ten, fifteen, maybe even twenty. Pretty little girls and bright little boys who'll have all kinds of new toys and games to play with."

"Really, Daddy?" Jimmy was awestruck by the astounding vision. Then doubt clouded his eyes. If there were all these marvelous playmates around, why hadn't he ever seen them? On the other hand, his daddy had never lied to him. "Where are all these boys and girls?" he asked hesitantly.

"In kindergarten," Amos answered triumphantly. It was immediately apparent to Amos from the baffled look on his son's face that Jimmy hadn't the faintest idea what kindergarten was. He quickly launched into a detailed explanation, describing with relish a big sunny schoolroom filled with children sharing toys, learning new things together, and becoming very special friends.

Jimmy's face glowed with excitement. "When can I go, daddy? Tomorrow? Can I go tomorrow?"

"Well, no, not tomorrow," Amos laughed. "But it won't be too long. Let's see now. Your birthday's October twelfth, which couldn't be better timing. You'll be almost five then, which is just the right age for entering kindergarten next September."

"Next September?" Jimmy repeated, stunned. "But, Daddy, that's forever away!" Tears of disappointment filled his eyes.

"Amos, maybe we could find a nursery school," Sarah offered desperately. "There must be some good ones around."

"I don't want a nursery school," Jimmy sobbed. "I want kin . . . kinergard!"

"Now you listen to me, young man," Sarah snapped with exceptional sharpness. "You don't even know what nursery school is, so you don't know whether you want it or not. Now dry those tears, open the rest of your presents, and let this family enjoy its Christmas! We'll talk about nursery school and kindergarten tomorrow."

"I think we just got our orders, Jimmy," Amos said solemnly. Then he turned and gave his son a little wink. Jimmy started to giggle. Then they all started to laugh, and suddenly it turned into one of the happiest and merriest Christmases they'd ever had.

But Jimmy never made it to nursery school, or kindergarten either. All the childhood diseases descended on him in one short, unhappy season. A bad cold that started soon after Christmas turned into whooping cough. He'd just barely recovered from that when he came down with the measles. And the following month he got the mumps.

"At least he gets to keep his daddy around," Sarah smiled tiredly as she and Amos took turns getting up at night to check his temperature and coax him to take liquids as he whimpered, "It hurts. It hurts to swallow." Much of the Midwest and the entire city of Cleveland, where they lived, had a major epidemic of mumps, which had caused thousands of fathers to leave their homes and camp out uneasily at hotels, motels, and houses of friends without children, because everyone knew if an adult male caught the mumps, he would become sterile. This was no problem for Amos and Sarah. Their son's health was.

"Nobody ever dies from mumps," Amos said firmly one night when Sarah broke down into tears. "Now it's just something he has to go through. He'll be fine."

"But he's so pale and weak. He never had a chance to get over the measles," she wept.

"He'll get over it. Now you go to bed before you come down

with it too," he scolded. "Because what will we do if you get sick?"

Sarah realized the sense of what her husband was saying and meekly took his advice, which not only pleased Amos but rather overwhelmed him since meekness was one characteristic conspicuously lacking in his wife's make-up. Things began to get better then. Neither Amos nor Sarah got sick, and by the middle of summer Jimmy was healthy and strong again, although Sarah fretted because he'd never gained back all the weight he'd lost and didn't seem to be growing very fast. The family doctor reassured her it was nothing to worry about. "Just give him a little time," he smiled. "He'll start shooting up so fast in another couple of months, you'll have to go out and buy him a brand new wardrobe."

Jimmy still hadn't done any noticeable growing by the end of summer, but he was happy and cheerful and increasingly excited as September grew near, because at last he would be going to kindergarten. It wasn't to be. The most severe influenza epidemic to hit Cleveland in a decade struck just before Labor Day, and a terrified Sarah wouldn't even allow her son outside the house, much less let him attend a school where he might pick up the virus from other children.

That year was the longest time of Jimmy's life. His parents did their best to help. Sarah gave up her part-time job at the library so she could spend more time playing with him. Amos, whose one vice was pool and was admiringly known as "one mean man with a stick," gave up his afternoon sessions at Hansen's pool hall where he and his friends from the post office regularly gathered after work to drink a few beers and kid around making bets on trick shots, so that he could come home and spend extra time with his son.

This made things a little easier on Jimmy, but it was still a long way from what he wanted. Then finally the waiting was over. The weather turned crisp and cool immediately after Labor Day. There were no flu bugs or even common colds around. Leaves began to change to beautiful autumn colors, warms russets and golds. The air was clear and fresh. And Jimmy Norton was ready to enter the first grade.

Jimmy bounded out of bed at six o'clock that Monday

morning, pulled back the curtains from his bedroom window, and beamed out at the sun that was just peeking over the horizon.

"I'm going to school today!" he announced joyfully to it. Then, hitching up his pajama bottoms, he ran into the bathroom and started running water into the tub. The room was still a little steamy from his daddy's shower, because Amos had to get down to the post office before seven. Jimmy cleared a small space in the steamed up mirror while he brushed his teeth and grinned at his image.

The tub started filling up and he turned around fast to shut it off before his mama heard it, because he wanted to surprise her. Then sliding into the tub so carefully he didn't even make a splash, he started scrubbing away, remembering at the last minute to wash behind his ears. When he was finished, he crept out stealthily, grabbed a big towel, and dried himself off before tiptoeing back to his bedroom.

The sun was bright now in the small bedroom, and Jimmy paused for a moment to admire his new outfit, which he'd just taken out of the closet and lovingly laid out on the bed. There was a handsome blue-and-white striped shirt with a collar that came to crisp, sharp points in the front; his very first long pants in gray flannel; a navy blue blazer with big shiny silver buttons; and, for the perfect finishing touch, a jaunty dark blue cap.

Slowly, almost reverently, he walked over and removed the cellophane covering from the shirt and the plastic bags from the pants and blazer jacket, stopping briefly to flick an invisible piece of lint from the cap.

The only mirror in Jimmy's bedroom hung above his dresser, so he had to climb on the bed in order to get a full view of himself in the new outfit. He almost fell off at the unexpected sound of his mama's voice.

"What in the world are you doing, bouncing up and down there like that?" Sarah demanded in shock as she appeared in the doorway. "And why is the bathtub full of water?"

"Uh, I wanted to surprise you," he said guiltily, barely managing to keep his balance. Then he grinned, too happy to worry about a scolding. "But don't I look beautiful, Mama?"

he said joyfully. "Nobody in the whole first grade is going to look better than me."

"Jimmy, I swear there are times I don't know what to do with you!" Sarah tried hard to sound stern, but her heart wasn't really in it. The truth was she thought he looked absolutely beautiful, too, and the expression on his face came close to making her cry. Her baby was finally going to get what he'd been longing for all this time.

She blinked and cleared her throat. "Now you get down off that bed before you ruin it along with all those new clothes, and come down to breakfast." She started to walk out, then turned around and gave him a little smile. "You might want to hurry up a slight bit, since it seems you got a present waiting for you there. Your daddy left it before he went off to work."

It took Jimmy all of three seconds to leap off the bed and give the covers a halfhearted smoothing over before racing out of the bedroom and down the stairs into the kitchen.

The huge package was sitting in the center of the table, wrapped in gold foil. Eyes wide with excitement, Jimmy pounced on it.

"No!" Sarah said firmly, coming into the kitchen behind him. "First you eat your breakfast. Then you open it."

"Aw, Mama!"

"Don't aw Mama me. Start eating!"

With a long-suffering sigh, he sat down, drained the glass of orange juice, poured milk from the pitcher into his bowl of cereal, and started gulping down the contents as fast as he could.

"You eat like a pig, you're gonna look like one," Sarah observed mildly as she walked over to the refrigerator. "Shame to have you show up your first day at school with food all over your new shirt, just like some little baby who was still too young to learn manners."

Horrified, Jimmy put down his spoon and craned his neck, searching desperately for spots on his new clothes. There were none, of course. His mama was putting him on. Still, there was no sense in taking any chances. He finished his breakfast with painstaking slowness, leaning well over the table and mopping up every potential dribble with his napkin.

"Got a little gift for you myself," Sarah said casually. "Didn't think it needed wrapping, though." She took something out of the cupboard and placed it on the kitchen counter, then stepped back so Jimmy could see it. "What do you think?" she asked with a trace of diffidence.

It was a lunch box, a smaller version of the one his daddy took to work every day but sparkling new, and it had a real Thermos tucked inside the lid. Jimmy was overcome with pride at the sight. It meant he was a real man now.

"Oh, Mama!" He was so thrilled, he couldn't think of another word to say.

"Well, now, we've got to fill it," Sarah smiled, delighted with her son's obvious pleasure. "What would Mr. First Grade like for his first lunch?"

"Peanut butter sandwiches with grape jelly, an apple, and ten chocolate chip cookies," he announced without a second of hesitation.

"What?" Sarah stared at him in shock. "Ten chocolate chip cookies? Jimmy, what are you going to do with *ten* cookies?"

"Why, I'm gonna share them with my new friends," he explained happily.

"Of course," Sarah murmured, turning away to wipe her eyes with the corner of her apron. "How could I have forgotten that?"

She came over to the table then to give him a hug. "And you're going to find so many wonderful friends, honey. Just remember you can bring them home anytime, because I want to meet them too. Now open your daddy's gift."

It was a briefcase with a tabbed zipper that whipped around the edges with a smooth gliding ease to reveal a panel of brilliantly colored, perfectly sharpened pencils tucked into a neat compartment on one side and a bright yellow lined pad tucked into a folder on the other side.

"Lots of room in there to keep all the books you'll start bringing home," Sarah said. "It's real leather, Jimmy, and you'll be able to use it all through school."

Jimmy ran his hands over the rich texture and then looked up. "I'm very lucky, Mama, aren't I?"

"You are not lucky, son, you are deserving!" Embarrassed at

her display of emotion, she quickly cleared the breakfast table. "But you're not going to be so lucky if we don't get you to school on time," she laughed. "Now pick up that briefcase and lunch box, and let's get this show on the road!"

The Nortons' house straddled a surveyor's line that separated their street into two different school districts. The closest elementary school was a short two blocks away. It was also old and run-down. Seven blocks away was a spanking new elementary school, built three years after the end of World War II to meet the needs of a large new housing development that had sprung up in the area. There was, of course, no question in Sarah Norton's mind which school her son would go to. She had enrolled him in the new school the minute the administration opened its doors for the coming semester, staring down their hesitant questions about exactly where her family lived with ferocious intensity.

Now she hustled her son out of the house and into the ancient but lovingly cared for family car, humming absently under her breath as she drove down the quiet street where they lived. She came to a halt at the main intersection that divided their neighborhood from the bustling new community that seemed to be growing almost faster than the eye could see.

The light at the intersection changed to green and Sarah pressed down on the accelerator, feeling the smoothness of the recently paved highway under the car's tires. The school was already in sight—a bright red brick structure with a high fence enclosing the large playground that featured a row of swings and seesaws, two jungle gyms, and, off to the far right, a baseball diamond.

"No, Mama," Jimmy said quickly as Sarah parked the car and started to get out. "I want to go in by myself."

"But, honey, you don't even know where to go!" Sarah protested.

"Then I'll just ask a teacher." He smiled shyly at her. "I'm a big boy now Mama."

"Well." She took a deep breath. "You are now, aren't you? All right, then, go along. Just be sure to be back here at this very same spot at two o'clock when I come to pick you up."

She leaned over to kiss him goodbye, but he was already out of the car and running eagerly toward the school.

The playground was crowded with children of all ages as Jimmy pushed his way through the gate and walked inside, staring around in wonderment. A tall, gangly redheaded youngster who'd been doing chin-ups on the jungle gym dropped to his feet and stared as he saw Jimmy wander in.

"Hey!" he called to the kids around him. "Hey, do you see what I see?"

Jimmy looked up in surprise as he saw the group of boys approaching him. Then his face lit up with delight as he realized they were coming to welcome him. Beaming with pleasure, he ran to meet them. But suddenly they slowed down. Only the big redheaded boy kept walking towards him.

"Hey, nigger, what you doin' at our school?" the redhead scowled.

Jimmy smiled uncertainly. "My name isn't Nigger. It's Jimmy. Jimmy Norton. What's your name?"

"Did you hear that?" the redhead yelped. "This dumb nigger doesn't even *know* he's a nigger!"

The entire group behind the redhead burst into wild whoops of laughter, punching each other with glee as they repeated their leader's remark. "A nigger who doesn't even know he's a nigger," they shouted hysterically. "Did you ever hear of a nigger *that* dumb?"

The redhead leaned over and grabbed the jaunty blue cap off Jimmy's head.

"Hey, nigger, let's see how good you are at catch." He tossed the cap over his shoulder to the boy behind him, who ran off to the side and then pitched it over to another boy.

"Don't!" Jimmy cried. "Please, that's my new cap. Please, please give it back." He started running desperately after the boy who'd just caught it. The redhead grinned and slyly stuck out his foot as Jimmy charged across the playground, tripping him and sending him crashing to the ground. The briefcase fell as he dropped, and the lunch box flew out of his hand and broke open, spilling the peanut butter and grape jelly sandwiches, the apple, and the ten chocolate chip cookies for his new friends all over the hard playground area. He started crawling over to pick them up, then cried out in anguish as the boys rushed over and stepped on his hands as he reached for them.

The school bell rang out suddenly, and in five seconds the playground was deserted. Except for Jimmy Norton. He lay in a small crumpled heap, his brand new blue-and-white striped shirt smeared and muddy, his precious leather briefcase scuffed and scarred, a long ugly rip in his gray flannel pants, three of the four once shiny silver buttons on his blue blazer hanging by a thread, and a steady stream of tears coursing down his bewildered, heartbroken face.

Late that night Sarah Norton crouched in bed and beat her fists against her husband's chest.

"I want to kill them!" she raged. "I want to go down there with a whip and cut them to ribbons! I want to make them bleed and hurt and suffer just the way they made our Jimmy do. I want to kill them!!"

"Sarah, you've got to stop carrying on like this. Please, honey, try to pull yourself together. You can't help Jimmy acting this way. You can't help anybody."

Sarah bent over, racked with terrible sobs.

"All right, then," Amos whispered. "All right, girl, go ahead and let it out."

A long time later Sarah straightened up and took the handkerchief Amos had waiting for her. "But what are we going to do now?" she said in despair.

"We're going to transfer him to that other school. I'll take care of it first thing tomorrow."

"But it's a terrible school," she cried. "They don't have any new equipment or teaching aids. They don't even have good teachers!"

"They don't have white bigots either," Amos said coldly. "Now listen to me, Sarah. If we don't get Jimmy out of that school right away, he could carry the scars for the rest of his life. Once he's settled into that new school, he'll have all the friends he needs."

Amos smiled at her encouragingly. "As for the teaching, well hell, honey, we'll tutor him at home if it's necessary. And by the time he's ready for high school, everything will have worked out just fine. He'll be a super scholar. I guarantee you that."

Sarah didn't speak, but her eyes said it all.

"Honey, you got to believe me when I tell you this is the right thing to do. You just got to stop crying now. This day was a lot worse for us than him. He's only six, you know. He'll forget all about it in no time at all."

But Jimmy Norton never forgot.

Three

THE April day had started out clear and bright but now gray clouds were threatening to obliterate the afternoon sun.

The photographer hired to take the picture of Jefferson High School's 1962 graduating class looked up anxiously at the darkening sky and found himself wishing for the twentieth time that he'd never taken on this damn assignment. He'd already wasted three rolls of film trying to get the large, unruly group of youngsters to stand still long enough for him to get them all into the frame, and if he didn't get them in this next roll the fucking skies were going to open up and pour down rain; which meant he'd have to come back another day, and that would blow his entire profit on the job.

"All right, now," he shouted. "Let's get it together and get it right this time. Girls, look this way and smile. Fellas, line up behind them. No!" he screamed frantically as an exceptionally tall boy slipped up behind the row of girls and leaned over, grinning widely as he hooked his arm around the shoulder of a pretty young girl in a yellow dress. "How many times do I have to tell you? The tallest stand in the back, the fourth row; next tallest in the third row; shortest in the second row behind the girls."

"Hey, man, this is my lady," the young giant said sullenly,

his grin vanishing abruptly. "And we want our picture taken together."

The photographer ground his teeth together, then took a deep breath. "Okay," he yelled. "If that's what you want, okay. As long as your classmates don't mind. Because . . ." He paused for a moment, then really yelled. "Because they won't even show up in the picture with you blocking them. Now if that's all right with them, fine, since this is the last picture I'm going to be able to shoot because it's about to rain. And then I'm leaving!"

The class of 1962 immediately exploded into furious outcries and accusations, and two husky youngsters plunged down through the rows and literally carried the belligerent Romeo to the back.

A few minutes later drops of rain began to fall and in seconds turned into a downpour. But by that time the photographer had his picture and was racing for his car.

It turned out to be a fine group composite. The football and basketball players, proudly wearing their letter sweaters, stood tall and strong in the back row, beaming at the camera. In the row just below them the cocky, confident young men who ran the politics of the school smiled coolly into the lens. The front row of girls showed some giggling, some smiling, some attempting a sophisticated aloofness, but essentially they all achieved a certain homogeneity. The students in the second row looked vaguely awkward and ill-at-ease, but almost all of them managed a game smile for the camera. The one exception was Jimmy Norton. Standing in the exact middle of the second row, he stared straight into the camera lens with a cold, distant frown.

Sarah and Amos Norton had considerably different feelings about the way in which their son had developed and grown up. However, since Amos never said anything about his feelings, Sarah believed in happy innocence that her husband also felt that their son was on his way to becoming the important success they'd dreamed of from the moment of his birth.

Sarah had some good reasons for believing that. From the time they'd taken him out of the new elementary school that had treated him so cruelly and enrolled him in the old one in their neighborhood, Jimmy had demonstrated an academic brilliance that had awed his teachers, who sent home handwritten letters along with his report cards to tell the Nortons how special their son was.

The letters and commendations kept coming in, and Sarah began to keep a scrapbook. But it wasn't just his scholastic achievements that delighted her. She knew it wasn't enough just to be brilliant; you had to have the kind of attitude that pleased and impressed the people who counted in order to get ahead. And Jimmy certainly had the right attitude. He was polite, well-spoken, neat, and clean, and never got into trouble. The only real worry she had was that he wouldn't have the chance to meet the people who counted. Everything depended on his getting into the right college, and she had begun sending away for applications to the best colleges in the country as soon as Jimmy finished his freshman year in high school.

It wasn't the shockingly high tuition costs of these fine colleges that upset her, for all of them offered scholarships. It was the academic requirements they demanded. It made no difference that he'd achieved top grades in every course he'd taken. It was the courses he hadn't achieved top grades in, simply because they weren't offered, that were going to destroy his future.

Sarah hated Jefferson High School with all her heart. It was a huge school with over two thousand students. It had won every city championship in football, basketball, and track in the past ten years. It had exceptionally advanced vocational training programs in subjects like auto mechanics. It also had one of the lowest rates in the city of students who went on to college after graduation, and seventy-five percent of its student body was black.

Sarah would have been horrified if anyone had told her she was a bigot. As she saw it, the facts were that the world was a black and white place where the whites held all the power. What you had to do was get to know the whites, get into their world, and then you'd have a chance to grab some of that power. Somehow she just had to get her Jimmy into that world. She kept writing to colleges.

Amos was proud of Jimmy's obvious brilliance, but nothing else about his son pleased him at all. He didn't want a neat, clean, studious boy whose polite smiles never reached his eyes. He wanted a boisterous, laughing boy who filled the house with his friends and got into minor scrapes and troubles just like any other normal kid. He wanted, with all his heart, the warm, open, loving boy who'd eagerly gone off to first grade that fateful September morning . . . and had never returned.

At first Amos thought it would just be a matter of time before Jimmy became his old self again. After all, the boy had been through a terrible experience. But when two years had passed and Jimmy had still made no friends at all, Amos realized the situation was much more serious than he'd imagined. In a desperate effort to help, he volunteered to coach the neighborhood's Little League baseball team in order to bring his son into contact with other youngsters.

Jimmy obediently went out for the team, but Amos was soon forced to admit that sports was not going to be the answer for his son. Jimmy was not only small for his age but totally lacking in athletic ability. Short and skinny, with a head that looked too large for his body, he was awkward and uncoordinated and all the patient hours of coaching Amos gave him so devotedly helped not in the slightest. Making matters worse was the fact that the other youngsters on the team were tough, scrappy, highly competitive kids. They made it painfully obvious they suffered Jimmy's presence only because they obviously loved and respected Amos, an excellent coach with a natural talent for bringing out the best in any boy . . . except his own.

Jimmy continued to come out for every game and sat stoically on the bench while his team raced to one victory after another, staring with a cold, distant look as the jubilant victors crowded around his father, beaming up at him as he hugged and praised them. Amos's efforts to help his son had been doubly disastrous, for not only had he failed to provide Jimmy with friends, he had made him feel rejected by his own father.

Not that Jimmy ever said anything. It wasn't his way. He simply withdrew completely from Amos.

In Jimmy's first year at Jefferson High School he found a friend. Sarah was delighted. She had tried hard to ignore the alarming fact that her son had gone through eight years of schooling without any social contact at all, comforting herself with the thought that he'd never found anyone who was his equal. How could he in those awful ghetto schools? Her Jimmy was waiting for the right contacts. And Lionel Pearson was certainly right. His father was a lawyer. That a lawyer let his son go to Jefferson High puzzled her until she found out that Lionel's father was planning to run for councilman in the district. He was a very smart man, showing that he didn't put on any airs or try to be pushy. She admired that.

Amos despised Lionel Pearson because he knew what Sarah never suspected. Lionel not only hated his father, he hated almost everything, and he was teaching that hatred to Jimmy. Amos realized it the first time Jimmy brought the boy home for dinner.

"Very nice to meet you, Mr. Norton." Lionel Pearson had smiled politely, offering his hand. "I understand you work for the post office. Do you find that a rewarding government subsidy for the crimes they've committed against us?"

"Actually, I find it a good job," Amos said evenly. "One that I earned, and one I enjoy."

"Really." Lionel raised an amused eyebrow, a smirk twisting the corners of his mouth; his expression made it clear he considered Jimmy's father not only an Uncle Tom but a fool.

The fierce rage that filled Amos vanished abruptly, replaced with the most heartsick feeling he'd ever experienced in his life when he saw his son give a little shrug and smile back at the young punk. His son, his flesh and blood whom he'd loved and cared for and devoted his life to, not only allowed a stranger to insult his father but actually condoned the insult.

Amos was not a religious man, but the day he heard that Lionel Pearson had transferred out of Jefferson High School he went to church, knelt down in front of the altar, and thanked God. He also prayed that Lionel had left before too much damage had been done. Cautiously, he approached his son, asking him if he missed his friend and still kept in contact with him.

Jimmy had stared at him for a moment, then smiled. "No, Dad, I don't hear from him. Which I know makes you happy. You never much liked him, did you?"

"I didn't like what he was doing to you," Amos answered bluntly. "You have a fine mind, Jimmy, bright and quick and strong. You can think for yourself, but it seemed to me you were letting Lionel do the thinking for you. That's the worst slavery of all."

Sudden anger flared in Jimmy's usually cool, withdrawn eyes. "Nobody controls my mind but *me*, Daddy!" he said fiercely. He leaned back in his desk chair, his eyes once again impassive. "Anyway, Lionel turned out to be a drag. He had some interesting ideas, but he never understood how to use them effectively."

Amos didn't really understand what Jimmy was talking about, but he found himself oddly comforted by the fact that his son had addressed him as Daddy. It had been years since Jimmy had called him that. He was also overwhelmingly relieved to learn that both Lionel Pearson and his dangerous influence were now things of the past. But he continued to worry about his son. Jimmy had returned to his solitary ways. He continued to get top grades but never voiced enthusiasm for any particular subject, and Amos often wondered if he really cared about any of them. There were times, in fact, when Amos wondered if Jimmy cared about anything.

The only thing that Jimmy had ever shown any real interest in was movies. From the time he was fourteen, Jimmy had spent every penny of his allowance at the ticket windows of movie theaters throughout the city. Amos enjoyed a good movie himself and in an attempt to get closer to his son had suggested maybe they could go together some time.

Jimmy had studied him silently for a minute, then shaken his head. "You wouldn't enjoy the movies I go to, Dad," he'd said finally.

Amos had protested, and so a few nights later they went together to see a movie. Jimmy was right. Amos didn't enjoy it at all. He didn't even understand it. The whole thing seemed totally amateurish to him, shot in grainy black and white, with actors and actresses nobody had ever heard of and a story you couldn't even follow. He was flabbergasted to hear his son rave about the picture when they left the theater, and could only nod numbly out of politeness.

"I warned you, Dad," Jimmy laughed.

Amos managed a weak chuckle in response, but privately he vowed never to tell Sarah about this. If she had any idea what her son thought was good, her whole life's dream would fall apart. Because her son had no taste at all.

But on this particular rainy April afternoon, the same afternoon that had finally seen the successful completion of the group picture of Jefferson High School's 1962 graduating class, Amos had more serious worries than his son's lack of taste and critical judgment. In two months Jimmy would be graduating from Jefferson High, and he still had not been accepted by any of the major colleges on the list that Sarah had so carefully and painstakingly drawn up after studying dozens of catalogues. Jimmy himself seemed indifferent to the stream of rejections from the various college admissions offices and even appeared reasonably cheerful about the prospect of entering Cleveland City College that coming September. Not Sarah, though. Each new rejection that arrived in the mail was like a personal blow to her.

It had gotten to the point where Amos actually dreaded coming home, for with each succeeding rejection Sarah grew more distraught. He always knew when another rejection had arrived the minute he walked inside. It was more than the fact that Sarah wasn't at the door to greet him, or that there were no warm cooking smells coming from the kitchen. It was a cold stillness that enveloped the whole house, as though all life had departed from it.

Amos braced himself now as he approached his front door and reached for his keys. There were still two colleges that hadn't been heard from, and logic told him they couldn't wait much longer to announce their decisions with high school graduation just around the corner. It was all too possible that both rejections had arrived in today's mail, and he had no idea how he was going to help his wife accept the fact that her dream was over.

The house was warm, filled with the delicious smell of fresh-baked bread mixed with the deep, rich odor of a slowly simmering pot roast and spiced with the scents of cinnamon and nutmeg.

"Sarah? Sarah honey?" Amos called out eagerly.

"Oh, Amos, it came! It finally came!" Sarah burst out of the kitchen, her face glowing with joy as she thrust the letter at him.

"Hey, what's going on?" Jimmy asked in stupefaction as he walked into the house and saw his parents hugging and kissing as they danced around the living room.

Flushed and laughing, Sarah broke out of her husband's embrace and held out the magical piece of paper.

"Look, son, look!"

Jimmy's body became rigid as he read it. "I don't want to go," he said in a dull monotone.

"*What*?" Sarah blinked in disbelief. "Jimmy sweetheart, what are you saying? This is from Cheviot Hills University. Cheviot Hills!" she repeated feverishly. "Don't you remember it?"

Jimmy remembered it very clearly. It was one of ten universities he and his parents had toured after he'd finished his junior year at Jefferson High. Located near the southern tip of the state, where an invisible border divided Ohio from Kentucky, it was a small, elite, ultraconservative college with impeccable credentials. Its unusually high rating on the college accreditation list guaranteed its students access to graduate schools of the highest caliber, and it featured an exceptionally attractive campus with acres of carefully tended lawns and flower beds, a brand new football stadium and track field, and handsome stone, brick and glass buildings that were an architect's delight. It also had a student body that was one hundred percent white.

In the brief second it took Jimmy to read the letter of acceptance, he relived that entire traumatic September day. As the memory swept over him, perspiration trickled down his armpits and his mouth filled with the copper taste of fear.

"Jimmy, say something!" Sarah pleaded. "Tell us what's wrong!"

But Jimmy couldn't tell them. He could barely stand to think about that day, much less talk about it. And the thought of ever having to go through another experience like it made him tremble with terror. That was why he hadn't minded all those rejections. Minded? Hell, he'd been delighted, barely able to keep from shouting out his relief each time another letter had arrived, politely turning down his application. No, that wasn't completely true. Four of those rejections had hurt and disappointed him deeply. They were from NYU, Columbia, USC, and UCLA; schools he, not his mother, had picked; schools he wanted desperately. Jimmy's one driving ambition was to become a filmmaker; these were the best film schools in the country.

But despite the fact that none of them had accepted him, there was a ray of hope. The dean of admissions at USC had written him a kind, sympathetic letter, praising him both for his ambition and his insights into what was happening in filmmaking, and suggesting that he take a couple of years to establish a good academic record at an accredited junior college and then reapply to USC.

Cleveland City College was not exactly world renowned, but it was accredited . . . and it sure beat the hell out of Jefferson High School when it came to academic status. So Jimmy had resigned himself to the two-year wait, and he was fiercely determined to make his academic record at Cleveland City such an outstanding one that USC couldn't possibly turn him down when he reapplied. But now this incredible, impossible letter of acceptance from Cheviot Hills had come along and fucked up everything. What the hell was he going to do about it, with his mother standing there staring at him that way with tears already beginning to spill down her cheeks?

As Jimmy looked at his mother's imploring face, he was suddenly overcome with a deep burning shame. Jesus Christ, he thought with self-loathing, you're not a six-year-old kid anymore, you're a man. So Cheviot Hills is all white. So what? If you don't have enough guts to handle that, you don't have enough guts to handle anything.

It also occurred to him that if USC was asking him to establish his credentials, he'd do it a lot better at Cheviot Hills than Cleveland City. In fact, one year at Cheviot Hills had to be equal to at least two years at Cleveland City. Excitement and hope filled him as he realized that he could be enrolled in USC's film school as early as September of 1963. All he had to do was make it through one shitty freshman term at Cheviot Hills, keep his cool, and get the best grades that snotty university had ever seen.

"Nothing's wrong, Mama." Jimmy smiled. "I remember now. It's just about the best on the list, isn't it?"

Jimmy managed to keep his smile all through the celebration dinner that followed.

Four

ERIN Connolly had known from the time she was fifteen that she'd be going to Cheviot Hills University, because virtually everybody who was anybody in her high school went there. Of course there were some exceptions. The boy who was president of the student council in Erin's senior year went on to Yale because everyone in his family had gone there for generations. The editor of the school newspaper went to Harvard because he planned to pursue a career in journalism, and the brilliant science student went to Johns Hopkins.

But all the bright, pretty, popular girls headed for Cheviot Hills, except Nancy Hollister, who stunned her friends by going to Smith. Who in their right mind would want to go to a girls' school, especially one of those snobbish Eastern girls' schools with their rigid rules and regulations and miserable little cramped dormitory rooms? Especially when you could live in the country club atmosphere of Cheviot Hills and meet all those handsome, wealthy young men who'd take you over the state line to Covington, Kentucky, where you'd not only experience some really swinging parties but could pick up several hundred dollars gambling. And what girl wouldn't enjoy having a little extra pocket money like that?

Registration for the fall semester classes at Cheviot Hills

University officially began on the third Monday in that September of 1962, and during the preceding weekend the campus was flooded with arriving freshmen. Most of them were chauffered there by their parents in Cadillacs, Lincoln Continentals, and an occasional Bentley, the cars overflowing with boxes and cartons containing record players, records, books, pictures and pennants, rugs, and lamps along with suitcases and wardrobes filled with clothes, to make the transition from home to college painless.

The steady stream of incoming cars caused a major traffic jam at the entrance to the school as two lanes, arriving from opposite directions, converged simultaneously at the wrought-iron gates. The campus security guard hastily summoned help through his walkie-talkie, and in a few seconds two young men, crisply attired in blue uniforms with a bright red stripe, arrived on the scene, giving friendly smiles and warm apologies as they directed the cars one at a time through the gates and down the winding road that led to the handsome dormitory buildings a half mile ahead.

Patrick Connolly drummed his fingers impatiently on the steering wheel as one of the traffic monitors held up his hand, stopping him as he waved through a car from the other lane. Then Patrick blinked in surprise as he saw the car that slipped in front of him and drove slowly through the gates. It was immaculately clean, and the way it gleamed in the warm afternoon sun made it obvious that it had been recently waxed and polished. But despite its shiny appearance, nothing could disguise the fact that it was nothing more than an old Plymouth sedan, probably at least five years old, and painted a bilious green.

Sheila Connolly was even more stunned as she looked at it. "Patrick, there are colored people in that car!" she announced in horror. "Do you think that means Cheviot Hills is allowing colored students in here?"

The major topic of conversation in the registration lines that following Monday morning was the unbelievable appearance of Jimmy Norton. Normal concerns—like what were the "cream" courses, who were the best instructors, and should you make a date now for the freshman mixer or take your chances and go it alone—were forgotten as the new students buzzed and whispered and speculated about what it meant having a black boy on campus. But in a few days the excitement and interest died. It turned out that he was the only black on campus, and since he had no athletic ability at all (there having been considerable nervous talk about what they'd do if he'd been recruited for the football or track team), they soon forgot him.

Erin was the only one who didn't forget him. Initially she was curious and more than a little admiring of this kid with three strikes against him. Jimmy came on cocky and abrasive in class, challenging every sacred precept of literature and drama and usually winning his point, then retreated to a small isolated table in the student union where he refused to lift his head for even the friendliest of greetings. Then she became intrigued by the sharp, incisive mind behind the arrogant facade and deliberately sought him out.

"Professor Whitley was really impressed with your discussion about Harold Pinter," Erin announced cheerfully as she pulled out a chair and sat down across the table from Jimmy, who was busily scribbling notes on a yellow lined pad as he studied the book in front of him. "Especially since nobody else in the class had ever heard of him."

Jimmy's head snapped up, and he stared in surprise at the vividly attractive girl who was smiling at him. Then his eyes narrowed. "And you?" he asked softly. "Were you impressed too?"

Erin grinned. "I was impressed with your ability to make points. There's a rumor going around that no one has ever gotten an A in Whitley's drama course, and I have a feeling you're about to make history."

"Rumors are rarely reliable." He bent over his book again. Several silent minutes passed as Jimmy attempted to concentrate on his notes and became increasingly irritated that this girl couldn't take the hint and leave. Finally he looked up and frowned.

"Is that why you came over here and sat down? To tell me you thought I impressed Professor Whitley?"

"No, that was just my excuse," Erin said with engaging frankness. "The real reason is that I'd like to get to know you, because I find you very interesting."

Alarm signals raced through Jimmy's nervous system at the words, making every hair on the back of his neck stand up.

Swallowing hard, he gazed directly into the brilliant green eyes surveying him and discovered an incredible truth. This beautiful, brash white girl wasn't even thinking of him as black. For a minute he couldn't believe what he was seeing. His own experience had taught him that when white people saw a black face, they immediately stopped seeing a human being. His friend Lionel had confirmed that it was true, although Jimmy had soon realized that Lionel couldn't see a human being when he saw a white face. But now it appeared that he and Lionel had been wrong.

Jimmy's instinctive assessment of Erin Connolly was totally correct. She had a great many prejudices, including a sweeping contempt for all people who weren't as bright as she, who were weak, and who allowed themselves to be used. But she was completely free of the stereotype prejudices, race and religion. The discovery of that fact was so exhilarating to Jimmy, it took him a long time to realize that just because Erin saw him as a person didn't mean she cared for him personally. And by the time he realized that, it was almost too late; for he'd fallen hopelessly in love with her. And in the process he let down his guard for the first time since he'd been a child, opening up not only his heart but his soul to her as he trustingly revealed the passionate hopes and dreams that drove him.

With a gentleness unusual for her, Erin made him understand that a love affair just wasn't in the cards. And she managed it with such delicacy that she not only allowed him to keep his pride but left him with the feeling that she needed his friendship. It wasn't compassion that motivated her, for compassion was not in Erin's experience. What motivated Erin to keep Jimmy's friendship was her fascination with his dreams. When he babbled about his love for her, he was as dull and boring as every other man who wanted her. But when he talked about Hollywood, the new Hollywood he saw coming, he was brilliantly articulate and almost mesmerizing as he painted word pictures of the coming power struggle between the established studio heads and the revolutionary young filmmakers. He told her about the New Wave in France, the directors like Truffaut, Godard, Chabrol, Rohmer, and Rivette. He introduced her to the works of Antonioni and Fellini. And he finally found an art theater near the university that was showing John Cassavetes's *Shadows.*

"Do you understand now what I've been talking about?" he exclaimed excitedly as they walked out of the movie house. "That was an American who produced that film! We're finally coming of age, and I'm going to be part of it!"

"I don't know," she said thoughtfully. "What he did was great, but he's never going to appeal to a mass audience with that kind of work, which means his pictures will never make a lot of money. And without the big audiences and the money, how can he ever become really powerful?" Erin looked up at Jimmy. "If I were going to be a producer, I'd go after it all. The awards, the money, the power, everything!"

Jimmy started to laugh. "Yeah, that would be your style, all right. And damned if I don't think you might make it, if you put your mind to it."

"Of course I would," Erin said serenely. Then she grinned at him. "So be glad I haven't decided to go into competition with you."

"Well, why don't you?"

"What?" Erin stared at him, momentarily confused.

Jimmy took a deep breath. "Erin, they accepted me at USC's film school. I'll be going there next fall. Why don't you enroll too? We could have such a great time there together!" He paused, feeling his heart pound as he gazed at her hopefully.

"Jimmy, I don't think I could do that," she said gently.

"Yeah, well, I guess it was a crazy idea," he mumbled, turning away so she couldn't see the bitter tears of disappointment that sprang to his eyes.

"But that doesn't mean we'll lose touch." Erin took hold of his hands. "We'll write to each other, and when I graduate I'll come out there. You'll be established by then, and you can introduce me to all the right people," she smiled.

He nodded, too dispirited to speak.

To Jimmy's surprise and delight, they did keep in touch. He wrote her a long letter his first day at USC, telling her in detail not only what the school was like but what California was like. He sweated long and hard over the letter, rewriting it four times before he was satisfied with the way it read. He wanted it to be interesting and intriguing, and it was. Erin responded quickly, eager to hear more. He answered immediately, telling her how much he missed her.

A month passed before he heard from her again. He realized by then that the only sure way to get her to write him was by keeping his letters bright, entertaining, and impersonal. It was humiliating in a sense but he was able to accept it, for he needed her letters. Life at USC wasn't much better for him than it had been at Cheviot Hills. He was still an outsider. Not that he faced outright discrimination; it was much more subtle. Blacks were considered losers in the Hollywood scene, and nobody wanted to be associated with a loser. So Jimmy retreated into himself once again, living in a run-down ghetto apartment at the edges of the USC campus, shunning contact with the other students, coming to life only in the classrooms, where he continued to challenge both teachers and classmates in brilliant debates that left them with a grudging admiration for his perception and ability.

During his junior year at USC, the letters from Erin began trailing off and then stopped altogether. He continued to write for several more months, then finally gave up. But his period of mourning for their lost friendship was very brief, for something so exciting happened to him he was swept up into a state of euphoria that wiped out all thoughts of her.

As his major class project for the year he produced a short film titled *Barrio*, using rented camera equipment and employing kids from the streets of East Los Angeles as actors. It swept USC's film school awards, and the prized trophy for best short produced by a student was personally handed to him by the guest speaker for the occasion, Martin Weinguard, powerful studio head of International Pictures.

"You are a very talented young man, and I predict a brilliant future for you," Weinguard had announced in his deep, booming voice. But it wasn't that public announcement that sent Jimmy Norton into a state of euphoria. It was the private conversation after the ceremonies, when Martin Weinguard drew him aside and told him International Pictures wanted him to work for them and would hold open a job until he finished school.

Martin Weinguard kept his promise. Two weeks after Jimmy graduated from USC, he was on the payroll of International Pictures as an assistant director. Two months later he was given his own picture to direct. A year later he changed his name to James Lee Norton, discarded his grubby jeans and T-shirts and replaced them with elegant, hand-tailored suits with wide lapels and flared pants, let his close-cropped woolly hair grow into a proud Afro, moved out of the roach-infested ghetto apartment (without leaving a forwarding address), and moved into a chic little house in Laurel Canyon, had his first screenplay optioned . . . and discovered that he'd been had.

It was the option on his screenplay that sent him hurrying to Martin Weinguard's office that hot, smoggy August day a year after he'd started working at International Pictures. He wanted very badly to make that picture, but he'd been continually put off by a number of executive producers who kept telling him to keep his cool.

"Jesus, man, take it easy," they said. "You know how long it takes to get a script approved for production. Just be happy that you're still getting properties to direct."

But he wasn't happy. The three films he'd directed were not only low-budget, unimportant pictures, they were a million light-years away from the kind of pictures he wanted to do. This script, which came straight from his guts, delivered the kind of personal statement he'd wanted to make all his life. He'd been so ecstatic when International had optioned it, he'd thrown open his house for a celebration party that had lasted over three weeks and included almost every employed and unemployed black actor and actress in Hollywood. But the celebration turned sour when first one month, then two passed and still no date had been set for filming.

"I'll go directly to Weinguard," he told his friends. "He's

the man who promised us this picture, and he's always kept his promises to me. It's just those fucking people who suck around him that are stopping us. Hear me!" he announced. "Hear me, and believe!"

Sylvia Hunter, Martin Weinguard's secretary, had called him back two days after he'd made his urgent request and told him she'd managed to squeeze him in at eleven forty-five the following morning. He showed up at eleven-thirty, knowing Weinguard often slipped out for lunch early, and determined not to miss him.

To his surprise, he found the anteroom completely empty. He had no way of knowing that Sylvia Hunter, suffering from a terrible bout with intestinal flu, had called desperately for a relief secretary and then, unable to wait a second longer, had fled to the ladies room. Nor did he dwell on her surprising absence long, because he immediately noticed that the door to Weinguard's office was half open, and he could see Martin Weinguard, his back to the door, standing at the window, apparently alone.

Elated by the thought that he would have an extra fifteen minutes to plead his case, he rushed across the thick plush carpet that muffled all sound and took a step inside the office, raising his hand to make a polite knock on the door. He was instantly embarrassed to discover there was another person in the room, hidden from sight by the angle of the door. He started to step back, then heard his name mentioned and froze.

"It's becoming a very real problem," Solomon Liebowitz said grimly as he got up from the couch and approached Martin at the window. "The government is putting on pressure you wouldn't believe about this equal-rights crap. I mean, they're getting to the point where they might actually subpoena our personnel records to see if we have a representative number of women and minorities in executive and managerial positions."

"You worry too much, Sol," Martin announced. "You always have." He glanced at the lawyer's pale face, which was now staring out the window alongside his. "Of course that's your job," he conceded. "You're our Washington representative."

Suddenly he chuckled and threw a friendly arm around Sol's

shoulder. "But you've got no worries with International Pictures. Guess I forgot to tell you about this nigger we hired a year ago. First-class nigger. Won all kinds of awards at USC, and just as ugly and black as any government busybody could ask for. Not one of those light-skinned pretty boys trying to pass. We got him on the books as a full-fledged director. Done three pictures already. Now, your Washington committees couldn't ask for more than that to prove we don't discriminate, could they?"

Martin Weinguard threw back his head and roared with laughter at the look of astonishment on Solomon Liebowitz's face. "Fooled you, didn't I?" he chortled triumphantly. "Thought I was too dumb to figure out this kind of problem was going to hit us soon. Well don't ever underestimate me again, my friend. International Pictures has created a perfect showpiece nigger in James Lee Norton, and we can trot him out to perform for us whenever we need him."

For one blinding second of rage, Jimmy Norton was prepared to leap into the office and launch himself at the throat of Martin Weinguard. What stayed him was hearing what Martin Weinguard had called him. James Lee. That's what he'd said. It had taken twenty-two years to change Jimmy Norton into James Lee Norton, and not even Martin Weinguard could take that away from him. He *was* in Hollywood, and he *was* a director, and he was here to stay. Because they'd made a big mistake when they let him in the door and then thought they could forget about him. They'd used him because they'd needed him. Well they still needed him, and now he'd learn how to use them. He would be very cool and very clever, and he'd get everything he wanted.

But he knew as he silently backed out of the office and walked quickly out of the anteroom and down the hall that he would never be satisfied until he took his personal revenge on Martin Weinguard. How or when that would happen, he didn't know. But that it would happen, he had no doubt.

Of course it was the furthest thing from his mind on that June morning almost a year later when he looked up from his table in the Film-Star Studios commissary and stared in stunned disbelief at the sight of Erin Connolly racing over to him, face alight with pleasure as she shouted, "Jimmy! Jimmy, is it really you?"

As it turned out, though, the unexpected reunion provided him with the greatest revenge he could ever have imagined.

XXX

Five

XXXXXXXXXXXXXXXXXXXXXXXXXXXXXXXXXXXXXXXXXXXXXXXXXXXXXXXXXXXXX

ERIN Connolly had meant it when she told Jimmy she'd be coming out to Hollywood immediately after graduating from Cheviot Hills, but she didn't actually arrive until over a year later. The reason for her delay was Eric Glass.

At the beginning of Erin's junior year, Cheviot Hills University expanded its American Literature program and lured Eric Glass away from Wesleyan University to teach the new course in contemporary American writers.

Eric was easily lured, having suffered through four years as an assistant professor at Wesleyan with no promotion in sight, despite all the professional accolades he'd received for his controversial paper titled "William Faulkner—Lost In Hollywood." A husky, well-built man in his early thirties with a shock of thick blond hair, bright blue eyes, and a slow grin that instantly melted the heart of every coed on the Cheviot Hills campus, he quickly became the most popular professor the college had ever had. He wore white turtleneck sweaters and tweed jackets with leather patches on the elbows, and it was rumored that he'd skied for the U.S. Olympic team, raced cars at Le Mans, lost his fiancée in a tragic fire (which was the reason he'd never married), smoked grass, and was in the process of completing a novel sizzling with sex that had already been optioned by a major Hollywood studio for $100,000.

His charm and good looks, combined with his romantic past and exciting Hollywood-bound future, totally enraptured Erin, and she pursued him with ardent determination. They were married in the spring of her junior year, had a glorious honeymoon in the Bahamas over Easter vacation, and Erin thought she was the luckiest woman in the world.

Three weeks after Erin Connolly became Mrs. Eric Glass, she found out that her husband had not only not skied for the U.S. Olympic team, raced cars anywhere, or tragically lost a fiancée, he hadn't even tried marijuana. He was frankly terrified when she brought home some prime Acapulco gold. "It's against the law," he'd stuttered. "Please, honey, get that stuff out of here before you get me in trouble."

Then she found out that the book he'd been desultorily working on for the past ten years was not only totally devoid of sizzling sex, it was totally devoid of anything interesting, including movie options. It was, in fact, the most boring book she'd ever read in her life, and it came as no surprise to her to learn that he hadn't even been able to find a publisher for it.

Making matters even worse was the discovery that Eric had not only been unaware of the glamorous rumors circulated about him but was faintly horrified by them, having a total lack of interest in such activities. He had no desire at all to become rich and famous, being a slow, easygoing, good-natured individual who had found his perfect niche in life and wanted nothing more than to stay in it.

Shortly after Erin received this dismal revelation, she was presented with an even more devastating blow. She was pregnant.

Erin stuck it out as a wife and mother for as long as she could, but six months before Eric Junior's second birthday she knew that if something didn't happen soon to change her life, she would go completely out of her mind. And the cold, clear logic that had guided her since she was a child told her that only one person could effect that change—herself.

Eric was obviously content to stay in this stifling, backwater place forever. Of course she could force him out of it, but where could they go? It would have to be to another university where he could teach his interminably dull classes in American Literature, because there was nothing else he could do. Long ago, he had set his sights low, and so teaching was all he was good for. But then what would happen to her? She would become just another faculty wife, struggling to impress the heads of departments on a minimum salary that barely covered the cost of the mortgage. And by that time there'd probably be another baby, maybe two, screaming for food and dry diapers while she raced out to the kitchen to replenish the avocado dip for their guests and worried about the ten dollars they'd spent on Remy Martin cognac because maybe the wife of the white-haired autocrat who controlled Eric's future in the English Department had switched her taste to Grand Marnier.

"No!" she screamed out loud in frustrated fury, setting down the bilious-looking bowl of pureed spinach on the high-chair tray with such force that it slopped over and frightened little Eric so much he burst into hysterical sobs.

"Oh hush," she said crossly. "It didn't hurt you. Besides, I just saved you the trouble of spilling it for yourself."

The baby continued to cry in great gulping hiccups. Erin glared at him, which only served to increase the volume of the cries. With a weary sigh she picked him up and held him against her shoulder, absently rubbing his back.

"All right," she murmured. "It's all right now."

Eric stopped crying immediately, blissfully happy as always to be in his mother's arms. He lifted his head and shyly patted her cheek, his eyes fixed adoringly on her, which caused Erin's own eyes to fill with tears.

"What am I going to do with you?" she whispered in despair as she carried him over to the kitchen table, sat down in a chair, and settled him on her lap. "You know I can't go on living like this. There's a great big world out there full of marvelous things: excitement and challenges and power. I was meant to be a part of that world!"

Eric smiled and nodded his fuzzy blond head with vigorous enthusiasm. He didn't, of course, understand a word of what his mother was saying, but he loved these moments when she took him on her lap and talked to him like this. Because he knew she was telling him important things, taking him into her confidence. They were special friends at these times.

It took Erin several weeks to figure out a way to handle both her personal salvation and her responsibility to the child she had given birth to. But she finally hit upon a plan that seemed virtually foolproof. Nevertheless, her mouth was dry and her heart was pounding erratically when she finally approached her husband in his study.

"Eric, there's something very important I have to talk to you about," she announced with a faint tremor in her voice.

"Hm?" He looked up from the stack of papers he was grading and gave her an absent smile, but it faded abruptly as he saw the look on her face. "What is it, honey?" he asked anxiously. "There's nothing wrong with the baby, is there?"

"No, no, he's fine." Erin nervously twisted her fingers together. "It's . . . actually, it's me."

"Good Lord!" Eric sprang to his feet and rushed over to her. "What did the doctor say? Whatever it is, I can't believe it's serious," he added feverishly. "You're the healthiest person I've ever known."

He peered at her apprehensively as he put his hand on her forehead. It was cool, her beautiful green eyes clear and bright, and her incredibly flawless complexion glowing with health. A sudden happy grin lit up his face as the truth dawned on him.

"You're pregnant!" he exclaimed with delight. "Honey, that's great. That's absolutely great! Why, you shouldn't have worried for a second about telling me," he assured her as he hugged her to him. "I always wanted a big family, and it looks like both the full professorship and tenure will be coming through by the end of this year, so we can certainly afford another baby. Maybe we can get a little Erin this time," he beamed. "I would really love to have a little girl just like you."

The whole discussion was getting totally out of control, Erin realized with desperation. "Eric, please let's sit down and talk," she said shakily.

"Of course." He was immediately solicitous, leading her

carefully over to the couch. "Morning sickness already?" he asked sympathetically.

"No, Eric, not morning sickness," she said tensely. "It's morning, afternoon, and evening sickness!"

"You're sick all the time?" He stared at her, dumbfounded. "But you've seemed just fine." He frowned then. "Well, there's certainly no need for you to suffer like that. If Dr. MacPherson can't come up with something to help you, we'll just get you another doctor."

"Eric, listen to me!" Erin screamed. "I'm not pregnant! I'm sick because of our life!"

"What?" Eric stared at his wife in bewilderment.

"Listen!" she repeated frantically. "Please, just listen to what I'm trying to tell you."

Eric listened with growing bewilderment. "But I don't understand," he said helplessly when Erin paused to take a ragged breath. "I thought you loved us. I thought we were so happy."

"I *do* love you," Erin protested. "I love you and little Eric more than anything in the whole world. It's just . . ." She made a gesture toward Eric's desk, piled high with books and papers. "It's just that I wasn't emotionally prepared for all this to happen so quickly. I mean, one minute I was a kid, a nineteen-year-old carefree coed, and then suddenly I was married, a mother, and a faculty wife.

"It's all going to work out," she said hastily at the look of horror on his face. "All I'm asking is a chance to get away for a while, to rest and relax and get my perspective back."

She slid off the couch and knelt in front of him, taking hold of his hands. "No, I'm not asking," she murmured huskily, "I'm begging. Not just for me, for all of us."

"Well." Eric cleared his throat, equally shaken by what Erin was saying and the terrible fear that he was going to break into tears. The past three years had been the happiest of his entire life. He loved his brilliant, magnetic wife to the point of distraction and adored his beautiful son. The thought of losing them was more than he could bear. With a tremendous act of will he forced back the threatening tears and managed a smile, drawing Erin up to the couch beside him.

"I know this has been as hard for you to tell me as it has been for me to hear," he said softly, stroking her hair. "But you're right, of course. I should have been more sensitive, realized what a change all this has been for you." He tilted up her chin and kissed her. "So go ahead, honey, have your well-deserved breather. I'm sure your folks will be delighted to have you and their handsome grandchild to themselves for a while."

Erin, who had been relaxing in relief at successfully accomplishing her mission, sat up abruptly at Eric's words.

"Eric, I'm not going to my parents. I can't imagine what ever made you think that. I'm going to California."

"California!" Eric exclaimed incredulously. "Have you lost your mind? That's over two thousand miles away, and you don't know a soul there."

"Of course I do," Erin said quickly, thinking of Jimmy Norton. "Don't you remember my telling you about my best friend in college who transferred out there to USC and wrote, inviting me to come visit?"

"No. I don't remember you ever mentioning a friend in California." Which was understandable, since Erin had never told him anything of the kind.

"Well, that's all right," she said magnanimously. "I probably told you about it during one of those times you were working on a new article and you just didn't hear me." She flashed him a teasing grin. "You know what you're like when you start writing. The house could fall down around your ears and you wouldn't hear it. Anyway," she continued a little breathlessly, "now you can see why I'm going to California. I mean, it's the perfect breath of fresh air I need. An exciting new place I've never seen, a chance to take a whole new look at me."

Eric stared at her with growing concern. A visit to her parents was one thing, but this sounded like something completely different. Completely and frighteningly different. "How . . . how long were you thinking of staying there?" he asked in a tight, choked voice.

"Maybe a month or two," Erin answered in a very small, quiet voice.

"A month or two," he repeated numbly, very clearly hearing

the sound of his house falling down around his ears. But then he realized how impossible it was.

"Erin, honey," he said slowly, "I certainly hope it's not going to take you that long to find this perspective you say you need. However, there's something else I don't think you've given serious thought to. This girlfriend of yours who invited you out to visit her was probably thinking you'd only be staying for a few days. Do you really think she'll want to put up both you and little Eric for a month or more? After all, from what you've told me, she's just a young girl starting out on her own. Probably living in a little one-room apartment. It will be hard enough for her to have an adult guest for any length of time, but a baby not even two years old yet? Honey, that just wouldn't work out at all."

This was the most difficult part of Erin's presentation, and for an uncomfortable moment she found herself unable to meet her husband's eyes.

"Well, that's the whole point," she said finally, lifting her head and facing him bravely. "I mean, I really need a breather from being a mother as well as a wife, so naturally I won't be taking little Eric with me."

"You're going to go off and leave your own son?" he said in shocked disbelief.

"I'm not leaving him," she snapped furiously. Instantly, she realized her mistake. Getting angry was the worst possible thing she could do. It would lead to a fight, and that would ruin everything. With an effort, she softened her voice and snuggled up to him.

"Darling, I'm not leaving him or you. What I'm doing is . . ." She cast about desperately for the right words and then came up with what she thought was an inspiration. "Well, I guess what you could call what I'm doing is taking a little sabbatical. Does that make sense to you?" she asked with a wistful little smile.

It made no sense at all to Eric. Professors took sabbaticals. Wives didn't. But it was obvious to him that Erin had made up her mind, and nothing he said was going to change it. So, confused and unhappy, he agreed to let her go.

The next two weeks held a peculiar, frenzied gaiety as Erin lavished love and affection on her soon-to-be abandoned husband and child and talked excitedly about how wonderful everything was going to be when she returned and they would all be together again. Of course she had no intention of returning. Her plan was to first get herself established in Hollywood and then bring her son out to live with her. She had even considered the possibility of having Eric come out too, because although she was no longer passionately in love with him, she was genuinely fond of him. He might not be the most intellectually stimulating man in the world, but he was extremely attractive, totally devoted to her, and surprisingly good in bed. It would be pleasant to have the comfort and security of a warm, loving husband waiting for her at home after a hectic day of meeting the demanding challenges of Hollywood.

However, Erin had to admit this was a rather remote possibility. For all his gentle docility, Eric had a certain stubborn streak when it came to family matters. He was, in fact, hopelessly chauvinistic. Men worked. Wives tended the hearth and home. Well, if it didn't work out, it wouldn't be all that upsetting. Hollywood was bound to be full of all kinds of fascinating men, and Eric could turn out to be a liability. Anyway, however it turned out, she would be generous. He would always have fair visitation rights with his son. She would probably even allow him to have young Eric for a full summer.

Erin's high spirits sank briefly when, four days before she was ready to start off for California, the postman returned her excited, exuberant letter to Jimmy Norton with a black stamp across it that stated, "ADDRESSEE UNKNOWN. RETURN TO SENDER." She had been counting on Jimmy to get her started in Hollywood. The bleak stamp on the returned letter made her realize just how much she'd been counting on him.

"Well the hell with you, Jimmy," she said defiantly as she turned the letter over in her hands. "So who needs you? I've always made it on my own, anyway."

The sun had barely peeped over the horizon on that July

morning four days later when Erin raced out of the house with one small suitcase in her hand and a large leather handbag slung over her shoulder, heading for the sporty 1960 MG roadster she'd bought with the two thousand dollars she'd withdrawn from the joint savings account she and Eric shared. The antique grandfather clock in the hallway, which Eric's parents had given them for a wedding present, bonged mournfully five times as she opened the front door, and she prayed it wouldn't wake Eric. She had left a loving note on the nightstand, explaining why she thought it was best to leave without any lengthy farewells. Now she cast a nervous glance up at the bedroom window. It remained dark and quiet. With a relieved sigh she jumped into the car, started the motor, winced at the loud sound of the engine as it coughed and turned over, and then quickly drove off.

Once outside the confines of the small Ohio town, Erin relaxed and settled back, luxuriating in her newfound freedom as she drove leisurely across the country. She also made a point of calling Eric every day to report her progress and to chat with her young son. But an unpleasant surprise awaited her on the eighth day of her odyssey. Her husband refused to put her son on the phone.

"He cries for hours after you call," Eric said angrily. "And it takes forever to get him to go to sleep afterwards. So we think it would be better if you didn't talk to him anymore."

"We?" Erin clutched the receiver so hard, her knuckles turned white. "And just exactly who is we?" she demanded.

"Nancy Burk. A friend of mine from the university who's helping me take care of him," Eric replied curtly.

"I see. Well, it didn't take you too long to replace me, did it?"

When there was no reply from Eric, nothing but a long, low humming on the wires, Erin banged down the phone, shocked to find tears streaming down her cheeks. Stop it, she told herself furiously. He's still your son, and one day very soon you'll go back and get him. Then he'll never have to cry again.

Six

ERIN drove slowly down Sunset Boulevard, gazing around in fascinated delight at the sights and sounds of the famous street. Immense billboards featuring top rock stars loomed overhead, dominating the skyline. Neon signs above storefronts pulsated with promises of exotic pleasures to be experienced inside their doors. Tiny patios, set up outside of restaurants and barely protected from the steady stream of sidewalk traffic by narrow railings, were crowded with people laughing and talking as they drank white wine and watched the passers-by. Music poured out of speakers mounted in front of record stores, and young girls with long blond hair stood on the curbs, thumbing rides and grinning at the drivers who turned and stared at them.

Suddenly Erin spotted the most famous sight of all, Schwab's Drugstore. Staring at it, she unconsciously allowed the car to slow almost to a stop until the irritated driver behind her blew his horn furiously. Startled, she edged over to the curbside lane and then found as she came up to the intersection that she was in a right-turn-only lane.

With a faint frown, she followed the lane off Sunset, intending to circle around and come back up, but as she drove down the long block, the sign in front of a large, two-story stucco building leaped out at her. "FURNISHED APARTMENT FOR RENT. POOL, AIR-CONDITIONING," it announced.

It's an omen, she decided happily. She parked the car, hopped out, and ran lightly up the steps to the building entrance.

Henry Jacobs, the manager of the apartment building, was an affable man in his late sixties who had recently retired from Sears, where he had been an accountant in the credit department. He was particularly pleased to be managing this particular building because it attracted such interesting people, including a number of pretty young girls with dreams of becoming actresses. Henry had always had an eye for pretty young girls, a fact that infuriated his wife, who had tried unsuccessfully to get Henry to accept a manager's job at a Santa Monica apartment complex catering to senior citizens. Failing in that endeavor, she was forced to satisfy herself by making a practice of personally interviewing all potential tenants who were young, female, and attractive. Under her steely eye, and faced with her pointed questions about their backgrounds, employment records, and credit references, most girls wilted and wandered away to seek other places to live. But Erin was in luck, for on that particular day Sophie Jacobs had rushed off to take advantage of a major store-wide clearance sale on sheets and towels at the May Company.

"Yes, it certainly is still available," Henry beamed as he looked at the lovely creature standing on his doorstep. "And I'm sure you'll like it. It's one of our very nicest units. Now just wait here a second while I get the keys."

It was just as nice as Henry had promised. It was so nice, in fact, that Erin was afraid she'd never be able to afford the rent. There was a big, sunny living room with wide glass windows overlooking the pool. Off to the right of the living room was a cheery little dining alcove which led into a modern kitchen with color-coordinated appliances. To the left was a hallway leading to the bathroom, which was large and spacious, featuring a handsome vanity counter which ran the full length of one wall and an adjoining walk-in closet with a built-in chest of drawers. The apartment was carpeted throughout, heavy lined drapes framed the big windows in the living room, and the furniture included a pleasant beige and brown couch that opened up into a double bed, a coffee table, two end tables with lamps, a comfortable-looking armchair, and a small dropleaf table with two straight chairs set in the dining alcove.

"It's beautiful, Mr. Jacobs." Erin walked around the room, touching the furniture, gazing out the window. "But . . ." She stopped and looked up at him. "But it may be more than I can pay. How much is it?"

The apartment went for $140 a month. Henry swallowed as he looked into the beautiful green eyes fixed hopefully on him. "If you're willing to sign a year's lease, I can let you have it for $110 a month," he said hoarsely.

"Oh yes, Mr. Jacobs!" Erin exclaimed joyously. "Of course I will!" She favored him with such a blinding smile, he found he didn't even care about the problems he was going to have when he tried explaining the rent to his wife and the building's owner.

Erin quickly scanned the lease, hesitating only when she came to the line requiring her signature. Then she took a deep breath and firmly wrote Erin Connolly. There was no longer such a person as Mrs. Eric Glass.

Two days after Erin moved into the apartment, she met Ron Fletcher. It had been a long, hot, and frustrating day for her. She had spent the morning poring over *Variety* and *The Hollywood Reporter*, and the afternoon answering every ad in the help wanted columns that promised even a possible entry to the movie industry. It had been a disillusioning experience. Employers who billed themselves as Hollywood producers turned out to be greasy little men looking for topless dancers. Employment agencies that guaranteed jobs at major studios wanted experienced secretaries who could type 80 words per minute and take shorthand at 120 words per minute. And every place she went, she found offices jammed with pretty young girls who glared with undisguised hostility at each new applicant who walked in the door.

It was almost six when she finally returned to her apartment, not sure whether her head or her legs ached the most. Collapsing on the couch, she kicked off her shoes and massaged her feet, then paused for a moment to look out the window. The pool sparkled in the last rays of the afternoon sun, a clear, clean inviting blue. It was exactly the therapy she needed, Erin decided. She got up and ran down the hall to the bathroom, stripping off her clothes as she went and leaving them in a careless pile behind her. A minute later, wearing an extremely brief bikini and carrying a brightly colored beach towel, she was out the door and down the steps.

The pool area was deserted as she dropped the towel on a chaise and dove into the water. It was cool and deliciously refreshing, and she forgot all about the aggravations of the day as she floated dreamily on her back for a moment before turning over and heading for the deep end, stretching out her muscles in a long, powerful crawl.

Ron Fletcher opened the sliding-glass patio door of his first floor apartment and walked over to the pool, testing the water temperature by tentatively dipping one foot over the side. Satisfied, he sat down on the edge and then slid in, wading slowly toward the center. Erin, completely unaware of him, had just completed a racing turn at the deep end and was now stroking vigorously back, arms pumping and head low in the water, when she rammed Ron dead center. He gave a queer gurgling gasp and sank toward the bottom.

Horrified, she dived down and grabbed him under his arms, bringing him to the surface. Paddling frantically, she carried him to the safety of the steps at the shallow end, where she flipped him over and started pounding on his back.

"Stop! You're killing me!" he moaned as he struggled to sit up.

"I thought I had," she panted. "Are you all right?"

"Maybe. I'm not sure." Cautiously, he put his hand over his heart, which was thumping at an alarming rate.

"Put your head down between your legs," Erin ordered.

He obeyed obediently and began to relax as Erin rubbed his back and neck.

"Better now?" she asked anxiously.

The ominous thumping began to subside. "Yeah." He finally managed to take an easy breath. He lifted his head and then his heart began thumping again, for he got his first good look at Erin.

"On the other hand, I could have a relapse any minute. I think you owe it to me to make sure that doesn't happen. So how about checking out my condition over dinner?"

"Well." Erin frowned and started to shake her head, but when Ron dramatically clapped his hand over his heart and began to choke and wheeze she couldn't help breaking into laughter.

"Okay! Just remember, though, that I'm the only one who will be doing any checking out."

It didn't work out quite that way, however. Halfway through their dinner at a small Chinese restaurant on Pico Boulevard, Erin discovered that Ron was not only a short, fat middle-aged man who was recently divorced and very lonely, but the head of publicity at Film-Star Studios.

And then for a brief, ecstatic period of time, Ron Fletcher forgot that he was short, fat, and middle-aged; and he was never lonely.

Seven

IT took two weeks, the shortest two weeks in Ron Fletcher's life and the longest in Erin's, before Ron was finally able to manufacture a job for her in his department. And by the end of the second week, Erin was about to give up. Ron's efforts were obviously going nowhere, and she didn't think she could stand one more night of his damp, groping hands and worshiping eyes. But that Friday evening when she opened the door after she heard his familiar and increasingly irritating cute little code knock, she knew that it had all been worth it.

"Congratulations, Miss Connolly!" he beamed, handing her a bouquet of red roses. "Starting this coming Monday morning at eight-thirty sharp, you will be an official employee of Film-Star Studios."

"You did it?" she cried excitely. "You really did it?"

"I did it," he smiled.

"Oh tell me!" She grabbed his hands and pulled him into the apartment, smothering him with kisses. "Tell me all about it."

"You'll be working with Andi Steiner, a very smart, very sharp little gal who handles the publicity releases on our major stars. Now Andi just happens to have her sights set on bigger things, and she's cultivated some pretty good contacts. So if you should turn out to be the most helpful assistant she's ever had, I'd be very surprised if you didn't get promoted right into her job. How does that prospect grab you?" he chuckled.

"I love you, Ron Fletcher!" At that moment, she really meant it.

Erin's heart skipped a beat as the studio guard scanned the list of names on the clipboard in front of him and frowned uncertainly.

"What was the name again, miss?"

"Connolly," she said tremulously. "Erin Connolly. I'm supposed to report to Mr. Fletcher in the publicity department."

"Oh, here it is!" He looked up and smiled at her. "Your first day, isn't it? Well, good luck."

"Thank you. Thank you very much." Erin gave him a radiant smile in return, and as she walked into the lobby of the arrogantly phallic glass and steel tower on the Film-Star lot, she knew she'd found the world she'd been looking for. The very air seemed charged with excitement, intrigue, and the heady scent of power. She paused for a moment, throwing back her head to drink it in before heading for the elevator.

"Welcome aboard," Andi Steiner said pleasantly, offering her hand. "Ron says you're a crackerjack at detail, and God knows we need someone like that. Our files are in a total mess." She waved her hand toward the back of the office. "Just look at that!"

Erin looked with horror at the mountainous pile of newspapers and magazines sitting in front of open file cabinets that bulged with yellowed clippings spilling out of their folders.

"It's not as bad as it looks." She grinned. "It's worse."

"Well, it does seem like it could use a little reorganization," Erin said shakily. "So maybe we should update files on our important stars first, and store the other files that are filling up those cabinets some other place until we have a chance to reevaluate them."

"That's good thinking, Erin. Very good thinking." Andi stared thoughtfully at her new assistant. "But how would you know who's important and who isn't?"

"I wouldn't, of course. I'd have to ask you."

"Right." Andi smiled coldly. "You will *always* check with me first before you ever do *anything*, because *I* am the one who makes the decisions. Just remember that, and we'll get along fine."

"Oh I will," Erin assured her. "And I want you to know how happy I am to have this opportunity to work for you. Mr. Fletcher said I'd learn more from you in two weeks than I would in a year from most people."

Andi snorted. "He did, did he? Well, that's the first bright observation the old fart's made in the past ten years."

She started to laugh as she saw the startled look on Erin's face. "Shocked you, did I? You thought because he's the head of this department and got you this job that he was a big wheel?" Andi shook her head pityingly. "Kid, have you got a lot to learn! Tell you what. Stow your purse and stuff in this desk, then trot your little fanny down to personnel to fill out the eight million forms they give all new employees. When you get back, we'll get you started on clipping stories out of this pile of junk, and then I'll take you out to lunch and fill you in on who's really important in this place."

By the time Erin finally completed the voluminous documents handed to her by the personnel director's assistant, she felt that Andi hadn't exaggerated by too much. Her fingers were stiff from writing the answers to endless questions about her background, and her head ached from keeping her lies straight about her fictitious work experience and single status, when she returned to the publicity department some forty minutes later.

She found a note on her desk from Andi. "Clip out every article on actors and actresses with a red check mark against their names on attached list," it stated tersely. A pair of scissors lay across the note, acting as a paperweight. Andi was noticeably absent from the office. With a resigned sigh, Erin began dragging the pile of newspapers and magazines over to her desk.

An hour after she began the tedious task, Ron Fletcher marched into the office, followed by two men talking rapidly and waving their hands. Erin looked up and smiled eagerly as he came up to her desk. He strode by without even saying hello. Cheeks burning with humiliation, she bent over the papers again, turning the pages without even seeing what was on them.

Two hours later she sighed, leaned back in her desk chair, and absently rubbed the painful crick in her neck. When she brought her hand back down to turn the next page, she saw with horror that it was stained black with the ink from the newsprint. Which meant that in rubbing her neck she had put a big, black, ugly stain on her blouse. Oh God, how could she go out to lunch with Andi Steiner looking like that?

Panicked, she fled to the ladies room, where she took off the blouse and examined it frantically. There was a definite smudge on the collar, but it wasn't too bad, she decided. She wet a paper towel with a squirt of liquid soap from the glass container over the sink and scrubbed vigorously. The smudge went away, and Erin smiled with relief as she hurried back to the office.

Another twenty minutes passed as Erin sat at her desk, lifting her head every few minutes to stare expectantly at the door. But there was still no sight of Andi. Her stomach growled, and she frowned as she looked at her watch. It was almost one-thirty. She got up and walked over to the girl who was sitting at the receptionist's desk busily polishing her nails.

"Excuse me," Erin said hesitantly, "but would you happen to know when Andi Steiner is expected back in the office?"

"Well, she usually gets back from lunch around one-thirty or two, unless she's had some special presentation to go to." The girl absently waved her hand in the air to dry the polish. "Today she just went out with some friends from the art department after their meeting this morning, so she should be back any minute now."

"She's already gone out to lunch?" Erin exclaimed.

"Well yeah, sure." The girl looked at her curiously. "Something wrong? I mean, like were you supposed to see her before?"

"No," Erin said in a small voice. "There's nothing wrong."

She returned to her desk, having learned her first important lesson about Hollywood. Promises meant nothing.

Two weeks later, Andi Steiner invited Erin to lunch again, and this time it actually happened. Erin had been kneeling in front of the file cabinets, stuffing old folders into storage boxes and replacing them with crisp, new, updated folders that she had painstakingly organized and cross-indexed when Andi tapped her on the shoulder.

"Hey, kid, I think you're due for a break. Another day buried in those files and you're going to forget your own name. Grab your purse and let's get out of here."

Andi took her to a small, pleasant restaurant with dark paneled walls and red leather booths. "Well, cheers," she announced as she lifted her martini glass.

"Cheers," Erin echoed with a smile as she picked up her glass of white wine. She took a sip and looked around the room with obvious pleasure. "This is really nice, Andi!"

"You deserve it, kid. You've been doing a hell of a good job for me, and I wanted to show you I appreciate it." Andi cocked her head, her bright inquisitive eyes peering out from the fringe of bangs that framed her small but attractive pixie face. "I'll bet this is the first lunch you've had since you started working here that hasn't come out of a brown paper bag."

Erin laughed. "You win."

"How old are you?"

"How old?" Erin looked at her uncertainly. "Why, uh, I'm twenty-two."

"Twenty-two. Jesus!" Andi stared into her martini. "I was thirty last week. Most depressing experience of my entire life."

"But thirty isn't old," Erin protested.

"Oh yeah? Maybe where you come from, Idaho or Iowa or whatever hick place, it isn't. But out here it's not only old, it's ancient." Andi moodily stirred the olive in her drink. "And if I don't get a break pretty soon, it's gonna be too late for me. Just too fuckin' late."

"Why?"

"All the rules have changed, kid. It's not like when I started here five years ago. Then publicity was a great job, a step up on the ladder. We had contract players, we produced fifty-two films a year. It was a production-line approach, and I was right in the middle of that production line and steadily moving forward every day. You don't have the faintest idea what I'm talking about, do you, kid?" she said with a crooked grin. She finished her martini in one large gulp.

"No," Erin admitted in bewilderment. "I really don't."

"Well, I'll try to explain," Andi signaled the waiter to bring another martini.

Erin listened intently as Andi recounted what had been happening in Hollywood over the past few years, realizing with a sudden shock of recognition that it was almost exactly what Jimmy Norton had predicted. She gave a gasp of horror as Andi told her that Film-Star was currently in debt to the tune of more than 70 million dollars.

"Take it easy, it's okay," Andi assured her. Then she gave a dry laugh. "Well, of course it isn't okay. What I mean is, it's nothing for you to worry about. Film-Star isn't in any danger of going out of business. Abe Lieberman is too smart to ever let that happen. Smart? Hell, he's a goddamn genius. Our studio is going to come out of this just fine."

She took a swallow of her martini and frowned. "But it's going to be a whole new ball game from now on. There's going to be a big emphasis on television, on syndication; and we're going to have a lot of independent producers coming in here with their own packages for feature films.

"So you see," she concluded gloomily, "with that kind of a setup, there's just no way to advance your career through the publicity department."

Erin could see all too clearly, and she silently cursed herself for her incredible naiveté in believing Ron Fletcher when he'd bragged about his importance. Well obviously there was only one solution. She had to get out of publicity and into another department, one with real power, as quickly as possible. But how? If Andi Steiner, who was a sharp, savvy woman with five years of experience and contacts at Film-Star, hadn't been able to manage it, what chance was there for someone as new and green as herself?

It was a sobered Erin who returned to the office to organize the files which just a few short hours earlier she had viewed with patient boredom, and now regarded with a passionate hatred.

Andi Steiner did manage it, though. A month later—a month that had seen a number of lunches between Andi and Erin, who had quickly decided that her only option at the moment was to cultivate a friendship with her ambitious boss in the hopes of gaining access to her contacts—Andi burst into the office and grabbed her around the waist.

"Erin baby, come with me!" she shouted ecstatically. "We are going out to celebrate!"

"I made it, kid," she announced, waving around her martini with such vigor that the icy cold gin slopped over the side of the frosted glass. "I finally made it! You are looking at the new production assistant to Leland Devereaux!"

"That's great," Erin said enthusiastically. "But who's Leland Devereaux?"

"Oh God, kid!" Andi groaned. "Haven't you learned anything since you've been here? Leland Devereaux just happens to be the most exciting, most gifted director Broadway has seen in the last decade. And Abe Lieberman got him! He's coming out here in three weeks to create and direct a special new series of quality programs for television. Major plays and dramas, documentaries, all top-drawer stuff. It's going to make Film-Star the most important, prestigious studio in this town, and it's going to give me a solid gold ticket to success!"

Andi sat back in the booth, a dreamy smile on her face as she envisioned the rosy future ahead of her.

"But what exactly will you be doing?" Erin asked curiously.

"Nothing much at first," she admitted with a little shrug. "A production assistant is really just a glorified gofer. But, you see, that isn't the point."

Andi leaned forward, her face intent. "The point is getting in on the ground floor of this kind of a project. Because if you're smart, all the opportunities are there. And believe me, kid, I'm going to take advantage of every one of them."

"*That* you didn't have to tell me. You'll be running the show in no time at all." A pensive look crossed her face. "I hope you'll remember me when you're big and famous."

"Of course I will," Andi said generously. "Which reminds me. The second reason I took you out to lunch today was to tell you that you're going to be running our little area in the publicity department for the next ten days."

"What?" Erin blinked in surprise.

"Then again," Andi said with a slow smile, "you do a good enough job while I'm gone, and I'll recommend you for the position on a permanent basis."

"But where are you going?"

"On vacation, my child." Andi lifted her glass and took a deep, pleasurable draught. "This little gal is taking off for Puerto Vallarta on the first flight out of here tomorrow, to have a ball while she can. Because once Devereaux arrives, there won't be any vacations at all. There won't even be any evenings off, if what I hear about him is true. He works his people twenty-four hours a day. So I'm going to get my batteries recharged in the next ten days, and come back ready to take on anything they throw at me."

"Puerto Vallarta," Erin said wonderingly. "Isn't that where Elizabeth Taylor and Richard Burton . . ."

"Right. And it works its wonders equally as well on us lesser mortals. It is *the* place to go for R and R. That stands for *romance* and recreation.

"Anyway," she continued, seriously, "I'm trusting you to handle things while I'm gone. And the most important task I'm assigning you is to keep your eyes and ears open about what's going on. Not that I really expect anything important to happen. But I'm giving you my vacation itinerary just in case, so if something comes up that's a problem, or something you think I should know about, you can get in touch with me immediately. Understood?"

"Understood."

"Good." Andi relaxed and picked up the menu, then peered over it. "By the way, I meant what I said about recommending you for my job."

"I really appreciate that," Erin said dismally.

• • •

Leland Devereaux arrived in Hollywood two weeks early, due to unexpected complications in his romance with the beautiful young actress-wife of a famous Italian producer. The producer, a highly excitable man, had arrived at Devereaux's hotel suite in the middle of the night, screaming and brandishing a revolver. "If you're not out of Rome before daybreak, you're a dead man!"

Devereaux prided himself on being a man of considerable physical courage; however, the present moment did not seem like the most propitious time to demonstrate it. He had packed hurriedly as the producer stood in the doorway tracking his every movement with the gun, and fled into a waiting cab, and off to Rome's Fiumicino airport.

During the long flight from Rome to Los Angeles, Devereaux repeatedly told himself that he had taken the only action possible; that it had been an act of wisdom, not cowardice. Nevertheless, the experience rankled; and he was anxious to put it behind him and forget about it. And the best way to accomplish that was by immediately plunging into work.

Having made that decision, he began to feel better almost at once. After all, he mused as he stroked his silky Vandyke beard, the work was all that really counted. The brilliant, creative work that only Leland Devereaux could bring to a world so desperately in need of it.

That realization so cheered him, he playfully pinched the luscious, pear-shaped buttocks of the stewardess who leaned over him to ask solicitously if he wanted another drink, and made a date with her for his first night in Los Angeles.

Executives at Film-Star were thrown into a state of total panic when Leland Devereaux charged into their offices two weeks ahead of schedule, full of ferocious energy and demanding that production start immediately on his first project, a screen adaptation of a highly acclaimed Broadway play. Frantic studio personnel shifted work schedules, grabbing people wherever they could find them to put together a staff for him. And the most frantic among them was Joel Gerson, the bright young man who had just been promoted to the coveted position of administrative assistant to the executive producer in charge of the new television series.

"Where is she?" he demanded frantically of the girl sitting at the receptionist's desk in front of the publicity department.

"Where's who?"

"Steiner! Andi Steiner! For God's sake, who else would I be asking about?"

"I . . . I don't know," the girl stammered, cowering back in her chair as he glared at her. "But if you want Andi Steiner, she's on vacation."

"Vacation? Oh Christ, I don't believe this," Joel moaned. He took a deep breath. "Okay then, we just have to get her back here. So where is she on vacation?"

"I don't know that either. I'm just the relief receptionist."

"Then who *does* know?" he roared.

"Her assistant." With a trembling hand, the girl waved behind her toward the desk where Erin was bent over, engrossed in cutting out articles from a pile of fan magazines.

"Thanks," Joel said curtly as he strode over to Erin.

"Hey!"

Erin continued clipping away.

"Hey. Hey you!" he shouted.

Erin dropped the scissors and glanced up in alarm at the frantic man looming over her.

"You Andi Steiner's assistant?"

Erin swallowed. "Yes."

"You know how to get in touch with her?"

"Uh, yes."

"Good. Then do it. Immediately! Get her back on the first plane from wherever she is and tell her we expect her back here tomorrow morning at eight o'clock sharp if she wants to keep her job as Devereaux's production assistant. You got that?" he yelled.

"I got it," she said faintly.

"Glad to hear that. Then I won't have to repeat it." He turned on his heel and marched out of the office.

Erin pulled open her top desk drawer, took out the envelope containing Andi's itinerary, and picked up the phone.

"Operator, I'd like to place a call to the Casa Del Mar Hotel in Puerto Vallarta, Mexico."

"Do you have the number for that hotel?"

Erin stared thoughtfully at the piece of paper in front of her which listed the name, address, and telephone number of the hotel in Andi's sharp, angular handwriting.

"I said, do you have the number?" the operator repeated impatiently.

"I'm sorry, operator. I've changed my mind. Cancel the call."

Erin hung up the receiver and then quietly stuffed Andi's itinerary under the pile of old magazines in her wastebasket.

Eight

ERIN set her alarm for six-thirty the next morning, and she was instantly awake and fully alert the second it went off. She bathed and dressed quickly, ate a hurried breakfast, and arrived at the Film-Star lot a few minutes before seven-thirty.

The studio guard blinked at her in surprise. "You sure are early today, Miss Connolly. Got some big project going on in publicity?"

"In a way, Harry," Erin smiled. "At least it's big to me."

"Well, good luck on it," he said cheerfully as he checked off her name on his clipboard. "I'll keep my fingers crossed for you."

And darned if I won't, he thought to himself as Erin blew him a kiss before hurrying past him into the lobby. She deserved the luck, because she was just as nice as she was pretty. Always greeted him with a smile, and usually took time to stop and chat with him a bit. Not like some of those stuck-up snobs who couldn't even take the time to get his name right. He found himself hoping that her project, whatever it was, would succeed, and he had a feeling it probably would. Over the years, Harry had developed a sense about the people who passed through his gates; and that sense told him Erin was one of the winners.

Erin was considerably less confident than Harry as she took the express elevator to the executive suites located on the twentieth floor, nervously fingering the strap on her purse as she rehearsed her speech.

Knowing that Devereaux had ordered production to start on his first venture promptly at eight o'clock, she had no doubts that Joel Gerson would be in his office at this early hour. But she had serious doubts about his response to her proposal.

Her mouth was dry, and she had problems swallowing as she stepped off the elevator and walked into his office.

"What do you mean, you couldn't reach her?" Joel screamed in outrage. "It's your job to reach her!"

"I've been trying, Mr. Gerson," Erin announced quietly. "I've called her hotel every hour on the hour since you came into my office yesterday. I even called from my home until midnight last night."

"Are you looking for an award or something? What the hell do I care if you called until midnight? All I want is to have Andi Steiner here. Now!"

Gerson poured water into a glass from the handsome silver carafe sitting on his desk, shook two pills out of a small vial and gulped them down, then broke into a sudden coughing fit as one of the pills lodged in his throat.

Erin leaned over and refilled the water glass, handing it to him hastily.

"Thanks," he said weakly as he swallowed and the choking spasm eased. "For something, anyway," he added balefully.

"I'm really terribly sorry about this, Mr. Gerson," Erin said earnestly. "But I'm sure I'll be able to contact Andi today. Unless, of course," she frowned, "Andi decided to accept that invitation from her friends in the area to spend the week with them. Unfortunately, she didn't leave me their name and phone number. Not that I think that would be a problem," Erin said quickly. "You know how dependable Andi is. I'm sure that whatever she's doing, she'll be checking in with her hotel. And I'll keep calling, naturally."

"Well, isn't that just swell," Joel said bitterly. "I can't tell you how much you've reassured me. Good old dependable Andi Steiner, who didn't even leave the name and number of unknown friends she might or might not visit, is going to call at some unknown time. And that is supposed to take care of my problem?"

He leaned over and smashed his fist on the desk so hard that the silver carafe leaped up and toppled over. "Well, it *doesn't* take care of my problem," he exclaimed furiously. "My problem is today! Today!! Do you understand?"

"Yes. Yes, I certainly do," Erin said apprehensively. "So that's why I decided to ask you if I could help out by taking her place until she gets back," she concluded in a shaky voice.

"*You*?" He stared at her incredulously. "*You* take Andi Steiner's place on the Devereaux production set?"

"I could do it, Mr. Gerson," Erin assured him feverishly. "I know I could. Andi and I have worked very closely together. She's even recommending me for her job in publicity, that's how much trust she has in me. And she's told me everything about this new job."

"You've got to be kidding," he said flatly. "You're a green kid who can't even manage to get hold of her boss in an emergency. How could I ever believe you could handle something like this, even for a few days?"

"I can't guarantee someone else's performance, Mr. Gerson," Erin said evenly. "But I assure you I can guarantee my own."

"Well." Joel sat back in his chair, a speculative look in his eye. "That's very interesting. Very interesting indeed. I wonder why it didn't occur to me earlier."

Erin felt perspiration forming under her arms as he continued to stare at her, a thoughtful smile playing around his mouth. Then without warning he abruptly brought his chair forward with a crash, and she jumped in fright.

"All right, little girl, we'll give you your chance. I'll call Faraday and tell him I've okayed your filling in for Andi Steiner for the next few days."

He stood up, placed his hands flat on the desk, and leaned over her, his eyes drilling into hers. "But just remember one thing—if I hear one complaint about you, if you so much as foul up a coffee order, you're through! Not just with the

Devereaux production, but with Film-Star Studios. Understood?"

"There won't be any complaints, I promise. And I want to thank you for this, Mr. Gerson. I just want to thank you so much."

"Stop thanking me and get the hell out of here and go to work!"

"Yes sir!" Erin leaped up from the chair and fled the office.

There were no complaints, of course. At least not from any of the production crew on the set, who found Erin an absolute treasure. She was quick, bright, efficient, unfailingly cheerful, and engagingly eager to do anything and everything they asked of her. There was one extremely bitter complaint, though, from an initially stunned, then outraged, and finally heartbroken Andi Steiner who returned a week later to find that her trusted assistant had completely, totally, and irrevocably stolen her one big opportunity.

"I'm telling you she never called me!" Andi cried in anguish to Joel Gerson. "You know me, Joel." Her eyes pleaded with him. "You know I'd never go anyplace where the studio couldn't get in touch with me any hour of the day or night."

"But I didn't know how to get in touch with you," he observed mildly.

"That's true." She reflected miserably that none of this would have happened if she hadn't deliberately withheld her vacation plans from him for fear that he might ask her to cancel them.

"I should have told you, and I apologize for not doing so. But I never dreamed there'd be any problems. I trusted that little bitch. I trusted her completely . . ." Andi broke off with a choked sob, then dug into her purse for a cigarette to help calm her. Her hand was trembling so much, she couldn't work the lighter.

Joel graciously leaned over and lit the cigarette for her. "Now just try to relax, Andi," he said soothingly. "You're not helping yourself at all by getting this excited."

"You do believe me, though, don't you?" she asked feverishly. "You do know I'm telling the truth?"

"Yes, Andi, I believe you," he smiled.

"Then why haven't you gotten her off that set?" she demanded hysterically. "She was only allowed to be there until I got back. Well I'm back now! I'm back, Joel! And it's *my* job!!"

"Unfortunately, they're into almost a full week's production by this time and the crew is used to Erin now. They really don't want a change."

"Joel, don't tell me that! You know as well as I that you can change a production assistant any time you want. Pull her out and put me back there!"

"I'm sorry, Andi," he said regretfully. "But I'm afraid I really can't do that. Devereaux himself has gotten used to her, and you can imagine how upset he'd get with any change in personnel."

"You cruddy fake!" Andi stormed. "What you're really saying is that you're sleeping with the bitch. I took you into my bed for a whole year, a year when you were nothing! I catered to your weird, kinky needs. I did everything for you! Well, if you think I'm going to keep quiet about this, you're crazy. I'm going to tell the whole world!"

"And the world will find it just as boring as I did," Joel said icily. "I took pity on you, which was obviously a mistake. You are a rather sad example of a woman trying to trade on a body that has seen better days. You are also, apparently, severely emotionally disturbed. I will try to be kind when I inform personnel why we must terminate you.

"By the way," he added as she started to cry hopelessly. "I have never been to bed with Erin Connolly. She made it on her own."

A friend of Andi's told her there was an opening in the publicity department at International Pictures. It was only an assistant's job and the department manager was dubious at first about hiring someone with Andi's experience, but a discreet check with Ron Fletcher reassured him that her leaving Film-Star was a political matter and had nothing to do with her work ability. Two days after the interview he offered her the position, and she accepted gratefully since there was absolutely nothing else available for her. Andi packed up her belongings, which seemed pitifully meager after five whole years, bade a tearful farewell to her co-workers, and made one brief stop before exiting Film-Star Studios forever.

"Hey, wait a minute!" the security guard protested as Andi pushed her way past him. "You can't go in there. It's a closed set."

"I've got an important message for one of the crew members," she announced grimly.

"Well, gee, I don't know," he began uncertainly. But Andi hadn't waited for his permission. She was already through the door and marching toward the front of the set before he'd finished speaking. He frowned, then started after her.

Erin was crouched by the side of the script girl, rapidly feeding her revised pages of the teleplay which she'd just run off on the Xerox machine, when she felt the sudden sharp pain of fingernails digging into her arm. She looked up in surprise, and then stared in disbelieving horror as Andi Steiner glared down and yanked so hard at her blouse that it was literally ripped off her shoulder.

"Bitch!" Andi hissed. "Filthy, lying, cheating bitch! I've got a message for you. I'm going to get you one of these days." She stood up and waved the torn scrap of Erin's blouse around the room. *"And I've got a message for everyone here, too. Watch your back when you're around this bitch if you don't want to end up with a knife in it!"*

The panting security guard came up and grabbed Andi around the waist as everyone in the studio looked on in stunned fascination.

"It's all right. I'll go quietly." She allowed the guard to lead her away, then turned around just before they reached the door. *"But remember what I told you,"* she screamed at the astonished faces. *"You let a killer in here, and you'd better watch out."*

"I . . . I'm so sorry," Erin stammered, crimson with embarrassment. "I can't imagine what she's talking about, but I apologize to all of you for having been the cause of this terrible interruption. Please forgive me," she added in a voice that sounded on the verge of tears.

"Hey, it's okay." Kevin Anderson, a burly stuntman who had become Erin's devoted slave from the moment she appeared on the set and took it upon herself to massage his back and neck between takes with a special liniment she'd bought, came over and roughly caressed her head. "Don't you know that you're nobody in Hollywood until you've made your first enemy?"

Both the cast and the crew broke into appreciative laughter, which was quickly stilled when Leland Devereaux smashed his gold-handled walking stick, a Devereaux trademark, across the arm of his director's chair.

"Perhaps we should ask Miss Connolly to make more enemies," he intoned glacially, "since this is the first genuine emotion I've seen on this set all day. Now shall we get back to work and see if *we* can produce some?"

Chastened, the crew scurried back to their cameras and the actors took their places as Devereaux snarled. "Action!" But their pace had been put off by Andi's appearance, and it was a bad take. They had to sweat through ten more takes before Devereaux was satisfied, and by that time everyone had completely forgotten about the incident, including Erin.

There would come a time, however, when Erin would remember it all too clearly, but by then it would be much too late to do anything about it.

During the next ten months Erin worked harder than she ever had in her life and loved every second of it, unhampered by a single unpleasant incident. She was at the studio every morning before eight and often stayed as late as eleven at night, even on days when the Devereaux unit wasn't shooting. Although she found television interesting and often exciting, only the creation of movies truly fascinated her and fired her imagination. So whenever she wasn't needed on a Devereaux project, she would appear on the set of whatever movie company was currently shooting, and shyly offer her services.

People soon grew used to the slim, long-legged girl with the glowing green eyes who was always available to bring them coffee and sandwiches and run errands for them; and Erin was allowed to roam freely throughout the studio.

She watched, listened, asked questions, and poked into every area of filmmaking; absorbing knowledge like a sponge. She saw how a film's soundtrack was recorded, mixed, and edited; became familiar with set design, costume design, and special effects; perceived the importance of a music score in creating atmosphere; discovered how a skilled cinematographer could command audience attention for a movie just through his control of light and shadow; and learned the vital function of the cutting room where, finally, all the confusing bits and pieces were shaped into a cohesive whole.

She also quickly realized where the real power lay in filmmaking. The people who designed, photographed, cut, and scored a picture were tools, absolutely necessary, but tools nonetheless. Power belonged to directors and actors, and absolute power to producers. No matter what the star status of an actor or the professional clout of an award-winning director, they were essentially hired help. Erin was determined to become a producer.

But when Erin confided her ambition to the friends she'd made at the studio they stared blankly at her for a moment, then burst into laughter.

"Honey, I think maybe you need to be told the facts of life," Mavis Coulter said with a kindly smile as she saw the crushed look on Erin's face. "We weren't making fun of you. It's just that we know your dream is totally impossible."

"Why? Why is it impossible?" Erin demanded. I know everything that goes into making a picture. There are kids coming out of film schools today who don't know half of what I do, and they're producing. So why shouldn't I be able to?"

"Because you don't have connections. Because you don't have money. Because you're a woman," Mavis added sadly.

"No, listen to me," she commanded as Erin started to protest. "I know how to make pictures just as well as you do. I've been a film editor here for the past two years and it took me eight years just to work myself into that position, even though I could have handled it perfectly after my first year here. As for producing pictures, well the studio executives would never give me a chance even though they know damn well I could do twice as good a job as some of these young hotshots who'd never get the film in the can without my help in the cutting room.

"But that's the way it is in Hollywood." Mavis sighed. "Women's Lib may have arrived in America, but it never made it into this town. Hollywood belongs to men, and the only power here is *male* power. You're just kidding yourself if you believe any differently."

"She's right, you know," Cheryl Green said glumly. "They told me the way to break into directing was by becoming a script girl. Well, I've been a script girl for seven years, and I'll probably die being a script girl. I mean, you can count the number of women directors in Hollywood on one hand and have four fingers left over. As for women producers—" She snorted. "Well, they don't even exist in someone's imagination. I'm telling you, Erin, there will never be a woman producer here!"

"You're wrong, Cheryl," Erin said grimly. "There will be, and her name will be Erin Connolly."

"Sure, babe. And I'll ride a pink elephant in the Rose Bowl parade."

Erin never mentioned her aspirations about becoming a producer to her friends again, and they assumed she'd given up the idea. She'd done nothing of the kind, of course, but she'd wisely decided that if the idea of a woman producer was that unpopular in Hollywood she could only do herself harm by talking about it. She would just bide her time until the right opportunity came along, and when it did she would take swift, decisive advantage of it.

But as the weeks went by and turned into months, she became increasingly discouraged. Because it didn't seem as though there would ever be any right opportunities. Not that her career was without progress. Lois Parton, the plump, rather homely, but thoroughly professional and totally dedicated script girl for the Devereaux production unit, had astounded everyone first by getting married and then by becoming pregnant. Leland Devereaux offered Erin the position when Lois left on maternity leave. It was considered by everyone except Erin to be an incredible honor, and she was deluged with congratulations.

Just a week later two different directors for independent production companies, whom Erin had worked for while they were filming on the studio lot, asked her if she'd be interested in joining them as an assistant editor.

"Jesus, you've really got the world by the tail!" Cheryl Green exclaimed with more than a touch of envy. "I mean, you've been at Film-Star less than a year and here you are with three incredible job offers. I worked five years before I got even *one* offer like that." She shook her head wonderingly as she stared at Erin. "It's unbelievable! What are you going to do?"

"I don't know." Erin forced a smile and tried to sound ethusiastic. "It's . . . well, it's all so exciting I'm just not sure what the right choice is."

"But television really isn't your thing, is it?" She flushed as Erin stared at her curiously. "What I mean is that I thought you were more into the film side. Major motion pictures, that kind of thing."

"You want the job as script girl for Devereaux, don't you?" Erin said softly.

Cheryl looked down at her hands, which were clutching a coffee mug with desperate intensity. "Yes," she admitted in a barely audible whisper. "The studio productions I'm working on now are dogs. I'd give anything to get on the Devereaux set."

She lifted her head and gazed at Erin. "Would you recommend me for the job if you decide to turn it down?" she said pleadingly.

"Of course I would, Cheryl," Erin told her as she stood up and absently patted her on the shoulder. "But right now I think I'd better go and get a bite to eat before Devereaux starts shooting again. Anyway, whatever I decide I promise to let you know about it first."

"You're a really nice human being," Cheryl said gratefully. "And whatever you decide, I want you to know how much I appreciate your help and understanding."

"Well, isn't that what friendship is all about?" Erin smiled as she walked out of the office.

But her smile faded abruptly as she made her way to the Film-Star commissary. In a few short days she would have to make a decision about the positions offered her, and the unhappy truth was that she didn't want any of them. They were all dead-end jobs that would lock her into obscurity. But there was no way she could turn down all of them without seriously jeopardizing her future in the business.

Erin was still frowning unhappily as she entered the commissary and glanced around the room for an empty table. Then her eyes widened in amazement as she saw the figure sitting at a small table in the back.

"Jimmy? Jimmy Norton, is it really you?" she shouted with delight as she raced over to him.

"My God! Erin!" He stood up and stared at her, "What in the world are you doing here?"

"I was just about to ask you the same question," she said happily as she pulled out a chair and sat down. Then she started to laugh. "We always seem to be meeting this way, don't we? Remember that day in the student union at Cheviot Hills?"

"Yes. Yes, I certainly do." He lowered himself slowly back into his chair, then reached out and took hold of her hand. "Just wanted to make sure you're real."

"Oh, I'm real all right," she assured him.

"And more beautiful than ever," he smiled. "You look absolutely terrific, Erin."

"You look pretty terrific yourself." Her eyes approvingly noted the casually elegant cashmere jacket, the custom-tailored shirt, the thin gold Rolex watch, and the perfectly manicured nails on the hand that rested lightly on top of hers.

"You sure have changed from that kid in jeans and a T-shirt I knew in college." She grinned. "It's a wonder I even recognized you."

"Well, the color's still the same," he said dryly. "That probably helped."

"Hey, what's with the hostility? This is me, Erin. Remember?"

He looked into the brilliant green eyes and saw that nothing had changed since that day in the student union. "I remember."

"Anyway," he continued briskly, eager to change the subject, "let's forget about the past and catch up on the present. What's been happening with you, and what are you doing here?"

"You first," Erin insisted. "Because you owe me an explanation. I wrote you the minute I knew I was coming out here and the post office returned the letter. You didn't even leave a forwarding address for me. That was mean, Jimmy," she pouted. "You promised to introduce me to Hollywood."

"Well, I've turned into a pretty mean dude. Especially when someone doesn't answer my letters for a whole year."

"Okay, truce time," she laughed. "Now tell me about you!"

"Oh, not all that much to tell," he said offhandedly. "Came out of USC's film school and went to International Pictures. I'm a writer and director now."

"A writer *and* a director?" Erin's eyes glowed. "Jimmy, that's marvelous. That is absolutely marvelous!" Then an expression of doubt clouded her face. "But how come I haven't run into you before if you've been working here at Film-Star?"

"Because I don't work for Film-Star. I'm under contract to International. They just loaned me out for a special project."

"Loaned you out?" Erin repeated puzzledly. "I never heard of a studio doing that."

"That's because you haven't heard about me. I'm a special project all on my own," he added with a wry smile.

"What?"

"Never mind," he said quickly. "It's just a management thing."

"Hey, James Lee! Great to see you here." A short, stocky man with iron-gray hair, who was dressed in a somber but impeccably tailored black suit, white shirt, and regimental tie, stopped at the table and offered his hand.

"We're really delighted to have this chance to work with you, James Lee. Please call me anytime if you have any questions or problems." He gave Erin a quick, quizzical glance before walking away.

Erin gazed in awe as he continued his brisk passage across

the commissary, pausing briefly to chat with a few people at the tables near the window. "That was Lee Golden!" she said breathlessly. "He's second-in-command to Abe Lieberman and just about the most powerful person in the whole studio!"

"I know," he replied tonelessly.

"You weren't kidding, were you?" Erin said admiringly. "You are really someone special." She looked at him inquiringly. "But why did he call you James Lee?"

"Because that's my name now. I changed it to James Lee Norton. Jimmy sounded too much like a kid."

"It's exactly the right name," Erin announced with a thoughtful nod. "Jimmy is who you were. James Lee is who you are now. A very successful man." She flashed him a quick, gamine grin. "So when are you going to introduce me to Hollywood, Mr. Success?"

"After you tell me what's been happening to you. No," he interrupted as she started to protest. "I won't do a thing for you until you bring me up to date on everything that's been going on in your life since we last saw each other."

"Well, if you insist." She sighed. "But it hasn't been all that exciting, I've got to warn you."

"I'm warned," he smiled. "So go."

A number of people would have been startled to hear Erin's account of her life over the past few years, especially Eric Glass, Ron Fletcher, and Andi Steiner. Eric Glass was portrayed as a lecherous college professor who took advantage of her innocence. There was no mention of her marriage to him, and certainly no mention of the child she had borne him. Ron Fletcher was a little more accurately portrayed as a lecherous studio executive, but his ultimate helplessness and rejection by Erin were quickly passed over. As for Andi Steiner, she was transformed into a paranoid middle-aged woman who tried to destroy Erin's career for no other reason than pathological jealousy.

"Well, you've certainly done well for yourself considering all those traumatic experiences," James Lee observed with a quiet smile. "I think congratulations are in order."

"What exactly do you mean by that?" Erin asked suspiciously.

He started to laugh. "Hey," he mocked her, "this is me, Jimmy. Remember?"

She glared at him indignantly, then gave up the pose as his wise eyes grinned at her. "Okay," she admitted. "So maybe I exaggerated things a little. But there's one thing I didn't exaggerate at all."

She leaned forward, staring at him intently. "Jimmy . . ." She checked herself immediately. "James Lee, I *know* I have the talent and ability to become a producer. And I want it more than anything in the world. Can you help me?"

"Erin, you're really asking the impossible," he said sadly, shaking his head. "Your friend Cheryl Green was right when she told you what it was like. You're a woman, you've got no contacts, no money. It just can't happen."

"Look, forget for the moment that I'm a woman," she said fiercely. "Suppose I could find the contacts and the money? Would that make it happen?"

He started to shrug, then froze as an incredible idea occurred to him. Was it possible? He looked across the table at the vibrantly beautiful woman who still made his pulse race, despite his knowledge of what she was really like and the hopelessness of any relationship between them. Yes, goddamnit, it is possible, he thought exultantly. Maybe Erin would never end up with her dream, but he would finally have his revenge. And what an exquisite revenge it would be!

"I think I might be able to help you after all," he said cautiously. "If you'll do exactly as I say."

Erin's green eyes blazed with hope. "Just tell me what you want and I'll do it," she promised excitedly.

"There's a party I'm invited to the end of this week. A very exclusive party at the home of Martin Weinguard. I'll take you with me."

"You mean Martin Weinguard the studio head of International Pictures?" Erin said wonderingly.

"The one and only." He smiled.

"And you'll personally introduce me to Martin Weinguard?"

"Oh, well you'll meet him too. But the really important person I'll be introducing you to is Anthony Wellington."

"Anthony Wellington?" She gave him a baffled look. "I never heard of him. Is he a new director or a producer?"

"No, he isn't even an important studio executive."

"I don't understand," she said uncertainly.

"I know you don't." He gave her a wolfish smile. "But just listen very closely as I tell you about Anthony Wellington, and then you'll understand perfectly."

Nine

ANTHONY Wellington fell in love for the first time in 1942. It happened at precisely nine-fifteen on a warm July evening in Stroudsburg, Pennsylvania, just after he had dipped into his bag of hot buttered popcorn in the Orpheum Theater and then stopped, transfixed, as he gazed upon the exquisite vision of Ingrid Bergman in *Casablanca*. He was thirteen years old.

His single-minded devotion continued into 1943, when *For Whom The Bell Tolls* came out, and was still going strong in 1944 with *Gaslight*. By 1946 and *Notorious*, his passion had expanded to include the whole world of show business, and it would be safe to say that there was no more star-struck a youngster in the entire United States than Anthony Wellington, who longed with all his heart to become a part of the marvelously exciting and glamorous world he saw on the screen of his local movie house in the small Pennsylvania town where he grew up.

Unfortunately, Anthony had no talent for show business. He couldn't act, sing, dance, or write. He couldn't even build a decent stage set. What he could do was make money. It wasn't something he wanted. It wasn't even something he worked at. It was just something that happened. Nature had played a very unfair trick on Anthony Wellington, giving him the passionate yearning soul of an artist but gifting him only with the Midas touch. And so it was inevitable that he wound up being the treasurer of the dramatic clubs he joined in high school and college, and then the business manager for the small, off-Broadway productions he became involved in when he wistfully followed his more talented friends to New York after their graduation from the University of Pennsylvania.

In an effort to keep his mind off the bitter disappointment of being forever a spectator and never a participant in the world he loved so much, Anthony started playing around with real estate in the free time he had between his chores of finding financial backing for his little theater groups. His real estate ventures flourished and began to pyramid. They also began to get so complicated, they demanded his attention almost full-time. Irritated at being taken away from his one true love, Anthony hired an accountant and reluctantly met with him once a week to look over his current assets and recommend the next move.

By the time Anthony Wellington was thirty, he was worth twenty million dollars. He listened glumly to his accountant's ecstatic report of the current value of his holdings. Then a sudden smile creased his face.

"Twenty million, you say?"

"At least!" Irvin Schwartz declared jubilantly. "Could be as high as twenty-one or twenty-two."

"Good. Then sell it all. Today."

"*What*? Are you crazy or something? Why would you want to do that?"

"Because with twenty million dollars I could be somebody in Hollywood," Anthony said triumphantly.

"It's true I can't act or write," he continued. "But with twenty million dollars I could become a producer. Now couldn't I, Irving?"

"Oh my God, the man's lost his mind!" Irving fell into a chair and groped desperately in his pocket for a Gelusil. "Now listen to me, Anthony. I know about your fantasy, but this is not the way to do it. Believe me, as your friend, it's not the way!"

"Why not?" Anthony asked pleasantly. "Don't you think twenty million dollars is enough?"

"It's not twenty million in cash. It's twenty million in assets. They're not the same thing! Don't you see that?" he said frantically.

"Well I guess we'll find out soon enough, won't we?"

"You're wrong!" Irving sobbed. "This is *not* the time to sell. You could lose everything. Wait, please! I'm begging you!"

But Anthony was adamant, and his perverse luck held. There was a sudden upsurge in the real estate market, and he came out with over fifty million dollars.

Hollywood executives were baffled by the tall slender man with the prematurely balding head, stooped shoulders, and apologetic smile who arrived in their midst late in 1959 and shyly offered them financial backing for their upcoming productions. For one thing, nobody had ever heard of him. He had no credentials in the entertainment industry on either coast. Even more disturbing was the way he approached them. It was totally unheard of for a potential investor to suddenly appear in a producer's office and open his checkbook. Things just weren't done that way. The standard procedure was to send out word that a certain party might be interested in making a deal; then, emissaries from both sides got together and cautiously explored the possibilities; finally a meeting was arranged where the principals, armed with their attorneys, would come together face to face. Anthony Wellington had ignored all these time-honored customs, and it made them very nervous. Either he was conning them, or the whole thing was a put-on. Suspicious and distrustful, they backed away from him, leaving him hurt, bewildered, unhappy, and very lonely. Then he met Marcia Weinguard.

It happened at a party thrown by Martin Weinguard to celebrate the nomination of two of his pictures for the 1960 Academy Awards. George Banner was an independent producer who was enjoying the unusual privilege of being courted by every major studio in Hollywood after his low-budget picture on California surfers had broken box-office records around the country. He was also one of the few people who really understood Anthony Wellington. Out of genuine liking, as well as pity for the gentle diffident man, he invited him along as his guest.

Anthony was so overwhelmingly grateful for the invitation that Banner immediately began to regret his impulsive kindness.

"Now look, Anthony," he warned. "Don't get any wrong ideas. I'm not taking you there for the purpose of meeting anyone who's looking for a financial backer. In fact, I don't want you to even bring up the subject. This is strictly for entertainment. Just relax and enjoy yourself."

"George, I wouldn't dream of talking about money at a party," Anthony said, deeply shocked. "How could you possibly have thought such a thing?"

Banner, who knew that money was always a major topic of conversation at every Hollywood party, shook his head at his friend's hopeless naiveté. "Well, it's been known to happen," he remarked dryly. "But don't you get involved in anything but a good time."

"You can count on that," Anthony smiled.

And at first Anthony Wellington not only had a good time, he had the time of his life. Beaming with wide-eyed delight, he shook hands with some of the most glamorous stars in Hollywood, almost beside himself with excitement. Then George Banner, after thirty minutes of shepherding his charge around the room, gently deposited him at a table and left him with a tray of delicacies from the buffet as he went off to take care of business. And Anthony Wellington stopped having a good time.

Initially he looked up and smiled eagerly at each person who passed by his table, and when he saw someone to whom he'd been introduced earlier he would leap to his feet and offer them a place to sit down. But it was like they'd all suddenly turned deaf and blind, gliding by him unseeing and unhearing, only to break into animated cries of pleasure at a voice that called to them from a table just beyond his.

Gradually his smiles faded and then disappeared altogether as he forlornly watched the party where, as usual, he was fated to be only a spectator, never a participant. He was on the verge of gathering together enough courage to leave his isolated corner and join the noisy, laughing crowd around the bar when the band filed into the room. They took their places on the stage and launched into a wild driving beat that brought everyone charging onto the small dance floor, where they exploded into joyous contortions.

Anthony blinked in confusion as multi-colored lights flashed on over the dance floor and the candle on his table flickered briefly before going out. It took several seconds before his eyes were able to focus again. Then he saw the woman sitting at the table next to him. She, too, was alone with a tray of food from the buffet sitting in front of her. But unlike himself, she was stuffing it into her mouth with ferocious energy.

"You must have found something better than I did," he smiled as he leaned toward her.

"What?" Marcia Weinguard looked up from her plate and stared at him blankly.

"Your selection from the buffet," he said, nodding toward her plate. "I was wondering what it is."

She cupped a hand around her ear. "You'll have to speak up. I can't hear a word in this racket."

"I said, I wanted to know what you're eating," he shouted. "Because you're evidently enjoying it very much."

Marcia, who was easily forty pounds overweight, pulled back and glared at him indignantly. "What the hell kind of crack is that? You trying to be smart or something?"

"I beg your pardon?"

The band's drummer executed a frantic paradiddle with his sticks as the guitarist, hips gyrating like Elvis Presley's, grabbed the microphone and let out a high, keening wail as he apparently experienced a major orgasm. A brief silence followed as the band's members fell back and lit up, the sweetish odor of marijuana mingling with the more conventional cigarette smoke in the room.

"Marcia, I've been looking everywhere for you!" An incredibly handsome young man in his early twenties came rushing up to her table. The ceiling lights reflected off the lustrous cap of dark curly hair and illuminated the sparkling blue eyes that glowed out of the tanned face. "Now you promised me a dance," he smiled engagingly. "So I'm claiming this next one."

"I never promised you anything, Rodney," Marcia said flatly.

"Well, I guess that's true." With an effort, Rodney managed to keep the smile on his face, his perfectly capped teeth gleaming whitely at her. "Maybe I just promised myself, because I was looking forward to it so much."

"Oh get off it, Rodney," Marcia said impatiently. "You've done your duty. Now go away and leave me alone."

"Marcia, what are you talking about?" He bent over and kissed her hand. "I *want* to be with you. Don't you understand that?"

"I understand very well," Marcia replied in a low, ominous tone. "But what you don't understand is that I don't want to be with you."

"I hear you," he answered nervously. "But your father . . ."

"It's all right, Rodney," she said wearily. "I'll tell him you came over and did just what he asked you to."

"Well, if you're sure . . ."

"I'm sure. So do me a favor and split!"

As Rodney turned and walked away, Anthony was horrified to see two big fat teardrops spill out of Marcia's eyes and roll down her cheeks. Whipping out a large white handkerchief, he pressed it on her and murmured, "I'm so sorry that young man upset you. Is there anything I can do?"

"No," she said with a muffled sob. "But thanks." She mopped her cheeks and handed his handkerchief back, then bent over her plate again.

"Forgive my rudeness in not introducing myself. I'm Anthony Wellington," he offered shyly.

"Marcia Weinguard," she mumbled as she shoveled a forkful of food into her mouth.

"Marcia Weinguard!" he exclaimed. "Are you by any chance related to Martin Weinguard?"

"Daughter." She began eating faster.

"Why, how exciting!" he beamed. "This is a real honor for me, meeting you."

She put down her fork. "Forget it," she announced curtly. "You'll just be wasting your time trying to play up to me, because nobody gets a penny out of Marcia Weinguard!"

He gazed at her in astonishment. "You think I'm interested in your money?"

Her eyes traveled over him coldly. "Well, it's pretty obvious that you're no actor, so you're not cozying up to me to get a part in a picture. That leaves money."

"Money," he repeated. Then as the incredible irony of the situation hit him, he started to laugh. And the more he thought about it, the funnier it became to him. His laughter grew into a roar, causing people at nearby tables to turn and stare.

"Hey! Hey, what's the matter with you?" Marcia asked nervously.

"Oh, my dear girl, if you only knew," he sputtered as another wave of laughter overcame him. He finally managed to bring himself under control, wiping his eyes with the handkerchief that was still damp from Marcia's tears. "You see, I've spent the last five months trying desperately to give away money. And now you think I want to *take* money. It's just too incredible!"

"What in the world are you talking about?"

"Well, I guess I do owe you an explanation," he said, embarrassed. He became aware of the fact that his loud laughter had attracted attention to them from every table surrounding them.

Hunching his shoulders and lowering his voice, he leaned close to her. "Actually, what happened was . . ."

Marcia listened in growing wonderment. At first suspicious, she quickly realized that Anthony was telling the absolute truth.

"It's the craziest thing I've ever heard. What are you going to do now?"

The leader of the band blew into his microphone and absently scratched his crotch as he announced, "And now a mellow number for the folk."

"I'm going to ask you to dance," Anthony smiled as the slow, easy sounds of a Bossa Nova wafted through the room.

"This is really nice," Marcia breathed softly into Anthony's rather storklike neck as they glided around the room.

"Yes, it certainly is." Anthony contentedly hummed off-key as they continued to circle. "Perhaps we could do it again. Would you by any chance, be free for dinner tomorrow evening?"

"Dinner?" Marcia was so startled she tripped over his foot. "You're asking me to dinner?"

"Why, yes." He looked at her a little uncertainly. "Is that all right?"

"Oh, Anthony, of course it is!" Her face lit up like a child's on Christmas morning. "I accept with pleasure."

Marcia Weinguard was so overwhelmed by the discovery that a man who had as much money as her daddy was seriously interested in her, she fell in love with him immediately. Anthony was so overwhelmed by the discovery that the daughter of Hollywood's most powerful studio head was seriously interested in him, he thought he fell in love with her. Martin Weinguard simply fell on his knees and thanked God that his homely, overweight daughter, whom he loved more than anybody or anything in the entire world, had finally found a man.

Marcia and Anthony were married three months later, on the occasion of her thirty-second birthday. "This way you'll never have an excuse for forgetting our anniversary date," she'd chuckled. It was the most spectacular wedding Hollywood had seen in two decades. Over a thousand people attended the reception at Martin Weinguard's palatial Beverly Hills mansion, and the guest list read like a who's who of the royalty of the entertainment industry. Anthony wandered around in a euphoric daze as the idols he'd worshiped from afar all these years came up to shake his hand and warmly offer him congratulations. At last he was a participant in the marvelous world he'd dreamed about and longed so much to become a part of.

But Anthony's euphoria quickly faded when he learned that

his new bride had no intention of holding parties where the elite of Hollywood would gather to discuss the future of the film business. She had no interest in the film business at all —past, present, or future. There were, in fact, only three things that interested Marcia Weinguard: eating, watching television, and sex.

Of the three, Anthony was most depressed by the sex. A shy, fastidious man, he was also a hopeless romantic who envisioned the act of love as a tender, exploratory adventure leading to heights of breathless pleasure that could only be expressed in terms of silent joy as the loving couple looked deeply into each other's eyes. That was not Marcia's way.

"Let's fuck, honey," she would exclaim happily as she threw herself upon him, her lips still greasy from the fried chicken she'd just gorged herself on. "Let's do it all, from top to bottom!"

Anthony dutifully did it all, but his heart wasn't really in it. And as time went by he became increasingly disheartened, not only by the way his marriage had turned out but by the way his entire life had turned out. For he was no closer to the magical world of show business now than he had been when he'd first met Marcia. Martin Weinguard had been kind but firm when he'd hopefully offered his services to International Pictures.

"Face it, Anthony, you weren't meant to be a producer. You know nothing about pictures, and I'm afraid you'll never be able to learn. You see, you just don't have a feel for the business." Martin had paused for a moment, then smiled. "But if you want the job of handling financial deals for our corporation, well, I could arrange that. Because money is something you really have a feel for."

"Thanks, Mr. Weinguard. I appreciate that, but it isn't exactly what I had in mind."

"Not *Mr. Weinguard*!" he chided him. "It's Martin to you, my boy. Got it?" he asked as he affectionately thumped Anthony on the back.

"Yes sir," Anthony said dispiritedly.

In an effort to keep his mind off the depressing specter of his failed dreams, Anthony began dabbling in real estate again and in the next nine years his net worth increased from fifty to almost one hundred million dollars. Two attorneys and three accountants worked full-time on his growing empire. And they were probably the happiest attorneys and accountants in Los Angeles, for Anthony was not only incredibly successful but astoundingly generous, offering them a share in his enterprises on top of the very healthy retainers he paid them. The only thing that troubled them was his peculiar reaction to success.

"I swear, he gets unhappier with every buck we make," Herman Weiss whispered to his partner. "It's not only unnatural, it's scary. Do you think we should talk to him?"

"No!" his partner announced decisively. "Let's not rock the boat. The more miserable he is, the more money he makes. It could be a disaster for all of us if he got happy."

"Yeah, you got a point," Herman admitted. "So we just leave him alone, right? And tell the others to do the same?"

"Right!"

Anthony was unaware of the decision made by his staff. All he knew was that they were considerate enough to handle more and more of the business on their own without bothering him, something that Irving Schwartz back in New York had never been willing to do. But occasionally something stirred inside him and told him he should call a meeting. He was always vaguely nonplussed to find these impromptu sessions sent his staff into a frenzy of activity with much scurrying around and exchanging of papers. But the end results were always the same. More money, more profits.

"Don't underestimate that man!" Herman Weiss hissed after one of those unexpected meetings. "The lawyers for Howard Hughes never saw much of him, either, but they were smart enough to realize he knew everything that was going on. I say we play straight with this guy!"

Everybody nervously agreed, and Anthony's empire continued to grow.

But his empire was the last thing on Anthony's mind as he peered into the mirror over the dressing table in his private bathroom on the second floor of the Bel Air estate he'd built for Marcia, and tried for the third time without success to knot his white tie properly. Because all he could think about was the fact that he was forty years old on this day, and he'd accomplished nothing. Not one of his dreams had come true.

"Here, let me do that for you," Marcia cried out as she burst into the bathroom. "You know you'll never get it right yourself."

"Probably not," he admitted. Docilely, he leaned over so she could reach the bow. "And how was your day, dear?" he inquired politely.

"Just like every day before one of Daddy's big parties," she muttered crossly. "Wearing myself out running all over town looking for a new dress, then putting up with all that tiresome fuss of fittings. And I had to wait a whole *hour* before Elaine was free to do my hair. I don't know why I bother. I never end up looking any better, anyway."

"Now that's not true, dear. You look lovely when you get dressed up, and you know your father always notices."

"Oh I suppose so," she said grudgingly. "But it makes a nervous wreck out of me, and I miss all my favorite television programs. I'm just so much happier staying home."

Her fingers paused in the act of tying his bow. "Hey, how about a quickie, honey?" she said hopefully as she gazed up at him.

"No!" he cried, cringing involuntarily. "I mean, we don't have time," he added hastily. "Your father was very specific about screening the new picture precisely at seven, and he'll expect us to be there to help him greet all the guests first."

Marcia looked momentarily dejected, then brightened. "Well, maybe it's better to save it for later when we can relax, and I don't have to worry about rushing to get dressed. It's more fun rushing to get undressed," she giggled. "Right, sweetie pie?"

"Right," he echoed dismally.

"I want you to promise me something, though. I don't want you going off and leaving me alone tonight. I know what you're like when Daddy screens a new picture. You get all excited and start trailing around after the stars and the director, pestering them with questions. And then you forget all about me. It's a terrible feeling," she said with sudden passion. "So please don't do that tonight. Promise?"

"I promise."

That night, for the first time in his life, Anthony Wellington broke a promise. Because the minute he laid eyes on Erin Connolly, he was transported into an ecstacy of feeling he hadn't experienced since that long ago evening in the Orpheum Theater in Stroudsburg, Pennsylvania, when he looked up from his bag of hot buttered popcorn and saw Ingrid Bergman . . .

Ten

"Now I'm not promising anything for sure," Erin warned an excited Cheryl Green as she sipped from her wine glass at the same restaurant that Andi Steiner had taken her to a year before. "But if things work out like I hope," she grinned, "then I'm looking at the new script girl for Leland Devereaux."

"Oh, Erin, that would be so wonderful!" Cheryl said as she lifted her glass of wine. "Is there anything I can do to help? I mean, you're so mysterious about the whole thing. Like, I get the idea it has nothing to do with your choosing one of those independent producers over Devereaux."

"Very perceptive, my friend. Very perceptive indeed." Erin grandly summoned the waiter to refill their wine glasses, and bestowed a kindly smile on Cheryl. "It's a whole lot bigger than that. And if it comes to pass, there could be some pretty exciting things in store for you. If you're the totally loyal person I think you are, that is," she said thoughtfully.

"Well, you know I am!" Cheryl looked faintly indignant. "I mean, you must know that!"

"Yes, I think I know that." Erin took another sip from her glass. "So I guess I can tell you I've set up a preliminary interview for you with Peter."

"Peter Faraday?" Cheryl squealed in excitement. "Devereaux's assistant director?"

"That's the man. But listen to me very carefully," she cautioned. "Devereaux doesn't know anything about this. So when you appear on the set this afternoon, as far as he's concerned you're just filling in for me while I'm out sick with the flu."

"And what will you *really* be doing?" Cheryl asked.

"Shopping for the sexiest dress a lady can wear."

"What?"

"Never mind. Just do well today and tomorrow."

"You're going to be out tomorrow too?" Cheryl exclaimed.

"Right. I'm giving you two days to become familiar with my job."

"Oh wow!"

"Don't get too carried away," Erin advised her dryly. "You don't have the position yet."

Cheryl flushed. "I know that. I wasn't suggesting . . . that is . . ." She swallowed. "Well, what I'm trying to say is I'll do just what you tell me."

"A wise decision. One you won't regret. Now, let's order."

Erin was feeling very pleased with herself as she dropped Cheryl off at the Film-Star lot after lunch and headed for Beverly Hills. She knew Cheryl was so eager to get the script-girl job with Devereaux that she'd do almost anything Erin asked. And Erin already knew what she was going to ask. It would be a little tricky to pull off, but Erin was certain it could be done. All Cheryl had to do was follow her instructions exactly. And then, Erin thought happily, I'll be on my way. Hollywood's first woman producer. After that, nothing could stop her from going all the way to the top.

Of course there was another little project to be accomplished before that could happen, she admitted as she pulled up to a stoplight and checked her appearance in the rear-view mirror. Project Anthony Wellington. But that wasn't going to be any problem at all, Erin decided as she grinned into the mirror. Her mirror image grinned confidently back. Absolutely no problem, it told her.

Then, as though fate had decreed that it was all meant to be, everything went right. The first shop Erin went into had the perfect dress. It was an exquisite white lace, cut low off the shoulders and gently undulating around the body.

"You look like a sexy angel," the salesgirl said admiringly as she saw Erin step out of the dressing room and pirouette in front of the mirror.

"Exactly what I want to look like." Erin smiled. "Now do you have shoes to match? And someone to adjust the waist and hemline?"

"Yes, of course!" The salesgirl scurried off, and a few minutes later both the shoes and a seamstress appeared.

"The dress *must* be ready by tomorrow afternoon," Erin told her.

"It will be," the small, elderly seamstress promised as she bent over and inspected the fit. "Ah, so lucky," she sighed through the pins in her mouth. "To have such a dress, and look like you. You're a very fortunate young lady."

"Thank you. I'm hoping to be."

"You will. You will. Take my word for it." The woman gently patted Erin as she pinned up the hem. "You've got the look of success about you."

Erin ran up the steps to her apartment, humming happily under her breath as she thought about the dress and the seamstress's remark. She stopped abruptly as she put the key in the door and heard the shrill, persistent ringing of her phone. It was only three o'clock in the afternoon. No one she knew would be calling her at home at this hour. Unless, she thought in sudden panic, something had gone wrong at the studio. Heart pounding, she flung open the door and raced inside.

"H–hello?" she stammered nervously as she picked up the receiver.

"Hello. Is this Mrs. Eric Glass?" a dry, precise voice inquired.

Erin froze, staring at the phone in stunned disbelief. "Who . . . who is this?" she finally managed to ask.

"My name is Samuel Perkins, and I'm representing your

husband, who is suing you for divorce and custody of the child on grounds of desertion."

"What?" Erin exclaimed wildly. "What did you say?"

"My name is Samuel Perkins and . . ."

"I heard you," she interrupted. "I just can't believe it! When? When is he planning to do this?"

"The court date is set for tomorrow afternoon."

"Tomorrow? You can't be serious! He has to give me notice. He can't do this to me overnight!"

"We have been trying to give you notice for several months, Mrs. Glass. However, that has proved impossible since you never bothered to give your family your Los Angeles address, and all efforts to reach a Mrs. Eric Glass have proved fruitless. Even your parents advised us that they have had no communication with you since you left your husband and child.

"All of which," he continued dryly, "has considerably strengthened our case for desertion. If your husband hadn't suddenly thought of the possibility that you'd taken back your maiden name, we wouldn't have been able to contact you today. I might add, only Mr. Glass's concern for notifying you prompted this call. It really wasn't necessary."

"You can't do this to me!" Erin screamed in rage. "I'll fight it all the way!"

"That is certainly your privilege." The attorney cleared his throat. "But if you plan to contest the divorce, it will be necessary for you to return here and appear in court tomorrow. Shall I advise Mr. Glass accordingly?"

Erin's hand trembled as she closed her eyes and thought about her son. She could see him in her mind's eye so clearly. The fuzzy blond head, the expectant, adoring look as he gazed up at her and shyly patted her cheek. Then she thought about what would happen if she went back to Ohio. She would miss Martin Weinguard's party. She would not meet Anthony Wellington. She would have to accept either the script-girl or assistant-editor job when she returned to Los Angeles on Monday. She would end up a nobody.

"Never mind, Mr. Perkins," she said quietly. "I've decided not to contest it."

After she hung up the phone, Erin sat motionless on the

couch for a long time. The light in the room gradually faded, and shadows crept in as the sun slipped over the horizon. From outside came the faint sound of voices, the splash of water against the sides of the pool, an occasional burst of laughter.

"He'll understand when he gets older," Erin told the dim, shadowy room. "I'll explain it to him, and he'll understand why I had no other choice. I'll be rich and famous then, and I'll make it all up to him."

The room had no answer for her, and she shook her head angrily. "It's all going to work out. It *is*," she said defiantly. "So I'm just going to stop worrying about it this very moment, because worrying is the worst thing I could do. It could upset me and ruin tomorrow night. And I owe my son tomorrow night."

Erin immediately began to feel better as she thought of matters in that light, and her voice was brisk and cheerful as she picked up the phone and called the exclusive Beverly Hills health club, scheduling an early morning massage and facial to be followed by an appointment with Simon, one of Hollywood's top hairdressers.

"You look too good to be true," an awed James Lee Norton said reverently as Erin opened the door of her apartment and invited him in.

"I am too good to be true," she grinned wickedly. "That's the basis of my charm. You want a drink before we go?"

"No. I want a hundred million dollars so *I* can have you instead of Anthony Wellington," he said huskily. Then he gave a quick, nervous laugh as he saw the startled look on her face. "Just a little joke," he assured her.

"Well, it would be nice if it weren't a joke," she murmured, kissing him on the cheek. "I think we'd make great partners."

"Partners!" he cried in mock anguish. "I wasn't talking about being *partners*."

Erin gave a relieved laugh as the familiar mischievous twinkle appeared in his eyes, replacing the intent hungry look that had been fixed on her. "Maybe someday we'll have a discussion about whatever you were talking about," she said lightly. "But right now I think we'd better concentrate on our current project. Any last minute tips on strategy?"

James Lee frowned thoughtfully. "Your biggest job is going to be separating Wellington from his wife. She sticks to him like glue, and he's too much of a gentleman to deliberately walk away from her. But unless you get him alone, you're never going to have a chance."

"Can't you distract her?" Erin asked as she picked up her purse, and they walked out the door.

"Nobody distracts Marcia Weinguard," he said wryly.

"But you can try, can't you?" she insisted as they got into his sporty white Porsche and drove off.

"Sure, babe." He down-shifted abruptly, tires squealing and motor roaring as he rounded the corner and then whipped out into the traffic of Sunset Boulevard, heading north for Martin Weinguard's home. "I'll do my best, but I can't promise anything. You'll understand better when you meet this broad," he told her with a crooked grin as they screeched to a halt at a red light. "In the meantime, start thinking."

Erin and James Lee rode in silence for the next ten miles, absorbed in their own thoughts. For Erin it was an exciting and slightly nervous time of planning her moves and dreaming of her final victory. For James Lee it was a time of grim satisfaction as he envisioned the humiliation long due Martin Weinguard. But no one would ever have been able to guess what was going on in their minds when they finally pulled up to the impressive gates outside Martin Weinguard's house and stepped out of the car. Their faces were as blandly gracious as those of all the other guests who arrived with secret thoughts hidden behind a smiling facade.

"James Lee!" Beaming, Martin Weinguard took a step forward and grabbed James Lee's hand, pumping it vigorously. *"So* glad you could come!" Then his smile faltered as he saw Erin. "And this is . . ."

"A business associate of mine at Film-Star," James Lee replied smoothly. "Miss Connolly, Mr. Weinguard."

Martin's face cleared. Having a black man in his home was one thing. Having a black man with a white girl as his date was something else altogether. It was unthinkable! But if she was just a business associate, well, that was different. As a matter of fact, he decided on reflection, James Lee had shown quite good judgment in bringing this girl. It would have been quite awkward for everyone if he'd shown up with one of those jungle bunnies he probably went around with.

"A pleasure to have you here, my dear," Martin said pleasantly. "And what is it you do at Film-Star?"

"I work with Leland Devereaux."

Martin's eyebrows shot up. "Well, that must be very exciting for you." He took a closer look at the lovely young creature standing in front of him. "I take it, then, you're directly involved in this exciting new television series that all of us in the industry are watching with such enthusiasm?" he asked with a speculative gleam in his eye.

Erin, aware of his sudden interest in her, played a hunch. "I have been very fortunate in that respect," she said demurely. "Mr. Devereaux has been kind enough to both guide and teach me, and as a result I've enjoyed the marvelous privilege of working personally on every project."

Martin had a difficult time restraining himself from jumping up and down and shouting with joy. That James Lee is some wonderful, smart nigger, he thought ecstatically. Every major studio in town had made surreptitious approaches to Leland Devereaux when they found out what was going on over at Film-Star, all to no avail. But James Lee had bypassed the obvious, zeroing in on Devereaux's new romantic interest instead. It was a stroke of genius, because the famous Broadway director was notorious for his slavish devotion to whomever was the current love of his life. Neither the love nor the devotion ever lasted very long, but while they did, he would do almost anything for the object of his passion. So all that was necessary was to cultivate this little girl with tender loving care, and she would deliver Devereaux to him. At that moment, Martin loved James Lee like a brother.

"I'm sure you're being much too modest, Miss Connolly," he announced softly as he took hold of both her hands and gazed intently into her eyes. "Leland Devereaux would never devote time to anyone who didn't show exceptional talent and promise. I would bet money that you are headed for some very big things, given the right opportunity. And I never bet money unless I know I'm going to win," he added with a chuckle.

"You're very kind," Erin murmured.

"Nonsense! All I am is right." He laughed then. "If you can forgive what sounds like an old man's vanity, I'd like to prove it by talking with you later. International Pictures is always looking for special people, and I think you might be exactly what we need for a major new project we're just starting."

"Daddy, the line of people is getting very long," Marcia whispered. She shifted her weight and tried flexing her toes in the shoes that were beginning to pinch painfully.

"What?" he said, startled.

"The *line*, Daddy!" she repeated irritably.

"Oh. Oh yes, of course." Martin coughed and released Erin's hands. "Miss Connolly, let me present my lovely daughter Marcia and her husband Anthony Wellington."

"A pleasure, I'm sure."

Anthony said nothing. His mouth was too dry to utter a word as Erin looked up at him, her luminous green eyes gently caressing his face. He vaguely felt the iron grip of his wife as she hooked her arm through his.

"Anthony, I want you to take care of this young lady," Martin announced preemptorily. "Get her a drink and get her comfortable. And make sure she has a good seat for the screening."

"I'd be delighted," Anthony said hoarsely, finding his voice with difficulty. He tried to offer Erin his arm, and there was a slightly awkward moment as Marcia continued to cling to it.

"Marcia!" Martin hissed.

Reluctantly she let go and then watched unhappily as Erin and Anthony walked off together. "Why did you do that, Daddy?" she whimpered.

"Because that little girl is going to do something very nice for me." He winked at her, a smug smile on his face. Martin would quickly find out how terribly wrong he was.

One week after the party at Martin Weinguard's home, all of Hollywood was buzzing about Anthony and Erin's torrid love affair, which was being carried on right in front of their delightedly scandalized eyes with a blatant lack of discretion.

"A toast to Hollywood's newest celebrity," James Lee chuckled, getting to his feet as Erin came out of the kitchen of her apartment and handed him a drink. "Long may she reign."

"Oh, she's planning to do that, all right," Erin said with a smile. "But not as a gossip item."

"Which, I imagine, leads us to why you invited me over tonight." James Lee sat back down on the couch and raised an inquisitive eyebrow as Erin curled up opposite him. "Am I supposed to guess, or are you just going to come out with it?"

"I've got it, James Lee!" she exclaimed, her eyes sparkling. "I've got the script for my first picture. But I need your advice on where to go from here."

He blinked in disbelief. "What do you mean, you've got a script? You don't even have a production company."

"Oh, don't worry about that." She waved an impatient hand at him. "Anthony has already agreed to set up one."

"Christ, Erin, you don't waste time, do you? How in the hell did you accomplish that in one week?"

"It wasn't all that difficult." She gave a tiny shrug. "All I have to do is marry him. Anyway," she continued eagerly, "let me tell you about this script."

"*Marry* him!" he shouted. "What the fuck are you talking about, Erin? We never planned on your marrying him!"

"I know," she admitted. "But that's because we didn't really understand what Anthony was like when we started this. He's awfully old-fashioned, James Lee, and the thought of having an affair would horrify him."

She leaned forward, clasping her hands together. "Believe me, this is the only way I can make it work," she told him earnestly. "Besides, it won't be all that bad. He's actually a very nice man."

"Jesus!" James Lee stared into his drink for a long moment. "You realize how much trouble you're buying yourself with this? I mean, it would be one thing if you had a little fling with him, got the money to produce your picture, and then returned him to his wife. But if you break up Marcia Weinguard's marriage, her father will never rest until he destroys you."

He took a long swallow of his drink and shook his head. "You have any idea of the power that man wields in this town? There's not a studio that'll let you in its doors to shoot this picture. There's not a single major star or director who'll sign with you."

"Those things occurred to me," she said with a wry smile. "Why else do you think I asked you to come over tonight? Obviously, I need some advice."

"Advice?" he repeated incredulously. "Erin, I thought you were listening to me. The only advice I can give you is not to marry Anthony Wellington, which you apparently refuse to accept. So that's it, babe. You're playing with a totally stacked deck, and you don't have one winning card."

"That's not quite true. I have *Merry-Go-Round*."

James Lee almost choked on an ice cube. "You've got to be kidding." He stared at her, unbelieving. "I mean, are you talking about the book that's been number one on the bestseller list for the past six weeks?"

"Of course," she grinned. "What else would I be talking about?"

"But Film-Star has the option on that! They locked it up cold before the book was even published. There's no way you could touch it!"

"Well, I found a way."

"How?"

"Actually, it was rather simple." Erin smiled. "I stole it."

Eleven

It hadn't been quite that simple. In fact, for a while it had looked like it was going to be impossible. Cheryl Green had proved surprisingly stubborn.

"No! Absolutely no! I'd do almost anything for you, Erin, you know that. But this is too much to ask. You have to be crazy to even think of it."

"Now just calm down, Cheryl, and listen to me," Erin said soothingly. "Then you'll see that I'm not asking much at all. This will be one of the easiest things you've ever done. And think of the rewards in store for you," she added warmly.

"*Easy!*" Cheryl shrieked. "You're asking me to steal the hottest property this studio has had in years, a property they guard like the Koh-i-noor diamond, and you have the nerve to tell me about the rewards in store for me if I do it? I'll tell you about the rewards I'll have in store. A jail sentence, that's what!"

"Cheryl, I'm not asking you to *steal* anything," Erin said. "I'm just asking you to borrow something. You make a Xerox copy of the screenplay along with the studio's contract and the writer's address and phone number, then return the originals to the office."

"Making Xerox copies of that screenplay is stealing. And you know it is."

"Only if you're caught. And you won't be."

"Can you guarantee that?"

For the first time in the long difficult lunch, Erin began to relax. If Cheryl was finally coming around to thinking in those terms, she could be persuaded.

"Of course," she smiled. "There's nothing to it. Now here's the plan. After your preproduction meeting in John Landers's office tomorrow morning, you pick up the wrong shooting script for that feature film he's doing, the first copy instead of the revised one. You discover your mistake a few minutes later when you're on the set and the cameras have started to roll. Naturally you're terribly upset and apologetic and offer to rush back to his office to get the right one. He'll yell at you, but since these things happen all the time, he won't yell too much. More important, he'll be so involved in blocking out scenes that he won't want to go back and get it himself. And since he trusts you, he'll hand over his keys. Which is all we need."

Erin leaned forward and handed her a small package. "You make a wax impression of the keys that fit his wall safe and office door, give this back to me, and I'll have matching keys made. Then the day after tomorrow, on your lunch hour, you let yourself into his office with the duplicate keys, get the screenplay and the studio's contract with the writer out of the safe, and run off a copy of each. I'll meet you in the ladies room just opposite the copying room, you'll hand me the copies, scoot back down to Landers's office to return the originals, and we're home free.

"Now isn't that just as easy as I told you it would be?" she grinned.

"I don't know," Cheryl said doubtfully. "I can do the thing with the keys, but why do I have to do the rest? I mean, you'll have the matching keys, so why don't you go into his office and get the material?"

"Cheryl, you're not thinking clearly," Erin reproached her. "It takes more than keys to get that material. The security guards know you, so if they see you going into Landers's office they won't question you. But they would certainly question me, since I've never worked on any of his projects."

"Well, let me think about it," Cheryl said unhappily. She pushed the food around on her plate. "It's something I've got to psych myself into, and I'm just not ready yet. Maybe I'll feel better about it next week."

"No!" Erin exclaimed sharply. "Next week is too late. You *have* to do it this week."

"But why?" she asked bewilderedly.

"Because Film-Star's option on *Merry-Go-Round* expires tomorrow."

"Oh, Erin, that's just a technicality," Cheryl said crossly. "Everybody knows they're going to renew it, and for a lot more money too. John Landers has already set up a meeting for this coming Friday with the writer and his agent, and they're holding a press party after to celebrate signing the new contract."

"It's a lot more than a technicality, my innocent friend," Erin informed her with a tight little smile. "It's a matter of forty-eight hours between tomorrow and Friday when *no one* will own the movie rights to that book. Now do you understand why you have to do it this week?."

It was a trembling, white-faced Cheryl Green who met Erin in the ladies room at twelve-thirty on that Thursday.

"Are we alone?" she whispered, her eyes darting nervously around the antiseptic, white-tiled area.

"All alone," Erin said reassuringly. "I checked it out." Her eyes fastened hungrily on the two large manila envelopes that Cheryl was clutching to her ample bosom. "You've got them in there?"

Cheryl nodded, then moaned. "Erin, I feel terrible. I think I'm going to throw up."

"Don't you think it would be better to wait until you return the originals to Landers's office?"

"Oh my God," Cheryl cried. "I still have to do that, don't I?" With a wild look in her eye, she charged toward the door.

"Wait!" Erin sprinted after her and grabbed her arm. "The copy. Which envelope has the copy in it?"

"I don't know," Cheryl sobbed.

Erin pried the envelopes out of her desperate grasp, checked the first page inside each, and then handed one back to her.

"Cheryl, I'm very proud of you. You've done a really first-class job here."

Cheryl's only answer was to clap a hand over her mouth as she rushed out.

Erin waited several minutes until she was sure that Cheryl would be out of sight; she didn't want to take the chance of anyone passing by to see them together. Then she quietly slipped out of the ladies room, took an elevator down to the lobby, and hurried out of the building to the parking lot, where she got into her car and drove to her apartment.

Once safely inside the apartment, she settled down on the couch and opened the precious envelope, scanning the contents. When she saw it was all there, she sighed with relief. Now came the tricky part. Taking a deep breath, she picked up the phone and dialed the number of Alan Corry, the brilliant young author of *Merry-Go-Round*.

"Who?" Corry said puzzledly as he picked up the phone in the den of his rented beach house.

"Erin Connolly, with Film-Star Studios. I'm terribly sorry to bother you at home, Mr. Corry, but something very important has come up about the picture and we can't reach your agent. Is there any chance at all that I might come out to your place late this afternoon so we can go over it?"

"Good Lord, there's no problem about renewing the option, is there?" Alan cried in alarm. "I thought everything was set. We're supposed to meet with you people tomorrow."

"Well, I wouldn't want to call it a problem," Erin said slowly. "But I do think we should get together as soon as possible."

"Oh my God! I told Harvey he was pushing too hard."

A long silence followed, intermittently punctuated by Alan's rapid breathing. "Look, Miss Connolly," he finally said in a nervous rush. "I'm a writer, not a businessman. Harvey, my agent, always handles that part. I– I really don't know what to tell you."

"Mr. Corry, please believe me when I say there's nothing to

be upset about. You have written an absolutely marvelous book, a book any studio would be proud to have. And speaking for myself, I would like to say I think it's the finest work any writer has produced in the last decade."

"Really?" Alan said shakily. "You really feel that way?"

"Without question! Now if we can just get together to iron out these problems, it will be smooth sailing from that point on."

"Well, if it's that important . . ."

"It is," she announced firmly.

"All right, then." He gave her directions to his beach house, realizing belatedly as he hung up the phone that she'd never told him what exactly the problems were.

Was it possible they were so bad she couldn't bring herself to mention them over the phone, he wondered anxiously. Surely they weren't going to refuse to renew the option, because if that was the case there'd be no reason for her to come out to see him. So what was left? The price they were willing to pay for the option renewal, that was one. Harvey had pushed for a hundred-percent increase. The start date on production of the picture, that was another. Harvey had inserted a clause in the contract that production had to start within three months, so that he'd receive his full money on the deal. Screen credits were the third. Harvey had insisted that the studio let him write the screenplay.

"Screen credits," he muttered. He began picking up books from the floor of the den and stacking them neatly in piles, blowing dust off the desk and polishing its surface with the sleeve of his shirt as he passed by. "They hate my script, and they want to bring in a new writer.

"On the other hand," he told the typewriter gloomily as its carriage caught the edge of his sleeve and tore a half-inch rip in it, "it could just as well be the production date. Maybe the studio is jammed with other pictures in production, and they're not going to start mine for another whole goddamn year."

Both thoughts were so depressing that Alan Corry gave up his halfhearted cleaning attempts and went into the small kitchen, where he took out a large glass, a bottle of vodka, a can of tomato juice, a tray of ice cubes, and a lime. After a moment of reflection, he returned the tomato juice and lime to the refrigerator and just poured the vodka straight over the ice cubes.

Alan Corry had a number of problems of his own. *Merry-Go-Round* was his first book, and he'd been stunned when it hit the bestseller list. In a feverish glow of excitement he had given his ex-wife a cash settlement, bought a three-thousand-dollar wardrobe, moved out of the dingy one-room apartment in New York that was located on the fringes of Harlem, and moved to California, where he rented a beach house and settled back to enjoy the good life while he wrote the screenplay for the picture. It hadn't turned out to be such a good life. The bills kept pouring in, but the money didn't.

"I'm a bestselling novelist," he'd screamed at Harvey, his agent. "So how can I be poor?"

"Because you never listen to me," Harvey had sighed. "I told you it would take time. You can be a hardcover bestseller and barely make any more than your advance. The money is in paperback and movie rights."

"So when are you going to get those for me?" he'd demanded.

"Soon, kid, soon. Trust me."

"Well I trusted you, Harvey, and you can see how far that's gotten me!" Alan shouted furiously as he got up and headed back to the kitchen for a refill, tripping over the stack of books on the way. As he bent down somewhat unsteadily to straighten them, the doorbell rang.

Oh Christ, that can't be her, he thought in panic. It's too early. I'm not ready. He peered at his watch, squinting to bring it into focus. Five o'clock. How could it possibly be five o'clock already?

The doorbell rang again, an impatient edge to it now, and Alan swallowed hard as he trudged down the hall to answer it.

"Mr. Corry, I can't tell you what a pleasure it is for me to meet the author of *Merry-Go-Round* in person," Erin announced sincerely as she held out a slim, tanned hand.

"*You're* Miss Connolly?" he blurted. Alan had been prepared for a crisply efficient, no-nonsense woman in her late thirties or early forties with horn-rimmed glasses and a matronly figure encased in a sensible tweed suit. This girl standing in front of him couldn't be more than twenty-two or twenty-three, and she was one of the most excitingly beautiful creatures he'd ever seen in his life.

"I hope you'll call me Erin," she smiled.

"Erin," he repeated in a daze. "A beautiful name. It's just right for you."

"Thank you, you're very kind." Erin gently extricated her hand from his grasp and took a firmer hold on the large envelope under her arm. "Do you think I might come inside?"

"Good Lord, of course. Of course!" He flung the door open wide. "Come in and make yourself comfortable wherever you'd like. I work in the den, but maybe you'd rather sit in the living room where you can see the ocean?"

"Wherever you're the most comfortable is where I'd be the most comfortable," Erin murmured softly.

"Well, what a nice thing to say." Alan led her down the hall, looked around at the dusty, cluttered living room, and thought about the equally dusty, cluttered den. "I'm afraid writers aren't every good housekeepers," he said with a nervous laugh.

"They're not supposed to be. Cleaning ladies are good housekeepers, but they rarely make great novelists. And I'm here to talk to a great novelist."

A sudden rush of heat engulfed him as he gazed into the luminous green eyes fixed on him. "That does put a different perspective on the situation, doesn't it?" he said huskily.

"The right perspective, I would say." Erin absently stroked his arm. "And one I'm very eager to explore."

"Yes. Explore." Alan felt suddenly dizzy. "How about a drink?" he stammered. "Would you like a drink?"

"That would be lovely."

"Good. Good. I'll go get it now." Alan went off toward the kitchen, then stopped abruptly. "All I have is vodka. Is that okay with you?"

"Vodka is all I ever drink," Erin assured him. She walked over to the couch and curled up on it. "Now isn't it a marvelous omen that we share the same tastes?"

"Very marvelous. Even absolutely marvelous."

But Alan's euphoria turned into puzzlement and finally

suspicion as he sat opposite Erin on the couch and listened to her.

"I don't get this," he growled. "I thought you were here to talk about my contract with Film-Star, but that's not what you're talking about at all."

"What I'm talking about is *you*," she said quietly. "And isn't that what's really important?"

"Yeah, to whom? You're asking me to kill a deal with a major studio like Film-Star to go with some totally unknown outfit, and you expect me to believe that's in my best interests? Boy, you must think I'm some dumb idiot!"

"Not dumb, Mr. Corry. Hopelessly stupid is more like it. Apparently you've never heard of International Pictures?"

He blinked in surprise. "International Pictures? You never told me International Pictures was involved in this."

"That's because it never occurred to me it was necessary. I thought everyone knew Anthony Wellington was the son-in-law of Martin Weinguard, the studio head of International."

"Anthony Wellington?" he repeated uncertainly.

"Really, Mr. Corry," she snapped. "Didn't you even read this contract?" Her finger stabbed at the letterhead on the piece of paper he was holding. "Anthony Wellington, a principal partner in Con-Well Productions."

"But what exactly does that mean?" he asked with a hesitant frown.

"I'm afraid it means I've wasted my time this afternoon." Erin removed the contract from his hand, collected her purse, and stood up. "It's a personal disappointment to me, because I believed so much in your book. However, you are certainly not the only bestselling novelist in this country. I can think of several, notably that world-famous author whose current book is edging you right out of first place on *The New York Times* bestseller list, who would be more than delighted to sign with us for half a million dollars. Anthony was right when he told me to contact him first."

Erin sighed. "Well, live and learn. In the meantime, thank you for the drink, and good day, Mr. Corry." She turned on her heel and marched briskly out of the living room.

"Half a million dollars?" Alan exclaimed in a strangled

voice. "Where does it say half a million dollars?" He stared at his empty hands where moments before the contract had rested. "Hey, Erin! Miss Connolly! Wait!!" He raced after her.

"What is it now, Mr. Corry?" Erin said impatiently. "It's late, and I must get back to my partner so we can make other plans. We have a production date to meet for our first release."

"I think we should talk more," he said breathlessly. "I didn't understand everything clearly at first. You know how writers are. We get all involved in what we're doing in our own little world and just don't relate properly to the business world outside. You do understand, don't you?"

Erin turned the car radio up to full volume as the Beatles latest hit came pouring out of the speakers, moving her body in rhythm to the demanding beat and pausing occasionally to caress the envelope lying beside her, which contained the signed contract from Alan Corry.

"It's going to be all mine," she shouted exultantly to the skyline of Los Angeles which began to appear in silhouette against the mountain ranges as dusk fell and lights winked on in the tall office buildings. "This whole place is going to belong to me!"

But it didn't work out the way she'd thought it would. Erin had been confident that once she owned the screen rights to *Merry-Go-Round* all the doors of Hollywood would open wide to welcome her. In fact, they remained locked tight. An enraged Film-Star Studios, in concert with an equally enraged Harvey Goldberg, Alan Corry's agent, filed class-action suits against both the fledgling production company and Erin personally, charging them with virtually every crime under the sun except murder; and Hollywood avoided Erin Connolly like the plague. Even secretaries hung up on her when she called. Trade papers had a field day with the lawsuits, reveling in the sensational background of the case; and the smart money in town predicted that *Merry-Go-Round* would shortly return to Film-Star.

It was a prediction that caused Erin increasing anxiety. "Anthony, are you *sure* this contract your attorneys drew up is fully binding?" she asked for the fifth time one evening as she paced nervously around her apartment.

"Honey, you just have to stop worrying yourself to death like this," Anthony said with concern as he walked over and put his arms around her. "The contract is as legal as any contract can be, and these are some of the best attorneys in the country."

"Then why does everybody say I'm going to lose?" she wailed.

"Well now, they're not law experts, are they?" he smiled. "They're just very opinionated people. And that's not the same at all. So come on and relax, honey. It's all going to work out."

"I wonder," she said dismally.

"There is one thing that's occurred to me." Anthony gave a gentle cough. "To help the situation, I mean."

Erin whirled around. "What, Anthony? Please tell me, because I feel like I'm at the end of my rope."

"The half-million dollars Alan Corry is claiming. I think maybe we should pay it to him."

"Are you crazy?" she exclaimed in shock. "I *told* you he misunderstood. That money was just a projected figure, based on his profit shares in the movie. *Nobody* pays an author half a million dollars just for the option rights to his book. Even Film-Star isn't contesting that!"

"I understand," he said with an apologetic smile. "But the young man does seem to believe he was getting that sum. And if we pay it to him, don't you think the controversy would go away? It would certainly make his agent happy. Ten percent of that is considerably more than Film-Star is willing to pay.

"Besides, we can afford it, you know. So why don't we do it, and take care of all these problems in the process?"

For one of the few times in her life, Erin was struck speechless. Half a million dollars had seemed an impossible sum to her, but Anthony was right. He could afford it. Which meant she could afford it. Until that moment, Erin hadn't fully comprehended just how much money Anthony really had. God, what a fool she'd been worrying about costs. Anthony could buy a small country if he wanted to.

"My love, my marvelous love, why don't I listen to you

more often?" Erin murmured as she wrapped her arms around him and nuzzled into his neck. "You are so brilliant, and you know how to take care of everything. Will you always take care of me?"

"As long as I live," Anthony promised fervently as her warm lips caressed him and her deliciously wicked tongue found its way into his mouth. "Oh, Erin," he groaned as she began stroking his body. "Oh, Erin, what are you doing to me?"

"Loving you, Anthony," she whispered. "Just loving you."

"Please love me more," he whispered back, and then dissolved into mindless ecstasy as she did exactly that.

Anthony's assessment of the situation regarding *Merry-Go-Round* was completely accurate, for the lawsuits were dropped immediately after Alan Corry received a check for $500,000. Without the support of the now delighted author and his equally delighted agent, Film-Star had no case.

But Erin, who thought her troubles were now over, quickly learned how wrong she was as James Lee's grim prophecy came true. When Martin Weinguard put a red-eyed, weeping Marcia on the plane for Reno a month after that fateful party, he promised her that Anthony and Erin would pay for what they'd done. And pay. He kept his promise. There wasn't a studio in town who would let her use its production facilities for shooting the picture. There wasn't an actor or actress who would sign with her. There wasn't a director who would talk to her. She couldn't even get a technical crew. And time was running out.

Against the advice of Anthony's lawyers, she had given Alan Corry a three-month option instead of the usual twelve-month contract. "Film-Star has already stalled him for a year on the picture," she had argued. "We *have* to offer him this in order to get him." It had never occurred to her she'd even need three months to exercise the option. Wildly eager to start filming her first picture and supremely confident that owner-ship of a bestselling novel combined with Anthony's money would open all doors, she had planned to start production immediately. Much too late she realized that Hollywood was a feudal society and it took more than money to buy it. Nor did it help to have Anthony apologetically remind her that he'd warned her of just this very thing, since he'd been similarly unsuccessful in buying his way into Hollywood.

"Don't tell me how *you* failed!" she'd screamed at him. "I'm *not* you, and I *am* going to make it. Do you hear me?"

"Yes, honey," he'd said unhappily. "I just wanted you to know that I understand and care."

"Then go somewhere else to understand and care, because you're not doing any good here!"

"I know. Somehow I never do."

Anthony wandered off sadly and Erin clenched her fists and rocked back and forth in an agony of despair. Two weeks, that was all she had left. Then the option would expire unless she'd started production by that time. "It just can't happen this way," she told herself fiercely. "It can't!" She leaned forward and picked up the phone.

"Yeah, babe, I've heard," James Lee said sympathetically. "But don't say I didn't warn you."

"Oh, James Lee, don't tell me that!" she begged, close to tears. "Tell me how to get out of this trap! Tell me how to save my picture. *Please*. I trust you. You're my only true friend."

"Jesus, Erin. Jesus, what are you asking?"

"I want your mind," she told him feverishly. "You've got the best goddamn mind I've ever known. You *have* to have some ideas!"

"Wow, you really ask a lot."

"Is it too much?" Her voice suddenly became soft and confidential. "Is it too much to ask for what we've been to each other all these years?"

He started to laugh. "Erin, I think you'd con the gravedigger on the day of your funeral."

"Does that mean you'll help me?"

"I guess it means I'll try." He hung up the phone and shook his head. "You're a prime fool, James Lee," he announced to himself. "You've gotten your revenge on Weinguard, so why the hell can't you leave well enough alone?" But of course he knew why. Erin was still in his blood. Sighing again, he picked up the phone and called New York.

• • •

"Tom Jeffries?" Erin looked up from the menu she had been absentmindedly perusing and regarded James Lee with a puzzled expression. "I never heard of him. What pictures has he directed?"

"He's a commercial director. Television commercials."

"*What*?" she cried in horror. "You want me to hire some hack who's spent his whole life with diapers and detergents to direct *my* picture? I'll give up the picture before I ever allow that to happen!"

"Well, that's your only other choice," he observed dryly. "But before you make the worst decision of your life, I suggest you listen to me for a moment."

"Listen to what? How I'll have the whitest whites and brightest colors of any movie ever produced?"

The preposterous statement, uttered in tones of anguished outrage, was too much for James Lee and he broke into helpless laughter.

"I don't see what's so funny," Erin said sullenly.

"I know you don't," he agreed, wiping his streaming eyes with the napkin. "Maybe someday you will. In the meantime, be a smart girl and listen to me like I told you earlier."

"Okay, but it better be good. This wasn't what I had in mind when you called today and said you had the answer to my problems."

However, as Erin listened to James Lee she realized he had indeed come up with the answer to her problems. Tom Jeffries was more than a talented, ambitious young man who aspired to the world of films; he was a craftsman who commanded such respect from his peers that they would literally follow him anywhere he went. Which meant he not only had his own services to offer, but those of camera crew, photographers, musicians, sound mixers and, most importantly, studio facilities and a first-rate lab to develop the film. He was also based in New York, with no ties to the Hollywood power structure.

"You're a genius, James Lee," Erin said gratefully. "I don't know how to thank you. But are you *sure* he knows how to direct a film?"

"I'm sure," he smiled. "I know it's hard for you to believe, but that's because you don't know anything about shooting television commercials. It takes an enormous amount of skill and professional know-how. Tom Jeffries will do a first-class job for you."

"Well." She leaned back against the booth and gave him a relieved grin. "It looks like I'm back in business. I've got everything I need now except the actors, and I'll bet we can get them from the New York theater."

"Not quite," he said slowly. "I'm afraid there's one very major thing you're lacking, and frankly I can't figure out any way to help you with it."

"I don't understand," she said with a puzzled frown. "What are you talking about?"

"Distribution."

"Oh my God!" The implications of what he'd just said sank in. "Those fucking studios control distribution, don't they? They'll never let my picture into the theaters. And what good is producing a picture if no one will ever see it?"

The realization that Hollywood, despite all her efforts and James Lee's help, still held the trump card was so bitter she had to blink back tears. Then anger and a grim determination replaced her momentary feelings of hopeless despair. All her life she'd had to fight to get what she wanted, and she wasn't about to quit now. Because Erin Connolly wasn't a quitter. She was a winner!

"I won't let them kill my picture," she told James Lee fiercely. "I'll beat them at their own game, and one day they'll all come crawling to me! There are independent distribution companies, aren't there? I'll go to them. I'll pay them to take the movie, if I have to."

"And you'll be wasting your money. Oh sure, you could buy some of the small outfits, but you know what that would give you? An exclusive showing at a drive-in theater in Steubenville, Ohio. No, babe, that isn't the way."

"Then what is the way?" she asked desperately.

"Make them want your product. There are only two major independent distribution companies. Forget about the rest. So what you have to do is create such demand for your picture, they'll be hungry enough for it to ignore the pressures from the big studios. But don't ask me how to accomplish that. You're saddled with an unknown director and no stars."

"I have a bestselling novel, though. I do have that, don't I?" she demanded.

"Right, babe. That's what you've got. Now try and figure out a way to capitalize on it."

It took Erin a week to figure out how to do it, but the idea she came up with was pure dynamite. It wasn't a new idea. In fact, it was one of the oldest ideas in Hollywood. But under these circumstances, it was a stroke of genius. *Merry-Go-Round* had the usual standard ingredients for a successful novel. There was sex and violence, salacious inside looks at the world of high fashion, a sinister suggestion of Mafia influence, and a glittering overlay of show-biz personalities. However, what catapulted it to the top of the bestseller list was none of these things. It was the love story between two characters who had captured the eagerly romantic hearts of America in a fashion that hadn't been achieved since Margaret Mitchell created Rhett Butler and Scarlett O'Hara in *Gone With The Wind*.

Erin instigated a nationwide talent search for the actor and actress who would play these sizzling roles. Ten million dollars of Anthony's money went into the promotion of that search. Hopefuls from Bangor, Maine, to San Jose California, applied for the parts. National magazines carried stories from their readers on their visions of the two characters. Television talk-show hosts interviewed possible candidates and asked their audiences for ratings on a scale of one to ten. The promotion built up to a feverish pitch a month after it had been launched, and then the word was leaked that the stars had been found.

By this time the country was in a state of tense excitement, because the identity of the stars was shrouded in mystery. None of the contestants who had appeared in public were being considered. A terse news release went out from Con-Well Productions. "We have just discovered the perfect two individuals who personify the incredible brilliance and sexual magnetism of the characters in *Merry-Go-Round*. You will meet them shortly."

Reporters jammed the small offices of Con-Well Productions in New York after that release.

"C'mon, Miss Connolly," a reporter from the *Daily News* pleaded. "Just give us a hint. When are you going to unveil them?"

"Soon."

"But when? You can't hold back much longer."

Erin knew that. The only thing she wasn't sure of was how to unveil them. The expensive public relations firm Tom Jeffries had introduced her to was hot on going with a public unveiling on a big television special. Erin wasn't convinced that was the best way to go. Then, watching CBS one night in her exclusive suite at the Plaza, she knew immediately what the best way to go was. A feature story on CBS's "60 Minutes." A hard news story on her personal achievement.

The Nielsen ratings went into double numbers when "60 Minutes" introduced the new stars of *Merry-Go-Round*, and an acerbic Mike Wallace found himself taken aback by the sheer sexual power of the two people Erin had found. But Erin didn't leave it there. During the entire six-month filming of the picture, America was treated to the explosive inside story of what was happening on the set. The male star was accused of fathering the child of the girl who tried to win him in the picture. The incredibly sexy female lead was threatening to leave the set if her co-star, who was now reputed to be her lover, didn't return to her. It was the story of *Merry-Go-Round* happening in real life, and the whole world thrilled to it. It was also the story of Hollywood at its best, and Erin reveled in every second of it.

Nine months after Erin Connolly appeared at Martin Weinguard's exclusive screening party in his palatial Beverly Hills mansion, Erin Connolly Wellington held her own screening party in the equally palatial Beverly Hills mansion that Anthony had bought for her. It wasn't as exclusive a party as Martin had held, and there was a distinct difference in the guest list. Martin Weinguard had successfully commanded the presense of major stars, important studio heads, big name directors and producers. Erin hadn't wasted her time inviting people who would turn her down. "Besides, who needs them?" she told herself exultantly. *"Merry-Go-Round* is breaking box-office records all over the country in its first week."

But Erin was anxious to make sure her picture continued to break those box-office records, so she'd opened her home to every important film critic and syndicated columnist in Hollywood. These were the people who could ensure her continuing success, and she was determined to make them welcome. The party had been publicized for weeks, promising not only the appearance of those dynamic young stars who had drawn audiences into the theaters by the thousands but the most opulent entertainment Hollywood had seen since Cecil B. De Mille had thrown one of his extravaganzas.

It was a wildly gala festival, and the crowds poured in. But as Erin stood by the door and counted the well-known faces who rushed up to kiss her on the cheek, she grew increasingly upset. Where was Randy Allen, Hollywood's most celebrated columnist?

"Hi, Mrs. Wellington," a breathless little voice announced. "I'm Lynn Powers, Randy Allen's assistant. He's terribly sorry he couldn't make it tonight."

No one would ever have been able to guess the cold fury that raged inside Erin as she graciously greeted the dumpy little Jewish girl who was so nervous she stumbled over her words as she tried to explain why Randy Allen hadn't been able to make it to the party. But as Erin, with a determined smile, continued to talk with Lynn Powers she realized that the terrified girl was considerably more than a dumb secretary. She was bright, perceptive, and astoundingly knowledgeable about Hollywood personalities. And then Erin flashed a very genuine smile as the idea came to her.

Of course Erin had no idea, as she set about to change Lynn Power's life forever, that she was about to create the deadliest enemy she would ever encounter.

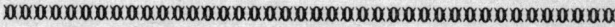

Twelve

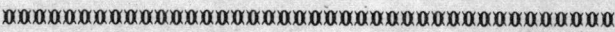

Lᴙɴɴ Powers officially came into existence on April 10, 1960, her creation inspired by a picture of a pretty young Hollywood starlet in the current issue of *Screen Romances* who bore the same name. Actually, however, she'd been around for some time before that. Nine years, eleven months, and thirty days to be exact. But during that time she'd been known as Shirley Silverstein, and that was a period of her life Lynn Powers wanted to forget about totally.

On April 10, 1950, a sweating, panting Sophie Silverstein gave birth to a baby girl after twelve hours of hard, painful labor.

"All right, Morris, you got your kid," she announced balefully as her husband tiptoed into the hospital room, clutching a wilted nosegay of flowers. "And I hope you're satisfied, because this is it! I'm never going through anything like this again!"

"She's beautiful, sweetheart. "I know it's been a terrible ordeal for you, but you must be feeling so proud now. You've given us the loveliest little daughter in the world."

"I'm not proud, and she isn't beautiful," Sophie said flatly. "She's probably one of the homeliest babies I've ever seen. If you can't recognize that, you'd better go and get new glasses like I've been telling you to ever since you ruined Leah Moscowitz's wedding dress by taking in the bodice a full two inches. The poor girl looked like a squashed melon on her wedding day, and we'll never get any more business from those people."

"That was *not* my fault!" Morris declared indignantly. "Her mother insisted on having the dress fitted like that, and you know it just as well as I do."

"Oh well, let's not argue." Sophie waved a weary hand. "The point is that you're the one who wanted a child, and now you've got one. So, since you're so happy about it, you can get up for the two o'clock feedings."

Morris got up for the two o'clock feedings as long as they lasted, which was quite a long time. And he was finally forced to admit that Sophie was right about their daughter. She was homely. The faint fuzz of reddish hair that had covered her scalp when she was born hadn't grown in at all. She also suffered from unsightly skin blotches, diaper rash, and colic. As she got older, she threw up more than she ate, usually on the person who was holding her at the moment. He took her to the pediatrician, who assured him Shirley would outgrow the distressing habit when her digestive system matured.

Morris found it increasingly difficult to cope as he kept nightly vigil over the crib that held his small daughter's feverish, sobbing form as she turned and tossed, and his wife snored peacefully in the next bedroom. When daybreak came, he wearily donned his clothes and went off to the tailor shop located on a quiet Brooklyn street where he bent over the sewing machine to complete alterations on suits and dresses that had been promised to customers first thing that morning. Finally he could cope no longer.

"All right, Sophie," he said on the night before Shirley's second birthday. "If you still want your mother to come live with us, it's okay with me. But make sure she understands she has to take care of the baby."

"Oh, Morris, I knew you'd come to your senses one of these days," Sophie exclaimed. "And you're going to be so glad you made this decision. I'll call her this very minute!"

"Remember to tell her about the baby. Those are my

conditions, and if she doesn't agree to them, she doesn't come."

"For heaven's sake, Morris, you think I have to tell her that? Mama will be *thrilled* to take care of her grandchild."

"Thrilled she doesn't have to be. I'll settle for willing. Especially between the hours of seven at night and seven in the morning."

"You don't have a thing to worry about," Sophie told him confidently. "You can count on Mama."

To his considerable surprise, Morris found out that Sophie had been right when she'd said he would be glad about his decision. Mama not only took over care of Shirley but the chores of house cleaning, shopping, and cooking; and she enjoyed the experience of looking after a family again so much that she rarely had a free moment to contract a disease or criticize Morris. As a result, Morris and Sophie came home every night to a clean house, a delicious hot dinner, and a contented child.

Everybody was happy, but no one was quite as happy as Shirley. For the first time in her life she was literally enveloped in love from dawn to dusk, and she thrived on it. The skin problems and stomach upsets went away. She began to explore her world, ask questions which were always answered, and gurgle with laughter at the games she now got to play. By the end of the day, she was satiated with pleasure and slept peacefully through the night.

"It's a miracle," Morris said wonderingly one Friday night, three years later, after the Sabbath candles had finally been blown out and Mama had lifted the sleepy child into her arms and carried her off to the bedroom they shared.

He picked up his glass of sweet wine and sipped it in contentment. "Sophie, we are very lucky. Our home is blessed, and our child is blessed. Isn't she lovely now?"

"No, Morris, she isn't lovely. She's just as homely as the day she was born. I wonder what will happen to her when she gets older."

"How can you say that?" he exclaimed in horror. "You're talking about your very own child!"

"So who knows better than a mother?" Sophie sighed. "Next year she goes off to school. I don't think she'll make it."

"You should bite your tongue! Such a beautiful, well-behaved little girl, a joy to her parents, and you're putting a curse on her like that? Shame on you!"

"We'll see, Morris. We'll see. Mama hasn't been feeling too good these days. If she goes, it's going to be hard on Shirley."

"What are you talking about?" he shouted. "Your mother has the constitution of a bull. I should be so lucky!"

"I hope so, Morris." Sophie gave a fatalistic shrug. "But I don't think so."

As usual, Sophie was right. Mama suffered a fatal coronary occlusion, ironically the only disease she hadn't diagnosed for herself, and died in the middle of the night before Shirley's first day at school. And Shirley's happy world died along with Mama. Sophie had to go back to shopping, cleaning, and cooking, as well as working at the tailor shop, and her disposition soured accordingly. She was snappish and irritable, and the house was filled with her constant complaining. Nor were matters helped by the fact that the funeral had been very expensive, and it turned out Mama didn't have any insurance. Morris had to go back to working twelve-hour days. There was also the problem of what to do with Shirley while both parents were at the shop. Hiring someone to look after her was out of the question. The money for that simply wasn't available. And Sophie certainly couldn't take off during the height of business to go home and sit with her. Which left only one possible solution. Shirley would have to come to the tailor shop after school where her parents could keep an eye on her.

At first Shirley was relegated to the small room at the back of the shop where she sat for endless, boring hours, on a hard chair in front of the scarred oak table at which Morris and Sophie ate their hurried lunch in shifts, listlessly filling in coloring books or just staring into space. But Sophie's thrifty nature soon rebelled at the waste.

"As long as she's here, she might as well do something useful. It's ridiculous to have her just sitting there doodling," Sophie frowned.

"What are you talking about?" Morris stared at his wife in shock. "She's only a baby, six years old. You're planning to bring back sweat shops with *our* child?"

"Oh for God's sake, Morris!" Sophie said disgustedly. "Always you exaggerate. You think it'll kill the kid to do a little sweeping up? Pick up the cuttings from the floor? It'll do her good to get a little exercise."

It wasn't long before Shirley graduated from sweeping the floor to stitching simple seams along the chalk marks her father had indicated on the cloth. And by the time she was nine, she was operating the sewing machine that repaired frayed cuffs on shirts. She was a quiet, obedient child who did her work well and never gave them any trouble; which was probably why Sophie was so outraged when she suddenly announced that she now expected to be paid for her work.

"Sophie, she has a right," Morris protested.

"What right?" Sophie screamed. "We feed her. We clothe her. We put a roof over her head. And do we ask to be paid for that?"

"Would you please calm down? All she's asking for is an allowance. The same thing as her friends have."

"She doesn't have any friends," Sophie replied grimly. "And she'll just waste the money on those trashy movie magazines, which are already addling whatever brain power she might have had."

"I'm giving her the allowance," Morris announced quietly. "And that's the end of this discussion."

It wasn't often that Morris made an announcement, but Sophie knew when he did there was no sense in fighting it. Her usually timid husband had an unsettling habit of coming out firmly on a subject once in a while, and there was no stopping him once he'd made up his mind. Unhappily, then, she agreed to Shirley's allowance. Her unhappiness increased tenfold a year later.

"Are you willing now to admit you were wrong?" she cried hysterically. "Your daughter has gone completely insane. Lynn Powers is what she insists on calling herself. She won't even answer to her own God-given name. And this is all your fault!"

"She only wants to make something of herself, like we once did. So what's the harm in that? And she's got friends now. You got to admit that, Sophie."

"Crazies just like her, sitting around every afternoon with their noses buried in that trash she collects instead of doing their homework," Sophie stormed. "I should do a public service, call their parents and tell them what's going on."

"You won't call anybody," Morris said sternly. "You'll let her do what she wants."

For a long time, all she'd known was what she didn't want. And what she didn't want was to be Shirley Silverstein. Because being Shirley Silverstein meant being fat, homely, and unpopular. It meant being poor. It meant a constantly aching back from bending over sewing machines, hand-me-down clothes, and the pervasive odor of boiling cabbage. Above all, it meant the continuous nagging criticism of her mother. Then one day she picked up a movie magazine left in the tailor shop by one of the customers, and then she knew absolutely and without a doubt what she did want. To go to Hollywood and make her mark in that fabulous, magic world. And she worked with single-minded devotion toward that goal.

She started collecting movie magazines when she was nine, and when she was ten she had a library of over five hundred issues. During her tenth year she bought a used filing cabinet from the money she earned at the shop and set up a comprehensive filing system on all the major actors and actresses of the day. By the time she was eleven, she was respectfully acknowledged by her peers as the leading authority on the careers and private lives of Hollywood's most important stars. She started her first fan club when she was twelve, and by the time she was fourteen she was the president of six different fan clubs and had received personal handwritten letters from those six glamorous stars her fan clubs were devoted to. She had power!

The day after her graduation from high school she packed a large suitcase with a few clothes and seven scrapbooks which held correspondence and publicity clippings on her fan clubs, drew her savings out of the bank, kissed her father but not her mother goodbye, and boarded a bus for Hollywood, confidently prepared to take the town by storm.

It took her less than forty-eight hours to discover she wasn't going to take anybody by storm, because she had no power at all. The letters from the stars that she had so proudly brought with her were fakes. Nobody had ever heard of Lynn Powers, and nobody wanted to hear from her. She went on a two-week binge of candy bars, cookies, and chocolate malteds before she finally pulled herself together.

"Enough already," she told the tear-streaked face in the mirror. "So you got fooled. A disappointment, sure. A disaster, no. You learned something. You go from here."

Lynn went to secretarial school, practicing her typing and shorthand by transcribing articles from *Daily Variety* and *The Hollywood Reporter* at night in her small, cramped studio apartment just off Fairfax and Sixth, an area that reminded her depressingly of the Jewish ghetto community she thought she'd finally managed to escape.

The counselor at the employment agency Lynn had signed with tore out her hair in frustrated rage as the stubborn, star-struck girl turned down one job after another.

"This kid's a potential gold mine," she wailed to her co-workers. "Types ninety words a minute, takes shorthand at one hundred eighty. And she can spell and punctuate, too. I got ten companies who'd hire her this very instant! Then I could switch her around to another job every three or four months and make a fortune in commissions. But the little pisher refuses to even consider a position unless it's connected with the movie industry. What did I do to deserve this?"

"My advice is to get her what she wants," the woman at the next desk told her unsympathetically. "Otherwise, you're gonna lose her."

"Yeah. Yeah, I know," the counselor sighed unhappily. "You're talking about that new listing that just came in."

The new listing was for a secretarial position with Randy Allen, the acid-tongued syndicated Hollywood columnist. The job paid peanuts, and the commission earned by the employment agency would barely cover the cost of a dinner for two at a good Los Angeles restaurant. The counselor had debated with herself for several days about letting Lynn Powers know about the opening, because it was such a waste of her talent and skills. But now she reluctantly conceded the wisdom of her co-worker's remark and dialed Lynn's telephone number.

Lynn was not particularly excited when she walked into the employment agency early the next morning. She was used to getting calls from the counselor telling her that just the right job had come up, only to find out when she arrived at her office that it wasn't right at all. But this time she was in for a surprise.

"Randy Allen!" Lynn cried, her eyes as wide as saucers. "You mean *the* Randy Allen, the famous columnist?"

"Yeah, that's the one I mean," she said glumly. "But I'm telling you, it's a lousy job. Just typing all day long, and the pay is really rotten."

"Oh how wonderful!" Lynn exclaimed joyfully. "I don't know how to thank you."

"Listen, kid, keep in touch with me," she begged. "I can get you twice this salary any time you want, with fringe benefits you wouldn't believe."

But Lynn hadn't heard a thing that had been said after the magic words Randy Allen had been spoken. "Oh hell," the counselor sighed as she watched the ecstatic girl race out the door for her interview.

Randy Allen hired Lynn thirty minutes after she walked into his office, which was the exact length of time it took her to take down his rapid-fire dictation and turn it into five crisply perfect typewritten pages. And for the next three months, he started every day with a prayer of thanks to the kind gods who had given him this jewel. Lynn was everything and more than she'd promised to be. No task was too big or too small for her. Her energy was inexhaustible and her cheerfulness constant. She had a real feel for the business too, bringing him little gems of gossip for his column and offering them to him shyly along with the fresh, home-baked pastries she brought with her every morning to serve him with his coffee.

But in the fourth month, Randy started feeling a little uneasy. Maybe Lynn was just a bit too good to be true. She handled a lot of his phone work now and was on a first name basis with most of his contacts. Was it possible she had ambitions of her own? At first he was embarrassed by such thoughts. After all, she was such a hopeless-looking klutz. Maybe his friends were right when they told him he had a tendency toward paranoia. He discussed the possibility at length with his psychiatrist, who just looked at him and said, "Hmm?" Which was no help at all. But then the fucker never had been any help, he thought angrily.

Randy was still trying to decide what to do about Lynn when Erin Connolly Wellington sent out her invitations for the extravaganza press party celebrating her first picture. He might have covered it himself if the incredibly beautiful young boy who'd become an overnight sensation in his first starring role (thanks in large part to Randy Allen's promotion of him) hadn't called in desperation and begged his mentor to come and see him because he was going out of his mind trying to decide whether he was really gay or not. Randy had a deep, personal interest in such discussions, so he sent Lynn out to Erin's party. He couldn't believe he would be missing anything important anyway. Erin Connolly was just a little cunt from nowhere who'd snagged that strange man previously married to Martin Weinguard's daughter. She wouldn't be around too long.

Lynn was so excited about the assignment, she couldn't eat or sleep or think about anything else. But when the day of the big party arrived, her feverish joy turned into teeth-chattering terror. Suppose they refused to let her in the door? After all, they'd invited the famous Randy Allen, not some dumpy little Jewish secretary from Brooklyn. And even if they did let her in, wouldn't they be furious to learn that Randy had snubbed them in this way?

"Nobody will talk to me," she moaned to the mirror. "I'll end up against the back wall with the catering service."

Lynn had a sudden terrible vision of herself huddled in a corner as a tall, imperious woman strode up to her and icily demanded to know where the tray of hot hors d'oeuvres was. "I'd probably go out to the kitchen and get them," she said sadly to her mirror image. "And then tomorrow Randy will fire me."

It didn't happen that way at all, although Lynn experienced a brief, heart-stopping moment of panic when she introduced herself to Erin. "Randy Allen's assistant?" Erin had said, staring at her through cold, narrowed eyes. "And just exactly what is it you do?"

Frantic to establish her right to be at the party, she'd babbled on about researching the material for Randy's columns and even co-authoring some of them; praying that what she was saying would never get back to Randy. He'd fire her quicker for that than for ending up serving hors d'oeuvres.

Several times Erin broke into her desperate recital with sharp, pointed questions. None of them caused Lynn any problems, because she really did know what she was talking about. In fact, although she was innocently unaware of it, she actually did perform the important functions she thought she was inventing for Erin's benefit. But at the moment, all she knew was an incredible sense of relief as the woman in front of her suddenly favored her with a warm smile.

"Well, my dear, we're certainly all sorry to hear about dear Randy's health problems, but it appears he's done us a real favor by sending you in his place. Colitis, was it?"

"Colitis?" Lynn repeated confusedly, still involved in relating the inside story of a famous television star who'd suddenly quit his hit series. "Gee, I don't remember any rumors like that about Paul Denton. It wouldn't go with his he-man image at all. Torn ligaments, caused by his doing his own stunts, is what I heard. Of course that's a lie. He made the whole thing up to get out of his contract, so he can sign next month with Peckinpah for that new picture. And to tell you the truth," she confided, "I think he's making a mistake. That picture is going to bomb!"

She flushed in embarrassment as Erin burst into laughter. "Well, maybe I'm mistaken," she mumbled. "You can't call them right all the time."

"That's not why I'm laughing," Erin assured her, still chuckling. "The colitis I was referring to belongs to your dear employer Randy Allen. Or at least that's what you told me. I mean, isn't that the reason he couldn't make it tonight?"

"Oh my God! How could I possibly have forgotten?" She swallowed hard and then bravely met Erin's eyes. "Especially since he's suffering from it so much. You must think I'm really terrible."

"No, I don't think that at all," Erin replied thoughtfully. "Why don't we get together for lunch next week and talk about it?"

"About Randy's colitis?"

"No. About why you forgot it."

Thirteen

"Wow, Mrs. Wellington! I mean, Erin," she corrected herself hastily as Erin gave her a friendly warning look. "I never *dreamed* you had anything like this in mind when you asked me to lunch. I . . . gosh, I just don't know what to say!"

"Why not say yes?" Erin suggested pleasantly.

"You really think I could do it?"

"Of course. You're a bright, sharp, ambitious girl, and you've developed a lot of very valuable contacts during the time you've worked for Randy Allen. All you need is a little financial backing to get started, and Anthony and I would be delighted to provide it."

"Wow!" Lynn reached absently into the basket of rolls on the table. She flushed as she saw it was empty.

"Gee, I'm sorry. I have this terrible habit of eating when I get nervous. I don't even realize I'm doing it."

"I think that's something you might consider changing," Erin said gently.

"Yeah, I know," Lynn mumbled, hanging her head. "Not that I haven't tried before, because I have. I really have," she told Erin earnestly as she looked up at her. "But giving up eating just seems to be the hardest thing in the world for me."

"Maybe you'll find it easier this time." Erin smiled. "After all, everything else in your life is about to change."

"That's true, isn't it?" she said wonderingly. "I still can't believe it, though. Fat, dumb Shirley Silverstein from Brooklyn becoming a famous Hollywood columnist. Boy, will that kill my mother!" she declared joyfully. "I can hardly wait to tell her!"

"Well, we've got a little work to do before you tell her." Erin laughed.

Under the warm, encouraging guidance of Erin Connolly Wellington, Lynn managed to diet off thirty pounds, learned how and where to shop for clothes, found the courage to have her nose done, changed her limp, mousy hair into a gleaming, sun-streaked California blond, and became Hollywood's most sizzling "in" gossip columnist, with her own radio and television show and a syndicated column that was carried by over two hundred newspapers across the country.

Erin's initial motivation in starting Lynn Powers on her career had been simply a matter of getting back at Randy Allen for his unforgivable snub in not attending the party for her first picture. But she soon found herself becoming genuinely fond of the gutsy little Jewish girl from Brooklyn who fought so hard to achieve her dreams.

In many ways, Lynn reminded her of herself. More important, Lynn was as loving and loyal as she was smart and ambitious. She never forgot for a moment that Erin had been responsible for her success, and she repaid the favor in a hundred ways. If there was a hot new star about to appear on the horizon, Erin was the first to learn about it. If a studio was in financial trouble with a picture or about to lose an important screen option, Erin heard about it before anyone else. And if the vitally important trade unions were considering a strike, Erin got the word about that in advance too.

For the first time in her life Erin had a woman friend, and she thoroughly enjoyed the experience, looking forward to the daily phone chats with their deliciously spiced tidbits of gossip, and sympathizing with Lynn over her one continuing failure. Because despite Lynn's astounding success, there was a very important thing missing in her life . . . romance.

It wasn't that men didn't ask her out, because they did. As a matter of fact, she could have had three hundred sixty-five dinner dates a year if she'd wanted to. The trouble was that all those eager, attentive men were only interested in Lynn Powers the columnist. No one was interested in Lynn Powers the woman.

At first, Lynn had eagerly accepted every invitation offered her in hopes that maybe this one would turn out to be different. But it never was. And she soon discovered that the loneliest feeling in the world was sitting across the table from a man who was ardently selling his client to you while at nearby tables couples touched and smiled, their ardor directed only at each other.

Soon Lynn began turning down almost as many invitations as she received, finding it infinitely more comforting to stay at home, curled up in the warm coziness of her small bed, watching old movies on television. And when lovers on the flickering screen came together in passionate embraces, causing tears of aching longing to stream down her cheeks, she could always get up and start writing her column.

Paradoxically, her sudden withdrawal from the social scene caused men to pursue her with frenzied desire. It became a real coup to get Lynn Powers to go out to dinner. Lynn was wryly amused by the accelerated courting she was receiving. It also made her accept fewer and fewer invitations. The only reason she agreed to have dinner with Garth Werner was because she was curious to find out what the man behind the talent was like.

Lynn had been genuinely impressed with the brilliant directorial work in the movie *CountDown*, which was based on the bestselling novel of the same name and had been handed over to a young unknown graduate of NYU's film school when budget problems and internecine battles within the giant studio that had optioned the book almost closed down production on the picture.

When the picture finally opened, Lynn devoted two columns to praising the director. She also discussed the film on both her radio and television shows. She didn't do this because any agents or public relations people had thrown themselves at her feet, abjectly begging for just a tiny bit of good press about the picture and promising to give her anything she wanted in return for the favor. No, she just did it because she liked the work. Which was one of the reasons Lynn Powers was so good. She couldn't be bought.

It also gave Lynn great pleasure to discover new talent. So when Garth Werner called her office in person to thank her for the reviews on his picture and ask her out to dinner, she hesitated only a few seconds before accepting. And it was the professionally interested syndicated columnist, not the wistfully lonely young woman, who opened the door of her apartment that night and smiled brightly at the tall, darkly handsome young director. But by the end of the evening Lynn Powers the columnist had been totally routed by Lynn Powers the woman, for she had fallen wildly, head over heels in love with Garth Werner. And, miracles of miracles, he seemed to really care about her too. Not her column, not her radio or television show, but her! She could hardly wait for Erin to meet him.

"Erin, you'll never guess what's happened!" Lynn cried ecstatically over the phone the next morning. "It's the most incredible, exciting thing you could possibly imagine!"

"You've met a man."

"Gee, how did you guess so easily?" she asked, crestfallen.

Erin burst into laughter. "Darling, what else could it be when you call at eight-thirty in the morning and tell me the most incredible, exciting thing in the world has just happened. Anyway, I think it's marvelous, and I told you it would happen one of these days. Now, who is he and how did it come about?"

Lynn happily launched into a detailed description of exactly how she'd met Garth Werner, where they went to dinner, what he said, what she said. Then she broke off in confusion when she came to the part about his coming back to her apartment.

"It was . . . well, it was everything I've ever dreamed about," she confided shyly. "If you know what I mean."

"Yes," Erin chuckled, "I know what you mean. So when are you seeing him again?"

"Tonight. I'm cooking for him. He says he hasn't had a good home-cooked meal since he came out to Hollywood. I hope I remember how," she added worriedly. "I haven't fixed a real dinner since I went on my diet."

"You'll remember," Erin assured her. "And you'll probably hook him for life."

"I'd like to. He's really something special. You know who he is, don't you?"

"Well." Erin paused for a moment. The truth was that the name Garth Werner meant nothing to her, but she didn't want to hurt her friend's feelings. Then she suddenly recalled the column Lynn had done on the movie *CountDown*.

"Of course!" she said enthusiastically. "He's the bright young director Continental Studios hired out of nowhere to take over that picture they were having such budget problems with. He not only brought it in on time, he brought it in under budget, didn't he?"

"He did more than that, Erin. He turned the whole thing around. They've already made their money back, and the picture's been in general release for less than a month."

"But he's got more going for him than that. He happens to be a personal friend of the guy who wrote *Street Scene*. Every studio in town is bidding for the screen rights to that book."

"Are you saying what I think you're saying?" Erin asked cautiously.

"You bet I am!" Lynn exclaimed. "He's got a lock on that book. And what he's looking for is a producer who will give him a piece of the action. I kind of think you just might be that producer."

"I kind of think you just might be right. So why don't we set up a little intimate dinner party, just you and Garth and Anthony and myself, to discuss it?"

"You've got it!" Lynn said jubilantly. "Just name the night!"

The last thought on Erin's mind when she set up that intimate dinner party for Lynn and Garth was taking away her friend's lover. Erin's only interest was in making a deal with the young director who could get her the screen rights to a picture she, along with most of Hollywood, had been hungering after.

Perhaps the chain of events that was set in motion when Garth and Erin met were inevitable. But it is equally possible that they could have been avoided if Erin herself had not been so terribly vulnerable at that time.

Over the past two years Con-Well Productions had become an established commercial success. This was due in large part to Anthony's money, which allowed the young company to expand in a manner that was beyond the means of most independent producers, who had to wait, hope, and pray for the financial success of their first picture before they could even begin to think of going into production on a second. With Anthony's virtually unlimited funds, Con-Well had been able to acquire properties and start filming them immediately after work had been completed on the previous picture. This kept Con-Well continually in the public eye, and distributors were more than happy to book its pictures, knowing that every one came backed with a good-as-gold, seven-figure advertising and promotion budget.

However, the Connolly-Wellington marriage was not enjoying the same success. Erin had initially been charmed by Anthony's quiet, wry humor, gentle, courtly manner, and wholehearted worship of her. It had made her carefully planned seduction of him more pleasurable than she'd dreamed possible. But after two years, she found no charm in him at all. His wry humor had become a bore, his gentle, courtly manner a drag, and his worship of her an almost intolerable irritant. He was, after all, almost twenty years older than she, and he had the body of an old man.

Erin was, by nature, a passionate, sensual woman. Curiously, it was the one thing she didn't understand about herself. All her life had been spent in fierce competition to win recognition and power, and in her headstrong battle to achieve those things she had sublimated her basic drives. Along the way she had cultivated people she could use and manipulate to help her in accomplishing those goals; the result was that she had spent her life surrounded by weak people. With the possible exception of her first love many years ago when she was in high school, Erin had never allowed herself to become involved with a strong, dominant male. She had never known a man who could challenge and excite her mentally as well as fulfill the powerful emotional needs and desires inside her that were clamoring with increasing urgency to be satisfied. She was about to meet that man, with devastating results.

"Well, here we are!" a glowing Lynn Powers announced the following Friday evening as Erin opened the door.

She threw her arms around Erin and hugged her, then stepped back and gazed up proudly at Garth. "And this is Garth Werner, the brilliant young director all Hollywood will soon be talking about. Garth, honey, my very best friends, Erin and Anthony Wellington."

Erin smiled, extending a welcoming hand, and then her breath caught in her throat as he took it. Her whole body tingled as though she'd suddenly touched a live electric current. Their eyes met and she stood there frozen, unable to look away.

Anthony gave a gentle cough. "I'm afraid he isn't going to think we're such good friends, dear, if we keep them standing out here on the porch."

Embarrassed, Erin flushed as she retrieved her hand from his warm grip. "Good heavens, forgive me," she said breathlessly. "Please come in. We're so glad to see you."

Lynn and Garth made themselves comfortable on the long, low circular couch while Anthony went over to the bar to mix drinks. Erin fussed with the tray of hors d'oeuvres, keeping up a steady and slightly feverish stream of conversation while trying unsuccessfully to keep her eyes off Garth.

Garth Werner was an extraordinarily good-looking man, in his late twenties. There was nothing pretty about him: his features were strong, bold, and totally male. He had an unruly mop of thick black curly hair, a dark slash of eyebrows over deep blue eyes that blazed with intensity, a square, stubborn-looking chin, and a low, husky voice with a rough, growling edge to it that gave it a distinctly sexual overtone. He was tall, two inches over six feet, and he had a lean, muscular body that always seemed on the edge of bursting free from some invisible bonds. He rarely sat still, prowling around the living room like a big cat as he talked.

Erin found herself fascinated with his hands. They were large and powerful looking with heavy-boned wrists, but the fingers were surprisingly long and sensitive. They were in constant motion as he talked, gesturing with such graphic precision that she could almost see them drawing pictures of the words he spoke. She shivered involuntarily as she thought about those hands moving on her body.

"Dear, I hate to mention it," Anthony whispered, "but I think Maria is getting a little anxious."

"Oh my God!" Erin leaped to her feet, and then smiled apologetically at her guests.

"Maria is not just a cook, she's the last great cook in Hollywood. Everybody is always trying to steal her from us. So, if you don't mind, I think we'd better go on in to dinner before we ruin her creation and she quits on us. They say no one's irreplaceable," Erin remarked as she led them into the dining room, "but then they haven't met Maria."

"This is marvelous!" Garth announced with a smile of pleasure as his fork cut effortlessly into the exquisitely tender beef with its rich wine-and-mushroom sauce.

"Absolutely superb," Lynn said. She leaned over and whispered desperately in Erin's ear, "Will Maria give me this recipe? Because my dinner didn't really turn out all that well."

"I'll get it for you," Erin whispered back. "But don't ever tell anybody I gave it to you."

"I won't. Cross my heart. Oh, Erin, you're a real lifesaver," Lynn said fervently. "Because this guy is nuts about good food."

"To Maria," Garth smiled as he raised his glass of wine.

"Indeed," Anthony agreed. "Say, Garth, maybe you'd like to tell her yourself how much you're enjoying this. She'd really like that."

Maria was brought into the dining room and blushed with pleasure as the two men stood up and complimented her on the meal.

"You got a real nice guest tonight, Mr. Anthony," she beamed. "I'll cook for him anytime."

"To Garth Werner." Anthony laughed as Maria retired to the

kitchen. "You may have just guaranteed me one of life's greatest joys, the delight of eating Maria's meals."

"I'd like to think so." Garth smiled. "Especially since I want the privilege of enjoying one of them again."

He finished his wine and set the glass back on the table. "So why don't we see if that's going to be possible. You want *Street Scene* and I want twenty-five percent of it. Can we do business?"

There was a stunned silence interrupted by Lynn's nervous whisper. "Honey, you can't just lay it on them like that. You have to lead up to it gradually, allow room for negotiation."

"That's a pretty big percentage you're asking for, young man," Anthony said. "Unless you're going to invest your own money in the production?" He gave Garth a quizzical look. "We hadn't been led to understand you were planning on that."

"I would if I could. Unfortunately, I'm not in a position at the moment to offer that. But what I do have to offer are the screen rights to a very powerful bestselling novel, and the very real possibility of an Oscar-winning picture for Con-Well Productions. I think that's worth twenty-five percent."

"Twenty-five percent is completely out of the question," Erin announced crisply. "That is not to say we are opposed to giving you some interest in the picture in exchange for your obtaining the screen rights. Lynn made it quite clear that's what you're looking for, and we agreed that would be part of the deal. What we had in mind was offering you five percent, which we feel is more than fair. And naturally you would defer your director's fee in exchange for it."

"Naturally I would defer my director's fee," he agreed. Then he started to laugh as a smug little smile crept over Erin's face. "But I won't take five percent. Or seven percent. Or even the ten percent you were probably willing to compromise on after haggling back and forth."

Garth leaned back in his chair and spread his large hands on the table. "Look, maybe Lynn didn't explain what a strange maverick I am. I don't believe in haggling. I believe in stating what I want, based on what I think is fair for what I have to deliver. People can take it or leave it. That, of course, is up to them."

"In that case there is absolutely nothing to discuss!" Erin snapped, white-faced from barely controlled rage.

"The other thing Lynn may have forgotten to tell you is that I hate making unpleasant scenes," Garth said lazily, his eyes gleaming with amusement. "So, since we can't agree on the picture, why don't we just relax and enjoy Maria's dinner as good friends."

"I'll drink to that," Anthony said quickly, distinctly alarmed by the furious look on his wife's face.

"Me too," Lynn echoed faintly. She was almost in tears over the unexpected confrontation between Erin and Garth that was changing her beautiful evening into a nightmare.

To everyone's surprise, Garth managed to switch the strained situation into the relaxed, enjoyable dinner he'd suggested. He began talking about his early days in New York, and he had some very funny stories about how he'd gotten into directing, including an incredible saga about his apprenticeship at a small New York ad agency that specialized in retail accounts for underwear manufacturers.

Everyone was still chuckling about his account of the inflatable bra that suddenly deflated right on live camera when Maria came in to clear the table, and they moved to the living room for coffee and cognac.

Anthony lit the fragrant pine logs in the fireplace and switched on the five-thousand-dollar stereo set that gently flooded the room with warm sound as he made his way to the bar.

"Wow, this is living." Lynn sighed as she curled up in a chair next to the fireplace.

"The best," Garth agreed as he sprawled out on the sofa, his long legs stretched out in front of him.

"And this is the best cognac in the world." Anthony beamed as he handed each of them a giant balloon-shaped glass of Tiffany's finest crystal, and settled into the chair opposite Lynn.

Erin crouched at the far end of the sofa, her emotions in turmoil. She now hated Garth with as much passion as she'd desired him earlier. He was a totally impossible, arrogant bastard who not only had the incredible effrontery to turn down the best offer he'd ever get, but to insult her in the process.

She gulped down the potent cognac in fury. Then she thought about what he'd said. An Oscar-winning picture for Con-Well Productions. Erin's first three pictures had all been solid commercial successes, but no one had ever considered them for an Oscar. And Erin wanted to win an Oscar more than anything in the world.

"All right, you get your twenty-five percent," she announced, and braced herself for the cocky, triumphant grin she knew was coming.

But Erin was wrong. There was nothing cocky or triumphant about Garth when he turned and looked at her. The expression on his face was totally serious.

"I'm glad," he said simply. "Because I want to do this picture very much. And I promise you it will be a fine picture." He reached out and took hold of her hand.

Once again his touch sent a tingling current of electricity surging through her body, and Erin's angry hostility dissolved, swept away by a rush of bewildering emotions.

"Well, this certainly calls for another drink!" Anthony exclaimed.

"Oh, Erin, I'm so happy you made this decision!" Lynn's face lit up like a Christmas tree. "You won't regret it, I promise you. He's going to give you your first Oscar. I just know it!"

For a while the four of them joined together to discuss the picture, all with their own eager suggestions for casting and locations. But gradually Lynn and Anthony became excluded from the conversation as Erin and Garth concentrated more and more on each other's ideas. And by the end of the evening, Lynn and Anthony found themselves sitting in silence as they stared at the vibrantly beautiful couple now sitting so close together on the soft, velvet sofa in front of the roaring fireplace that their heads almost touched as they continued to talk, totally engrossed in each other.

One week after Erin's intimate dinner party for Lynn and Garth, Hollywood's major trade papers reported that Con-Well

Productions had scored a major coup by obtaining the screen rights to *Street Scene*. A small paragraph at the bottom of the story announced that the director on the picture would be Garth Werner, a young director who'd made his debut with Continental Studios' trouble-ridden production of *CountDown*.

One week after that, the major trade papers, along with every sensational tabloid, gleefully reported that a sizzling romance between Erin and the young director was about to break up the Connolly-Wellington marriage. It was the most delectably exciting news since Erin Connolly had broken up Marcia and Anthony's marriage and formed Con-Well Productions. Because without Anthony's money, how could Con-Well Productions survive? They waited with breathless anticipation to see what would happen.

Lynn Powers went back to spending her evenings alone in her small apartment. But she no longer wasted her time watching old movies on television. She was much too busy planning a way to destroy Erin Connolly.

XX

Fourteen

XXXXXXXXXXXXXXXXXXXXXXXXXXXXXXXXXXXXXXXXXXXXXXXXXXXXXXXXXXXX

THE rain beat down steadily on the roof, sounding a counter-point to the massive roar of the surf as the big waves crashed against the shore. There was a sudden sharp hiss as a gust of wind sent a shower of raindrops down the chimney where they sputtered furiously as they hit the red glowing logs in the fireplace.

Erin sat up, buttoned her blouse, and ran her hands through her hair. "We never even made it to the bedroom, did we?" she said shakily.

"No, we didn't." Garth smiled at her. "But then I always did want to make love on a fur rug in front of a roaring fire while a storm raged outside."

"Don't ever try to be a writer," she laughed. "They'd murder you for lines like that. Besides, this is hardly a fur rug." She grimaced as she brushed ineffectively at the lint on her custom-designed silk blouse.

"Complaints already?" he grinned.

"I wouldn't say that."

Suddenly uncomfortable with the memory of her total and ectastic capitulation to his erotic demands, she got to her feet and walked over to the sliding-glass doors that opened on to the deck overlooking the pounding surf.

"This isn't bad for a tacky little beach house, Garth," she said lightly. "But you'll be able to afford a much more impressive place after *Street Scene* comes out."

"Maybe I like my little tacky beach house." He stood up and stalked over to where she was standing, grabbing her arm. "Did that ever occur to you?"

"Garth, stop it! You're hurting me."

He let go of her so abruptly she fell against the glass door. "I'm sorry. I didn't mean to do that. Are you all right?"

"I'm fine," she said stiffly. "But it's getting late. I have to leave."

"No. I'm not going to let you leave like this," he murmured huskily as he reached out for her.

"Garth? For God's sake, Garth, what are you doing?" He unbuttoned her blouse and leaned down to kiss her breasts. But her protests suddenly turned into moans of pleasure as his mouth closed around her nipple and he sucked deeply, his hands moving caressingly down her body.

He picked her up easily and carried her back to the living room, setting her down gently in front of the fireplace, his mouth traveling from her breasts to the soft swell of her stomach as his lean, sensitive fingers slid between her thighs, separating the moist, curled pubic hairs and exploring the hot pink tenderness underneath them.

"No," she said faintly. "No, we can't. It's so late. I have to . . ."

She broke off, gasping involuntarily as he found the delicate bud that was the fountainhead of her ecstasy.

"Sit on me," he growled. "Ride me."

"Oh, Garth, I can't," she begged. "I really have to go."

"Not yet, love. Not yet. Now come to me," he demanded as he pulled her on top of him. "Take it and come to me!"

Helplessly, Erin allowed him to pull her forward towards his thick, erect penis, then shuddered as it touched her. Wild now with desire, she lifted her hips and plunged down on him as his hands gripped her buttocks and rotated them with increasing intensity.

"More," she sobbed. "Give me more."

"Can you take it, babe? Can you take still more?" he panted.

"Yes. Oh yes!"

She braced her hands on his chest, throwing her head back in exultation as she felt him becoming harder and longer, stroking every nerve inside her body. It was an incredibly exquisite sensation, feeling him grow like that inside her, as though she'd been empty and hungry all her life and was finally discovering the miracle of being filled.

"I'm going up the mountain," she cried.

"Climbing with you, my sweet bitch. Climbing with you all the way."

Erin reached the crest of the mountain and swung dizzily, wildly on the edge. Instead of falling off, she spiraled up to another peak. And then went up again and again to new peaks, never discovered before, until she finally exploded into the stars.

"Honey? Hey, honey, are you okay?" Garth asked with concern as he leaned forward and kissed the tears off her face.

"I don't know," she said tremulously. "I've never felt this way before."

"It's all right," he told her gently. "I won't ever hurt you, Erin. All I want to do is give you pleasure and make you happy."

And for the next few weeks Garth more than kept his promise. Erin drifted through them in a state of delirious bliss, totally caught up in the rapture of their relationship. They saw each other every day, meeting for lunch in small, out-of-the-way restaurants and then driving back with feverish impatience to his beach house to make love, clinging to each other until the last possible moment, when she reluctantly pulled herself away from him to get dressed and head back to the big Beverly Hills mansion where Anthony innocently awaited her.

It was a magical time, a world filled with lovely dreams and desires that grew more beautiful with each meeting, because the incredible chemistry between them became stronger each time they came together. And it was made possible by a set of unusual circumstances.

Anthony's lawyers were busy negotiating contracts with the tough agent who represented the author of *Street Scene*. Anthony was busy supervising his real estate empire, making sure there would be enough liquid capital to launch a major production effort for what he fondly thought of as his and Erin's first Oscar winner. Con-Well Productions, having completed its current picture, was in a holding action; waiting for the new film. Garth Werner had fulfilled his contractual agreements with Continental Studios and had not signed up for anything else, awaiting production to start on *Street Scene*. And Erin, for the first time in her life, had no demanding schedules to meet, no challenges to face, nothing, in fact, that would force her to make a choice between her fierce, driving ambitions and deep emotional needs. But all this was about to change.

"But why can't you tell me over the phone?" Erin insisted.

"Because it's too important to discuss over the phone. I have to talk to you face to face."

"It's nothing bad, is it?" she asked, suddenly apprehensive.

"No, my love," he said in that husky growl that still sent shivers through her every time she heard it. "I would say it's something very good."

"Oh, Garth, suspense drives me crazy! I don't know how I'm going to wait!"

"Well, you won't have to wait very long. It shouldn't take you more than thirty minutes to get here from your place. You know how to get to Donkin's, don't you?"

"I think so," she said uncertainly. "Although it's been ages since I've been there."

"Just take the freeway to Marina Del Rey and turn off on Marquesas Way. You'll run right into it."

"All right, darling. I'll see you in a bit." She blew him a kiss and hung up, then ran to her bedroom to get dressed.

It actually took her just a little over twenty minutes to reach the attractive restaurant located on a choice piece of land overlooking the huge marina and Pacific Ocean beyond. Traffic had been relatively light on the busy San Diego freeway system and Erin, eager and impatient to hear Garth's news, had raced the powerful cream-colored Mercedes at a steady eighty miles per hour down the outside fast lane.

She pulled into the restaurant's parking lot with a muted

squeal of brakes and leaped out of the car before the parking attendant had a chance to open the door for her.

"Hey, take it easy. He'll wait for you." The attendant grinned. Then his eyes widened as he got a good look at her, and he stared in open admiration. "Hell, anybody would wait for you," he said fervently. "Probably forever."

"You're sweet." She gave him an absentminded smile and patted him on the cheek. "Now take good care of the car, okay?"

"I will. You can count on it! How long . . ."

Erin whipped by him without waiting to hear the rest of his question, and he gazed after her as she disappeared inside the restaurant.

There was no sign of Garth in the lobby or at the bar. Erin glanced around anxiously, and then she looked through the wide glass doors leading to the deck and saw the solitary figure standing at the far end.

Garth was leaning over the railing, watching the sailboats tacking back and forth in the channel on their way out to the ocean. It was one of those rare perfect Los Angeles days where a hot, bright sun illuminated a pure blue cloudless sky and the air sparkled like champagne, miraculously free of even a taint of smog. A fresh breeze stirred off the ocean, causing the sails of the sleek long boats to dip gracefully as they heeled over. Garth's head rotated slowly, following their fluid motion. Then he sensed Erin's presence and turned around to face her.

He looked so handsome, her breath caught in her throat. The sun had burned color into his face, making his eyes a startlingly vivid blue. His eyebrows slanted black above them, and one lock of crisp dark hair fell over his forehead. His sports coat, a casual but elegant dark blue cashmere, hung easily from his broad shoulders, revealing a glimpse of the blue-and-white striped shirt under it; and his custom-tailored white slacks showed the lines of his long, lean body to perfection.

He smiled with pleasure as he saw her and walked over quickly to meet her, his arms outstretched.

"You look beautiful," he said as he took hold of both her hands and leaned down to give her a light kiss.

"You're looking pretty great yourself," she replied a little breathlessly.

She linked her arm through his and started walking back toward the restaurant, then glanced up in surprise as he firmly guided her away from the door and led her over to one of the tables set up on the outdoor dining deck under a gaily striped umbrella.

"We're going to eat out here?" she exclaimed.

"Yes, why not?" he smiled. "It's such a beautiful day."

"Well." She wet her lips and looked around nervously at the crowd of people now filling the dining area, to see if there was anyone she recognized. "It's . . . it's not very intimate."

"No, but it's very bright and clean and open. Which is what I'm in the mood for today."

Erin was gripped by a sudden feeling of uneasiness. "Does this have something to do with what you want to talk to me about?"

"In a way." He pulled out a chair and seated her, then beckoned to a waiter. "What would you like to drink?"

"Just white wine, I think." She fumbled inside her purse for her cigarette case, found it, and dropped it as she pulled it out.

"Relax, honey," he told her as he picked it up, extracted a cigarette from it, and lit it for her. "Nobody's going to bite you."

"Oh, I've never objected to a bite from the right person," she said with a slightly shaky laugh. "As long as it's friendly, that is."

"I don't think that's ever been in question."

Erin blushed under his knowing look.

She took a quick drag on the cigarette and fidgeted with the ashtray as the waiter brought the wine and then waited for Garth's approval before filling their glasses. The minute he left, she ground out the cigarette with a quick, jerky motion and folded her arms on the table, staring at him.

"Okay, now tell me what this is all about."

"First, I got a call from Derek Marston's agent. Derek wants the lead role in *Street Scene*. In fact, he wants it so much, he's willing to negotiate on price. You know he usually won't even talk about doing a part unless he's been guaranteed a million dollars up front."

"My God!" Erin was so excited she almost leaped out of her chair. "Oh, Garth, that's incredible! That is absolutely, totally marvelous! The hottest young star in Hollywood, and he wants to do *our* picture!"

Her triumph faded when he said nothing. "Is there a problem?" she asked uncertainly. "I mean, I know he has a reputation for being difficult on a set. And there are rumors about his being heavily into drugs.

"You're not going to turn him down, are you?" she said in sudden horror. "Garth, please don't tell me that!"

"No, I'm not going to tell you that. It's true he's difficult, if not impossible, on a set. And he is into drugs. He's also an animal."

Garth leaned back and lit a cigarette, thoughtfully studying the smoke as it drifted lazily up toward the sky. "But he's a wildly talented animal," he said quietly. "He has more raw force and power than I've ever seen in an actor. And I know how to harness that force and power and turn it into what will be the greatest performance of his life. I think he knows I can do it, too. So I don't foresee any insurmountable problems in working with him."

He smiled at her then. "Besides, I said this was just the first thing I had to tell you."

"And what's the second?" she asked faintly.

"The author of *Street Scene*, Joel Greenberg, is my friend. His agent refused to let him do the screenplay because he's involved in a new book. And we've been bogged down for weeks trying to find a top Hollywood screenwriter who's free now."

Garth took a sip of his wine and grinned. "Well, we don't have to worry anymore. Joel wrote the screenplay on his own with nobody but the two of us even knowing he was doing it. He just finished it, and it's dynamite! It's the best script I've ever seen!"

"That's wonderful, Garth," she said slowly. "Both pieces of news are wonderful. But now let's get to the third act." She looked at him quizzically. "I assume there is a third act?"

"Of course. There's always a third act."

He propped his elbows on the table and tented his fingers, staring at her across them. "You realize that what I've just told you means we're ready to go into production. Which also means we'll be working like dogs every day from early morning until night, till the picture's finished. There'll be no more time for lunches like this. No more time for lazy afternoons on the beach. No more time for us to be together like we've been."

"W—what are you trying to say?" Erin's voice shook so badly she had to stop for a moment and fight for control. "Are you telling me that we're through?"

"Jesus Christ, no!" He leaned across the table and grabbed her hands. "How could you possibly think that? Don't you know how much I care about you?"

"But then what are you saying?"

"That I want you to leave Anthony. That I want you to come and live with me."

"Oh, Garth," she whispered. "I want that too. And I will, after *Street Scene* is completed."

"*After Street Scene?*" he shouted. "Erin, didn't you hear a thing I said? It's *now* that you have to do it. That's the whole point."

"I understand, darling," she said quickly. "Of course I understand. But there are some things *you* don't understand."

"Like what?"

"Like this very important picture we both want so much to do. We can't do it if I leave Anthony."

"You're right," he said flatly. "I don't understand. Maybe you'd be kind enough to explain?"

"Darling, please don't look at me that way," she begged. "Believe me, I know what I'm talking about. We *need* Anthony for this picture. It won't be as terrible as you predict. I know how busy you'll be, but we'll always find a way to get together."

"Really? A quickie in wardrobe between shoots?"

"I don't think that comment was necessary," she replied stiffly.

"Well, what about us?" he demanded. "Are *we* necessary? Or have I just imagined this whole thing?"

"You know better than that," she said quietly. "You know how I feel about you. I also know how important this picture is to you. So why are you trying to destroy it?"

"I guess because I really *don't* understand. Why would it be destroyed if you left Anthony?"

Erin gave an unhappy sigh. "The only thing that's made Con-Well Productions possible is Anthony's real estate money. Money I have no access to. Anthony's attorneys took care of that," she added bitterly.

She took a cigarette out of her case, and as Garth lit it she inhaled deeply, the smoke jetting out of her nostrils in twin streams. "I'm not saying that Con-Well Productions isn't a success. We've done very well. All of our pictures have shown a profit. But there simply isn't enough money in the company to launch a major production like *Street Scene*."

She looked at him gravely. "Now do you understand?"

"That's the big problem?" He started to laugh. "Honey, you've been worrying your head about nothing. We don't need Anthony's money. Any one of the major studios would jump at a chance to back this picture."

"I don't think so, Garth." She smiled wryly. "I'm not exactly the most popular producer in Hollywood."

"What the hell difference does that make? Studio heads don't invest money on the basis of popularity contests. They invest on the basis of getting winning properties, and who's got a more winning property than us? A bestselling novel. A screenplay by the author of that bestselling novel. And Derek Marston, the hottest star in Hollywood. To say nothing of a brilliant director," he added with a mischievous twinkle. "So how can we lose?"

"It's not that easy, Garth. My first picture was based on a bestselling novel with the author doing the screenplay and I had Anthony's money backing me as well. I thought I had it made, but the major studios almost killed me."

Her eyes clouded as she remembered that struggle. "This can be a very nasty town, darling, and the people here have long memories."

"Hey, lighten up, love. That's ancient history. Who cares now that Martin Weinguard's daughter lost her husband to you? You're exaggerating the whole thing."

"You can say that because you weren't here when it happened. But I was, and I know what it was like."

She took another deep drag on her cigarette and frowned. "Besides, let's not forget that Con-Well Productions is as much Anthony's as it is mine. He could make things very difficult. He could tie up the whole company in litigation, and no investor would touch us with a ten-foot pole."

"I don't think Anthony would do that," Garth said softly. "And I don't think you believe it either. He's a very decent person, and he knows Con-Well Productions is your creation. I think he'll sign the whole thing over to you."

"Probably," she admitted reluctantly.

"Well then why are you creating these barriers?" he demanded. "Anthony will give you control of the production company. We'll take the property to a major studio and get financial backing. Then we'll make our Oscar-winning picture."

He reached over to touch her. "And we'll be together," he said huskily. "All the way. You and me. We'll make it, babe. You can count on that. So what do you say?"

"I'm afraid to take the chance," she said miserably. "Oh, Garth, I want this picture so much! You have no idea how much I want it!"

"I'm beginning to get an idea," he answered grimly. "It's the picture that's really important to you, isn't it? Not me."

"No, that's not true!" she cried. "You're both important. The two most important things in my life. Why can't I have both? Why do I have to make a choice? It's all there for us if you'll just be a little patient."

"I'm not a patient man. But I warned you about that when we first met. Remember, I told you I didn't believe in compromises, negotiations, or haggling over deals."

"Are you saying our relationship is a deal?" she exclaimed.

"No. You are."

"I don't believe this conversation. I really don't believe it!"

"Believe it," he told her quietly. "Because I mean it."

"You're crazy! You're not making any sense at all."

Her hand trembled as she reached for another cigarette. "You'll change your mind when you have a chance to think it over."

"I won't change my mind." He leaned over to light her cigarette, then stood up.

"Goodbye, Erin."

She stared in shock as he threw two twenty-dollar bills on the table and walked away.

Fifteen

"HELLO? Hello?" Erin said feverishly.

"Hi there, Mrs. Wellington," a cheerful young voice announced. "This is Tina Andrews from *The Hollywood Reporter*, and we'd like your comment on the story that Derek Marston has just signed with Con-Well Productions for considerably less than his usual million-dollar deal, just so he can get the juicy role of Wyeth in *Street Scene*. Is it really true he agreed to cut his price in half?"

"How did you get my private number?" Erin demanded furiously.

"Oh well, that's a trade secret. We couldn't reach you at the office, so we go where we have to in order to get the news. Is it true?" she insisted.

"Of course it's not true," Erin said coldly. "And if you want to find out what he signed for, I suggest you ask his agent."

She banged down the phone and then leaned over the desk and started to cry. "Goddamn you, Garth," she wept. "Why do you have to be so stubborn? Why won't you call me?"

It had been a week since that luncheon at Donkin's restaurant, the most miserably unhappy week of her life. The ache of missing him was so intense she felt it as a physical pain, like a cancer clawing at her insides. She couldn't eat or sleep. She'd

187

lost five pounds. There were dark smudges under her eyes, and her face looked gaunt. An anxious Anthony had begged her to go to the doctor.

"There's nothing wrong with me," she'd snapped, and then burst into tears in front of his astonished eyes.

"Erin, my dearest Erin, what *is* it?" His face filled with alarm, he'd put his arms around her and patted her ineffectually. "Please tell me. Let me help you."

"You can't help," she'd sobbed. "You're the very last person in the world who could help."

Erin had been filled with sudden remorse as she saw the look of naked pain in his eyes at her unthinkingly cruel words.

"Forgive me, Anthony," she'd said contritely. "I didn't mean that."

Forcing a smile, she'd leaned over and given him a quick kiss. "Put it down to preproduction nerves. You know how much I want an Oscar for this picture, and we both know how tough that's going to be with the way this town feels about me."

His face had brightened perceptibly. "Well, don't you worry about that!" he'd assured her. "We're going to produce such an outstanding film, they won't have any choice but to vote you that Oscar."

Beaming fondly, he'd hugged her to him. "And we're going out this Friday night to that ridiculously overpriced Beverly Hills restaurant where all the so-called Hollywood powers congregate to show our faces and celebrate the production start of *Street Scene*. And I bet you'll start feeling better immediately!"

The antique grandfather clock in the foyer solemnly bonged five times. Erin raised her head from the exquisite Queen Anne desk in her study, wiped the tears from her face, and glared at the phone she had just recently answered with such hope.

"Well, fuck you, Garth!" she announced savagely. "I don't need you! I'm going to that restaurant tonight and everyone there is going to get the news that Erin Connolly Wellington is about to become a major power in this town!"

But her mood of defiance faded as she went upstairs to dress, and looked into the mirror at her strained, unhappy face.

"Have you missed me at all, Garth?" she whispered forlornly. "It's five o'clock now. Are you remembering how special that time was for us? We'd stand out on the deck of that little beach house of yours and look out over the ocean. It was always so beautiful at that hour. The sky all aglow as the sun hung in it like a big ball of fire. Then the wind would come up, we'd turn and see the faint shadow of the moon rising, and you'd turn and grab me. 'Give me tomorrow,' you'd always say. 'Give me another tomorrow with you.'"

Erin suddenly slammed down the hair brush that she had been listlessly pulling through her hair. "Goddamnn you, I know you haven't forgotten!" she said fiercely. "You're suffering just like I am. It's only that stupid male pride of yours that's keeping you from me."

"All right then, Mr. Macho." Erin began carefully applying her make-up. "Two can play at that game. And I can wait as long as you. You'll be coming to me before long."

"You look absolutely beautiful!" Anthony said reverently as he escorted her into the jam-packed restaurant.

"Thank you, sweetheart." Erin gave him a glowing smile for the benefit of the crowd as they were led to their table. "Now, who's here?" she hissed as they sat down and she pretended to study the menu.

"Well, let's see." Anthony glanced around the room and then broke into a big grin. "Erin, look!" he exclaimed delightedly. "Well, now we really will have a celebration!"

Erin looked, and felt her heart stop. Walking through the door was Garth, and by his side was an exquisitely beautiful young girl with an angelic, heart-shaped face, wide, cornflower-blue eyes, and a mass of silky blond hair. Her arm was tucked through his, and she was gazing up adoringly at him.

Anthony leaped to his feet as they approached the table. "Garth, what a pleasant surprise!" he cried happily. "Erin and I are here to toast the beginning of production on our picture this coming Monday. You must join us!"

Garth's eyes rested briefly on Erin, then moved away as he introduced the girl at his side. "Thank you, Anthony," he said pleasantly. "But I hope you'll excuse me if I ask for a raincheck. Melissa and I have some private things we need to talk over."

"I can certainly understand that," Anthony chuckled. "If I were with a gorgeous young lady like Melissa, I'd want to keep her to myself too, instead of spending the evening with an old married couple like us. But I do hope that sometime soon you'll give us the pleasure of getting to know her."

"That's a promise," Garth said with an easy smile. "Because if things work out the way I expect them to, Melissa and I will be seeing a lot of each other."

He nodded politely then before walking away, and Erin felt a sharp pain as her fingernails dug into the palms of her tightly clenched hands.

"They certainly make a lovely couple, don't they?" Anthony said admiringly as he sat down and gazed after them.

It took every ounce of will power Erin possessed to keep from screaming. "Yes, I suppose they do," she said through gritted teeth. "Although I must say I never envisioned our director as a cradle-robber. The girl can't be more than nineteen."

"Oh my, do I detect a little feminine cattiness here?" he asked with an amused twinkle in his eye. "After all, you're not much over nineteen yourself. And that makes me a considerably more serious cradle-robber."

"I'll be twenty-six this September," she answered grimly. "And that's a lot over nineteen."

"You'll also be the most beautiful twenty-six-year-old woman in the world, or for that matter the most beautiful woman of any age, twenty-three, twenty-one, or even nineteen."

"Do you really mean that?" she asked with a desperate eagerness. "Do you really think I'm still beautiful?"

"Of course I do!" He leaned over and took hold of her hand. "My dear Erin, how could you doubt it? Don't you ever look in the mirror? You're not just beautiful, you're the most exciting woman I've ever met!"

"Thank you, Anthony."

"Well, you hardly have to thank me for it," he smiled. "It's something mother nature blessed you with."

He picked up his menu and then peered at her over it. "I must say it pleased me to see Garth and the young lady here tonight. Not that I ever believed the rumors, but still it was nice to see them together."

Erin's head snapped up. "Rumors? What rumors?" she asked sharply.

"Oh well." He shrugged apologetically. "You know how this town is. When they don't have any real news, they start making it up. Things about you and Garth having . . ."

He coughed suddenly and looked down at the menu. "Something between you. That sort of thing."

"You must be joking! I would sooner become a nun than become involved with that impossibly arrogant and obviously emotionally retarded excuse for a man!"

"Good Lord, Erin," he exclaimed in obvious alarm. "I didn't know you felt that strongly. I mean, I know the two of you didn't hit it off too well at first, but I somehow assumed you'd patched up your differences. You're not thinking of bringing in another director on the picture at this stage, are you?"

"No, I'm not thinking of doing that." She gave him a wintry smile. "After all, how could I? He owns twenty-five percent of the picture."

"Well that's true, isn't it?" He fingered the menu nervously. "But if you really don't want him to direct it, aren't we going to run into major problems?"

"No," she replied curtly. "As long as he does his job and we do ours, there will be no problems. Now let's order, Anthony, and then get the hell out of this place!"

Anthony hastily summoned the waiter, who urged them to try the house specialty, veal scallopine with prosciutto ham in a white wine sauce.

"Will it take long?" Anthony asked anxiously.

"Oh no, sir. It's ready right now."

"Order it!" Erin commanded him in a savage whisper.

Anthony gave a nervous little cough. "Well then, I guess we'll both try it."

"You'll enjoy it very much," the waiter promised.

Erin doubted that seriously as she gazed bleakly after the waiter, who was now busily making his way through the crowded room toward the kitchen. She followed his progress, then found her eyes drawn like a magnet toward the small table at the far end of the room where Garth and Melissa were talking animatedly, their heads close together. A sick helpless rage filled her at the sight. I'll make him pay for this, she vowed silently. Somehow I'll make him pay.

Anthony tried valiantly to carry on a conversation as the waiter returned with the steaming hot plates of veal scallopine and placed them on the table, then discreetly withdrew; but he soon trailed off disconsolately when Erin continued to reply in curt monosyllables.

They finished the meal in silence, a silence which continued as Anthony paid the check, led his wife out of the restaurant, and drove home.

"I understand there's an excellent drama on PBS television tonight," he offered tentatively as they walked inside. "One of those splendid BBC productions. Would you like to watch?"

Erin stared unseeingly at her husband, her eyes still filled with the vision of Garth and Melissa. She suddenly focused on him.

"No, Anthony." Her hand reached out to caress him. "No, I don't think we'll *watch* a splendid production. I think we'll *stage* one. I want you to make love to me, Anthony."

"Oh, Erin!" he said worshipfully as she moved close to him.

"Well then, what are you waiting for?" she laughed. "Come on, race me to the bedroom."

Anthony charged up the stairs after her. When he arrived, breathless, at the door of their bedroom, she was already naked and waiting for him.

"My dearest love," he moaned as he flung himself on her. "My dearest, sweetest love."

"Is that good? Do you like that?" she whispered as her hands and mouth roved over him.

"Oh God, yes. Yes, yes, yes!"

It was over in less than a minute. Anthony sat up, his hands trembling as he tried to stroke her hair. "I'm so sorry," he whispered. "It's just that it's been so long. I tried to wait, but I couldn't."

He leaned over to kiss her, then flinched as she pushed him away. "A little time," he begged. "Give me a little time and I'll make it right for you."

"It's not your fault, Anthony," she said dully as she got out of the bed. "Go to sleep."

Erin barely made it to the bathroom in time. When the last retching spasm had passed, she stood up unsteadily and washed out her mouth.

Anthony was lying quietly in the bed when she returned. He'd gone to sleep just like she'd told him to do and he slept, as he always did, stretched out on his back with his arms folded peacefully across his chest and his feet crossed neatly at the ankles. It occurred to her, with sudden revulsion, that he looked like a corpse laid out in an undertaker's parlor, and she knew she couldn't possibly get back into that bed with him.

Turning around and running soundlessly across the thick carpet to her closet, she grabbed a pair of chocolate-colored suede slacks and a bulky white turtleneck sweater and pulled them on, then fled from the bedroom, down the stairs, and out of the house to her car.

Erin had no conscious plan of what she was going to do or where she was going to go. All she knew was that she had to get away. After an hour of mindless driving, pushing the accelerator of the powerful car harder and harder toward the floorboard, feeling the scream of the wind as she tore down the freeway at seventy, eighty, ninety miles an hour, she was aghast to discover herself in front of Garth's small beach house.

Oh no. I must be losing my mind. What in the name of God possessed me to come here?

She looked up and saw lights in the window. "He's still awake," she murmured to herself. Then her hands tightened on the steering wheel. "Of course he's still awake. He's in there with that bitch Melissa, and they're doing all the things we used to do. Except we never did them at night," she sobbed. "We never had a night together."

She started to shake and fumbled desperately in her purse for a cigarette, dragging the smoke so deeply into her lungs after she lit it that she felt a sudden sharp pain in her chest.

"Get out of here, Erin," she told herself fiercely. "Get out while you still have a shred of pride left."

But her hands refused to release their tight grip on the steering wheel and put the car into gear; and she knew that subconsciously she'd planned all along to drive up here and confront him.

But with what? she asked herself in anguish. It was all my doing. Am I going to go up to that door and make a complete fool out of myself?

"Well, apparently that's exactly what I'm going to do," she admitted out loud. She turned off the engine, got out of the car, walked slowly up the steps to his place, and knocked on the door.

"Who the hell is it?" Garth yelled.

Erin swallowed hard and knocked again.

"Listen, if you've got a flat tire, why don't you try hiking down the road half a mile to that gas station instead of bothering people in their homes." He flung open the door.

"My problem isn't a flat tire," Erin said unsteadily.

"Jesus Christ!" Garth stared at her. "Jesus Christ, Erin, what are you doing here?"

"I'm not sure," she said miserably. "I think maybe . . ."

She never had a chance to finish her statement. He opened his arms and reached out for her. Not that he had to reach very far. She rushed toward him, trying to fit her body into every turn and curve of his, feeling him, touching him, stroking him.

Erin had no clear memory of what happened next. One minute she was standing in the doorway. The next minute she was in the living room in front of the fireplace trying to undress him when she felt him surge inside her.

They were so hungry for each other, they came in jolting spasms, like a wild horse bucking his first ride.

"That was hello, Erin," Garth said huskily. "That was just hello. Now come here and let me get to know you again."

Vaguely, Erin heard the same chord playing over and over again on the stereo. "Garth. Garth, the record's stuck."

"Let it stick," he growled. He stared deep into her eyes.

"Just like this, babe. Just like this." He was holding her now so that she lay on her side, one leg resting high on his as he slowly moved in and out of her.

"Stick it a little more, sweet bitch?" His hands caressed her firm, round buttocks, manipulating them ever so gently. Close, closer, letting him slide into her, then drawing away until the tip of his cock nuzzled at the edge of her open thighs, almost leaving her.

"Look, Erin!" he commanded. "Look at us."

She looked, and gasped. She could see him, actually see him as he filled her.

He leaned over and kissed her, his tongue deep in her mouth as he began moving faster and faster in and out. The room was filled with brightly colored lights that kept changing into different patterns.

"It's a kaleidoscope, Erin," Garth whispered in her ear.

He knows what I'm feeling, she thought in wonderment. He knows exactly what I'm feeling. And then the patterns went round and round and round.

"I think we passed out for a minute," Garth said in a hushed voice. "I think we goddamn passed out from that incredible fucking we do to each other."

They were both lying on their backs, and Erin felt like she was floating a foot above the floor. She reached out to find him. He was right there, and she took hold of his hand.

"You know now, don't you?" he said quietly. "You know you can't ever leave me."

"Yes, I know," she replied with a soft, contented sigh. Then her eyes suddenly narrowed and she struggled to sit up. "But what about that bitch? What about her?" she demanded furiously.

He stared at her. "What bitch? What are you talking about?"

"Little Miss Puberty," she hissed. "Melissa what's her name who, you so happily informed us tonight, would be spending a lot of time with you."

Garth threw back his head and burst into laughter. "Oh, *that* bitch. Well, honey, actually she's not a bitch at all. She's a very sweet girl."

"I don't care if she's Joan of Arc reincarnated." Erin

pounded on his chest with her fists. "You're not spending a lot of time with her. In fact, you're not spending *any* time with her. She's out of your life permanently as of this moment. Do you hear me?"

"How could I help hearing you?" he grinned. "They can probably hear you all the way to San Diego."

"It's not funny!" she stormed. "I don't know what your relationship with her was, and I don't want to know. I just want you to tell me it's over. What was your relationship?"

"That's what brought you up here tonight, isn't it? You saw us together, and you couldn't stand it. You had to find out what was going on."

"What would you have done if you'd found us here together?" he asked. "Pulled out a gun and shot us?" He picked up her purse and started rummaging through it. "Let's see, is the murder weapon in here somewhere?"

"Don't, Garth," she said tensely. "Don't tease me like this, please. I really can't take it."

"I have a feeling you can take anything," he said slowly as he gazed at her.

"That's not true." Erin's eyes filled with tears. Then she suddenly sat up straight and wiped them away.

"I need you, Garth," she said bravely. "I think I need you more than you need me. It's a difficult thing for me to admit, but I guess it has to be said. And if it's too late, well then I have to accept the blame for that." There was a certain quiet dignity about her as she looked squarely and unflinchingly into his eyes.

"Oh, babe, do you have any idea how long I've been waiting to hear you say that?" Garth reached out and gathered her into his arms. "I love you, Erin. I love you with all my heart. There's never been anybody else since the second I met you."

"But what about . . ."

"Hush," he said softly, rocking her in his arms. "Hush, love. Melissa is an actress. A young, talented actress a friend of mine saw playing in a little theater on Santa Monica Boulevard. I want her for the part of Janine in *Street Scene.* That's all our relationship amounts to."

"That's really all?" she said incredulously.

"That's really all," he smiled. "Now why don't we go to bed?"

"Bed," she repeated uncertainly. "But it's so late. I should be going . . ."

"No," he said firmly. "You're not going anywhere except into my bedroom. To sleep with me. To be with me. Always."

He gripped her by the arms and stared at her. "You do understand that, don't you?"

"Yes, master," she laughed.

"Good. Come on, then."

The bedroom drapes in Garth's rented beach house were made of a cheap, flimsy fabric that offered no protection against the strong morning sun as it rose up over the horizon and bounced rays off the glittering blue ocean below.

Erin sat up with a start as the demanding light streamed through the windows and illuminated the small room.

"Garth. Garth, wake up." She poked him in the ribs. "It's morning, and I've got to leave."

"Nuh," he mumbled indistinctly, burrowing deeper into the covers. " 's night. Go back to sleep."

"It's not night," she insisted, poking him harder. "Look!"

"Jesus, babe," he grumbled as he turned around and squinted at her. "It can't be more than five o'clock. You call that morning?"

"It's not five. It's almost six-thirty."

"I don't believe this," he moaned. "I fell in love with an early morning freak."

He dug his knuckles into his eyes, shaking his head at the same time. "Honey, I'm crazy about you, but this is too much. If you're one of those up-at-dawn beach joggers, you're just going to have to go out and do it by yourself."

"What I have to do has nothing to do with jogging, Garth," she said softly. "I have to go home and talk to Anthony."

"Oh Christ!" He bolted upright and stared at her in dismay. "Erin, you must think I'm the most insensitive clod of all time. I don't know what to say except I just forgot all about Anthony for the moment."

He reached out and put his arms around her. "Honey, you

want me to go with you? It'll only take me a couple of seconds to get dressed."

Erin gazed at him affectionately. "You're a darling to offer, and I appreciate it. But this is something I really have to do alone."

"You'll call me?" he said anxiously. "You'll call me right away after you've told him?"

"Of course." She leaned forward and kissed him, then slipped out of the bed and pulled on her slacks and sweater.

"Remember, I love you," he told her earnestly.

"I'll remember." She smiled and started to walk out of the room, then stopped by the doorway and turned around. "And I love you too," she said softly. Then she was gone.

It was a few minutes past seven-thirty when Erin pulled into the driveway of the handsome Beverly Hills mansion, parked the cream-colored Mercedes in the garage next to Anthony's long, black, gleaming Lincoln Continental, and walked through the breezeway into the spacious French country-style designer kitchen.

Anthony was waiting for her. He was perched on a stool at the breakfast bar, his eyes fixed on the door.

"Where have you been?" he asked tonelessly.

"Well." She swallowed nervously. "As a matter of fact, that's exactly what I want to talk to you about."

"I'm listening," he said in the same monotone.

"Is there . . ." She looked around distractedly. "Is there any hot coffee?"

"No."

"Oh." She forced a smile. "Then maybe you'd like me to make some?"

"I don't want you to do anything except tell me where you've been."

"This isn't easy for me to say, Anthony." Erin set her purse down on the counter and stared at it.

For a long moment there was no sound in the room except for the faint ticking of the kitchen clock that was mounted on the brick wall over the open-hearth fireplace.

"I guess the only way is to come right out with it," she finally announced shakily.

Erin looked up at him. "I've been with Garth, Anthony. And I want to be with him. All the time."

"Are you telling me you went to him last night after making love to me?" Angry red splotches stained Anthony's normally pale cheeks.

Erin stared at him in alarm and briefly considered lying to him, telling him she'd just left the house that morning. But as he glared at her, she realized it would be futile. He *knew* what time she'd left the house. Oh shit, she moaned silently. This is going to be much worse than I imagined.

"I'm waiting for your answer," he told her coldly. "Is that what you did?"

"I love him, Anthony," she whispered. "I didn't want to. I never expected anything like this to happen. I swear to you, I never expected it. But I can't help it. I can't help how I feel. Can you understand at all?" she pleaded.

"Just what is it that you're saying?"

"I want to live with him."

"You mean you want to leave me."

"Well." She looked at him helplessly. "I would have to leave you under those circumstances, wouldn't I?"

"Yes," he said dryly. "You certainly would. And since you've figured out everything else, have you figured out how you're going to do that?"

"That's what I wanted to talk to you about."

"Of course. It must have been very much on your mind." He offered her a glacial smile. "Then let me resolve your unanswered questions. You may walk out of this house at this very moment. You are free to go to your lover. You may even take your clothes, your jewelry, and the car I bought for you."

He rocked back on the stool, crossed his long, storklike legs, and hooked his fingers around one knee. "But's that's all you'll take," he said evenly. "If you want any more, you'll have to go to court and fight me for it."

"But, Anthony, what about Con-Well Productions?" she cried in horror. "You *know* that's my company!"

"Ah, yes. Con-Well Productions. I wondered when that subject would come up."

He rocked back and forth on the stool, seemingly oblivious of the fact that it was in immediate danger of toppling over, a faraway look in his eyes.

"Most women would be concerned about getting the house," he mused. "Or alimony."

He grabbed hold of the counter seconds before the stool lost its precarious hold on gravity and crashed to the floor. "Not you, though," he said thoughtfully as he gazed at her. "No, the only thing you're concerned about is Con-Well Productions. I'm finally realizing that's the only thing you've ever been concerned with, from the very beginning."

"Anthony, it's hard for me to believe this is you talking," Erin said shakily. "You've always been the kindest and gentlest of men. I really thought you'd understand. I never imagined you'd turn out to be so hard and cruel."

"There are apparently a number of things you've never imagined." He stood up and leaned over the counter, his long, bony fingers closing on her wrist like surgical pincers. "For example, that I have feelings."

His fingers tightened, and the flesh around her wrist turned white. "If you'd been honest with me from the start, if you'd told me about this when it began, I would have understood. I might even have been able to forgive you.

"But you lied to me!" The red splotches on his cheeks spread, and his breathing became labored. "You sat in that restaurant last night and said there was nothing between you and Garth. Then . . ."

His chest heaved, and he had to stop for a moment to get his breath. "Then," he said between clenched teeth, "you deliberately seduced me when we came home. You used me and you made a mockery out of my feelings for you. And after you'd used me and discarded me, you walked out of my house and drove to your lover's house. Where you made love to him.

"You did make love to him, didn't you?" he shouted.

"Yes," she whispered.

"One truth." He let go of her wrist and sat back down on the stool. "Finally one truth out of you," he said heavily.

"Anthony, what are you going to do?"

"I'm not going to help you pack, if that's what you mean."

"You know that's not what I mean."

"Of course I know that." He looked at her, his eyes now cold and forbidding. "We're back to Con-Well Productions again, aren't we? Well, I'll tell you what I'm not going to do. I'm not going to give it to you. However . . ." He paused.

"What?" she said desperately. "What, Anthony?"

"However, I am willing to sell it to you. For six million dollars."

"Six million dollars! What kind of a sick joke is that?"

"I assure you, my dear, it is not a joke. Even I don't joke about six million dollars. That's my offer. Take it or leave it."

"But where would I get six million dollars?"

"Oh that won't be a problem." He regarded her with a thoughtful little smile. "I may no longer be the kindest and gentlest of men, as you so perceptively observed a few minutes ago, but I'm still a very generous man."

He plucked a small note pad from the shelf over the counter and began jotting down figures on it. "According to my accountants, the current net worth of Con-Well Productions is six million dollars. The studio complex I built for you in the San Fernando Valley represents three million of that. One million for the land, two million for the buildings and equipment. The other three million dollars is in cash receivables, profits realized from our pictures."

Anthony looked up at her. "I'll take the three million in cash receivables as a down payment, and you'll sign a note for the remaining three million, using the studio property as collateral. The interest on the note will be at ten percent a year, payments to be made quarterly. At the end of three years, the entire note will become due and payable.

"That seems a reasonable amount of time to me," he said reflectively. "Because if you haven't made enough money in the next three years to pay off a three-million-dollar loan, then you really don't belong in the movie industry, do you?"

"It's too bad you waited so long to become a bastard," Erin observed quietly. "Because if you'd started earlier, you might have become a genuinely interesting man."

"Unfortunately, my timing has never been very good." He stood up and peered at her. "Well, what's your answer?"

"I don't have much choice, do I?"

"Not if you want the screen rights to *Street Scene*."

"All right, Anthony, you've got your deal."

"Good. I'll have my attorneys draw up the papers."

He started to walk away, then turned around and stared hard at her. "There's one more thing. When the divorce is final, I want you to take back your own name. Wellington no longer belongs to you."

Sixteen

"WOULD you please quiet down?" Bobby Franken begged. "Just come up one at a time, give me your name and assignment, and we'll get back to you as soon as possible."

The young unit manager was standing at the entrance to Con-Well studios' Sound Stage 3, gripping his clipboard desperately to his chest as the angry crowd of film technicians and extras swarmed around him.

"They said shooting was starting today!" A burly extra in faded blue jeans and a tight white T-shirt strode up to Bobby and shook his fist threateningly in front of his face. "I turned down a chance to work in a television series, got up at four o'clock this morning, and drove fifty miles to get here. And now you're telling me you don't know *when* they're going to start shooting? What the fuck is going on, anyway?"

"Listen, just take it easy, will you?" Bobby wiped his arm across his forehead and it came away damp with perspiration. "There's a temporary problem with the script," he lied, improvising wildly. "The director isn't satisfied with the way the riot scene reads, and he wants it rewritten. They're working on it now."

"Bullshit!" a furious voice shouted. "You don't need a script for a riot scene. All you need are actors, a camera crew, and a director who knows what the hell he's doing. So maybe," the voice sneered, "what you're telling us is that we're stuck with a director who doesn't know his ass from a key light and is afraid to start shooting!"

"What's your name?" an authoritative voice barked out.

The crowd, which had started to catcall, abruptly fell silent as Garth came through the door of the sound stage and glared down at them.

"I'm waiting," he said softly into the sudden quiet. "I'm waiting to meet that unrecognized genius who knows all about directing. Would that gentleman like to step up here and be recognized?"

There was the muted sound of shuffling feet and a few nervous coughs.

"No? He prefers to remain unrecognized?" Garth smiled coldly. "Well, I think that's a wise decision.

"Because he doesn't know what the shit he's talking about!" Garth's voice cracked out like a whip over the crowd. "The only one who knows is me! *I'm* your director. *I* will tell you what to do. And *I* will tell you when and where you'll do it. Now if that's too tough for you to take, then go back to your unions and ask for another assignment where things will be safe and easy. Where you won't have to put out all the way. Because I don't want you on my set. I only want winners."

He turned to Bobby. "Take their names. Anyone who still has complaints, pay them off immediately. And tell the unions to make a note of those names. We don't want them sent out to us ever again." Then he stalked away.

Garth's bluff worked. The men, now grinning sheepishly, formed an orderly line and gave their names to Bobby, who checked them off against the list on his clipboard, then they got into their cars and trucks and drove away.

But Garth's proud, arrogant pose disappeared as soon as he stalked out of their sight and walked into the sound stage. Shoulders slumping and a worried frown on his face, he made his way down the corridor to Erin's office.

She was sitting behind the large mahogany desk, a tight unhappy smile on her face as she talked into the phone.

"No, Sol, I'm afraid I don't understand. What high risk?

There's no more bankable star in Hollywood than Derek Marston. And there's no hotter property than *Street Scene*. May I also remind you that Con-Well Productions has never lost money on a picture? Which is more than any other studio in this town can claim," she added bitingly.

She paused for a moment to light a cigarette and smile up at Garth, then bent down once more to the phone. "I'm sorry, Sol, I didn't catch that. You said what? Oh," she said heavily. "Of course I can see how it would make a difference. Yes, Sol, it was nice talking to you, too. Goodbye."

"Not going too well, I take it." Garth sighed.

"That, my love, is the understatement of the century," she said grimly. "Would you like to try for total failure?"

"But how can they turn it down?" He smashed his fist on the desk in frustrated fury. "They've got to know this is a potential Oscar winner, which is every investor's dream. They're not denying that, are they?"

"No, they're not denying that." Erin took a drag on her cigarette and stared moodily at the swirling smoke. "They're denying me."

"That's crazy!" he said furiously. "How do they do that?"

"Very politely." She gave him a wintry smile. "By an extremely odd coincidence, every important motion picture investor has just recently committed his money to a picture being produced by someone else. Which obviously ties up all his available funds, don't you see?"

"What about the major studios?"

"They don't even bother to be polite," she said distantly. "I have yet to get past a secretary to a production chief."

"Well hell, it's only Monday, isn't it?" He forced a cheerful smile and leaned over to kiss her. "Come on, babe, we haven't even begun to fight. We'll beat them yet."

"How?" she asked dismally. "Anthony really stripped this place. I don't think we even have enough money to pay the electric bills."

"We'll find a way," he said fiercely. "We have each other, and we have a great picture. We'll make it together."

"Will we?" She looked up at him miserably. "Will we really?"

"Yes, we will." Garth took a deep breath, then stared intently into her eyes. "But you're going to have to go to New York."

"What?" she said confusedly.

"New York," he repeated. "There's more money on one single street in Manhattan than there is in this whole fuckin' cow town. You go to New York, babe," he told her softly, "and you'll get our money for us."

Erin flew to New York the next day and spent two exhausting weeks talking to bankers, investors, promoters, anyone and everyone who had money. But it was all in vain. No one had any faith in the stability of Con-Well Productions now that Anthony Wellington and his money had withdrawn, and no one wanted to risk money on a picture that every major studio in Hollywood had refused to back. The ultimate humiliation for Erin was facing their thinly veiled, although always politely expressed, contempt for her. Because the contempt was based solely on the fact that she was a woman, and their comments made it clear they thought she was not only out of her depth but out of her place in trying to negotiate what was obviously a man's business.

An oil-rich Texas entrepreneur brought the matter home to her in a particularly painful fashion after a dinner at New York's famous Four Seasons restaurant where she had first argued, then explained, and finally almost begged him to back the picture before giving up and reaching for her purse as the check arrived.

"Now just stop right there, little lady." He'd smiled, whisking the check away from her. "The day that Jeb Stanton can't buy a pretty girl a dinner is the day that Jeb Stanton is in deep trouble."

"Mr. Stanton, you are not buying a pretty girl a dinner," she'd said through clenched teeth. "You are having a business discussion at a dinner where you are the invited guest. *I* will take care of the check."

"Honey, you're real cute when you get mad," he'd chuckled. "Always did like a spirited woman." He'd winked at the waiter then, who'd smiled back, taken Jeb's money as he totally ignored Erin's efforts to pay him, and walked away. "But can I give you a little advice? Don't push your luck, honey," he'd said earnestly, leaning toward her. Find a good strong man to handle these things for you. You'll be a lot happier and a lot more successful that way. Believe me, old Jeb knows."

Erin had barely restrained herself from picking up her wine glass and throwing it right into the smug, fatuous face. She'd taken a cab back to her hotel after icily refusing Jeb's offer of his chauffeur-driven limousine, thrown herself on the bed where she'd pounded the pillows in rage before picking up the phone to book a seat on the first morning flight back to Los Angeles.

Glittering rays from the sun burned through the airplane's window as TWA's Flight 502 passed through its fourth time zone on its journey from New York to Los Angeles. Erin turned away from the painfully bright light, pulling down the shade as she took off her watch and set the hands back three hours.

"We are now approaching Los Angeles International Airport," the impersonal, antiseptic voice of a stewardess announced. "Please extinguish all cigarettes and make sure your seat belts are fastened. It has been a pleasure to serve you, and we hope to see you again soon on TWA."

There were two sharp bumps as the plane landed and then taxied up to the terminal. Erin stood up and collected her belongings, and then was almost knocked off her feet by the impatient crowd surging toward the door as she stepped out into the aisle. When she finally reached the exit and walked down the ramp leading to the airport lobby, she saw Garth waiting for her and ran toward him.

"Hey!" He grinned as she rushed into his arms and hugged him fiercely. "If this is what happens when you're away from me for a couple of weeks, maybe I should send you on more trips."

"Oh, Garth, I missed you so much. I'm so glad to be home. I *hate* New York!"

"It was that bad, huh?"

"Worse," she said tersely. "It was so awful I don't even know how to describe it. The filth. The noise. And those people you call New Yorkers are even worse than their rotten, filthy city! I can't imagine how you could have lived there all those years."

"Okay, okay now," he said soothingly. "Take it easy, honey. You're back where you belong."

"That's for damn sure! And I'm never going back to *that* place. Ever!"

"I'm sorry, Erin," he said as he picked up her overnight case and led her out of the airport. "I'm really sorry. I truly thought it would work out."

"I know you did," she said contritely, squeezing his arm. "And probably what's really bothering me is that I failed to make it work, because I didn't know how to handle stupid bastards like Jeb Stanton."

"Who?"

"Never mind. That's a story for later. Right now all I want to do is go home and sleep for two days. I am so tired I can't believe it."

She offered him an apologetic smile. "After that, I'll start getting things together again, I promise."

"Do you think you could settle for five hours instead of two days?"

"Five hours? What do you mean, five hours?"

"Well." He hesitated for a moment. "The thing is that in a little over six hours we're due at a party Derek Marston's throwing."

"Oh no, Garth!" she moaned. "Not a party tonight. Especially not the kind of party Derek Marston throws. I just couldn't face it."

"I'm afraid you're going to have to."

An expression of alarm crossed her face. "He's not giving us any problems about the picture, is he?"

"Not nearly as many problems as Barney Lipsky, his agent is," Garth said grimly. "Lipsky's threatening to pull Derek out of his *Street Scene* commitment on the grounds that Con-Well Productions has failed to live up to its part of the contract by canceling the originally scheduled production start without sufficient prior notice, and being further delinquent in not providing a new production start date."

"Jesus Christ!"

"I don't think we can count on him to help us."

"And going to this party will?"

"I hope so, babe. I sure hope so."

"How?" she demanded wildly. "What do I tell him after this fiasco in New York?"

"First of all, he doesn't know that New York was a fiasco. Second, I don't think it would be all that important to him."

"Not important?" she said incredulously. "Garth, what are you talking about? We don't have any money. And without money we can't start production. You're telling me that won't be important to him?"

"Look, honey, you don't know this kid. You've never met him, so you don't understand where he's coming from. He's a New York street kid. He grew up being hassled by his parents, his teachers and the cops. Now he's being hassled by his manager, his agent, and his accountants, and he resents the hell out of it. He'd like nothing better than to stick it to all of them. He's got sympathy for the hassle we're going through. Besides, he really wants to do this picture."

"But he's not a total idiot, is he?" She stared at him. "I mean, it's nice to know he'd like to stick it to the establishment, but he's not about to throw away his career to do it. Is he?" she insisted.

"No," Garth admitted. "No, he isn't about to do that."

"Then what in God's name do you expect *me* to do at this party tonight?" she asked despairingly.

"Buy time for us. Just buy time for us, Erin, and pray."

Derek Marston's house, set on a gently sloping bluff overlooking the ocean, was located in the Trancas area of Malibu, several miles north of Zuma Beach. As Garth and Erin approached it, they could see red-jacketed valet-parking attendants running frantically up and down Pacific Coast Highway, dodging traffic as they crossed the busy lanes.

Both sides of the highway were lined with parked cars stretching out for almost a mile in either direction, and the variety of the vehicles attested to Derek's eclectic taste in friends. Rolls Royces nudged bumpers with dusty Chevy pick-up trucks. Volkswagens crouched nervously in front of massive Harley Davidson motorcycles. Cadillacs sniffed at the tails of campers.

Erin gazed at the endless line of vehicles in stunned disbelief. "My God, do you think there's anyone he *didn't* invite?"

"Just his Malibu neighbors, who are undoubtedly busy once again filing complaints with the sheriff's department."

They pulled up to the gate and handed their car over to one of the attendants, then walked onto the spacious grounds. The house was set back a good five hundred feet from the entrance gate, surrounded by flower beds and a velvet green lawn. Off to the right was a regulation tennis court where a heated doubles match was in progress, cheered on by a crowd of spectators. To the left of the house was an Olympic-size pool and Jacuzzi encircled by a huge free-form deck. A volley ball net stretched across the shallow end of the pool, and a noisy crowd leaped up and down in the water, screaming and laughing as they batted at the ball. At the far end of the deck a rock group blasted away while a frenzied crowd of dancers performed in front of them. Occasionally an unwary dancer would get too close to the edge of the pool, whereupon a hand would reach up out of the water, grab the hapless dancer by the ankle, and flip him into the pool.

People of every size, shape, age, color, sex, and costume clustered around the chaises set up on the deck and the lawn, their voices loud and shrill as they drank and talked. Three nude couples paddled dreamily in the Jacuzzi, the glazed expressions on their faces making it clear they were stoned out of their minds.

"Apparently they're holding the party out here," Erin observed. "Do you see our host?"

Garth shook his head. "No, all you're seeing is the fringe element. The real party, as always, will be going on inside."

"If this is just the fringe element, I don't think I want to meet the real party," she said faintly.

"Don't worry. I'll look out for you."

Derek answered the door in response to Garth's knock. He was dressed in white shorts and a white silk shirt that was open to his navel. A gold chain hung from his neck, gleaming dully against the golden tan of his powerful chest. The short sleeves of his shirt were tight around his swelling biceps. His strong muscular legs were covered with golden sun-bleached hairs, but they were darker than the thick shock of white-blond hair that fell in careless disarray over his forehead. His eyes, the same tawny gold as a lion's, blazed out of his sensually handsome face. Those golden cat eyes now opened wide in admiration as he saw Erin.

"Well ol' buddy, so this is what you've been hiding away at that little pad of yours. Can't say I blame you. If I had her, I'd hide her away too."

He reached out to Erin, the tips of his fingers lightly caressing her cheek. "You ever get tired of this old grouch, you let me know. Because I'd be mighty happy to take care of you."

"Down, boy." Garth was smiling as he spoke, but there was a definite edge of warning in his voice.

"Hey, man, take it easy." Derek threw up his hands in mock fright. "Would I invade a friend's turf?"

"Of course you would."

"Of course I would," Derek agreed with an amused grin. "But not without the lady's permission." He looked speculatively at Erin. "I guess I don't have that, huh?"

"I'm afraid not. But it was nice being asked." The warm smile she gave him took any sting out of the rejection.

"Well, maybe I'll ask you again sometime. People have been known to change their minds."

He started to laugh as Garth made a low growling sound. "But not tonight. Tonight is just for friends. So stop hanging around the door. Come on in and enjoy yourself."

"He really is a magnificent animal," Erin murmured as they followed their host inside.

"Just don't forget the animal part."

"Darling, you're not upset about what he said, are you?" She looked at him in genuine surprise.

"You mean, am I jealous?" He smiled. "No, honey, I'm not jealous. I don't have any reason to be, do I?"

"No. No, you certainly don't."

"I didn't think so." He kissed her absently, then frowned. "It's just that I have to warn you about something. I should have guessed that Derek would come on to you like that. The problem is that I'm not kidding when I say he's an animal. He sees something he wants, and if he gets any encouragement at all he'll go after it and forget everything else. So don't tease him. He doesn't understand that. Forget the flirting you might carry on with a normal human being and concentrate instead on appealing to the rational part of his brain that wants to do this picture."

"You're serious, aren't you?" she said in amazement.

"Very serious."

"Okay. Message received and understood." They walked into the living room behind Derek.

"Hey, listen up!" Derek yelled to the crowd sprawled around the large sunken living room. "These are my friends Garth and Erin, so treat 'em nice. You hear?"

"Yeah, man, we hear." The crowd clapped enthusiastically, then two exceptionally pretty young girls and a short black man with a beard sprung up and raced over. The two girls embraced Garth, and the black man took Erin's hand and bowed low over it.

"What's your pleasure, ma'am? You name it, we got it. Just tell this humble servant, and he will bring it to you."

"Well." Embarrassed and confused, Erin tried to pull her hand away. "I . . . I don't know."

"You gotta know," he said urgently. "You gotta tell me, so I can bring it to you." His eyes, preternaturally bright, burned into hers.

"Scotch. Scotch and water would be fine."

"Brand?"

"I beg your pardon?"

"The brand. What *brand* of Scotch?"

"Oh, the brand." She cast a desperate look at Garth, who was trying to fend off the amorous advances of the two girls. "Well, how about the house brand?"

"Very good, lady. *Very* good." Chuckling gleefully, the black man danced off.

"What's the matter, baby?" Derek's eyes were gleaming with amusement as he looked at her. "Don't you like my catering service?"

"Well, they're certainly different."

Derek threw back his head and roared with laughter. "You can say that again, baby. As a matter of fact . . ."

The rest of his sentence was drowned out as someone turned up the stereo and the raw, elemental sound of Mick Jagger screamed through the house. He grinned and shrugged, mouthing the words "Later, baby" as he plucked the two girls off Garth, holding one in each arm, then wandered off with the girls clinging to his neck and giggling.

"Garth, I want to go home," Erin announced. "Right now."

"We can't, honey. We haven't accomplished what we came to do, yet."

"You're out of your mind if you think we're going to accomplish anything in this madman's zoo," she snapped. "Unless you count getting out alive as an accomplishment. And I think our odds on that are getting slimmer with every second we stay here."

He started to laugh. "Honey, it's not all that bad. You'll get used to it. Just try to relax."

Erin jumped in fright as the short black man with the beard suddenly appeared in front of her and pressed an ice-cold double old-fashioned glass against her lips.

"House brand, ma'am," he chanted happily. "House brand." He abruptly let go of the glass, and Erin caught it bare seconds before it crashed to the floor. "Good," he said approvingly, then disappeared as quickly as he'd appeared.

"Relax? I'll get used to it? Is that what you said?"

Garth tried valiantly to keep a straight face, but Erin's outraged expression as she held the dripping glass was finally too much for him and he broke into helpless laughter.

"I'm delighted you find me so entertaining," she said frigidly. "Especially considering the competition I have all around me. And if you run out of chuckles here, come on home and we'll see what else we can do for you." With those words she turned on her heel and started marching toward the door.

"Wait!" He grabbed her by the arm.

"For what?"

"Hey, honey, I'm sorry," he said apologetically. "I didn't mean to laugh at you." His face was completely serious now as he looked at her. "Erin, I know how unpleasant this is for you, but you have to believe me when I say it's important."

"Then explain it to me!" she snapped, still furious.

"Derek wants to talk to us. He wants some assurance that we'll be producing this picture."

"*Talk* to us? You can't even hear yourself think in this place, much less talk. If he wants to talk, why doesn't he come to our offices?"

"Because it's not his way." Garth frowned unhappily. "I know it sounds weird to you, Erin, but you have to trust me. We had to show up here tonight, show him we were willing to meet him on his own turf, as he puts it. We have to do this if we want to save the picture."

"But what are we supposed to tell him?"

"That we believe in him."

"For God's sake, Garth, we'll probably never even see him again tonight. Look at this crazy party!"

"We'll see him," Garth said confidently. "He'll be coming over to us in a bit. In the meantime, let's go and sit down."

With a gentle but firm hand, Garth led her over to the long curving sectional couch that filled almost half the living room and faced both the fireplace and the huge glass windows that looked out over the ocean. An exquisitely fashioned antique coffee table, its rich, hand-rubbed surface brutally scarred with cigarette burns, sat in front of the couch. Silver cigarette boxes lined with cedar were open on it, offering a colorful variety of marijuana cigarettes. Some were wrapped in bright red, white, and blue Uncle Sam stripes. Some had smart Mondrian designs. A few were in dark chocolate-brown paper with sharply twisted ends. In the center of the table was an expensive crystal bowl filled with a fine white powder. Half a dozen small gold spoons surrounded it.

"Want to do a little coke?" A slim young boy who couldn't

have been more than sixteen sat down next to Erin and politely offered her the bowl.

"No!" Garth said harshly, pushing it away.

"Hey, man, what's the matter with you?" the boy protested. "I was just trying to be nice."

He shrank back against the couch as Garth glared at him. "Jesus, the weirdos you get at these parties," he muttered, dipping his spoon into the bowl and inhaling. Then a sudden smile illuminated his face. "Peace, man," he sighed happily.

"Chow time!" A heavy-set man in his middle thirties with a swarthy complexion and the physique of a professional body-builder stood in the middle of the living room, bellowing through a megaphone. *"Everybody to the dining area! These are orders!"*

Erin stared in astonishment as everyone stood up obediently and filed out. In less than two minutes the entire room had been cleared, and a soft gentle silence fell as someone turned down the stereo and changed the tape. Then the voice of Sinatra quietly crept into the silence. It was vintage Sinatra, from an album recorded in 1954, and the sound was mellow, rich, and confident as the wistful lyrics of "My Funny Valentine" wafted through the room. The only other sounds were the distant roar of the surf outside and the hiss and sputter of logs burning in the fireplace.

"So what's happening?" Derek appeared abruptly from a side door and sat down on the couch, crossing his legs yoga-style as he dipped a gold spoon into the crystal bowl and inhaled.

"Well, it's really a fascinating party," Erin began.

"Fuck the party," he interrupted impatiently. "I mean, what's happening with the picture."

"Oh." Erin wet her lips nervously and glanced at Garth.

"Hey, don't look at him!" Derek grabbed her arm, forcing her to turn and face him. "Look at me! I'm the one asking the question."

Erin stared into the demanding eyes and tried desperately to think of something to say. Nothing came to her, and suddenly she felt too tired to even try making up any lies.

"Nothing," she said simply. "We still haven't found any backers."

"Okay, that's straight," he announced grudgingly. "I would have been pissed if you'd tried to waltz me around."

He leaned over and picked up one of the chocolate-brown joints from the silver box in front of him, inhaling sharply as he lit it and holding the smoke for several seconds. "These are the best," he told Erin as he passed the joint to her. "The fancy wraps are just low-grade shit."

Erin took a slow drag, waiting until the lighted tip glowed red before passing it on to Garth. Then her eyes widened in shock as it hit her.

"What's the matter, baby?" Derek laughed. "Not used to this grade?"

"No," she said dazedly. "It . . . it's certainly different from what we used to smoke in college."

"College?" He peered at her curiously. "You telling me that's the last time you lit up?"

"Yes, I guess it is," she admitted.

"Weird!" He shook his head. "I never figured you for such a square."

Erin flushed with anger at the casual contempt in his voice. "Not square," she snapped. "Just too busy with important things to waste time getting strung out."

"Really?" He smiled tauntingly. "Don't look to me like all that important busy work of yours has gotten you too far. Or we wouldn't be sitting here with a dead picture."

"It's not dead!" she said furiously. Then she bowed her head to hide the unexpected tears that filled her eyes at the thought he might be right, and her picture really was dead.

"Hey," Derek said awkwardly. "Hey, I didn't mean to upset you like that. Come on, now," he urged. "Garth tells me you're a really good fighter. You're not going to give up now, are you?"

"No." She looked up and managed a smile. "No, I'm not going to give up. But what about you?"

He shrugged uncomfortably. "I'm getting a lot of heat. From a lot of people. You know what they're telling me?"

"What?" Erin asked quietly.

"That I can't handle this part. They say I'm too young. That I don't have enough experience yet."

He scowled at Garth. "Is that true, man? I mean, shit, I'm twenty-four years old!"

"It doesn't have anything to do with age," Garth told him. "It has to do with discipline and dedication."

"Hell, then there's no problem," he grinned cockily. "When I want something, I'm the most disciplined, dedicated son-of-a-bitch in the whole world."

The grin faded as Garth regarded him thoughtfully. "You wouldn't fuck me around, would you? I mean, you really don't think I'm too young?"

"Of course not," Erin interjected crisply. "Do you know how old Marlon Brando was when he appeared on Broadway in *A Streetcar Named Desire*? Twenty-three."

"No shit!" Derek gazed at her, obviously impressed. "Brando was only twenty-three when he played Stanley Kowalski?"

"That's right."

"Well, whaddya know!" The grin flashed across his face. "Wait'll I tell those cocksuckers that! Twenty-three!"

He turned suddenly and stared at Garth. "You think I could be as good as Brando?"

"Yes, I think so. And *Street Scene* could do for you what *Streetcar* did for Brando."

"Then we gotta make it!" he announced. "So where do we go from here?" he asked, turning back to Erin.

"I'm not sure."

"You tried everybody you know, right? Hollywood *and* New York?"

"Right."

"Well, maybe I know somebody you don't," he said slowly. "Somebody who'd be willing to come up with the bread. If you're willing to deal with him, that is."

"Willing?" Erin exclaimed. "Derek, I'd deal with the devil if he had the money."

"Yeah? In this case you probably would be."

"Are you serious? You *really* know someone who would back the picture?"

"Sure I'm serious. But it'll have to be on his terms. You gotta understand that from the beginning."

"What exactly does that mean? If he insists on owning rights to the film, we can negotiate that."

"Oh, fuck the rights, baby. That's not what he's interested in. Personal favors is what he's interested in.

"Not yours," he assured her laughingly as she looked at him in alarm. "He couldn't care less about sex. Power is his turn-on. Political power. Not that he'll back the picture without financial return. You'll pay through the nose for his money. Probably thirty or forty percent. And if you don't come up with the money when it's due, you'd better be prepared to leave town in a hurry. Unless you want to pick out your cemetery plot in advance."

"I don't understand. What personal favors could I possibly do for him?"

"Just one I know about. But I think it's pretty important to him."

Derek dipped the gold spoon into the crystal bowl once again and inhaled deeply. "Beautiful," he said dreamily. "Cleanest high in the world."

"But what about this investor?" Erin asked desperately.

"Still interested, huh?" Derek smiled lazily at her. "Well just 'cause you're so pretty, I'll tell you about him."

Seventeen

No one in Hollywood was quite sure when Arnold Scorsi arrived in their midst. It seemed as though one minute he didn't even exist, and then they turned around and found him everywhere. Tall, lean, tanned, gracious, and smiling, with his lovely wife on his arm, he turned up at the most select parties. And he was always in the company of the most important personages.

But people quickly learned not to try and pry into his background. There was an aura about Arnold Scorsi that made even the most nosy, impertinent questioner stammer nervously and decide suddenly to retreat to another part of the room.

Ostensibly, Arnold Scorsi was an eminently respectable corporation lawyer who had left New York to settle in Beverly Hills because, as he explained smilingly, "My wife fell in love with California on our first trip out here, and I've never been able to deny her anything."

However, Arnold Scorsi's real job was much more important than any ever held by a corporation lawyer; for Arnold Scorsi was consiglieri to the most powerful man in organized crime in the country. He had been carefully groomed for his present assignment over the past ten years and was now entrusted with over five million dollars to invest in the right places in Hollywood. His immediate responsibility was to control the vital pipeline that led from Hollywood to Washington. His ultimate responsibility was to make sure the "right" man was elected as the next President of the United States.

Now he looked up from the folder lying on his desk that contained the contracts for *Street Scene* and various legal documents detailing the corporate structure of Con-Well Productions, a faint frown on his face.

"I sympathize with your problems, Miss Connolly," he said carefully. "But I'm afraid I don't see any way in which I can help you."

Erin swallowed twice before she spoke. Arnold Scorsi was the first person she'd ever met who made her feel afraid. "Mr. Scorsi, I want to produce this picture more than I've ever wanted anything in my life."

She leaned across the desk, her luminous green eyes fixed on him. "And I would do anything to make it possible," she said in a low, husky voice.

"I'm sure you would," he remarked dryly. "But as I said before, I'm afraid you've come to the wrong person for help."

"Someone told me you represent a number of clients who look to you for advice on investing their money. I was hoping that one of them might be interested in backing a major film with the potential of winning an Academy Award."

"My dear lady, all the people I know invest in stuffy things like municipal bonds. They would be terrified at the very thought of putting their money into something as flamboyant as movies," he said with a laugh. But his eyes were cold as stone as he looked at her.

"I understand Senator Ryan is quite enamoured of the young girl who starred in my last picture." Erin wet her lips. "Unfortunately, she is as shy as she is beautiful. It's almost impossible for anyone to get to meet her. However, she will be coming to a little informal get-together I'm having this weekend."

Arnold gazed thoughtfully at her for several minutes. "Were you planning on inviting the senator?" he asked finally.

"I've never been formally introduced to him," Erin replied quietly. "So I fear it would be presumptuous of me."

A small smile lifted the corners of Arnold's thin lips. "Well that is a problem, isn't it? Perhaps I could be of help to you in this particular matter."

Senator Johnny Ryan thoroughly enjoyed himself at Erin's intimate gathering at Garth's beach house that following weekend, even though he did leave early. Of course he didn't leave alone. The stunningly beautiful eighteen-year-old girl who had starred in Erin's and Anthony's last picture left with him. An hour later the phone rang.

"We start production on Monday!" Erin shouted ecstatically as she hung up the phone and raced into the living room.

Wild cheers went up from five of the six people who were comfortably sprawled around the big oak coffee table sipping wine and nibbling on cheese and crackers. The sixth, Garth, was conspicuous by his silence.

"Hey, man, what's the matter with you?" Derek punched him on the arm, an exasperated expression on his face. "Didn't you hear Erin? We've got our picture!"

"I just wish we could have gotten it some other way," he said moodily. Garth had been strongly opposed to soliciting Arnold Scorsi's help after discovering what was involved in making a deal with him, and it had taken Erin and Derek a full week to talk him into it. From the look on his face now, it was clear he regretted giving into them.

"Listen, my friend, I do not think there is anything wrong here." Paul Marriott, the brilliant French cinematographer Garth had signed up for the picture, smiled gently at his host. "It appeared to me that the young lady left most willingly with your handsome senator."

"You think so too?" Garth turned abruptly toward Melissa, the girl with the angelic face and mass of silky blond hair he'd introduced to Erin and Anthony that fateful evening many weeks earlier. "The two of you are good friends. She came here today mostly because of you. Are you happy about her going off with him?" he demanded.

Melissa flushed, nervously twisting the strands of her hair. "It was her choice, Garth, just as you insisted it would have to be. Besides," she added with a shy smile, "I don't think it was all that difficult. Johnny Ryan is as charming as he is good looking. It's not like you turned her over to some dirty old man."

"Absolutely right." Tom Sanders, a veteran character actor, gave an amused chuckle. "What you did was turn her over to a dirty *young* man, and that makes all the difference in the world. Believe me, I know."

"Okay." Garth grinned in spite of himself. "It's obvious I'm outnumbered and outvoted. So let's get on with the picture."

"Right, man!" Derek exclaimed exultantly. He stood up and filled everyone's wine glass, then extracted a bottle of pills and several glassine envelopes from his shirt pocket, throwing them down on the coffee table. "Now let's get this party rolling in style," he laughed delightedly. "Because we got a lot to celebrate!"

Garth's hand smashed down on the table, crushing the drugs. "We celebrate when we get the Oscar," he announced coldly. "In the meantime, we work our butts off. And the only high you're allowed is what you get from doing a good scene. Now, are there any questions?"

"No suh. No way, massa." Tom Sanders cringed in mock fright, then turned and grinned at the others. "I think we just heard the voice of God."

"Damn right you did!" Garth glared at them for several seconds, then allowed a small smile to creep across his face. "I don't have to tell you how good you are, because you all know it. And I don't have to tell you what I'm expecting from you, because you know that as well. Together, we're going to sweep the Academy Awards. You know that too, don't you?" he shouted.

"Yes!" they shouted back.

"Good." He leaned back against the couch and laced his fingers together behind his head. "Now get the hell out of here and enjoy your last free day before shooting starts," he ordered.

There was tremendous tension and pressure on the set from the very first day, and it increased steadily every week. The primary reason was the time problem. Because of Erin's difficulties in obtaining financial backing for the picture, the originally scheduled production start date had been delayed a full month. Under normal circumstances, a one-month delay would not have made any particular difference. But these were most definitely not normal circumstances. For *Street Scene* was being produced as an Oscar contender, and that meant the picture had to be completed by the end of the year in order to qualify for the Academy Awards that would be presented the following spring. Which gave the cast and crew only five months to put together a highly complex and demanding film that would ordinarily have taken over a year to produce.

Two months into shooting, the time problem was compounded by a money problem. It was not that Arnold Scorsi had been stingy. He hadn't been particularly generous, but the financial backing he'd provided had been well within the accepted budget range for a major release. Erin had been forced to siphon off some of the funds in order to meet the quarterly interest payments to Anthony for his sale of Con-Well Productions to her, but that wasn't what caused the problem. It was the demands of the distributing company, who'd handled all of Con-Well's previous pictures.

"You can't be serious, Harry!" Erin had exclaimed in shock when the short burly owner of the distributing company had shoved her contract back across his desk without signing it, and stated his terms. "Con-Well Productions has been dealing with you for over two years, and you've never asked for anything like this before. You've made a goddamn fortune on us!"

"Yeah, well, that was the old Con-Well. This is the new Con-Well." He chewed stolidly on the soggy end of his cigar, his small pig eyes regarding her coldly. "You get my drift, or do I have to spell it out for you?"

"No, you don't need to spell it out," she snapped. "You've made your meaning very clear. But has it occurred to you that you could be making a very important mistake?" she said furiously. "This picture is going to win the Oscar, and then Con-Well Productions will never need you again. Or forget this blackmail!"

"So?" He shrugged indifferently. "You win some, you lose some. You wanna take your business elsewhere, be my guest."

All Erin wanted at the moment was to kill Harry, preferably by strangling him with her bare hands. The possibilities of accomplishing that were very slight, she had to admit grimly. Harry's thick bull-like neck was probably twice the circumference of both her hands joined together. Even less possible was taking Harry's bored suggestion to place her business elsewhere. Because Harry owned the biggest independent distributing company in Hollywood, and without him she would never be able to get a successful release for *Street Scene*.

"All right, Harry. We'll go with your terms."

"Two million up front for advertising and promotion, right?"

"Right."

"And I see it logged on your books," he demanded. "Not a cent goes out from that account for production. It stays right there!"

"Yes, Harry. It stays right there." Erin pushed the contract back across his desk. "Just sign on the dotted line," she said dully.

Garth was stunned when she came home and told him. "My God, Erin, how could you have done that to us? We're already over budget by half a million. I was counting on that money," he told her, an anguished look on his face. "I need it, babe. I've got to have it!"

"Don't tell me you need it," she yelled at him. "Because we don't have it anymore."

"Okay, okay now. Just take it easy," he murmured as he put his arms around her. "We'll manage. Somehow we'll manage."

They managed, but barely, in the month that followed. A cameraman quit on the spot when he dropped a lens and was faced with the accusing eyes of both the cast and his fellow crew members. Two young supporting actresses walked off the set in tears after Garth screamed at them, "The reason this is take twenty-two is due entirely to your unbelievable stupidity. Didn't anyone ever tell you how to hit your marks?"

Paul Marriott found another cameraman, and Derek came up

with replacements for the two supporting actresses, who were now filing a suit with the Screen Actors Guild, charging undue harassment. The shooting went on, with the pressure mounting visibly every day. By this time only three people were holding the production together: Garth, Paul Marriott and, amazingly enough, Derek. No one had expected him to survive the intense pressure without blowing up, but he not only kept his cool, he helped everyone else keep theirs. He showed up promptly at five every morning and stayed late into the night, even when his scenes weren't being shot, cajoling and encouraging the rest of the cast. Then everything blew sky high when Erin got the second piece of devastating news from Harry.

"Will everybody please hold it down? I have an important announcement to make." Garth's face was white as chalk, and it was only with the greatest effort he managed to keep his voice steady as he stood up and addressed the cast and crew after Erin had run onto the set and whispered frantically in his ear.

"First of all, I want to tell you what a fantastic job each and everyone of you has been doing. I know what it's taken out of you just trying to keep up with this ball-breaking production schedule. But you've not only kept up with it, you've turned in consistently superior performances. At the rate we're going, we'll not only meet our December twenty-fourth deadline but bring in a picture we can all be very proud of."

There were a few scattered cheers. However, most of the people remained silent, looking up apprehensively at Garth. A strange chemistry comes into being between a strong director and those he's directing. It's almost as though their nerve ends become linked, and whatever happens to one is instinctively felt by all. Now, although none of them had the slightest idea of what Erin had just told Garth, they sensed there was a serious problem with the picture.

Garth knew they sensed it, and he took a deep breath before continuing. "Unfortunately, I'm going to have to ask even more from you," he said heavily. "We're going to have to complete filming earlier than we'd planned. Our new release date is November twenty-second."

"*What?*" Derek screamed in rage. "Have you lost your total fuckin' mind? We can't do that, man. We just can't do it!"

"We *can* do it. It won't be easy, but we can do it."

"*No!*" The outraged cry from Paul Marriott, the brilliant cinematographer, seemed even louder than Derek's, because he had never been known to even raise his voice. "You are asking the impossible," he said hoarsely. "You are asking us to destroy our film."

"Goddamnit, shut up and listen to me for a minute!" Garth yelled as a sullen swell of anger began to grow in the crowd. "There isn't going to be any film unless we meet this deadline. The distributor has just informed us that every major theater chain across the country is booked solid with Christmas releases from the big studios. Our only chance to get a decent showing and qualify for the Academy Awards is to break the picture before Thanksgiving."

"Jesus Christ, Garth, that's less than two months away! How can you stand there and tell us we can make a November twenty-second deadline when we need at least five more weeks of shooting? Or were you planning to forget editing and printing, and just send out the daily rushes?" Derek asked with an angry laugh.

"I can stand here and tell you that because we don't have any other choice."

"Well that's where you're wrong, ol' buddy," Derek snarled. "Because we do have a choice. And I for one do not choose to ruin my career and kill myself in the process by volunteering for a suicide mission that will only result in a hopelessly botched-up picture. The Academy Awards come around every year. I can wait for the next one." He turned around and stalked off the set.

"He'll be back," Erin reassured Garth with a nervous smile.

"I hope so," Garth said bleakly. "But I wouldn't count on it. I've already pushed him harder than I ever thought I'd have to, and I'm afraid he's reached his limit."

Garth's gloomy prediction proved to be right. Derek didn't show up the next morning or the one after that, and he refused to answer any phone calls. After a full week had gone by, the morale on the set hit rock-bottom. In desperation Garth tried shooting around the missing star, but it became harder and harder to do. For one thing, the upcoming scenes demanded his presence. For another, everyone on the set had stopped believing in the picture after he left, and their performances were leaden and uninspired.

"Maybe he's right," Garth said wearily the following Sunday night as he and Erin picked dispiritedly at their TV dinners in front of the fireplace in his beach house. "The Academy Awards do come around every year. So maybe the smartest thing for us is to follow his advice and wait for next year."

"Garth, we can't!" Erin's face filled with panic, and she clutched at his arm. "My God, darling, you said it yourself when you told them this was our only chance. And you know it is," she said feverishly. "We can't wait a year. Con-Well Productions will be dead in a year. The only way we can survive is to make the picture *now*!"

"Do you mean we? Or just Con-Well Productions?"

"I didn't think there was a difference." Erin retreated from him, a stiff, hurt look on her face.

"Oh, babe," he sighed. "I guess you don't deserve that. We wouldn't be in this mess today if I hadn't insisted on your leaving Anthony."

"Are you sorry?"

"No." He smiled at her. "Of course I'm not. But are you?"

"You don't have to ask that. I think you know you don't have to ask that." Her hands reached out to him again, her fingers gently tracing the sharp planes of his face before moving down to caress his body.

He moved away abruptly. "I'm sorry, honey," he said miserably. "This goddamn picture is really taking it out of me. I hope you can understand."

"I'm trying, but it's not easy. It's been almost a month since you made love to me."

"Well, give me one more month and then I'll make it all up to you." He grinned at her. "In fact, I'll not only make it up to you, I'll have you begging for mercy."

"Is that a promise?" she asked huskily.

"You can count on it! After we wrap this picture, we'll go away somewhere. Maybe Mexico. I've got a friend who has a

place in Mazatlan. We'll lie in the sun, drink Tequila, and—"
He broke off abruptly and gave a short, harsh laugh. "What the
hell am I talking about? We don't have a picture to wrap. One
more week like this past one and I'm going to have to shut
down production."

"Oh, Garth, please don't do that!" Erin knelt in front of him,
her eyes begging.

"Babe, you know I don't want to, but what choice do I
have?"

"You have a choice," she told him fiercely. "Get Derek back
on the set."

"I'm afraid that's something I don't know how to do."

"Then I'll do it," Erin announced grimly.

Eighteen

THE voluptuous young girl who opened the door of Derek's beach house in response to Erin's knock gazed at her uncertainly.

"Gee, you sure look different from the other ones Sylvia's been sending over. Did she clue you in on the action?"

"Not exactly." Erin felt herself flushing under the girl's scrutiny and had to fight a desperate urge to turn and run away.

"Well she should have, because it's really a weird scene. I don't mean to put you down, honey, but maybe you should split while you have the chance." Her hand went up and absently fingered a large bruise on the side of her mouth. "After all, we're sisters, aren't we? And who'll look after us if we don't look after each other?"

"Nobody," Erin agreed.

"Hey, where the fuck is that new bimbo? I heard the door! Now get her in here!" The furious voice of Derek echoed through the house.

"Listen, honey, you can split right now," the girl whispered nervously. "And I'll tell Sylvia you showed up too late. That he was busy with somebody else and didn't have time for you. It'll be okay, I promise."

"No, that's all right. But thanks anyway." Erin gave the girl a tentative wave as she stepped past her into the house and walked down the hallway toward the sound of the steady, pounding rock music.

Derek was lying stark naked on top of the rumpled sheets in a huge circular bed that sat in the middle of the bedroom under a mirrored ceiling. His eyes were closed and he was puffing on a water pipe, his head nodding in slow rhythm to the beat of the music. The air in the room was rank from the pungent reek of sex mixed with the stifling odors of stale booze and hashish.

As he heard the click of Erin's high heels on the parquet floor, he raised one arm and beckoned indolently.

"You can start by going down on me, chickie," he said in a bored voice without opening his eyes. "Then if you do good, we'll have a present for you later on."

"That's terribly generous of you, but I think I'll pass," Erin announced dryly.

Derek's eyes snapped open and he bolted upright in the bed, staring at her in disbelief. "Jesus Christ, Erin, what are you doing here?"

"Well, I'm not on assignment from Sylvia, if that's what you mean."

His face reddened with embarrassment as he groped ineffectively at the tangled sheets and tried to cover himself. Erin started to laugh at his desperate attempts to extricate the top sheet, which was trapped under his leg, and his eyes suddenly darkened with rage.

"Shut up, cunt!" he said tightly. "Nobody invited you here, and nobody wants you here. Now get out before I have you thrown out!"

"I didn't mean to upset you, Derek." She instinctively backed away as he got out of the bed and advanced threateningly toward her.

"What the fuck is that supposed to mean?" he demanded furiously. "You come in to my home, insult me, and expect me not to get upset? Where the hell do you think you're coming from?"

"I said I was sorry. And I know it was probably wrong of me to come here like this, but it was the only way I knew to reach you. Now would you please calm down and put on some clothes, so we can talk?" she asked quietly.

"It just so happens I *like* being naked."

"All right," she said equably. "You stay naked, and we'll talk." Erin walked past him and sat down in one of the boudoir chairs, then looked up at him with a pleasant smile.

Derek gave an unwilling laugh. "You got more balls than most men I've met." He went back to the bed and arranged himself cross-legged on it, staring down at her. "But this time it won't work, baby. I'm not going back to the set, and that's final."

"Why?"

"Oh, come off it! You know exactly why."

"Preserving your artistic integrity was the way I heard it." Erin's eyes coolly surveyed the filthy, disheveled bedroom. "This is what you meant by artistic integrity?"

"Listen, don't you talk down to me, bitch! I know what I'm worth, and I'm not about to compromise it."

"It's apparent to me you've already compromised it," she said curtly. "If I'd had any idea how fast you could slide downhill, I would never have come to you with this offer. Because it's painfully obvious you could never handle it."

She stood up. "Good luck on your B-pictures, Derek. And I hope you can keep them going. At least they're a little better than straight porno."

"Hey, you don't walk out like that!" Derek leaped out of the bed and grabbed her. "I know you're conning me," he whispered viciously as he fastened his hands around her neck and began to shake her. "But you don't get out of here until you admit it. You understand that?"

"What I understand is that you're through as a major star."

"Shit, I don't need this crap." He pushed her away. "Just get the hell out of here."

"With pleasure. And when they draw up the list of once talented actors who blew it, they'll mention the name of Derek Marston, who had a chance to do the final cut on an Academy Award picture. If they can remember you, that is."

"*What*?" He stared at her, completely dumbfounded. "Repeat that!"

"Why bother? It would just be a waste of time." She headed for the door.

He jumped in front of her, barring her way. "Well, you're going to repeat it whether you want to or not, if you expect to leave here," he announced grimly. "Now let's hear it again loud and clear."

"Final cut." She smiled at him coldly. "Now do I have permission to go?"

"Jesus Christ, you really did say that." He shook his head. "Erin, that's just not possible."

"I don't see why. It's happened before."

"Are you kidding?" he exclaimed incredulously. "Maybe three actors in the whole history of filmmaking have been granted that honor, and they were all superpowers. You know damn well that the final cut belongs to the director. It's his personal stamp on the picture, the signature that marks the film as his creation. I can't believe Garth would ever give that up."

"Perhaps that's because you're not thinking very clearly." Erin quickly reached out and put her hand on his arm, patting him soothingly. "I don't mean because of this, uh, party you're having today," she said hastily. "I was referring to your very legitimate concern about jeopardizing your career by being denied the proper time to build and develop the character you're playing."

Confusion replaced the belligerent look in his eyes. "What's that got to do with Garth giving me the final cut?" he asked in honest bewilderment.

"For heaven's sake, Derek, it has *everything* to do with it." She gazed at him earnestly. "Don't you see? If you have final cut, then the picture can't be released without your approval. And that means there's no way in the world your career can be jeopardized. Because only you will have the power to judge your performance. If it's not up to the standards you insist upon, then you'll have the right to demand more time. So you can't lose. You can only win. Right?"

"I guess so," he said uncertainly.

"Oh, Derek, what do you mean you guess so? You know perfectly well this will make you the power on the set. I can't believe you're suddenly getting modest at this stage of the game."

"Yeah, well, it still seems strange to me," he muttered dubiously. "That picture really belongs to Garth. I just can't see him giving it up like this."

"The picture belongs to both of you," Erin said softly. "And Garth knows that. I thought you knew it too. Don't you remember him telling you this would make you the next Marlon Brando? And don't you also know that is the dream of every director? To find an incredibly talented young actor and bring him to the peak of his career? To create a major motion picture star? What's a little ego thing like the final cut compared to that kind of achievement?"

"He still thinks I can be as good as Brando?"

"He doesn't think it. He knows it!"

"Jesus, I don't know what to say." Derek ran his hands through his hair. "I promised Barney I'd start that new picture next week."

"Barney?" Erin stared at him in alarm. "You mean your agent?"

"That's the only Barney I know. You know some other Barneys?"

"But you can't do that!" she exclaimed in horror. "You're still under contract to us."

"You want to bet on that? Barney's broken more contracts than I've ever had."

Erin took a deep breath. "Well, we won't fight your agent," she said in a voice that remained steady only through tremendous effort. "If you recall, he never had any faith in you from the beginning of this picture. He was the one who said you wouldn't be able to handle the part. We *know* you can handle it. So we'll just have to leave the decision up to you."

"Okay, let's say I take your offer." His eyes drilled into hers. "There are less than seven weeks left before the November twenty-second release date. That means shooting will have to be finished in two weeks maximum, to allow time for editing and printing. Do you agree to release me from my contract in two weeks, whether we complete shooting or not, and also agree that I can refuse to let the picture out if I'm not satisfied with it?"

"I guess I have to, don't I?"

"Damn right you do," he announced, grimly triumphant.

"All right. You've got it."

"Then we've got a deal."

"You won't regret it," she said fervently. "This is going to be your Academy Award picture."

"I don't know about that. There's so much work still to be done, and so little time." Then he smiled at her. "But I promise you this. I'll give it my damnedest."

"I know you will," Erin said warmly. She stood on tiptoe and gave him a light kiss, then gasped as his arms went around her and his mouth fastened hungrily on hers. He had tremendous body heat, and she could feel it burning through the thin silk dress she was wearing. His tongue searched deep as his hands moved down and grabbed her buttocks, rubbing her against his hardness with slow, rhythmic strokes.

"Oh God, Derek. Stop! Please stop!" She struggled frantically to get away, fighting her own unconscious response as much as his attack.

He released his hold on her so abruptly that she almost lost her balance, then reached out and steadied her with one powerful, muscular arm.

"One of these days I'm going to get the final cut on you too, baby," he grinned. "But just like this time, I'll wait for you to come and offer it to me."

"I'd appreciate that," she said breathlessly, trying to regain her composure. "In the meantime, can we just concentrate on the picture?"

"Sure we can," he laughed. "We'll pick up this particular scene at a later date."

"And you'll be on the set first thing tomorrow morning?"

He shook his head wonderingly. "You are some tough broad. You never lose sight of what you want for a minute, do you?"

"I never lose sight of what all of us want," she answered crisply. "And isn't that what you want in a producer?"

"Depends." His eys regarded her cynically. "For example, I

would hate to be that poor son-of-a-bitch Garth. But I feel just fine being me."

"You don't know what you're talking about, so I'll just ignore that last comment of yours," she said frigidly. "All I ask is that you continue to feel fine, so you'll be able to do your best."

"Oh, I'll do that all right," he agreed laughingly. "Now I'd offer to be a gentleman and walk you out of here, but I think you already know your way and would prefer to do it on your own. Did I figure that correctly?" he asked mockingly.

"Absolutely," she snapped. "See you first thing tomorrow morning."

"And have a good night," he called out cheerily as the staccato click of her heels echoed down the hallway.

Erin found her hands trembling so badly on the steering wheel of the powerful Mercedes as she drove it out of the circular driveway of Derek's beach house toward the access road leading to Pacific Coast Highway, she was forced to pull off to the side and stop.

The pervasive decadence of the orgiastic scene inside the beach house had affected her more than she'd realized, she decided. But as she lit a cigarette and leaned her head back against the car seat, waiting for the pounding of her heart to subside, Erin was forced to admit it was more than the ugly atmosphere that had upset her. It was the overpowering animal savagery of Derek himself that had left her weak and trembling.

She could feel her cheeks burning with humiliation as she remembered that brief moment when her body had treacherously responded to his raw maleness. Worst of all, he'd *known* she'd responded. The amused, mocking look in his eyes as he'd held her off and surveyed her had made that painfully clear.

Cut it out, Erin, she commanded herself fiercely. After all, it was just for a moment. It didn't mean anything. It has nothing to do with your real feelings. You wouldn't even waste the time of day talking to that arrogant young prick if it wasn't for the picture. You might as well blame yourself for responding when a hot wire touches you.

She lit another cigarette and moodily regarded the glowing tip. "And it wouldn't have happened at all if you'd had more of a prick these days, Garth," she muttered aloud.

Erin jumped as a car pulled up beside her, the horn beeping as the voluptuous young girl who'd greeted her earlier leaned out of the open window and called. "Hey, are you okay?"

"Oh, yes. I'm fine."

"Well, listen, you can't just park here," the girl announced with a worried frown. "The guard will be coming around soon."

"No problem," Erin assured her. "I'm leaving right now."

"And everything's okay?" the girl repeated anxiously.

"Couldn't be better." Erin forced a smile and waved as she started the engine and pulled out of the access road. But the smile faded quickly as she headed down Pacific Coast Highway and thought of the task that lay ahead of her. When she'd first conceived the idea of offering Derek the final cut on *Street Scene*, she'd felt confident she could bring Garth around to accepting it without too much trouble. However, Derek's reaction had severely shaken that confidence.

She recalled the incredulous look on Derek's face as he'd exclaimed, "You know damn well that the final cut belongs to the director. It's his personal stamp on the picture, the signature that marks the film as his creation. I can't believe Garth would ever give that up."

Was Derek right? Would it really mean that much to Garth? Or would he be able to see, as she did, that it was only a symbolic gesture, a necessary concession to Derek's overweening ego? Surely he would be able to see that and put the whole thing in perspective, she told herself desperately. After all, it wasn't as though she was letting Derek direct the film. The little bastard probably didn't even know how to do a final cut. He'd undoubtedly end up standing around helplessly while Garth did the real work.

Erin found herself cheering up at that thought. It would be a shock to Garth, of course, when she told him what she'd offered Derek. But after they'd talked it over, he was bound to admit she'd done the only thing possible to save the picture. Why, he'd probably end up chuckling over the clever way they'd manipulated their cocky star.

The smile was back on her face as she drove into the narrow garage underneath Garth's place and parked behind his battered MG roadster, then ran up the steep steps at the side of the garage that led to the small beach house perched on stilts above.

"Hello?" she shouted excitedly as she burst through the door. "Is anybody home?"

Garth poked his head around the bathroom door. He was naked except for a brief pair of bikini shorts that hugged his hips, and his face was covered with shaving cream. He looked like an improbably lean, muscular Santa Claus.

"Hello yourself," he grinned, his lips very red within the lathery white beard. "Come in and tell me what happened."

"Oh, Garth, I'm so glad to see you!" she exclaimed, putting her arms around him, slipping to her knees and kissing the small of his back.

"Hey, watch that!" he warned her laughingly. "I could cut my throat if you keep that up."

"Then put the razor down," she said huskily. "Because I plan to keep it up." Her hands slid inside the waistband of his shorts, caressing him, and as he turned around to face her she knelt in front of him, pulling off the brief scrap of cloth that covered him and taking him into her mouth.

"Please, Garth," she begged. "I want you so much."

Without saying a word, he knelt down next to her on the narrow bathroom floor and began to undress her. She quivered uncontrollably as he removed her panties, which were soaking wet from her need, and touched her. "Hurry," she moaned. "Oh hurry, darling."

He cradled her in his arms as he entered her, and she came immediately. Sobs of disappointment racked her body. "No!" she cried as she tried frantically to hold on to the spasming ecstasy. "It's too soon! It's too soon!" She had waited so long, she had been so hungry, it couldn't be over all ready. It was too cruel to endure.

"Hush," Garth murmured. "Hush, love. It's only the beginning." He began moving inside her with slow, even strokes that steadily increased in intensity, and she felt the sweet pleasure start to build once more. In less than a minute, she came for the second time. But he didn't stop. Now he was pounding into her, and she was coming again and again. At the end she was mindlessly screaming his name over and over, her arms flung behind her head and her arched body streaming with perspiration.

"Jesus, babe," he whispered in awe. "You are really something else!"

"You're not too bad yourself," Erin panted as she tried to sit up and then collapsed back on the floor with a happy sigh, one languorous hand reaching up to touch his lips.

Unexpectedly he started to laugh, and she drew back in confusion. "What's so funny?" she asked defensively.

"You! Look at you!" He pulled her up and turned her towards the mirror.

"Oh my God!" Her face was covered with gobs of Garth's shaving cream, her eyes peering comically from the fuzzy froth of beard. "Oh, I don't believe this!" she cried, breaking into hysterical laughter. "How could you make love to someone who looked like this?"

"I must have been concentrating on some other area," he grinned. "Now let's see what you look like down here." He leaned over, his tongue tracing a path between her breasts and then down to the soft mound of pubic hair.

"Stop!" she pleaded, laughing helplessly at the same time. "I can't take any more."

"Not even a little?" His tongue probed insistently.

"No! No! I give up."

"Finally she admits it. The lady has met her master."

"I knew that from the first moment I met you," Erin said softly. "You knew it too."

"To tell you the truth, I wasn't all that sure." He gazed at her quizzically. "And you still haven't told me what happened today when you went to see Derek."

"Oh. Well . . ." Flustered, Erin grabbed a handful of Kleenex and started wiping the gobs of shaving cream off her face.

"I guess I didn't have to ask," he said ruefully. "If it had been good news, you would have told me the minute you walked in."

He patted her comfortingly. "Don't feel too badly, honey. I never really thought there was any chance of getting him to change his mind."

"Then I've got a surprise for you." She gave him a nervous smile. "Because he did."

"It's a tough break," he continued. "But it's not the end of the world. We'll—" He broke off abruptly as her words registered. "What did you say?"

"He changed his mind."

"He's coming back to the set?" Garth exclaimed incredulously.

"First thing tomorrow morning."

"My God, I can't believe it! That's fantastic!" he shouted gleefully as he swept her up in his arms, dancing her around the bathroom. "You're a goddamn miracle worker, Erin. You're a bloody genius! How did you do it? And why didn't you tell me right away?"

"I guess I got carried away with another priority."

"That you did, lady. That you most certainly did!" He shook his head wonderingly. "Jesus, babe, this is such marvelous news I hardly know what to say. We've got to celebrate!

"Come on," he announced as he set her down and took hold of her hand. "First we are going to open that bottle of champagne in the refrigerator, and then we're going out for the most lavish dinner you've ever had!"

Erin had to run to keep up with his long, excited strides as he pulled her out to the kitchen. The cork came out of the champagne bottle with a big, satisfying pop and the wine shot up to the ceiling in a golden spray. Beaming delightedly, he filled two glasses and handed her one. "To us, first. And then to success and the Oscar."

He gulped down the effervescent bubbles, laughing as they tickled his nose. "Okay, now tell me how you accomplished this miracle, you beautiful little thing."

"I just did what you told me to do," she said with a tentative smile. "I appealed to his ego."

"Oh sure," he replied mockingly. "Simple as that, huh?" He leaned over and refilled her glass. "Now cut out the false modesty and tell me what you really did."

The renewed confidence Erin had felt when she'd arrived back at the beach house some thirty minutes earlier now deserted her totally as she looked at Garth.

"Well, darling, actually there was only one major problem to overcome," she began nervously. "And once that was taken care of, the rest was easy."

"Hey, enough with the suspense! Out with it, now. Bottom line!"

"I promised him . . ." She stopped and swallowed. "I promised him he wouldn't have to worry about the stepped-up release date forcing him into a bad performance. You do know that was the only thing he was really concerned about, don't you?" she said feverishly.

"Of course I know that." He looked at her strangely. "But what could you possibly promise him that would allay his fears on that score?"

"Nothing that's of the least importance to you and me," she said quickly. "But you know his impossible ego. So I told him he could be in on the final cut of the picture and decide for himself if his performance was up to par."

She reached out and put her hand on Garth's arm. "Oh, darling, you would have laughed if you could have seen the expression on his face when I offered him that. He was so thrilled! He respects you so much, it was like I'd given him the keys to the kingdom."

"Erin, stop right there!" Garth stared at her, his eyes suddenly cold. "Just how many keys to the kingdom did you give away?"

"I don't know what you mean," she stammered. "I just told you. He gets . . ."

"Final cut. That's what you gave him, isn't it?" he shouted. "You bitch! How could you do that to me?"

"Darling, please let me explain," she begged. "It doesn't mean anything at all. You know that."

"It means nothing to you. I understand that all too well. Anything for the picture, right?"

"Garth, I can't believe you're reacting this way before you've even given me a chance to explain," she said frantically.

"Explain?" he yelled. "You think a man needs an explanation of what happened when his balls are cut off?"

He smashed the bottle of champagne down on the counter so hard that it broke into pieces, sharp splinters of glass flying everywhere, and he stalked out.

Erin ran after him as he disappeared into the bedroom and started dressing. "Garth, you're exaggerating this whole thing. Won't you at least listen to me?" she pleaded.

"Listen to what?"

"The reason. The reason, darling. Surely you can see why I did it."

"Of course I can see that." His eyes raked her with icy contempt. "Any fool could see that." He turned away and continued dressing, then headed out of the bedroom toward the front door.

"What are you going to do?" she asked as she followed him.

He stopped and uttered a short, harsh laugh. "What I'm going to do is get the hell out of here and try to get my head straight. But obviously that's not your real question, is it? You want to know what I'm going to do about the picture."

"That's not true. I love you, Garth."

"Sure you do." He laughed again but it was a cold sound, and there was no smile on his face. "Well I can tell you this much. I'm not going to walk out on the picture and let you hand it over to some other director. I've invested too much of myself in it to allow that to happen. I'll be on the set tomorrow morning and every morning after that until it's completed. And when I say completed, I mean completed the way I want it to be. Not the way you want it or Derek wants it or anybody wants it except me," he added fiercely. "Because this is *my* picture, and I'm not going to let anybody forget it."

He paused for a moment, a sudden bleak look on his face. "After that, I don't know what I'm going to do. I just don't know."

"Oh, darling, everything's going to be all right," Erin cried desperately. "Please just give it a chance, and you'll see we're going to be all right."

"Erin, we'll never be all right again." He turned and walked out the door.

Nineteen

"No!" Derek shouted angrily. "What the shit is your problem, anyway? I mean, didn't you even read the fuckin' script? Janine is trying to *seduce* me, for Christ's sake. And you're acting like a constipated virgin."

"Janine is trying to seduce a human being!" Melissa screamed. "Not some hairy animal. And, besides, who ever gave you the right to be a director?" She burst into hysterical sobs and ran off the set.

"Jesus! That's all we need. A stupid broad in a supporting role who suddenly becomes a prima donna."

"She'll be back," Garth said quietly from his chair behind the set. "But she's right. You're pushing her too fast. You have to let her come to you."

Derek flushed as he stepped out of the circle of bright lights and made his way over the complicated lines of cables snaking around the floor to Garth's chair.

"Yeah, I know," he grunted as he flopped down in the chair next to Garth. "And she was right about that last crack she made, too. I'm not the director, and I should have kept my damn mouth shut."

"It's okay." Garth smiled and gave him an affectionate punch on the shoulder. "The way you're going, you just might turn into a respectable director one of these days. In the meantime, you doing one hell of a job with the character you're portraying."

"You mean that?"

"I mean it."

"Jesus, man, that's great to hear." Derek hunched over, absently cracking his knuckles. "Because I'm giving it everything I've got. I just hope to God it's enough."

"Keep on going the way you have been and it will be."

"You know something, man?" Derek exclaimed suddenly. "You are something special. I mean, *really* special. Because I know damn well, no matter what Erin said, that giving me the final cut wasn't your idea. It was something that little conniver dreamed up herself. And you could have been shitty as hell about it, riding me on the set, slicing me up every time I goofed. But you've been just the opposite. You've gone out of your way to help me, to teach me stuff. So . . . well, I just wanted to tell you how much I appreciate it, and thank you for it," he finished awkwardly.

For a brief second, Garth's expression turned cold and forbidding. Then he shook his head and smiled at the young actor. "I'm the one who should be thanking you. You're not only giving a magnificent performance, you're sparking everyone on the set to do the same. If we get an Oscar for this picture, it will be because of you."

Derek ducked his head, suddenly embarrassed. "Yeah, well, we won't get it with me parking my ass here," he mumbled. "I'd better get back to work."

He stood up and walked back to his marks. "Okay, you guys," he yelled. "Let's hit it! We're going after a perfect take this time."

To everybody's delighted surprise, it was a perfect take. Melissa returned to the set, still seething with rage over Derek's crude but absolutely accurate assessment of her last scene, and turned in a bravura performance as the shy, lovestruck young girl whose terror at losing the boy she's adored since childhood goads her into a desperate competition with the woman he's turning to.

Derek and Melissa received a standing ovation from the cast

and crew when they finished the scene. Erin, who'd quietly slipped into the sound stage a few minutes earlier, joined in the applause. And, as she'd done every day for the past ten days, once again crossed her fingers and gave thanks for the miracle occurring before her eyes.

After Garth had walked out of the beach house the previous Sunday, she'd been numbly prepared for total disaster. It had seemed impossible then to believe the picture could ever be saved. But it was not only being saved, it was achieving a brilliance she could hardly believe. The scenes shot before Derek had stalked off the set had been so good she'd despaired of ever matching them. The most she had been able to hope for was that the remaining scenes would go smoothly enough to allow a clever editor to cut and segue them into the earlier footage. But there was no chance of doing that, because Garth scrapped all the film shot the week before Derek left the set and started every scene over again to build the proper momentum. She'd been horrified when she saw what he was doing.

"My God, Garth, have you lost your mind?" she'd cried. "You're throwing away our only insurance on this picture."

"If you want another director, tell me now," he'd snarled. "Otherwise, shut up!"

She'd shut up after she saw the rushes. They were superb. She also stopped coming around to see the dailies three days later. She'd appeared as usual that evening, peering intently through the viewer at the tiny frames of film, and then announced in shock, "This shadow is terrible! Why hasn't someone cut it?"

There was a sudden grim silence in the room, and she had turned around to find three pairs of eyes staring at her hostilely. Sarah Lawton, the film editor, dropped her eyes when Erin looked at her but Garth and Derek had continued to glare at her.

"I—I'm sorry," she'd stuttered nervously. "Obviously everyone here has noticed it also. I should have realized there hasn't been time to fix it yet."

The oppressive silence continued and she stood up and fled from the room, knowing that she was not only not needed but not wanted. And she stayed away. But she couldn't make herself stay away from the set, even though Garth pointedly ignored her presence.

He turned around now as he heard the door open and she waved eagerly, a bright smile on her face as she made a circle with her index finger and thumb indicating how pleased she was with the scene. He regarded her unsmilingly for a moment, then curtly turned back to the set; and her arm dropped awkwardly to her side.

"It's my picture too," she whispered. But no one was paying any attention to her. With an unhappy sigh she slipped out of the room as quietly as she had come in and made her way to her car, which the guard had waiting for her immediately outside of the sound stage.

It was three o'clock, and she was due at the advertising agency in Beverly Hills for a three-thirty meeting. She'd be late, but at least she didn't have to fear any disapproving looks from them, Erin thought with a bitter smile. They'd wait for her until midnight, if necessary, and still greet her with enthusiastic cries of pleasure.

"No love so true as that bought with money," she murmured to herself as she drove out of the lot and onto the Ventura Freeway that led, through convoluted ribbons of asphalt, into the cold heart of Hollywood's show business capital. "As long as you don't lose the money."

The steel radial tires on the Mercedes hummed confidently along the sharp curves of the freeway as Erin stepped hard on the accelerator, racing along at ninety miles per hour. A check in the rear-view mirror showed a distant speck of black moving up fast. It was a highway patrol car. Erin quickly released the pressure on the accelerator, letting the car glide around the turn approaching the San Diego Freeway, and breathed a sigh of relief as the patrol car whipped by her.

"For Christ's sake, Erin, take it easy," she admonished herself. "The last thing in the world you need now is a speeding ticket." She looked up to check the rear-view mirror again. Sometimes the highway patrol cars traveled in packs. But the only image in the mirror was her own white, strained face. As it looked back, it seemed to mock her. And what's the first thing in the world you need, it asked.

"Oh shut up!" she said furiously. "I'm going to get my picture. That ad agency is going to produce the most exciting campaign that's ever been seen. I've given them the money to produce it and the product to back it, and I'm going to get that Oscar!"

And what about Garth, the image asked implacably, are you going to get him too?

"I don't know. You know I'm trying. God know's I'm trying!"

It was true. Erin had been doing everything within her power to show Garth how much she loved him, believed in him, and wanted him. No matter how late he got home from the studio, she was always up and waiting for him; and as soon as she heard him drive into the garage she hurried into the kitchen to fix him something hot to eat.

At first she had tried to discuss the day's shooting with him, offering herself as a sounding board for his ideas and thoughts, but she quickly realized that was the last thing in the world he wanted. Gray-faced with exhaustion, he could hardly keep his head up while he ate. All he wanted was sleep. So she would serve him quietly, clear the table when he was finished, pick up the dirty clothes he flung off as he fell wearily into bed, and lay out fresh clothes for the morning, then go out and clean up the kitchen.

Her own days were frantically busy as she rushed from one meeting to another, coordinating the massive advertising and promotion campaign that would launch the picture. In between conferences with copy and art directors, recording sessions for the radio and television commercials, and luncheons with syndicated columnists and film critics, she managed to make time for meetings with Con-Well's accounting staff, which assured Garth a steady flow of money to keep his production going smoothly. It was an almost impossible task, trying to keep everything going successfully at the same time, but somehow she did it. And she never bothered Garth about it. If there was good news, she told him. If there was bad news, she kept it to herself. And every free moment she was on the set, cheering him on.

But he doesn't seem to notice at all, she thought glumly as

she walked into the office of the Beverly Hills ad agency, smiled absently at the eager young account executive who bounded out to meet her, and then frowned as he led her into the conference room and presented her with the layout.

"I don't know," she said hesitantly. "It seems exploitative somehow."

"Exploitative? My dear, I can't believe you said that!" Josh Engels, the silver-haired president of the ad agency sprang forward and seized her hands. "Look again," he urged her. "Sensual, yes. But never exploitative. And the *power* of the concept! It will turn on everyone who sees it. They'll stand in lines eight blocks long at the movie theaters for a chance to find out what's behind this ad!"

Erin shook her head. "I'm sorry, Josh, but you're going to have to change it. Get that hungry look off her face, and put some more clothes on her. I'll be back at ten tomorrow morning to okay the revision."

The art director groaned involuntarily and Erin turned around, giving him a sympathetic smile. "I know. It means you'll be working through the night to get it ready, and I am truly sorry. But this is a very important ad, and it has to be exactly right. I hope you can understand."

"Don't worry," Josh said gamely. "We'll do it, and it *will* be right. You can count on us."

"I'm sure I can." She made a point of shaking hands with everyone in the room and thanking them personally for their cooperation.

It was an effort to come up with a warm, personal comment for each individual, but she decided it was well worth it as she walked out of the agency to her car and recalled the appreciative smiles on their faces. It wasn't that she was worried about getting them to work all night. Josh was the original slave-driver. If the money was right, he'd work his people to the bone and then bring in his mother, wife, and children to finish the job when they dropped in their tracks. But although you could force people to work to death, you couldn't force them to be creative at the same time. She desperately needed that creativity, and she knew the only way to get it was to impress them with a sense of their own importance. Hopefully, she had now accomplished that.

But the brief surge of energy she'd felt faded as she climbed into the car and put the key into the ignition. Her head ached almost unbearably from the pressures of the past two weeks, her stomach was a tense knot of pain, and she found herself constantly rubbing her eyes, which felt like they were full of sand.

She lit a cigarette and leaned her head back against the seat of the car, trying to relax for a few minutes before she headed into the bedlam of homeward-bound traffic as thousands of irritable commuters poured onto the congested freeways. The lazy spiral of smoke drifting up from her cigarette had a hypnotic effect, and she began to nod off. She came to with a start as the cigarette burned down, singing her fingers.

"Goddamnit!" she shouted, flinging it out the window and nursing her fingers. It was the most minor of accidents, but for some reason she found tears springing to her eyes. Oh for Christ's sake, pull yourself together. This is no time for an attack of nerves.

She started the engine and drove down Wilshire Boulevard to the freeway entrance, telling herself that all she needed to do was hang on for another sixty minutes and then she'd be home. At which time I'll pour the world's largest drink, empty a whole bottle of bubble bath into the tub, and collapse in style until Garth gets back tonight, she promised herself. It was such a pleasurable image, she found herself smiling in anticipation.

The smile changed into an expression of terror as she drove into the garage underneath the beach house and saw Garth's car. Heart pounding, she raced up the steps and burst into the living room.

"What's wrong, Garth?" she cried in panic.

He was sitting on the couch, his long legs stretched out in front of him, staring unseeingly at the cold ashes in the fireplace. He lifted his head at her cry and regarded her blankly.

"Wrong?" he repeated vaguely.

"My God, darling, what happened?" She rushed over to him. "Is there a problem on the set?"

"No, there's no problem."

"But you're home! It's only six o'clock."

"Oh, that." He gave her a tired grin. "That's not a problem. It's a plus. You see, I think we can finish the shooting tonight. So I gave everybody five hours off to rest and prepare themselves. We go back to the studio at ten and film straight through tomorrow morning. I think we'll have a wrap then."

"Garth, that's incredible!" Erin's face lit up with joy. "Oh, darling, I can't tell you how proud I am. To think you've brought it in a day early! It's a miracle."

"Yeah, well, save your praise until next week. We still have to cut and edit. That will be the real test. When we see just what we've got."

"It's going to be superb," she announced confidently. "I just know it."

"Maybe. Maybe not. We'll have to wait for that." He started to stretch and then winced.

"What is it, darling?" she asked anxiously.

"Getting old, I guess," he said ruefully. "At this moment I feel like a geriatric case. Every bone in my body aches."

"Let me help." She moved quickly over to the couch and started massaging his neck.

"Hey, you don't have to do that."

"I know," she said softly. "But I want to. Now lie down. Come on, Garth, lie down," she insisted as he looked at her quizzically. "It's going to feel good, I promise."

He shrugged, then did as she ordered. A minute later he gave a low groan of pleasure.

"I told you you'd like it," she smiled. Her hands patiently kneaded the tight muscles at the base of his neck. His skin was warm and smooth, and she could smell the clean, fragrant odor of his thick black hair. With an effort she restrained herself from burying her face in it.

"You want more there, or should I do your back now?" she asked. There was no answer, and she realized he was fast asleep. "My poor tired baby," she whispered, leaning over and kissing him gently. "Sleep well, and have pleasant dreams."

Erin let him sleep for a little over two hours before waking him. He sat up with a start when she shook him by the shoulders. "Jesus, what time is it?" he demanded.

"It's still early," she reassured him. "Just a little after eight. Dinner will be ready in twenty minutes, so you have plenty of time to shower and dress."

He rubbed his eyes wearily, then blinked as he looked around. While he had been sleeping, Erin had cleaned up the small living room, lit a fire in the fireplace, and set two places for dinner on the oak coffee table. There was a basket of crisp French rolls in the center of the table, along with an uncorked bottle of red wine. Candles glowed softly at each end.

"Hey, this is really nice!" He smiled at her then. "You've been pretty nice too. And I appreciate it."

It was all the reward she needed. "My pleasure, darling," she said happily.

She was humming contentedly under her breath as she went back to the kitchen and started fixing the salad, after checking the casserole which was bubbling nicely in the oven. It's going to be all right after all, she told herself confidently. Everything's going to work. The picture, and us.

Garth finished the filming that night just as he'd hoped. Then came the backbreaking work of editing and cutting. The release date was now less than a month away. Hesitantly, remembering her earlier rejection in the cutting room, Erin offered her services.

"I don't know," Garth had said dubiously. "God knows we need all the help we can get, but what can you do?"

"Whatever you order me to." She'd smiled at him diffidently. "I don't claim to be an expert, but there's lots of scut work I can do. After all, there was a time when I got job offers as an assistant film editor."

"You did?" He looked at her in surprise. "I never heard about that."

"Well, it wasn't one of my starring roles," she'd admitted with a small grin. "But they thought I was good enough to give me a try. And I don't think I've forgotten how to do it. So what do you say?"

"Are you kidding?" He'd grinned back at her and grabbed

her arm. "Come on, lady! We've got ten cans of film waiting just for you."

It was a mind-numbing process, and there were times Erin thought she wouldn't be able to stand one more hour of viewing the endless reels, marking off the next section of cuts. But somehow she managed. More important, she also managed to keep her mouth shut when Garth, the film editor, and Derek announced their decisions about the editing. Her role was as a lackey and she kept it that way, rushing off with each completed can of film to the lab that was now working twenty-four hours a day to print it.

Con-Well Productions delivered the finished prints to the distributor one hour before the deadline, and Erin threw a party to end all parties to celebrate the event. The main sound stage at the company's San Fernando studio was thrown open to welcome the cast and crew along with their families and friends. Dom Perignon champagne flowed freely. Two rock groups played continuously. Enough food to feed a small country filled the wide-planked redwood tables set up around the area. But despite the lavish and almost frenetic display, most people left early. The simple fact was that they were exhausted. Completing the picture had taken almost every ounce of energy they possessed, and after eating and drinking they just drifted off.

"Do you think they liked it?" Erin asked anxiously as she and Garth drove away.

"Sure," he said absently, concentrating on the traffic in front of him.

"Well, but maybe I should have waited a week or so," she persisted. "When everybody had a chance to rest up first."

"Erin, would you please stop harping on it?" he said irritably. "You gave the party when it should have been given, it was a fine party, and everybody appreciated it. Now can't you just let it go at that?"

Hurt, she subsided and leaned back against the seat, staring out the window at the cars roaring by. They drove the rest of the way home in silence. But once they reached the beach house, Erin's spirits revived.

"I don't know about you, but I'm not through celebrating

yet," she announced gaily as they walked inside. "Why don't you light a fire and put on some music while I fix us a couple of drinks?"

She dropped her evening wrap and purse on an end table and walked briskly into the kitchen, where she arranged a variety of bottles and glasses on a tray.

"How's this for a dazzling array?" she laughed as she walked back into the living room. "Not that I expect us to drink all of it, but you never know what the night might . . ."

She trailed off uncertainly as she looked around the empty room. There was no fire, no music, and no sign of Garth. "Darling?" she called nervously. "Where are you?"

"In here," he called back, his voice sounding slightly muffled.

"Garth, what are you doing?" she exclaimed in shock as she appeared at the doorway of the bedroom and saw him backing out of the closet with a load of clothes in his arms.

"I thought I told you." He pulled a suitcase out from under the bed and started packing the clothes in it. "Don't you remember I said that as soon as the picture was completed I was going to take a vacation in Mexico? At my friend's place in Mazatlan?"

"Of course I remember!" She clapped her hands in delight. "But I thought *you'd* forgotten. You've never mentioned it even once since you first told me about it."

She ran over and hugged him. "What a marvelous surprise, darling! But you really shouldn't have sprung it on me like this. I know you men only need some slacks and shirts and a change of underwear to be off and running, but us women folk like to do a little shopping first. I don't have even *one* decent outfit I can wear down there. Or did you think I could buy the clothes once we got there?"

"Erin, I thought you understood," Garth said slowly. "We're not going there together. I'm going by myself."

"We're not going there together?" she repeated numbly. "But you told me . . ."

"Things were very different when I told you that. And you know it."

"No, I don't know it. We've been together practically every

minute in the past two weeks. We've been as close as two human beings can get. How can you say things are different?"

"Please, Erin, don't make things more difficult than they have to be," he sighed. "It's true we've been close these past two weeks. But that was a professional relationship. We were working together to save the picture. That's not the same as a personal relationship."

"I don't understand what you're saying!"

"No, you probably don't." He smiled sadly. "To you, there's no separation between your feelings for your business and your feelings for people. But to me there's a big separation. And that's why I'm leaving you."

"I don't believe you! We mean too much to each other. Is this some last minute macho move on your part to try and prove something to me?"

"If it makes you happy to think that, then go ahead," he said indifferently as he snapped the clasps on his suitcase.

"Garth, don't do this to us," she pleaded. "You know you love me."

"Past tense, babe. I did love you."

"Then how could you stop?"

"I didn't stop, Erin," he said evenly. "You killed it."

"That's bullshit, Garth!" She glared at him. "All right, I admit we've had some rough times. I've done some things you didn't like, and you've done some things I didn't like. But I never stopped loving you because of it. I love you just as much today as I did when we first met."

"Then I feel sorry for you," Garth said quietly.

Her face went white at the cutting words. "How *dare* you tell me that?" she spat furiously. "No one *ever* has to feel sorry for Erin Connolly, because she doesn't need anyone!"

"I'm sure that's true. Which is probably the problem."

"What the hell is that supposed to mean?"

"Nothing you'd understand in a million years." He carried his suitcase over to the door. "I'll be gone for at least six weeks. You're welcome to stay here while I'm away, but I'd appreciate it if you'd find another place to live before I return."

"You needn't worry about that!" she snapped. "I'll be packed and out of here before you get to the airport tonight."

"Suit yourself." He picked up his suitcase and walked past her through the doorway.

She stared after him in numb disbelief. It couldn't end like this. It just couldn't! She willed him to turn around, come back and put his arms around her and tell her he couldn't leave her. He continued walking steadily through the living room to the front door. She heard it open and then slam shut. It was a very final sound. She began to shake uncontrollably.

It's just that it's cold in here, she told herself. I'll light a fire, and then I'll be fine.

She moved stiffly into the living room and crouched down in front of the fireplace. The gas jet came on with a hiss, and flames leaped up as she held a match under it, causing long ominous shadows to fill the silent room. She quickly adjusted the flow of the gas, and the old charred logs sputtered feebly before collapsing through the grate in a smoldering pile of ashes. They gave off no warmth at all.

"What am I going to do?" she sobbed. "Where am I going to go?" The thought of a lonely, impersonal hotel room was more than she could bear.

Then sudden rage seized her and dried up the frightened tears rolling down her cheeks. "No one walks out on Erin Connolly," she announced fiercely. "Erin Connolly walks out on them. I'll show that bastard!"

She stood up, walked over to the phone, and dialed. It rang, over and over again. She was about to give up when finally a sleepy voice answered.

"Derek? It's Erin. You gave me an invitation once. If the offer's still open, I'd like to take you up on it."

XX

Twenty

XXXXXXXXXXXXXXXXXXXXXXXXXXXXXXXXXXXXXXXXXXXXXXXXXXXXXXXX

THE dream came back for the fourth night in a row. It always started the same way. She was walking on the narrow strip of sand in front of Garth's beach house. It was a dangerous place to walk, a "wet beach" as the residents called it. What it meant was there was no beach at all except at very low tide. The rest of the time the ocean pounded up against the pilings of the structures that sat above it, and riptides threatened everyone who ventured out on it. It was high tide again, and the waves were throwing her relentlessly underneath the building as large rocks began to dislodge from the foundation and slide inexorably toward her.

Then just before the rocks rolled over her and crushed the life out of her body, a light would come on in the beach house above and Garth would appear on the deck. "I'm back, Erin," he would call out to her, his voice so strong she could hear it clearly over the raging surf. "I've come back for you. Just hold on, darling. I'll be right there."

He always reached her just in time, taking her in his arms and holding her so tight that the heat of his body flooded her with warmth. And once again, as in all the other dreams, the miracle occurred. The moon came out, pouring bright golden light on the ocean, and the waves gently receded, leaving an incredibly wide smooth beach in their wake. "I love you, Erin," he murmured, his voice now as soft as the water caressing the gold-flecked grains of sand. "Please love me back."

"Oh yes, Garth. Always." Moaning with pleasure, she lay back as he entered her and began moving with slow, delicious strokes. The light from the full moon covered her with glory, and then she began to reach her own glory. "Oh my love," she cried in wonderment, "my very dearest love. Garth! Garth!!"

Suddenly the dream went wrong. His hands, which had been caressing her breasts, moved up and fastened tightly around her neck, and his thumbs pressed cruelly against her windpipe. She couldn't talk. She couldn't even breathe. She began to thrash from side to side in bewildered terror.

"Bitch! Bitch! You ever say another man's name when you're coming with me and I'll kill you!"

Erin swam out of one nightmare into another. Derek was kneeling over her, his cock hard inside her and his hands shaking her like a rag doll. They were lying in his big circular bed in the master bedroom of his beach house, and the faint luminous glow from his bedside clock cast an evil green light over his face. His golden cat eyes glowed ferociously at her.

"Jesus Christ, Derek, what are you doing?" she gasped.

"Fucking you while you sleep." His hands relaxed around her neck and he smiled, a feral smile, his teeth very white and sharp as he gazed down at her. "And you were responding. You were fucking back like there was no tomorrow."

His hands tightened around her neck again. "Do you know who's fucking you now? *Do you*?"

"Yes," she said.

"Good. For that you get a reward. I'm going to take you on a carousel ride."

He rolled over on his back, pulling her with him, then gripped her around the waist and lifted her up in the air.

"No!" she protested, struggling to get free. But he was enormously strong and held her easily.

"Relax, baby. You'll like coming this way. You'll come again and again."

He lowered her until just the head of his cock entered her,

then began slowly rotating her around his thick, engorged penis.

She willed herself not to respond, but the sensation was so exquisite it was impossible to resist. Helplessly, she gave in to it, shuddering as she climaxed over and over. And with each new orgasm the pleasure became more intense, like oil burning on water that blazes brighter and brighter as it spreads.

"What's my name, bitch?" Derek panted. "Who's fucking you?"

She was still coming and it was difficult to talk. "King Cock," she gasped.

He laughed harshly. "And there's only one. Don't ever forget that!" He grabbed her, pulling her down on him, and she felt him plunge through her. He was bucking wildly now, his teeth clenched and his eyes squeezed shut. He was throbbing so hard, it shook her entire body. She could feel the intense heat penetrating her as he plunged deeper and deeper. And then she exploded into a million pieces.

"God!" Derek fell back against the bed as she collapsed on top of him. "What an incredible fuck. You are *prime*, baby," he said reverently. "I'll never understand how Garth could have left you."

"Don't you *ever* say that!" she screamed in sudden fury, sitting up and beating him on the chest. "He didn't leave me. I left him! And you'd better get that straight right now!"

He grabbed her wrists and flipped her over, leaning down and staring hard into her eyes. "Listen, Erin, I don't give a shit who left whom. All I care about is that you're mine now. So tell me. Tell me you belong to me."

She glared at him defiantly, refusing to answer, and unexpectedly he chuckled. "Damned if you aren't the most stubborn, independent broad I've ever known. But that's all right. I like you that way. Matter of fact," he added huskily as his fingers gently traced the outline of her delicately modeled face, "I'm crazy about you, baby. And I'll take good care of you. You'll never be sorry you came to me." He patted her. "Now let's get some sleep."

He turned on his side, bunching the pillow under his head and yawning, then bolted upright as light flooded the room.

"What the *hell* are you doing?" he exclaimed.

Erin had switched on the lamp on the nightstand and was now sitting up against the headboard, lighting a cigarette. "I'm too wide awake to go to sleep," she said crossly. "So I thought I'd read some scripts."

"Jesus Christ, Erin," he groaned. "Do you realize it's three o'clock in the morning?"

"Well, whose fault is that?" she snapped. "*I* wasn't the one who woke us up at this hour."

"Oh come on, baby," he pleaded. "I'm really tired, and I've got a meeting with my agent at nine this morning."

"All right, I'll go into the living room," she said angrily, starting to get out of the bed.

He reached over and pulled her back. "Hey, you don't have to do that. I've got a better idea. Something that will make you feel really special, and then you'll sleep like an angel."

"What?" she asked suspiciously.

"This." He opened the drawer of the nightstand on his side and pulled out a small tin. "We'll do a little coke. Be great for both of us."

"I don't know, Derek." She hesitated. "I've never tried it."

"No time like the present." He scooped up a small pile of the fine powder on his index finger. "This isn't too classy a way to do it," he apologized. "But it works just as good."

She stared in frightened fascination as he brought it to her.

"Go on," he urged. "Just inhale. I promise you'll dig it."

She leaned over tentatively and sniffed, and for a brief second everything was icy cold and numb. Then she felt her whole body lift up and float away.

"Derek, this is marvelous!" She gazed at him in wonderment, feeling as though her eyes had never opened so wide nor seen so clearly. "Everything is so bright! Everything is so lovely!"

"Yeah, ain't that the truth," he grinned. He scooped up another small amount of the fine white powder and drew it sharply into his nostrils, sighing with pleasure as it hit him. "The whole world is beautiful," he said dreamily. "And we're the most beautiful things in it."

"Especially us! Especially us!" she announced in delight as

she climbed out of the bed and headed for the desk in the corner of the room.

"Hey, what are you doing now?" he asked as he watched her bend over and pull out a large black scrapbook from the bottom drawer of the desk.

"It's our picture. Look, darling, look!" She dragged the thick book back to the bed and opened it.

It was an impressive volume. Erin had diligently collected every press notice on *Street Scene* from the moment it had been released on November twenty-second. It had opened to extremely favorable reviews, and the box office had responded with enthusiasm. In its first few weeks the film had audiences waiting in theater lines all across the country to see it.

Derek looked at her in amazement. "When did you put all this together?"

She blushed. "Oh, a couple of weeks ago when I had a little free time." Actually Erin worked on the book every single day, hungrily combing the newspapers and magazines for every scrap of news about the picture. But it was a secret passion, and one she would never have admitted to anyone if it hadn't been for her euphoric cocaine high. Now the high began to recede as Derek continued to look at her quizzically. "Please, Derek," she whispered to herself. "Please don't laugh at me and spoil it all."

She needn't have worried. He began flipping through the pages and quickly became absorbed in the clippings. There were reviews from every major film critic and columnist in the country: Gene Shalit of NBC-TV, Archer Winston of *The New York Post*, Rex Reed of *The New York Daily News*, Vincent Canby of *The New York Times*, Rona Barrett of KABC-TV, Charles Champlin of *The Los Angeles Times*, Jack Kroll of *Newsweek*, and Richard Schickel of *Time*. He paused at a full-page newspaper ad featuring his picture. "STREET SCENE IS A WINNER!" it proclaimed in bold type. "AND DEREK MARSTON MAKES IT A WINNER! GOLDEN GLOBE AWARD FOR BEST ACTOR!"

"How about that?" he exclaimed gleefully. "Derek Marston makes it a winner! That's *me* they're talking about."

"It certainly is. And you are a winner, darling. Just like the picture." A troubled expression crossed her face, and she rubbed absently at her forehead.

"What's the matter, baby?"

"I don't know," she said hesitantly. "All of a sudden I feel . . . empty or something."

"Don't worry about that," he reassured her. "You're just coming down. It happens that way all the time with coke. You'll sleep now," he told her soothingly. "Turn off the light and snuggle up here. You'll be fine."

"But we still haven't gotten any Academy Award nominations."

"You're jumping the gun, baby. The academy hasn't even announced them yet."

"But when they do, we will be nominated, won't we?" she asked anxiously. "You do believe that?"

"Sure I do."

She relaxed and smiled at him. "That's good. Because you have to have faith in order to make things work." Then she curled up next to him as he'd told her to do, and promptly fell asleep. And all her dreams for the rest of that night were about her picture.

Two weeks later, on a cold, rainy February morning, Erin sat behind her desk in the executive suite of Con-Well Productions' business office, located in Century City, and stared tensely at the phone. There were three other people in the suite with her. Paul Marriott crouched on the edge of his chair and chain-smoked steadily as he gazed unseeingly at the carpet; Melissa was curled up in a tight ball in the corner of the couch; and Derek was restlessly pacing up and down from one end of the room to the other.

It was the third Monday in February, and in less than fifteen minutes the doors of the Motion Picture Academy on Wilshire Boulevard in Beverly Hills would open to admit the hundreds of domestic and foreign journalists who were crowded around the entrance. Inside the building, academy staffers had worked through most of the night preparing the announcements on this year's Oscar nominations. The noise from the crowd began to build as the time came closer.

"Derek, you're driving me crazy!" Erin snapped. "Can't you sit down?"

"No!" he snapped back.

"Can't say I blame you. Jesus, when will they call?"

"When they know," Paul muttered somberly as he lit another cigarette. "You have good people there?"

"The best. They'll be right in front, and get the news first. Oh God, I'm not religious, but do you think it would help if we prayed?"

"It's too late," Melissa sighed. "Either we got it or we didn't. They've already made their decisions."

The phone rang then, and everybody in the room jumped. It rang again and Erin reached out for it, but her hand was shaking so badly she dropped it before she could bring it to her ear. When she finally managed to pick it up, there was only a dial tone. "There's no one there."

"Jesus Christ, Erin, you disconnected them!" Derek shouted. "Let me handle this." He leaped over and reached for the phone, but she shoved him away sharply.

"They'll call back, and I'm the only one who's going to answer," she announced, her face white. "It's my picture."

As though she'd ordered it, the shrill ring sounded once again in the room, and she grabbed the phone. "Yes, Andy, I'm here," she said hoarsely. "Yes, I can hear you. What? *What?* Oh, Andy, I can't believe it. Say it again. Yes. Yes, I've got it. And thank you, Andy. Thank you!" She hung up and leaned back in the chair, an expression of pure bliss on her face.

"For Christ's sake, Erin, tell us!" Derek shouted.

"Six," she said ecstatically. "We got *six* nominations. Best Picture. Best Director. Best Screenplay."

She turned and beamed at Paul. "Best Cinematographer."

He was so overcome that tears sprang to his eyes, and he went into a coughing fit to try and hide them.

She turned back to Derek and Melissa, and grinned mischievously. "I said six, didn't I? Now let me think . . ."

"Erin, please!" Derek groaned.

"Best Actor and Best Supporting Actress!" she finished triumphantly.

The room exploded with noise as they screamed with joy and began dancing around, hugging and kissing each other first and then running over to embrace Erin and Paul.

"Any chance I could get in on this party?" a warm, deep voice inquired.

They whirled around to face the door, and Melissa's eyes lit up with delight. "Garth!" She raced over and threw her arms around him. "Oh, isn't it the most incredible news? Isn't it just fantastic?"

She stepped back and shook her finger accusingly at him. "But where have you been all this time?" she demanded. "We haven't heard *one* word from you in months!"

"Well, Mexico turned out to have more charm than I expected," he said with an easy smile. "But it looks like I came back at the right time."

"Hey, man, you can say that again!" Derek bounded over and pounded him enthusiastically on the shoulder. "Any better timing and we could make you an actor."

"No, no!" Paul protested laughingly as he came forward. "We need him too much as a director." He took hold of Garth's hands. "Congratulations, my friend," he said softly. "We pulled it off after all, didn't we?"

"Yes, we did. Thanks to all of you."

"Enough of this sentimental slop!" Derek yelled. "We are going to celebrate!"

"Right!" they all shouted, grinning like idiots at each other.

Erin watched them from a distance, a painful lump in her throat as she gazed at Garth. He was deeply tanned from his two and half months in Mexico, and he had never looked more handsome. All the strain lines in his face, the exhausted slump of his body, had disappeared. He stood tall and proud, the crisp black hair curling over his forehead and the intense blue eyes glowing out of his smiling face.

"I still love you," she whispered. "And I'll do anything you want if you'll just give me another chance."

He looked up and met her eyes, then walked over to her. "Well we really did make it, didn't we?"

"Yes," she replied unsteadily. "Yes, we did. And I'm very

glad you're back. It wouldn't have been the same without you."

"It's not something I would have missed." He smiled. "Looks like we're both on our way now."

"And there's so much we have to talk about," she said eagerly. "Have lunch with me, Garth."

"Thanks, Erin, but I'm afraid I'm tied up. I have a lady waiting for me."

"Oh." The sudden pain that pierced her chest was so sharp she was unable to breathe for a moment. She closed her eyes, feeling beads of perspiration break out on her forehead as she tried to swallow.

"Erin? Are you all right?"

She opened her eyes and forced a smile. "Of course. I think it's just all the excitement. It made me a little dizzy there for a second."

"You're entitled. It's a very exciting day."

"Yes it is, isn't it? Well, I'd better let you run along," she said brightly. "You should never keep a lady waiting. See you at the awards, Garth."

"Right. See you then."

Erin kept the smile on her face as she watched him walk away, telling herself it would be absolutely ridiculous of her to cry. How could she possibly cry when everything she'd dreamed of and worked so hard for was finally coming true? This is the happiest day of my life, she told herself fiercely. The very happiest day of my entire life.

Twenty-one

Street Scene swept the Academy Awards, winning Oscars in every single category for which it had been nominated, and Erin became famous overnight. Not only was she the only woman producer to ever achieve such honors, she was young, beautiful, and a highly controversial figure in the Hollywood film industry. The press fell on her with cries of delight, and she was courted, catered to, and eulogized. Her photograph made the cover of both *Time* and *Newsweek*, and her phone rang constantly. Literary agents, including some of the biggest and most powerful in the business, called to offer books and scripts. Theatrical agents, who controlled an impressive stable of stars, begged for a moment of her time to discuss future projects. And, the sweetest triumph of all, major executives from three of Hollywood's top studios made overtures to discuss a possible deal on her next picture. She basked happily in the glory for a full month. Then on a warm, sunny May day while she was sipping a glass of wine on the patio of an exclusive Beverly Hills restaurant and smiling across the table at the eager reporter leaning toward her, she felt the first grip of pressure.

"So, Miss Connolly, the big question for all of us is what you're going to do now. Rumors are flying all over the place about the next picture you're going to produce, but you still haven't given us any definite word."

He smiled engagingly. "And I don't have to tell you how important that word is. You've got options on some of the biggest properties around, and everyone is waiting breathlessly to see which one you choose. Because you made a commitment when you won those Oscars; a commitment to excellence, and another Academy Award for Con-Well Productions next year. No producer in the history of this industry has ever had the courage to make that kind of commitment, and I don't need to tell you what kind of excitement that's generating in this town. Everyone, and I do mean everyone, is watching and waiting."

"Well, I can't believe I ever put it in such egotistical terms as that," she said with a nervous laugh. "Every producer is committed to excellence, and I think I was talking about all of us if I did say anything like that. So we'll just have to wait and see what next year brings."

"Come on, Miss Connolly, surely you don't expect me to believe that. You know as well as I do that this next film is crucial, because now that you've been proclaimed the best, you can't get away with just producing good pictures. You've got to top your own performance, and everybody in this town will be gunning for you."

"That miserable little creep!" Erin stormed later that night as she and Derek sat on the couch in the living room of his beach house, having their usual evening cocktails while they waited for dinner to be prepared. "First he comes out with this preposterous statement that I've challenged the entire film industry to a new standard of excellence, and actually has the nerve to claim he's quoting me, and then he finishes up by telling me if I don't have another Oscar next year, I'll be washed up in this town."

"Welcome to fame, baby," Derek grinned. "Ain't it fun?"

"No. It isn't fun at all. I've won my Oscar, I've established myself, and now all I want is to be left alone to make more pictures."

"What? Is this the same Erin Connolly who's been spreading

herself around like a smorgasbord for the press that I hear talking now?" he inquired with a mocking gleam in his eyes.

"That's a pretty lousy remark, Derek, especially considering that you've been spreading yourself around as a smorgasbord for considerably more than the press." Her eyes surveyed the living room. "But perhaps I should thank you for cleaning up before I get home. Or is there a surprise waiting for me in a bedroom or bath somewhere?"

"Hey, take it easy." He took the glass out of her hand, got up and walked over to the bar to refill it, then leaned against the counter and gazed at her curiously. "I didn't know that bothered you. You've never mentioned it before."

"You mean the girls you run in and out of here every day? No, that doesn't bother me, Derek," she said coldly. "True love was hardly one of the conditions we had when I moved in with you."

"Then what is bugging you?" he asked, genuinely puzzled.

"That the little prick might be right," she muttered, reaching for a cigarette. "I've read so many books and scripts, I'm going blind. I don't know what to choose for the next picture. I don't know what's the right one. Do you?"

"Jesus, Erin, don't ask me. I can't make that kind of decision."

"But you've read the material I've given you, haven't you?"

"Uh, sort of." He shrugged uncomfortably. "Actually, I let my agent do it. I mean, he's more into that scene."

"Oh my God, I don't believe this! You took all those scripts I gave you and handed them over to Barney Lipsky?"

"Well what the hell did you expect me to do?" he said defensively. "After all, he's the one who knows what works best for me."

"Really? What about the fact that he wanted you to turn down *Street Scene*? What about the fact that he could have lost you the Oscar?"

"That was different. I had Garth's guarantee on the picture."

"*Garth's* guarantee?" she said furiously. "What about *mine*? *I* was the one who bought that property, in case you've forgotten."

He turned away, refusing to meet her eyes, and she sighed.

"All right, Derek, maybe you have a point. I know how important the director is to an actor. So what if I go to Garth with these properties? Let him read them and make the decision?"

"You can't."

"Of course I can. We may not be lovers anymore, but we're still professionals. We can work together. As a matter of fact," she said with sudden enthusiasm, "I don't know why I didn't think of doing this sooner. We'll get hold of Paul Marriott and all the rest of the crew that worked on *Street Scene*. We'll bring the whole winning team back together again, and we'll produce our second Academy Award picture. How does that sound to you?" she asked him, her eyes sparkling with excitement.

He shook his head. "You're too late, Erin. Garth is going into production on his own picture at the end of this month."

"*What?*" She stared at him in shock. "But . . . but he never even mentioned it to me. He never said a word! How could he do a thing like that?"

"Well, Erin, I hardly think he felt he needed your permission," Derek said dryly. "And as far as the Academy Awards go, I think he's planning to win them on his own next year without your help."

"With you? He signed you?"

"No. Not that I wouldn't have signed if he'd asked me. He's the greatest director I've ever worked with. But the part just isn't right for me. I could see that when he explained it to me."

"You went to him without telling me? Knowing what I'm going through?"

"Jesus Christ, Erin, what is all this shit?" he said irritably. "We live together, but that doesn't mean you own my career. And if you think it does, then maybe you'd better move out right now."

There was no question but that he meant it, Erin realized as she looked at him. And with the realization came panic. He was her ace in the hole for her next picture. She *had* to have him and his incredible box-office magic. And up until this moment it had never occurred to her that she'd have any problems getting him. Because despite the constant parade of young girls he brought into the house while she was away, she knew how dependent he was on her, how important she was to him. The casual sexual encounters were nothing more than ego gratification, a way of proving to himself that he was wanted, desired, a star. Invariably he was always hungriest for her on the days of those sexual encounters; making love to her fiercely and demanding that she tell him how much he pleased her. She also knew why she was so important to him. He saw her as someone superior to himself, and he desperately needed the reassurance that a superior being could want him. But now she saw by the way he was looking at her that she'd lost that superior status, which meant she could lose him. And that couldn't be allowed to happen.

"Darling, I think you missed my point," she said lightly, taking a sip of her drink. "Of course I don't think I own your career. What I was saying was just the opposite. No one but you owns your career, and no one else should try to. Not Garth, and certainly not Barney Lipsky! You're much too major a talent for that.

"By the way," she added idly as she lit a cigarette, "what was the role Garth turned you down for?"

"He didn't turn me down," Derek scowled. "He just said it wasn't right for me."

"But what was it?"

"Andrews. In *The Olympic Connection*."

"He turned you down for *that*? Good God, Derek, you would have been magnificent!"

"He said I was too young. And I think he was right," Derek said defiantly. "After all, the guy's over forty."

"Forty is too old for you to play? Derek, did you ever see James Dean in *Giant*? He was only twenty-four years old when he appeared in that, and the character he played aged over fifty years during the course of the picture."

"Yeah, well, I'm not gonna be any new James Dean in Garth's picture," he said morosely. "Because I'm not gonna be in it."

"Frankly, I think that's Garth's loss," she told him crisply. "Don't feel badly about it, darling. I've learned these things work out for the best. It simply wasn't meant for you to play that part because somewhere there's another picture, a much more exciting picture, that's going to be offered to you."

"You really think so?"

"I don't think so, I know so. And that's something you can count on. Because I'm Irish, and we have special gifts for seeing into the future."

"I sure hope you're right," he sighed, hunching over and staring into his drink. "Because I get a little crazy between pictures. Like, I don't know what to do with myself."

"It won't be much longer now."

"But what if a picture comes along that I feel is right and it isn't *your* picture?" he challenged. "Say it comes to my agent from some other producer and I want to sign. Are you going to hassle me about it?"

"Derek," she said leaning forward to caress him. "I am never going to hassle you. All I want is the best for you, and I'll back you in any decision you make."

"Jesus, I almost believe you," he whispered as she gently stroked him.

"I'll forget you said almost, darling. And now why don't we forget the whole subject for a while and concentrate on something more immediately rewarding?"

Rosa, the short, plump Mexican maid who had entered the living room to announce that dinner was ready, pursed her lips in disapproval at the scene in front of her. Erin and Derek were sitting on the floor giggling while they dipped tiny gold spoons into the crystal bowl of cocaine that rested between them. She hesitated for a moment, wondering whether to interrupt them or not. When Derek unzipped his fly and moved on top of Erin, she turned around and fled from the room.

Erin picked up the clock on the nightstand and gave a despairing sigh as she saw the illuminated hands pointing to four o'clock. Derek was sound asleep beside her, lying on his back and snoring gently as he had been for the past five hours while she'd tossed and turned restlessly. Unlike her first experience with cocaine, this one had left her tense and almost suicidally depressed when she came down. There was a tight band of pain around her head, and her neck ached unbearably no matter what kind of position she tried. She massaged it distractedly while her mind continued to plague her remorselessly with its dismal litany. You've got to find a picture soon, Erin, it repeated monotonously. If you don't find a picture, you'll lose Derek to another producer. If you don't find a picture, Garth will beat you out for the Oscar. If you don't find a picture, you'll be a nobody in this town again.

"I've got to get some sleep," she whispered frantically. "If I don't get some sleep, I'll go out of my mind!" She reached over and took one of the chocolate-colored marijuana cigarettes from the small box on the table next to her. The pungent, acrid smoke burned her throat as she lit it and inhaled, and she almost gagged. Angrily, she mashed it out in the ashtray and then got out of bed, making her way uncertainly to the bathroom through the dark of the bedroom.

She flicked the switch and the bright overhead light went on, and she peered hesitantly into the recessed mirrored cabinet above the handsome onyx washbasin. The shelves were crowded with bottles of pills. She took them out one by one, carefully examining their labels.

When she found the one filled with fat red-and-yellow striped capsules that stated TAKE FOR SLEEP AS NEEDED, she gave a moan of relief, uncapped it quickly and swallowed two of the pills. And, although she knew it made no sense, it seemed to her that her body was beginning to relax already. Turning off the light, she tiptoed quietly back to the bedroom and slid into bed. There was a brief moment when she felt suddenly warm and slightly dizzy. Then she didn't feel anything at all.

"Hey! Hey, say something! Do something!"

Erin opened her eyes with effort and gazed blankly at Derek, who was shaking her vigorously. "What?" she muttered thickly.

"Jesus, Erin, what's wrong with you?" he asked anxiously. "Are you okay?"

"I think so." She shook her head, trying to clear it. "I took some of your sleeping pills last night, and they really knocked me out."

"How many?" he asked, a note of concern in his voice.

"Oh, just two." She smiled ruefully. "But if I'd known how strong they are, I would have made it one. God, I really feel wiped out. How long before they wear off?"

"What time did you take them?"

"A little after four."

"Well, baby, you might as well go back to bed. Because those little mothers are going to stay with you for at least another four hours."

"Another four hours?" she exclaimed in horror as she looked at her watch. "But I've got a meeting in less than two hours."

"Better cancel it," he advised her. "You won't be in any shape for it."

"I can't! It's very important." She sat up and started to get out of the bed, then had to grab at the headboard for support as a wave of dizziness swept over her.

"Goddamn!" she swore. "Derek, be an angel and buzz Rosa for me. Have her bring a hot pot of coffee in here while I shower."

"You're gonna need more than that." he laughed as he observed her. "Believe me. If that meeting of yours is really important, I'd better get you an upper."

"Another pill? Oh no, Derek," she announced firmly. "I've had it with pills!"

"Suit yourself, but I'm telling you, it's the only thing that will help."

"How?"

"The best way possible. It'll take the sleeping pills right out of your system. You'll feel absolutely great, on top of the world."

"I don't know." She hesitated. "I mean, isn't it dangerous?"

"Dangerous? Hell no, baby, it's perfectly natural, as long as you don't overdo it," he assured her. "Like, you know what happens to your body if you feed it too much food one day then the next day you go out and run two miles. What you do is burn off the extra calories. Well, it's the same principle here. The uppers work with your body to burn off the effects of the sleeping pills. Simple as that."

Erin didn't believe for one moment that it was as simple as that, but she knew she had to make the meeting this morning.

Besides, Derek had a definite point when he said there was no danger as long as you didn't overdo it. One time couldn't possibly hurt her. Look at him. He'd been using these drugs for years, and he was in incredible condition.

"All right. I'll try your wonder cure."

"You'll thank me." He grinned as he padded out to the bathroom and then returned with the pill and a glass of water. And thirty minutes later she couldn't thank him enough. The headache, nausea, and dizziness had completely disappeared. Her mind had never been sharper or clearer, her body was in perfect control, and she had never felt better in her whole life. Energy and confidence surged through her as she looked at him across the breakfast table.

"I should never have doubted you, darling," she said gratefully. "You've known what's best for me from the minute we met. And you've never let me down."

She smiled warmly at him. "I'm never going to let you down, either. Somehow, I just know that when I get home tonight I'm going to have that perfect picture for you. It's going to be waiting on my desk when I go in this morning."

It wasn't waiting on the desk, it came in on a telephone call from Joel Wiseman. "Are you ready for this?" he shouted ecstatically into the receiver. "The only novel that won both the Pulitzer Prize and the National Book Awards, and I'm giving you first chance at the screen rights to it."

It was like an answer to her prayers, and she barely restrained herself from letting out a cry of delight. "I don't know, Joel," she said slowly. "It sounds interesting, but I've practically committed myself to another project, and I don't think I want to take on a second one at the same time."

"Sweetheart, you owe it to yourself to look at this before you make *any* commitment. Because I am talking quality here. I am talking prestige here. I am talking Oscar potential! Now have lunch with me today. And I won't take no for an answer."

"Joel, you literary agents are bigger hucksters than all of Hollywood put together," she laughed.

"So where do you want to eat?"

"The Bistro? At one?"

"You've got it, sweetheart. Ciao."

She was still laughing as she hung up, then a slight frown crossed her face as she realized he hadn't told her what the book was. She punched down the intercom button on her phone and buzzed her secretary.

"Nancy, what novel won both the Pulitzer Prize and the National Book Award this year?"

"I haven't the foggiest," Nancy admitted cheerfully. "But give me a few minutes and I'll find out."

Fifteen minutes later Nancy walked into her office. "The book is called *Body Count* and boy is it controversial!" she exclaimed. "Eight publishers turned it down flat before the author found someone who was willing to go with it. And even then they only printed a minimum number of copies. The critics had to ferret it out on their own. By the way, in case you're interested, the guy who wrote it was coming straight from where it happened. He was a Marine lieutenant in Vietnam, and he had to take over a squad or platoon or whatever the hell they call them when the captain in charge of the outfit was killed. By his own men."

"Are you serious?" Erin said incredulously.

Nancy shrugged and gave her an apologetic smile. "Hey, don't blame me. I just do research here."

"But why haven't I ever heard about it? I mean, something that explosive should have been on all the bestseller lists."

"It never made the bestseller lists, Erin. The *L. A. Times* book editor I talked to said that people in this country just weren't ready for unpleasant facts about Vietnam. In fact, they didn't want to read *anything* about Vietnam. The whole subject was still just too close for comfort, and they wanted to forget about it. He said the book is unfortunately a case of being ahead of its time."

Nancy looked at her uncertainly. "Are you considering this as a property?"

"I don't know right now. I really don't know."

"This book was a loser right from the moment the author started it," Erin stated coldly as she looked across the table at

Joel Wiseman. "So what the hell are you trying to pull by peddling this thing to me?"

"Nothing that wins the Pulitzer and the National Book Award is ever a loser," he replied with equal coldness. "My mistake was in not realizing that you're a coward just like most of the other Hollywood producers."

He signaled briskly to a waiter as he drained his drink. "So order, and we'll call it quits. You get a nice lunch, and I learn a lesson."

"That's the first intelligent recommendation you've made all day. I'll have the filet of sole, and please ask them to bring it as quickly as possible, because I have a great deal of *important* matters awaiting me back at the office."

"Two filet of sole," he said glumly to the waiter who came up to their table at that moment. "And we'd like them served right away. The lady's in a hurry."

The waiter nodded understandingly and was back with their orders in less than ten minutes. They ate silently; then Joel gave an unhappy sigh.

"It's really a goddamn shame." He absently pushed the uneaten portion of his fish around on the plate. "Derek Marston is absolutely perfect for the part of the lieutenant. With that raw, primal energy of his, he'd *make* the picture. The author wants him for the part in the worst way. That's why he asked me to come to you."

Joel sighed again before looking up at her. "I suppose you have him under contract?"

She glanced at him sharply, the unwelcome feeling of panic stabbing at her once again. But it was obvious from the expression on his face that he wasn't testing her. He clearly believed she had Derek locked up.

"Joel, is that a serious question?"

"No, not really," he admitted ruefully. "There's no way you'd let him out of your clutches after the performance he gave in *Street Scene*. Everybody knows that."

"Well I don't think having him in my clutches is quite the way I'd put it. But if you mean has he signed with Con-Well Productions for his next picture, the answer, naturally, is yes."

He lifted an eyebrow and regarded her with a knowing grin,

and she blushed with embarrassment as she realized it was apparently common knowledge she and Derek were living together. Flustered, she gathered her purse and pushed back her chair.

"Joel, would you forgive me if I leave you to settle the check? I really do have the most frantic schedule ahead of me this afternoon."

"If you'll do me one favor."

Halfway out of the chair, she paused for a moment and looked at him in surprise. "Favor?"

"Read the book." He reached into his briefcase and pulled out a copy of the novel, holding it out to her. "Erin, just do this one thing for me."

"But, Joel, I don't see any point to it. I've already explained to you why Con-Well Productions isn't going to option it. The material is simply too controversial. My reading it isn't going to change my mind at all. In fact if the book is anything like what I've heard, it will just confirm my decision."

"I'll take my chances." He leaned forward quickly, laying the book on the table and taking hold of her hands. "*Please*, Erin," he said imploringly. "Just read it. That's all I'm asking."

He released her hands then and gazed at her. "Surely that isn't too much to ask, is it? A few hours of your time? They could be the most important hours you've ever spent."

Uncomfortable with the naked intensity in his eyes, she nodded. "All right, Joel. I'll read it."

"Thank you. And I promise you, you won't regret it."

Erin was quite sure she wouldn't regret it, because she hadn't the slightest intention of reading the book. She took it from the agent dutifully and then tossed it on the front seat of her car. As she drove away from the restaurant and back to her office, she felt a headache developing as she thought of the pile of scripts waiting for her there. God, let there be one winner among them.

There weren't any. At least none that she could see. She sent Nancy out for coffee and then burrowed back into the pile. As she opened her third pack of cigarettes of the day, it seemed to her that every script she picked up got progressively worse. And she was feeling progressively worse right along with them. The exhilarating effects of the pill Derek had given her that morning had worn off several hours earlier, and she was now so exhausted it was an effort to focus her eyes on the pages in front of her. "Oh shit!" she finally exclaimed in disgust. "You don't even know what you're reading anymore. Give it up for the day."

"I've had it, Nancy," she announced as she walked into the reception area. "If anything important comes up, you can reach me at home."

"Bad day, huh?" Nancy said sympathetically.

"There may have been worse, but I can't remember them at the moment."

"Tomorrow will be better," Nancy smiled. "It's in our horoscope."

"Well, let's hope the horoscope is right." She managed a weary smile in return, then gave Nancy a brief wave and left the office.

It was still fairly early when Erin drove through the tunnel at the end of the Santa Monica Freeway and headed north up Pacific Coast Highway to the beach house. The sun sparkled off the ocean, the air was warm and balmy, and she felt her spirits reviving. Maybe Nancy's right, she thought, and tomorrow will be better. In the meantime, I think I'll treat myself to a nice lazy afternoon by the pool.

As she pulled into the long circular driveway, turned off the motor, and started to get out of the car, her eyes fell on the book lying on the seat beside her. She hesitated for a moment, then shrugged philosophically and picked it up. Since she had the rest of the afternoon free, she might as well give it a look. It wouldn't take her very long to skim through it, and then she could report back to Joel tomorrow and get him off her back.

But to Erin's surprise, she found she couldn't just skim through it. The writing was intense, compelling, forcing her to read it in depth. It was also haunting and deeply disturbing. She shook her head as she came to the part where the Marine captain is executed by his own men. Her initial reaction had been right. The subject matter was simply too controversial for a movie in this day and age. A shame, though. God, what a powerful film it would make. And Joel was right. Derek would be outstanding as the young lieutenant. Sighing, she laid it down on the chaise, stretched out, and let the last warm rays of the sun caress her as she drifted off to sleep.

"Hey! Hey, Irish!"

She sat up with a shock of surprise as the exuberant voice boomed in her ear, and stared in confusion at Derek who was leaning over her, grinning from ear to ear.

"What?" she said bewilderedly. "What did you say?"

"Irish." He picked her up and hugged her so hard, she had trouble breathing. "Don't you remember? You told me this would be my day! The day I found my picture. Because you're Irish, and you can see into the future. Well, you were right, baby, because I did find it. I went into Barney's office today and he handed it to me. And it's perfect! Just like you told me it would be. Isn't that great?" he crowed as he set her back down on her feet.

"You signed a picture contract today?" The color drained from her face as she looked at him. "No, you couldn't have!"

The delighted joy on his face abruptly faded. "Goddamnit, Erin! I came home to celebrate, not to get hassled. You told me you wouldn't hassle me."

"I'm not hassling you," she said faintly. "It . . . it's just a little unexpected, that's all."

"What do you mean, unexpected?" He glared at her. "Didn't you tell me it would happen today?"

"Yes, I certainly did." She walked back to the chaise and picked up the book. "The only thing I didn't expect was that you'd get two pictures in one day." She held out the book to him. "This is your next Oscar, Derek. Did Barney guarantee you an Oscar too?"

"Listen, Erin, I'm in no mood to be conned. So what the fuck is this thing you're handing me?"

"To tell you the truth, I'm not sure," she said quietly. "I just think you should read it."

"You're not sure? Then why the hell should I bother?"

"Because I'm Irish," she told him with an oblique smile. She laid the book down on the table next to the chaise, picked up her beach towel, and walked off the patio.

He stared after her as she disappeared into the house; then, with a grudging curiosity, he reached out for the book and flipped it open to the first page.

When Erin reappeared on the patio an hour later after bathing and dressing, she found Derek stretched out on the chaise, a frown of concentration on his face as he slowly turned the pages of the book.

"Do you want a drink, darling?"

"Yeah," he muttered without looking up. "Bring it out here."

She mixed the drinks herself and carried them out, setting the two glasses down on the table next to him as she curled up in the lounge chair opposite. "Gin and tonic okay?" she asked.

"Sure," he said absently. He reached out for the glass, took a brief gulp, and returned to his reading.

He was still reading when Rosa came out to the patio forty minutes later to announce dinner, and he carried the book with him into the dining room. The plump Mexican maid gazed uncertainly at Erin.

"It's all right, Rosa," Erin assured her. "Just serve the meal."

Derek read steadily through dinner, grunted irritably when Rosa tried to clear his plate away, then pushed back his chair and stood up, still holding the book. "Bring my coffee to the study," he ordered.

At midnight Erin gave up her vigil, as Derek continued reading, and wearily made her way into the bedroom. She fell asleep almost immediately. Then she groaned in protest as a bright light blazed in her face and she found Derek leaning over her, shaking her.

"For God's sake, Derek, what are you doing?"

"You were right, Erin!" he announced feverishly. "This *is* my picture. It's absolutely dynamite! I want it. I want it more than I wanted *Street Scene*. I want it more than I ever wanted anything in my whole life!"

She was fully awake now as she looked at his flushed,

excited face. "I thought you'd feel that way. But what about the contract you signed today?"

"Oh that's no problem," he shrugged. "I just finished talking to Barney and told him to get me out of it."

"You woke Barney Lipsky in the middle of the night to tell him you're breaking the picture deal he just finished making for you?" Erin let out a peal of laughter. "My, how I would have loved hearing his reaction to that."

"He wasn't exactly delighted."

"I'll just bet he wasn't. Well, darling, you've made my day with that little tidbit of news. Now let's get some sleep."

But as Derek turned off the light and climbed into bed next to her, Erin's feeling of glee about Barney was replaced by a sudden cold shiver of apprehension; and she found herself wondering if she had paid too high a price to keep her box-office star.

Erin's apprehension turned into grim reality as work began on *Body Count*, for the production was plagued by major problems from the outset. Joel Wiseman explained that one of the conditions the author insisted on, in selling the property to Con-Well Productions, was that he would get to write the screenplay. Erin agreed readily, because both her first picture and her Oscar-winning picture had come from screenplays written by the authors of the original books. And since both of those screenplays had been excellent, she naively assumed that good novelists automatically make good screenwriters. When she saw the first draft of the script for *Body Count*, she found out how wrong that assumption was.

"It's a disaster, Joel!" she'd moaned over the phone. "It's so bad, I can't believe it came from the same man who wrote the book. We can't *possibly* go with this!"

"Now calm down, Erin. I'm sure you're exaggerating. Besides, remember our deal."

"Have you read this?"

"Yes."

"And you have the nerve to remind me about our deal after

seeing this piece of crap? Have you gone completely bananas?"

"Look, Erin, the man is a novelist. A highly talented novelist. There's no one writing today who can equal his power in rich narrative interior scenes, evocative descriptions, and character delineation."

"Then let him go write another novel," she'd said furiously. "And let me get somebody who knows a few simple things like dialogue and camera action!"

"Sweetheart, I think you're blowing this whole thing out of proportion," he'd said soothingly. "Of course you can go out and get someone who knows those technical things. I would *expect* you to. After all, this is just a first draft. So please feel free to turn it over to one of your professional craftsmen for polishing."

"Professional craftsmen? And what about the screen credits for this particular professional craftsman you're referring to so casually? What exactly does he get out of this?"

"Well." A nervous cough had followed. "Equal credits?"

"He does all the work and then has to share the credits? You're crazy, Joel. No first-class screenwriter would touch it on that basis."

"He'll have to," Joel had replied unhappily. "Because my man wants those screen credits. Without them, there's no deal."

It took Erin two months to find a screenwriter who would agree to those terms. The top writers turned her down flat, as she'd expected, and it was unthinkable to hire a second-rate hack for such an important and complex film. Finally she found a competent professional who was having severe financial difficulties at the moment and agreed to do it if she would pay him double the going rate. Another three months passed before he completed the revisions, because the author of the book had become totally paranoid at the thought of having another writer work on his script and insisted on going over every word the exhausted screenwriter wrote with a fine-tooth comb. By this time, production on *Body Count* was five months behind schedule and not a single foot of film had been shot. Then the real problems started.

Erin had hoped that with this picture she would be freed at
last from the onerous responsibilities of financing and distribution and could concentrate solely on producing. But the major
studios who had made overtures to her earlier were frankly
appalled by the property and backed away from it in horror,
warning her with much head shaking that she was crazy to even
consider making such a film. "There are much easier ways to
commit suicide," one told her dryly. Their reactions, although
they depressed her somewhat, didn't surprise her; and she
glumly prepared to take on the whole burden once again. What
did surprise her, and seriously depress her, was the reaction of
Con-Well Productions' comptroller.

"That's ridiculous, Max!" she'd snapped. "We grossed over
thirty million on *Street Scene*. So how can you possibly tell me
I'm in trouble if I finance this picture?"

"Look at the figures," he'd said gloomily. "You had to pay
Garth Werner twenty-five percent of the profits for his share in
Street Scene. You had to pay off the loan to the backers, and
you know the interest rate Arnold Scorsi wrote into that
contract. Then you had the payment to Anthony Wellington on
his note. After subtracting all that, plus expenses and taxes,
you've got less than five million left."

"Well come on, Max," she'd smiled. "Five million is hardly
peanuts."

"The way you're going, it'll be peanuts any day now," he'd
said sadly. "You're over budget on script. You're over budget
on casting. And you still have location shooting ahead of you.
That's going to cost a fortune." '

"Then we'll just tighten our belts."

"You'd better, Miss Connolly." He'd frowned, absently
pushing up the glasses which had slid down his nose. "Or
you're going to run out of money before this picture is
finished."

She hadn't counted on being so much over budget on
casting. Derek had wanted the picture badly enough to waive
his usual million-dollar fee, just as he'd done on *Street Scene*.
Unfortunately, the other actors hadn't waived their fees at all.
In fact, they'd increased them. Con-Well Productions had just
turned out an Academy Award winner, and all the actors'

agents had demanded top dollar for their stars on that basis. It wasn't something that Erin could negotiate. She desperately needed the draw of top actors for this highly controversial film, and so she had to pay what they demanded. But as their contracts rose in price, Derek's had to rise also. Because his ego demanded that he make a minimum of fifty percent more than anyone else. He was, after all, the consummate star. So casting costs, which had originally been figured at two million, rose to three million. Erin just swallowed hard and paid them. Then came the problem with the director.

Anson Konrad was a dark, saturnine man who never smiled. In fact, his usual expression was a ferocious glower. But he was generally acknowledged as one of the few directors in Hollywood who deserved the title of genius. Erin paid a small fortune to get him, and then her investment went up in smoke the second week of filming.

"If he does not do as I say this time, I leave!" Anson hissed as she came on the set.

"If you keep this cocksucker on the set one more minute, *I* leave!" Derek yelled.

"Please, can't we just sit down and talk about this?" Erin begged.

"No!" they shouted in unison.

She looked at the director first, then at Derek. There was no doubt about the rage in his eyes. It wasn't at all like his occasional fury with Garth. He clearly hated and distrusted this director.

"I'm really sorry, Mr. Konrad," she sighed. "But Derek stays."

"Your problem, Miss Connolly," he said icily as he stalked off the set.

"Oh shit, Derek, what do we do now?"

"You got nothin' to worry about, baby," he said confidently. "I know a really first-class director. A guy who can bring this whole thing together. I'll have him come over tonight and talk with us." He smiled then and gave her a hug. "You're first class too, baby. You stood up for me when it was important. I won't forget that."

Erin was less than enthusiastic about the director who

showed up at the beach house that night. "All he did was agree with everything you said," she said as they got into bed. "Goddamnit, Derek, you need direction, and I can't see that man offering any!"

"Did it ever occur to you he agreed with me because I was right?" Derek retorted angrily. "Or have you forgotten how closely I worked with Garth on *Street Scene*? I learned a hell of a lot on that picture, and Garth himself told me I had the makings of a fine director."

"Oh, darling, I'm not questioning your ability for a moment. You're not only enormously talented, you have a sixth sense about what makes a scene work that's really extraordinary. And no one is more aware of that than I. It's just that the role you're playing in this picture is so demanding, I worry about you taking on any additional responsibilities. You should be free to concentrate totally on it."

Mollified by her words, he smiled and patted her hair. "Your problem is you worry too much. Believe me, I can handle it. Now let's do a little coke and relax. And you'll see that everything is going to work out just fine."

But Erin saw with increasing despair that everything was not working out fine. In fact, it wasn't working at all. Derek assumed more control over the set every day, to the detriment not only of his role but the picture as a whole. He was blowing up his part to ridiculous proportions, invalidating the integrity of the character he played and reducing the rest of the cast to one-dimensional figures. The director meekly went along with him. She tried on numerous occasions to point out what was happening, but he became instantly hostile at the mere suggestion of criticism. Finally she was forced to admit the unhappy truth that she couldn't control him. He would either do it his way or quit. Garth would have been able to whip him into line in one day, but there was no Garth on the set. It was extremely painful to her to realize how little real power she had. Of course she could hire and fire, but that was meaningless compared to the power of creating a successful picture. Only a strong director could do that, and although she was strong in many ways, she wasn't a director.

As the weeks and months went on, she worried more and

more. Costs went up and the money supply from Con-Well Productions shrank, with Max nagging at her constantly. The trades were filled with stories about problems on the set. Two major actors had quit when Derek slashed their parts. The distributor was making ominous noises about theater chains that didn't want to show the film after hearing what it was about. She found herself drinking too much, smoking too much, and jumping at sudden noises. It was a problem trying to sleep. When she finally dozed off, terrible nightmares would bring her awake with a start, trembling and drenched in perspiration.

She began taking barbiturates so she could sleep through the night. Then she started taking amphetamines to get her going the next day. The only real pleasure in her desperate, fevered existence came when she allowed herself a little coke, and soon she could hardly wait to get home and indulge herself in that blissfully peaceful high. She had begun avoiding looking at herself in the mirror, because the face that looked back at her was so ugly with its puffiness and dark bruise marks under the eyes. She attributed her ravaged appearance to exhaustion and the frantic pressures of the job. It never occurred to her that her appearance was caused by the drugs she had unwittingly become so dependent upon.

"Erin, you look like shit!" Derek announced the night before they were due to leave for location shooting. "I don't think you'll make it down there."

"Darling, we all look like shit by this time." She laughed as she scooped up the fine white powder and inhaled it appreciatively. Then she lay back on the bed and smiled up at him. "Thank God for such nice shit."

"Hey, baby, I don't think you're hearing me," he frowned. "You're really in terrible shape. I think you should stay here."

"What? And miss the most important part of the film? Not a chance, Derek. This producer is going all the way with her picture."

He shook his head. "Erin, forget it. Mexico is really tough about dope. You can't take a chance by going down there."

"Dope?" She struggled to sit up and groped for a cigarette.

"What the hell are you talking about, Derek? We're not talking about dope. We're talking about my picture."

"You're hooked, baby," he said unhappily. "So why don't you just admit it? You can't do us any good down there."

"Hooked? What kind of nonsense is that? You know perfectly well that cocaine isn't addictive. Besides, you take it all the time."

"Not like you do, baby, I can take it or leave it. You can't get along without it."

"That's not true," she whispered, white-faced. "That's not *true*, Derek!"

"Then prove it to me. Stop."

She tried. She tried very hard. She lasted all of two weeks. They were shooting the final scenes of the picture on the Yucatan peninsula in the southern part of Mexico, where the tropical jungles and marshes offered a close approximation of the Vietnam geography. At the end of the first week on location, over half the cast and crew had come down with dysentery. Erin was far and away the hardest hit. The local doctors, seriously concerned about her extreme dehydration and generally weakened condition, insisted she return to California for treatment. She spent three days in Cedars-Sinai Hospital and was released only on condition that she stay in the Los Angeles area for a ten-day convalescence period.

She went crazy pacing around the empty beach house, worrying about what was happening to her picture. It was almost impossible to get phone calls through to the location site, and when she did the news was invariably bad. More cast and crew members had come down sick. Equipment broke down and replacements had to be flown in from California, causing crucial delays in shooting. Worst of all, neither Derek nor the director ever returned her frantic calls, and she found herself reduced to screaming over the phone to some minor assistant.

After three of those frustrating sessions, she turned in desperation to the soothing comforts of the fine white powder. It helped. In fact it helped so much she wondered why she'd waited so long. With renewed confidence, then, she announced to the doctors at Cedars-Sinai that she was cured and was going back to her picture. They tested her and reluctantly agreed. The virulent bug was gone. But they warned her it could attack her again with even more serious consequences if she went back. She laughed them off. "This time I'll be tougher."

She returned to the location shooting without the bug, but she carried something almost as virulent with her. Her personal doctor, the one who supplied her with cocaine, had understood her needs and provided her with a clever disguise for carrying the white powder into Mexico. It was concealed in capsules that he placed in prescription bottles, whose labels stated they contained medication for her dysentery. As it turned out, the effort wasn't really necessary. The Mexican custom officials, after inspecting her special visa, passed her through without any checks, smiling and apologizing for the inconvenience their country had caused her and wishing her better health.

The white powder was the only thing that kept her going in the next few months, because there was nothing but disaster on the set. An unexpected rain of monsoon proportions closed down shooting for four weeks. When it finally let up, the sick and despondent crew members and cast who'd remained on the set had no energy for anything. Neither the director's pleading nor Derek's raging could force them into giving viable performances. Foot after foot of film was scrapped as scenes had to be reshot.

The picture was now more than a year behind schedule, and it had long ago missed the deadline for the next Academy Awards nominations. Erin found some small comfort in knowing that Garth's picture was suffering similar problems. He'd been on location for six months, and it was reported that he had at least one more month of shooting ahead before filming would be complete. So at least he wouldn't be one up on her. They'd be competing at the same time—both a year late—for the Oscar.

But as it turned out, Erin was denied even that small comfort. Her picture, which had opened to mixed reviews and bombed at the box office, didn't get a single Academy Award nomination. Garth's got eight. She hung up the phone in her Century City office after the call came through and stared at the people who were sitting in front of her, gazing tensely up at her.

"We didn't make it," she said bleakly. "We got nothing."

Derek let out an anguished scream and ran out of the office. The rest of the people continued to sit there and look at her.

"Go home," she said harshly. "There's nothing here for you."

Derek didn't come back to the beach house that night or any of the following nights that week, but Erin was barely aware of his absense. Numb with grief and despair, she spent hours huddled on the couch in the living room, staring unseeingly out at the ocean, refusing Rosa's frightened pleas to eat something, rousing herself only when the room grew completely dark, to make her weary way to bed where the welcome oblivion of drugs awaited her.

On the fourth day of her self-imposed exile, she accepted the mail from Rosa and listlessly picked up *Daily Variety*. There was a feature story on the Cannes Film Festival. A picture she'd never heard of had swept the awards. She shrugged, started to glance away, then blinked in surprise as the familiar name registered.

"*Cyclorama*, written and directed by James Lee Norton and produced by James Lee Studios Ltd.," the article read, "has proved to be not only this year's biggest sleeper but one of Hollywood's most unsettling surprises. The brilliant but decidedly controversial James Lee has not been heard of in this town since he walked off an International Pictures set two years ago and instigated a lawsuit against that studio for infringement of civil rights, claiming that minorities were not only discriminated against but were threatened with blacklisting if they filed any complaints. The suit never reached the courts, and most Hollywood insiders agreed that James Lee had committed professional suicide. Several months later he moved to France, confirming that opinion. But he's certainly turned the tables now! He's kept his American citizenship, entered *Cyclorama* as a U.S. (read Hollywood) entry, won all the awards in sight, and is now being courted by every major film producer in Europe. By the way, he never withdrew that suit against International Pictures. So watch out, Hollywood!"

"Well, you finally made it," Erin murmured. "Hungry little Jimmy turns out to be a winner after all." She knew she should feel happy for him. She tried for a moment, but it was too much of an effort. The truth was she didn't care. No, that wasn't quite the truth. The truth was she hated him for succeeding when she was failing. Because she, Erin Connolly, was the one who should be winning. She was the one who had it all! The talent, the dedication, the drive. So why were all these losers from her past making it when she couldn't? Even that miserable excuse for a man she'd married, Anthony Wellington, was doing well. He'd moved back to New York and, infuriatingly, for once in his life had done something right. The first play he'd backed had turned out to be a smash box-office hit, he was now producing a new play, and there were rumors of romance between himself and the leading lady.

Forget it, she told herself tiredly. It doesn't matter. Nothing really matters anymore. She turned the cover page of the green and white tabloid, then froze in shock as the headline on the second page leaped up at her.

"DIRECTOR AND STAR OF *THE OLYMPIC CONNECTION*, NOMINATED FOR EIGHT ACADEMY AWARDS, PLAN JULY WEDDING." The print blurred as she began reading about Garth's upcoming marriage.

"Miss Connolly, there's a phone call for you." Rosa stopped abruptly in her tracks as she saw Erin's shoulders shaking, tears streaming down her cheeks. "I—I'm sorry, ma'am," she stammered. "I'll tell them you're busy."

"No." Erin looked up at her, wiping away the tears and forcing a smile. "No, Rosa. You don't have to tell them that. I've had my final piece of bad news, and nothing can be any worse. It's time to pull myself together and make a new start. I'll take the call."

It turned out to be the greatest mistake of Erin's life.

Twenty-two

"I DON'T care if she did it with three midgets while she was standing on her head!" Lynn Powers snapped with considerable irritation into the phone. "I'm not running a sleazy gossip column here. What movie stars do in the privacy of their homes is their private business. All I report on is their public business. Now if you can't understand that important distinction, I have a number of suggestions as to what you and your hot little tips can do. And my favorite is drop dead!"

She slammed down the phone without giving the stunned caller a chance to answer, then sighed as she saw every extension line on the panel light up.

"Hey, Sally, which one should I pick up now?" she asked as she walked into the adjoining office.

Sally was frowning fiercely over the small switchboard as she punched down buttons and talked into the receiver. She looked up with a startled expression. "What?"

"The next call," Lynn said patiently. "What's the most important?"

"Well, Andi Steiner's on three and she says she has something vitally important to talk to you about."

Lynn raised a skeptical eyebrow. "Andi Steiner? The woman at International Pictures? Sally, I think you're losing your touch. The day that a studio publicist has anything vitally important to say is the day I'll go into another business, because the flacks will have taken over this one. Now let's try again."

Sally, who'd been with Lynn ever since she left Randy Allen and started her own column, and who probably knew more about her famous and powerful employer than anyone else in the world, hesitated a moment before speaking.

"Andi's not calling to push studio product," she said finally. "Andi wants to talk to you about Erin Connolly."

"Oh." The sound of the word as Lynn uttered it was not unlike the surprised gasp of someone who has unexpectedly been hit in the stomach. She recovered quickly, her eyes narrowing in speculative interest. "In that case, Sally," she said softly, "I think you got your priorities right."

She turned around, walking quickly back into her office, and settled into the swivel chair before punching down line three and picking up the phone.

"Andi, how *are* you?" she exclaimed warmly. "I swear, I don't know where the time goes. It's been *ages* since we've talked. What are you people up to these days?"

"Did Sally tell you why I'm calling?" the tense voice asked.

"Why, no, I don't believe she did," Lynn replied innocently. "She just said you had something very important to relate. A new picture, darling? Is that it? Or are you about to confirm the rumors that you've stolen Frederick Landsman from Columbia?" she chuckled. "You do know I had that story first, don't you?"

"Actually, it's none of the above, as they say," Andi laughed nervously. "It's Erin Connolly I want to talk to you about."

"Erin Connolly?" Lynn said vaguely. "But whatever for, darling? She's washed up. Her last picture bombed terribly. Surely you people aren't considering bringing her into the studio as an independent producer? I mean, I wouldn't consider that a news story. More like a requiem mass, I'd say."

"Please, Miss Powers, don't play games with me," Andi implored her. "I want to destroy Erin Connolly, and I think you do too. Just let me come to your office and I'll tell you how we can do it."

"That's a very strange statement," Lynn announced coldly. "I assure you I have no interest in destroying anyone, much less Erin Connolly. She's accomplishing that quite well on her own. I think this phone call of yours was a big mistake. For your sake, I'll try to forget it."

"You owe it to your public to give them the facts," Andi pleaded. "Won't you at least let me come to you with those facts?"

"You're very determined, aren't you?" Lynn said curiously.

"Very determined," Andi answered grimly.

"Well, that in itself is rather interesting," Lynn said slowly. "All right, Andi Steiner, I'll see you in my office at two o'clock tomorrow. But please don't be late. It will be enough of a problem just finding time to fit you in."

"I won't be late, Miss Powers," Andi promised fervently. "And you won't be sorry you took the time, when you see what I have for you."

"This is your big story on Erin Connolly?" Lynn said incredulously. "That she takes drugs?"

"It's been enough to ruin a lot of people in this industry," Andi replied defensively.

"But you have no proof! You expect me to go with a column based on nothing but gossip? Hell, if I published blind items about suspected drug users in the movie industry, I'd be out of business in two weeks from libel suits alone."

Lynn leaned back in her swivel chair and stared thoughtfully at Andi. "What is it with you, anyway? Why do you want to bring her down?"

"It's a long story, and it happened a long time ago," Andi said bleakly. "Suffice it to say that I trusted her, I thought she was my best friend. Then she betrayed me and stole the one thing I wanted more than anything else in the world."

"I see," Lynn remarked quietly. She closed her eyes for a brief moment, remembering with pain how Erin Connolly had done exactly the same thing to her.

When she opened her eyes and looked at the unhappy

woman sitting in front of her, Lynn's expression was kind and gently pitying. "I'm very sorry, Andi. I know how much something like that can hurt. But I don't see any way I can help you. I just don't print unsubstantiated rumors."

"But what if they aren't unsubstantiated?" Andi's hands twisted nervously in her lap. "What if you got a sworn statement from the doctor who supplies her with cocaine?"

"Doctor?" Lynn asked sharply.

"Warren Felber. Surely you've heard the stories about him? That he supplies half of Hollywood with its drugs?"

"Yes, I've heard that," she frowned. "I've never wanted to believe it, though. Warren is an excellent doctor and a very nice human being. I went to him to have my nose done, as a matter of fact. Did you know that?"

"No, I didn't." Andi dropped her eyes.

"Well, that's neither here nor there," Lynn said with sudden briskness. "Anyway, what you're suggesting is totally preposterous. Even if Warren is involved in the drug trade, he's hardly about to jeopardize his position by admitting to it, no matter what guarantees I give him about confidentiality. And I have no interest in doing an exposé on the man. I'll leave that up to those so-called investigative reporters."

"He'll sign that statement for you," Andi said. "Just as soon as you show him this." She reached into her large handbag, drew out a manila file folder, and laid it on Lynn's desk. "Once you read that, Miss Powers, you'll never doubt for a minute that he'll sign it."

Andi stood up, a twisted smile on her face. "And all I can ask from you is to do what's right." She walked out of the office.

Lynn stared after her in confusion. The phones began to ring again. She looked down at the brightly lit buttons, started to punch one of them and pick up a call, then shook her head. "Damned if the woman hasn't gotten to me," she muttered as she opened the file folder. Her eyes immediately widened in shock as she saw the headline in the first article. "Jesus Christ!" she exclaimed. "Jesus Christ, Warren, how did you get away with this for so long?"

• • •

Warren Felber, a small, dapper man with warm, friendly eyes and quick, deft hands, was Hollywood's most prestigious plastic surgeon. Stars who were outraged at the thought of having to wait for anything—a salesperson at Gucci's, a table at the Bistro, or even a traffic light—meekly signed up six months in advance to get an appointment with him.

Part of the reason for Warren's fame and popularity was that he did truly marvelous work on sagging faces and bodies. But mostly it was due to the way he took care of his patients. As a plastic surgeon, he had legal and almost unlimited access to the very best cocaine. He was also a very considerate man. The street price for an ounce went as high as $3000. Warren charged only $1000. And no one begrudged him his considerable profit, even though they knew the pharmaceutical companies gave him the standard professional rate of $27 an ounce. After all, he was a doctor and he could be counted on to warn an overenthusiastic sniffer when his or her septum was in danger of being destroyed. It gave his patients a comfortable feeling of being cared for.

Most of the time Warren was a very happy man. He made $250,000 a year legally, and $600,000 a year illegally. And he didn't have to pay one penny of tax on the $600,000.

But there were nights when suppressed fears broke through his guard, emerging in the form of nightmares which brought him awake, sweating and trembling, to find his wife bending over him anxiously.

He and his wife never spoke at these times, for there was nothing comforting to say. She would simply hold him against her breast, stroking him gently until he fell back to sleep. And the next day he would try to forget that even the $250,000 he earned was basically illegal.

Warren Felber, once a brilliantly promising young surgeon, had lost his license to practice medicine when he was thirty years old and the nurse at his hospital tearfully admitted to her superior that he had performed an abortion on her. The matter was quickly hushed up by the hospital's governing board, and he'd gone three thousand miles away to try and forget the whole terrible experience.

During the next five years, he surreptitiously practiced medicine in a small New Mexico town. No one ever challenged his credentials. Emboldened by his luck, he moved to Arizona and worked openly for a government-sponsored clinic. A full year passed, and there wasn't even the slightest ripple of suspicion about him. Excited and hopeful, he took his family to Los Angeles and opened an office in Beverly Hills.

Business was very slow at first. Then one day an aging and almost forgotten actress came to him. When he'd asked her curiously who had recommended him, she had smiled wryly and replied, "The *Yellow Pages*." Later, she admitted that she'd called fifteen plastic surgeons before him, but he was the only one she could afford.

It had been a number of years since she'd worked, and she'd been existing on her Social Security checks and a small savings account. Then her agent called with a job offer for a TV commercial. "It's absolutely perfect for you!" he enthused. "The only thing is," he added apologetically, "you'll have to get rid of those bags under your eyes."

The operation was a success and she not only got the part in that commercial but was soon signed up for three other commercials. There was only one problem. Under the fierce lights of the camera, the sensitive new skin around her eyes dried and tightened, causing her excruciating pain. Warren, who had become genuinely fond of the spunky little woman, compassionately gave her a prescription for the anaesthetic cocaine to ease her suffering. She was tearfully grateful and promised she'd find some way to show her gratitude.

A few months later, Warren was astounded to find new patients pouring through his doors, all recommended directly or indirectly by the aging actress. "Who would ever have imagined she knew all these people?" he said wonderingly to his wife. But it didn't take him long to realize that most of them were more interested in his prescriptions than his surgery. He agonized briefly about how to handle the situation, then decided since he was living on borrowed time anyway he might as well make the most of it.

It had worked out very well. The world he operated in was a very protective one. His patients needed him more than he needed them, and so everything was kept very quiet. There had never been a hint of scandal or trouble. Warren comforted himself with the thought that he had never been responsible for anyone's addiction. He had never "turned on" anyone in his life. They only came to him after their drug habits had been well established. Actually, he told himself, he was performing a humanitarian service. For God knows what might happen to those people if he sent them out into the streets to buy the dangerously polluted drugs that sold there.

But Warren's rosy-eyed view of himself was about to be brutally shattered as he walked into his examining room, where Lynn Powers waited for him.

"Well, Lynn, what brings you here today?" he asked cheerfully. "Nothing serious, I trust." He reached out a gentle hand to touch her face. "Nose bleeds? Trouble breathing?"

"Don't!" Her voice held a peculiar mixture of command and entreaty as she pulled away from him.

Baffled, he dropped his hand and gazed at her with concern. "Good heavens, my dear, what's wrong?"

"Warren." She stopped and swallowed. "Warren, there's nothing wrong with my health. I'm here on business. I want to talk to you about Erin Connolly. And her drug habit."

His face went as white as the immaculately starched surgical smock he wore. "I . . . I don't think I understand."

"Yes you do, Warren. You understand perfectly."

"What is it you want?"

He looked so stricken, so bewildered, she had to turn away for a moment. When she finally managed to speak, her voice was unsteady. "I'm really sorry to involve you in this, Warren. Please believe me when I tell you I mean you no harm. All I want is to see justice done. Erin Connolly is a vicious, unprincipled creature who deserves to be punished. And with your help she'll get that punishment. All you have to do is acknowledge she's a heavy drug user. I won't use your name, I promise! And her attorneys won't be pressing any charges after they see the statement you sign," she added with a wintry smile.

"Are you crazy?" Warren said hoarsely. "I would be committing professional suicide if I signed a statement like that. You don't know what you're talking about when you say you'd protect me. I wouldn't have any protection at all! I'd be indicted on so many counts, I can't even add them up."

He collapsed on the small stool in front of the examing table and buried his head in his hands. Then after several long moments, while he forced himself to take slow, shallow breaths to reduce his frantic hyperventilation, he raised his head and looked at her.

"But I can't imagine why we're even having this conversation," he said evenly. "You've come to me with a completely unfounded charge. One that you most certainly can't prove and one that I will deny categorically, " he added with sudden grimness. "Now I think you should leave."

"No, Warren. You're not going to kick me out. Not after you read this." She handed him the manila folder.

He took one look at it and uttered a groan like a mortally wounded animal. "Oh God. Oh dear God!" He gazed at her with haunted eyes. "Where did you get this?"

"Does it matter?"

"No," he said dully. "No, I guess it doesn't." He sighed and passed a trembling hand over his brow. "You can give me the statement now."

She took it out of her purse and started to hand it to him, then paused. "Wait a minute, Warren. I think I have a better idea." She nodded thoughtfully to herself, a small smile beginning to play around her mouth. "Yes indeed, Warren. A *much* better idea." The smile grew into a broad grin as she looked at him. "And this time I really can guarantee you'll be safe. Your name will never come into it. Now listen to me very carefully."

"Are you sure, Rosa?" Erin asked with a puzzled frown.

"Yes, Miss Connolly. A Dr. Felber. He says it's important."

"Well, I think I geared myself up needlessly to take this call," she laughed ruefully. "I was all prepared to bravely confront Harry who's announcing my picture is being withdrawn from distribution or, at the very least, to hear Max inform me I'm on the brink of bankruptcy."

The maid stared at her uncomprehendingly, and Erin gave

an apologetic shrug. "Never mind, Rosa. It's all right. I'll take the call in the study. And maybe I'll have a little lunch afterwards. One of those special enchiladas of yours with salad."

"Oh yes, Miss Connolly!" Rosa beamed, the gold tooth in the front of her mouth gleaming. "I go start that immediately!"

"Hello? Warren? Are you there?"

"Yes. Yes, I'm here. I hope I didn't catch you in the middle of something."

"No, nothing important. Just looking over some scripts." She hesitated. "How are you, Warren?"

"Me? Oh, I'm just fine." He coughed. "Well actually, not perfectly fine."

"Good Lord, Warren, what's wrong?"

"Well, certainly nothing serious." He gave an uneasy laugh. "Mostly my wife's nagging. She thinks I'm overworking. But then, I guess all wives feel that way."

"Yes, I suppose they do," Erin said uncertainly.

"Well, I don't want to bore you with all this," he announced with sudden vigor. "The point is . . . well, the point is that I'll be leaving at the end of this week for a medical conference in Switzerland, and my wife insists we stay there for a long holiday. Maybe two months. Or more."

"Two months or more?" Erin gasped. "But . . ."

"I know," he interrupted quickly. "It was the first thing I said to my wife. How could I possibly leave my patients alone without treatment for all that time? Well, obviously I'm not going to do that. Which is why I'm calling you."

"I appreciate that," Erin said shakily. "I really appreciate that. What . . . what do you suggest in my case?"

"A visit as soon as possible. So I can do a thorough check on your condition before I take off. Do you think you could make it into my office tomorrow morning?"

"Of course. Of course I can. What time?"

"Would ten o'clock be convenient?"

"Yes. Ten would be fine."

Erin leaned back against the car seat and drew a quivering sigh of relief as she patted her purse, which bulged slightly from the large package inside it, before starting the engine and driving out of the underground garage that served the exclusive Beverly Hills medical building where Warren Felber's office was located.

"God, what if I hadn't taken that phone call?" she muttered. "Warren would have left the country without being able to reach me, and that would have left me . . ." She shuddered at the thought of where that would have left her. Well, it hadn't happened so there was no sense dwelling on it. She had what she needed, and with a little care it should last her almost three months. By which time Warren would be back and everything would return to normal. Although, she reflected thoughtfully, maybe it would be a good idea to continue this stockpiling even after Warren came back. It would save her all those weekly trips to his office, and wouldn't it be marvelous to know she had a full two- or even three-month supply on hand at all times!

Then she shook her head and reluctantly dismissed the idea, smiling in spite of herself as she imagined Warren's reaction to that proposal. He would be horrified. He was such an old fussbudget, insisting on constant physical examinations for his patients. Well that was probably as it should be. It was why she and several hundred other people went to him. He took good care of them, and he never let them down in any way.

The traffic light at Topanga Canyon and Pacific Coast Highway flickered a warning yellow before changing into red. Erin was only a few feet away from the intersection and going very fast. She took a chance and sped through it. Seconds later she heard the siren and saw the Highway Patrol car zooming up behind her. "Oh shit!" she exclaimed in disgust. As the car approached her, she slowed down and pulled off on the shoulder of the highway.

"Could I see your driver's license, ma'am?" the officer asked politely as he peered through the open window at her.

"The light was yellow, officer," she said earnestly. "If you were behind me, you could see that. The only safe thing to do was go through it."

"Yes, ma'am. Now, your driver's license?"

She heard footsteps crunching on gravel, looked around in

surprise, and saw a second uniformed cop circling her car. "What's he doing?" she asked in confusion.

"Please, ma'am, just give me your driver's license," he said stolidly.

She opened her purse and reached for her wallet. The cop's eyes narrowed sharply as he saw the package inside. "Step outside the car," he barked suddenly. "Don't make any sudden moves. Open the door, and come out as I direct you."

Erin stared in terror at the gun pointed at her.

"Isn't this one of your patients?" Warren's wife asked.

She had unfolded the newspaper left by the room-service waiter who'd just brought the breakfast tray into their elegant suite in New York's Plaza Hotel, where they were resting up before catching their flight to Europe.

Warren stared at the headlines which screamed, "FAMOUS HOLLYWOOD PRODUCER IMPLICATED IN DRUG RING." With a sick feeling, his eyes dropped to the story below.

"The Los Angeles police received an anonymous tip at ten-thirty yesterday morning that Erin Connolly, the brilliant and beautiful twenty-eight-year-old Hollywood producer whose film *Street Scene* swept the Academy Awards two years ago, had just picked up a large shipment of cocaine that would later be sold and distributed by Miss Connolly to various members of the film industry whom she has been supplying for several years. When California Highway Patrol officers stopped and searched her car on Pacific Coast Highway shortly after receiving the anonymous phone call, they discovered . . ."

The newspaper print blurred in front of Warren's eyes and he bolted from the table, reaching the bathroom barely in time.

XXX

Twenty - three

XXXXXXXXXXXXXXXXXXXXXXXXXXXXXXXXXXXXXXXXXXXXXXXXXXX

THE oversized metal key jangled harshly in the lock as the guard opened the door of the large, crowded holding cell. Erin was numb and sat with her head bowed, not even bothering to look up. During the first few hours of her confinement, she'd leaped to her feet and run forward eagerly each time the door had opened, sure that this would be the time someone had come to release her. But as the slow, agonizing hours of the afternoon passed into night with no sign of reprieve for her, she gradually began sinking into a state of hopeless depression.

"Why, oh why," she moaned for at least the fiftieth time, "was I so incredibly stupid as to call the beach house instead of my attorney?" In her first frightened panic, all she'd been able to think of was getting hold of Derek. But of course he wasn't there when she called, and Rosa came completely unhinged at learning Erin was in jail, breaking into tears and lapsing into rapid Spanish so that Erin was unable to make any sense at all out of talking to her. Nor was her desperate pleading with the police to allow her another phone call of any avail. The law allowed her one call. She'd made it, and that was all she'd get.

"Connolly. Erin Connolly," the guard shouted.

Absorbed in the miserable litany of self-castigation, her mind screened out the words. She rocked back and forth, continuing to moan softly to herself. The guard, an impatient edge to his voice now, yelled her name again.

"Hey. Hey, honey, ain't that you?" the woman next to her whispered, nudging her.

"What?" she said blankly. Then as the guard yelled her name once more, the words suddenly penetrated.

"Here!" she cried frantically. "Here!" She stood up and ran toward the door.

"You're Connolly?" he asked suspiciously.

"Yes."

"Well, it sure took you long enough to answer," he grunted, examining her carefully. "Still strung out, huh?"

"Is that a legal question, Officer?" she asked with a sudden cold bite to her voice.

He shrugged. "None of my business, lady. Come on, there's someone waiting for you."

Erin gazed unbelievingly at the trim, dapper figure who came forward to meet her, his hands outstretched in a welcoming gesture.

"Well, my dear, this is hardly the occasion I would have chosen to renew our acquaintance." Arnold Scorsi smiled. "It certainly doesn't compare with that delightful party you gave after your picture won the Academy Award, where you so graciously entertained my wife and myself."

"Arnold, what are you doing here?" she asked in a stunned voice.

"Surely that's obvious, isn't it? To get you out of this dreadful place. Come on, now," he said soothingly, "we have a few papers to sign, then you'll be free and we'll go somewhere to talk."

"But I still don't understand," Erin said as Arnold led her out to his car and considerately held the door open for her. "How did you hear about this? And why did you come down to help me? We haven't talked to each other since that party."

"My dear Erin, there's no time limit on friendship," he chided her gently. "As to your first question, I happen to know several police reporters quite well." Then his eyes narrowed and a sharp frown creased his forehead as he got his first good look at her in the bright sunlight.

"What's the matter?" she asked as she saw the sudden change in his expression.

"You," he said bluntly. "You look terrible, Erin."

"A night in jail isn't exactly a beauty treatment."

"Hm. Well let's get you a decent meal, and then we'll discuss what we have facing us."

"Are you going to defend me, Arnold?" Erin asked hesitantly as they walked into the restaurant and sat down in a booth at the back of the room.

"Of course. Why else would I be here?"

"The thing is . . ." Erin paused as the waiter set the large seafood salad in front of her. "The thing is," she continued in a small, unhappy voice, "I'm not sure I can afford your fees. I know you're very expensive, and I've had some financial setbacks lately. Actually, I don't really know what my financial status is at the moment."

"Don't worry about it, Erin. Just consider this a favor between friends. I'm confident you'll find a way to repay that favor one of these days."

Erin felt a cold shiver go through her at his words. The thought of being in Arnold Scorsi's debt was the most awful thing she could imagine. No it wasn't, she realized suddenly with a choking feeling of terror. Being sent to prison was much worse. Anything, anything at all, was preferable to that. And there was no doubt in her mind that she could be sent to prison. The police had made that all too clear. Would her attorneys be able to save her from that? They were careful corporation lawyers. They wouldn't even know where to start on a case like this. They probably wouldn't even care, she admitted miserably to herself. Con-Well Productions was their only genuine concern. So that left Arnold Scorsi as her one hope.

"Thank you, Arnold," she said huskily. "I accept your favor with gratitude, and I promise to repay you whenever and however I can."

"It never occurred to me that you wouldn't. But you must do exactly as I tell you."

"Well . . . well, that goes without saying," she stammered, unnerved by his swift and unexpected change from warm, comforting friend to cold, demanding accuser. "What is it that you want me to do?"

"First, you move out of that beach house. I don't want any continuing connection between you and Derek Marston. It will only hurt our case. Everyone knows Derek is into drugs. It's an angle I may be able to play up."

He paused for a moment and gazed at her quizzically. "Unless you feel a need to protect him?"

"No." Her throat was very dry, and it took her a few seconds to swallow. "No, I don't need to protect him."

"Good," he said approvingly. "That's one problem out of the way. Now, the next thing you're going to do is move into this apartment in Westwood. A friend of my owns the building, and the penthouse apartment is currently available. You'll love it."

"But how can I afford it?" she asked in shock.

"Erin, I already told you not to worry about these things," he said a little impatiently. "I'm taking care of everything." He handed her a card. "Here's the address of the building and the name of the manager, who'll be expecting you. I want you to move in there today. Is that understood?"

"Yes."

"All right. Now, after you get settled in I want you to make an appointment with this doctor." He flicked through his wallet and pulled out another card. "He'll give you a complete physical, start you on vitamin shots, and get you back into shape."

Arnold leaned back in his chair and surveyed her for a moment. "Finally, I want you to knock off the booze and drugs. And I mean completely. When we go into court, you have to look like a clean, healthy, all-American girl."

Erin flushed angrily. "I resent that remark, Arnold. It's totally uncalled for."

"Oh no it isn't," he said softly. "It's very much called for. Just take a look in a mirror, Erin. You're only twenty-eight years old, but you'd never know it from that face. It's the face of a forty-year-old woman. A boozer and a junkie. One who's been around the track too many times," he added cruelly.

"How dare you talk to me that way?" She started to rise from her chair. "I don't have to put up with these insults!"

"Of course you don't. Go on, then. Get up and leave. And good luck."

She sank back into the chair. "Do I really look that bad?" she asked pitifully.

"I'm afraid you do." Then his cold smile grew warm. "But it's hardly fatal, my dear. You're young and basically healthy. We'll have you looking the way you should in no time at all. And that, believe me, is very important." There was a sudden faraway look in his eyes. "Very important indeed."

The strict health regimen Arnold Scorsi's doctor put Erin on worked wonders with her appearance. In just a little over a month, she had recovered completely from the debilitating effects of the drugs and alcohol. The vitamin shots, plus a carefully planned diet and a special therapy and exercise program, had restored the luminous glow of health to her complexion. She had gained ten pounds, which did away with the gaunt, haggard look that had aged her and gave her back her natural youthful vitality. She was sleeping well, her brilliant green eyes once again sparkled with life, and she had never looked more beautiful. Arnold was visibly delighted.

"If I weren't a happily married man, I think I'd fall in love with you on the spot."

"In that case, let's hope the judge is an unhappily married man."

He threw back his head and laughed. "Well put, my dear. I shall endeavor to find such a judge." He gazed at her appreciatively. "You have spirit, Erin Connolly. I like that."

She smiled as she thanked him, then the smile faded as she thought of what was still ahead of her. "Have they set a date for the trial yet?" she asked a little tremulously.

"I've got us on the docket for next week. Now don't worry," he said quickly as he saw the sudden apprehension in her eyes. "Do exactly as I say, and everything will work out just fine."

Arnold Scorsi was as good as his word. He presented Erin as an innocent victim, an unknowing courier for Derek Marston. It was on his instructions, Arnold told the judge, that Erin had driven into the city that day to pick up the package. She had no idea what was in it.

His defense was skillful and extremely persuasive, with witnesses who swore that in all the times they had been at Derek's beach house Erin had never used drugs. That in fact she had tried to persuade Derek to stop using them, and believed she had succeeded in that endeavor. What finally convinced the judge was his quiet but impassioned plea to consider the facts of what had happened when Erin was stopped by the police and subsequently taken into custody.

"Now, your honor, you know as well as I that people who deal in drugs are all too well aware of the consequences if they get caught," Arnold said softly. "Which is why they always have attorneys on tap to rush to their rescue. An unfortunate situation," he added sadly, "because all too often those attorneys manage to free them and then they go on peddling their dangerous wares.

"But that didn't happen in this case!" he announced, his voice rising sharply. "Erin Connolly, like everyone else in these circumstances, was allowed only one phone call. And what did she do with that one phone call to freedom? Did she call an attorney, who could be counted on to race down and bail her out of jail? No! She did what any normal, bewildered, frightened, and *innocent* person would do. She called the man who had sent her after the package, in the trusting belief that he would come down and explain the whole nightmare away. Of course he didn't. He didn't even accept the phone call from her. And so this poor woman was forced into the incredible humiliation of spending a night in jail, not even understanding what had happened."

Arnold wearily let his arms drop to his side at this point. "Your honor, I will leave it up to you to decide where justice lies in this case."

The judge, who had become increasingly mesmerized by Erin's glowing green eyes, which had been fixed soulfully on him during Arnold's entire speech, almost lost his grip on the gavel as he pounded it down and announced with more than a trace of huskiness, "The court finds Erin Connolly *not* guilty. Case dismissed."

"You were wonderful, Arnold," Erin said gratefully as he escorted her out of the courthouse and drove her back to her apartment. "I can't thank you enough. But how in the world did you manage to keep Derek from contesting that charge you made against him?" she asked curiously.

"Oh it wasn't all that difficult," he said casually. "After all, *he* wasn't on trial. You were. And when his attorney pointed out to him how messy things could get if he came into court, he immediately saw how wise it would be to disappear for a while until things blew over. Besides, by the time the police showed up at his beach house with a search warrant, there wasn't a trace of drugs to be found anywhere in the place. So then it comes down to a case of his word against yours, and since you've been tried and acquitted I rather imagine the police will simply drop the whole matter.

"Of course," he added with a dry smile, "I must tell you that Derek does not harbor particularly warm feelings toward you at this juncture. I hope you were not planning to continue your relationship with him."

"No. It occurred to me during the trial that would not be a very feasible idea. Nor one that even interests me," she announced with sudden grimness. "It's a chapter of my life I would like to put behind me and forget as soon as possible."

"A highly intelligent decision." He pulled up in front of her apartment building. "Because all the good chapters are still ahead of you. Now take care, and we'll be in touch soon."

Erin felt a sudden cold chill go through her at his words. "In touch soon?"

"Well of course. You don't think I'm just going to desert you at this point, do you? I'll want to know how you're getting on. And if you have any problems, please feel free to call me."

"Yes, Arnold, I'll do that. When . . . when do you want me to call you?"

"Good heavens, my dear, only when and if you need to. What in the world did you think I meant?"

"I–I don't know. I thought maybe . . ."

"Erin, I can see this trial has been a terrible strain on you. You need time to relax, to pull yourself together. Go on, now," he commanded, leaning over to open the car door.

"Start building those nice chapters in your life. All I ask is that you remember I'm a true friend, ready whenever you need me."

As the next few months passed and Erin slowly began picking up the shattered pieces of her life and putting them back together again, she forgot all about Arnold Scorsi. He never called, wrote, or even made his presence known at the apartment building he had found for her. The manager of the building appeared during the second month of her occupancy and somewhat diffidently asked her if she wanted to sign a lease on the place.

"As you know, ma'am, the owner's original lease is up now," he said with a shy smile. "And apparently he's not going to renew it." He cleared his throat. "I know you've been subletting, something we don't ordinarily allow, but you've been such a fine tenant that we'd be happy to turn the lease over to you, if you're interested."

She signed the lease immediately, because she'd fallen in love with the beautiful, spacious penthouse apartment that offered spectacular views of both the city and the ocean. She also signed it because she was finally able to afford it. The recent sessions with Max, Con-Well Productions' comptroller, had been as grim as they were exhausting; but she was forced to admit that everything he said made sense. She really had no choice except to follow his advice. His gloomy predictions about *Body Count* had come true with a vengeance. The picture had come close to forcing her production company into bankruptcy. Only the money from the foreign-distribution sales of *Street Scene* had saved Con-Well Productions from going under. But that money had just about run out, and the upkeep on the Century City business offices and San Fernando studio was slowly but surely bleeding the corporation to death.

"Which is a ridiculous situation," Max said with considerable asperity. "You could be realizing a considerable profit by renting out the studio to independent producers. It's an excellent facility. Anthony did a first-rate job when he built it. I know at least ten companies who'd pay top dollar for the use of it."

He took off his glasses, polished them vigorously, then frowned as he put them back on. "The same is not true of these offices," he said as he looked around. "They are, to put it bluntly, a total waste of money. We have no business to transact in them. Ergo, we have no business being in them. Close them down. Lay off the staff. And the sooner the better!"

"I know you're right, Max," Erin sighed. "But where does that leave Con-Well Productions?"

"Alive, and isn't that what you really want? A year from now, when all this unpleasant publicity disappears, you'll be in shape to start producing again. *If* you're careful about the way you handle your money."

"You don't have to worry about that," she assured him with a grim smile. "This town hasn't seen the last of Erin Connolly. I'm going to be back bigger and better than ever. And if it takes a year of scrimping and saving to accomplish it, well then, I'll be the best scrimper and saver you've ever met."

It wasn't in Erin's nature to scrimp and save, and she loathed every moment of it. But she did it, knowing she had no other choice. Even if she had money, there was no way she could produce a successful picture at this time. Arnold Scorsi had saved her from a jail sentence, but there was no way he could save her from the harsh judgment of Hollywood. She was a pariah now in that close-knit society. She'd originally forced her way into it as an unwelcome outsider, which was a sin in itself, and then compounded that sin by becoming notorious in an ugly drug scandal. Half the town wouldn't even speak to her. The other half licked its chops in eager anticipation of destroying her the moment she tried invading their ranks again.

Less than a week after Erin gave her reluctant approval, Max had rented out all three sound stages at the San Fernando studio, and she realized wryly that he'd had the prospective tenants lined up all the time. But she could hardly complain. The combined revenues from the six-month leases would put Con-Well Productions solidly in the black for a full year, and Max assured her there would be no problem in either renewing the leases at the end of the six-month period or bringing in new tenants.

Erin then closed down the Century City offices, laying off all the staff except her secretary Nancy, and rented a tiny, cramped suite in an old run-down building whose only virtue was its Beverly Hills postal address.

"Well, Max, Con-Well Productions can't go completely out of business for a whole year," she said defensively when he found out what she'd done.

"For all the business you'll be doing, you could work out of your apartment and be a lot more comfortable," he told her bluntly.

"But I wouldn't be. I just wouldn't be, Max."

"Oh all right," he grumbled. "If it's that important to you, go ahead. The amount of rent you're paying for the little rattrap isn't enough to make any difference anyway."

Erin had to admit Max's description of her new offices wasn't too far from the truth, as she looked around that first day after the movers left.

"You think you can hack this place, Nancy?" she asked doubtfully.

"I've seen worse." Nancy grinned at her. "Come on, boss, cheer up. It's only temporary. You'll put me back into the style I'm accustomed to in no time at all."

The phone rang, and they turned and stared at each other in shock. Then they both began to laugh.

"My God, Nancy, if that surprises us so much, we're in worse shape than I thought," Erin said ruefully, wiping the tears of laughter from her eyes.

"Are you expecting a call from anyone?"

"No, not even a bill collector."

"Well, in that case I guess it's safe to answer it." Nancy made her way around the packing boxes to the desk and picked up the phone.

"Good afternoon, Con-Well Productions," she said brightly. "Yes, I believe she just came in. May I tell her who's calling? Thank you, sir. Just a moment, please."

Nancy cupped her hand over the receiver and looked up at Erin. "Someone named Arnold Scorsi. You want to . . ." She broke off abruptly as Erin's face turned a deathly white. "Erin? What's the matter?"

"Arnold Scorsi? Is that what you said?"

"Hey, take it easy," Nancy said in alarm. "I'll tell him you're not here. Now sit down before you fall down, and I'll get you a glass of water."

"No, it's all right." Erin took a deep breath. "I have to take the call." She walked stiffly over to the desk and held out her hand.

Reluctantly, Nancy handed over the phone, her eyes wide with concern as she watched Erin take another deep breath before speaking into it.

"Hello? Arnold?"

"Hello yourself. How's my favorite client doing?"

"Just fine," she said faintly. "How are you, Arnold?"

"Couldn't be better. Understand you signed a lease on that apartment. Glad to hear it. I knew you'd love it."

"Arnold, I know I still owe you for the first month's rent on it." She swallowed. "As a matter of fact, I was planning to call you about that this week. I'm really sorry it's taken me so long, but my financial situation is just beginning to get straightened out. However, I have some really good news," she continued feverishly. "It looks like I'll not only be able to pay you back for the apartment but take care of your legal fees as well. Just tell me what they are, and I'll get a check off to you immediately."

"Erin, Erin, what is all this ridiculous talk?" he protested. "Didn't I tell you all that was just a favor between friends? Surely you don't think I'm calling to ask you for money?"

"Well, you certainly have the right to." There was complete silence on the other end of the telephone, and Erin felt herself starting to perspire. She plucked at the blouse that was clinging damply to her. "Arnold? Are you still there, Arnold?"

"Sorry, my dear," he murmured. "One of those infernal transatlantic calls finally came through and my secretary inadvertently switched lines to take it. Please forgive me for keeping you on hold. Now, where were we?"

"Talking about the money I owe you," she replied tensely.

"No, no." His voice was a brisk reprimand. "How many times must I tell you that was a favor? Ah, now I remember! This time it is I who have a favor to ask of you. I do hope you're free this coming Wednesday evening."

"What?"

"Wednesday evening. You are free, aren't you?"

"I'm sure I can arrange it."

"Wonderful!" he exclaimed enthusiastically. "I can't tell you how much I appreciate it. I know it's terribly short notice, but Senator Ryan made a special point of asking to have you there. He was most impressed with you when he met you, and this is quite an important party for him. He'll be announcing his official candidacy for the next Presidential race, and he's eager to have all his friends there."

Arnold chuckled. "I don't think you'll find going too much of a burden. It promises to be a most delightful party, and I can assure you that you won't be asked for any political contributions. This is simply a fun occasion."

"A party?" Erin was so giddy with relief to learn that all Arnold Scorsi wanted from her was to attend a party with him that she started to laugh. "Arnold, you've got a date!" she told him happily. "I'm long overdue for a good party."

It wasn't until the next day that she realized how strange the invitation was. Why would Johnny Ryan, a Presidential candidate, request the presence of a Hollywood producer who had been involved in a drug scandal, been on the verge of bankruptcy, and was being avoided like the plague by everyone in town? It made no sense at all. It was crazy!

There was only one answer. They wanted something from her. But that's just as crazy, she thought. Because she had absolutely nothing that could be of any possible use to them.

Twenty-four

THERE were over three hundred guests at the party, including some of the biggest names in Hollywood, but the man who commanded the most attention, after Johnny Ryan, was an advertising executive named David Bernstein who was rapidly becoming known as one of the prime movers and shakers in the world of politics.

All the experts agreed that his stunningly creative campaign had been responsible for putting this President of the United States into office, and David had been besieged by offers from both parties when the incumbent President decided not to run again. To date, David had not announced that he'd accepted any of the offers, but his presence at the party caused reporters to buzz around him.

Erin had always been fascinated by men with power. She made her way quietly but determinedly through the crowd that surrounded David until she found an opening left by a harried waiter fighting his way back to refill his drink tray. She slipped into the vacant spot and stood there looking up at David, her green eyes glowing with interest. She had no idea that Arnold Scorsi was watching her from the far side of the room, a quiet contented smile on his face, as David turned away from a particularly obnoxious reporter, met her eyes, blinked, and then took her by the arm and moved her out of the crowd.

They left the party together and David took her to a restaurant named Chianti's, which she'd never heard of before.

"It's my hideaway," he told her. "I never bring anyone from the business here. So I'm trusting you to keep it a secret."

It was a small, elegant, formal place, and the food was superb. The other patrons were quiet, expensively dressed couples who murmured to each other in soft voices and seemed several light-years away from the frenetic world she knew. She couldn't imagine that they had ever had to fight for anything in their whole lives, and that impressed her. She was also very impressed with David Bernstein. He was nothing like she'd imagined advertising executives to be. Everything about him suggested quiet, confident authority. He also possessed an immense charm and warmth that relaxed her and drew her out. For the first time she could remember, she actually talked about herself instead of manipulating the conversation into areas designed to make the other person open up and reveal himself. And by the time the cappucino was served, Erin thought she'd discovered the man she'd been looking for all her life.

During the next few weeks Erin existed in a state of delirious happiness, oblivious of everything but David. He was all she thought about, all she cared about. When she wasn't with him, she daydreamed about him, lovingly recalling the way his dark intense eyes lit up when he was excited about something, seeing the delicious curve of his lips as he grinned in amusement, hearing the rich sensual quality of his resonant voice, feeling his hands as he cradled her head between them and leaned down to kiss her, his mouth so warm as it fastened on hers.

Nancy sighed as she watched Erin staring dreamily into space, the contract on her desk lying just as she'd placed it over an hour ago, still unread.

"Hey, I'm all for love, but don't you think you're carrying it a bit far?" she announced from the doorway.

"What?" Erin blinked and gazed at her vaguely.

"That thing on your desk. You're the one who asked for it, remember? The television deal for your pictures."

"Oh that." Erin smiled. "Well, it's not really such a good deal, is it? I mean, they're insisting on the rights to *Street Scene* before they'll agree to pick up the other pictures. But *Street Scene* won't be available for another three months. So I think I'll just wait out those three months and auction off the rights to the highest bidder. And double my money in the process."

"I guess I should give thanks you haven't forgotten everything."

"Nancy, I never forget anything."

"Are you sure?" Nancy hesitated for a moment, then took a deep breath and resolutely plunged in. "Listen, Erin, I know it's none of my business, but you do know the guy's married, don't you? And he's got kids. I mean, I just don't see any future for you."

"You're really concerned, aren't you?" Erin said wonderingly.

"Are you kidding?" Flushed and embarrassed, Nancy tried a cocky smile. "It's my future we're talking about here, too."

"Of course it is. And I'm not going to let you down, Nancy. This thing between David and me is the best thing that's ever happened to me. It's making me stronger, more sure. Everything is going to work out for the best. Not just for me, but for the business and you as well. I promise you that."

"But what if he lets you down? What happens then?"

"David will never let me down."

The call from Arnold Scorsi came two days later. "Well, I think you enjoyed that party even more than I promised you would," he announced genially. "David Bernstein is a most enchanting fellow, isn't he?"

Erin felt an instant flash of apprehension, her instinct telling her that Arnold Scorsi was finally calling in his debt.

"Yes," she said cautiously. "He seemed quite pleasant. Actually, everyone did. It was a delightful party."

"Come now, my dear. Pleasant is such an anemic word.

According to my sources, you're finding David a great deal more than pleasant."

Erin hesitated, unsure of how to answer. She and David had been very discreet. Did Arnold really know anything or was he just making an educated guess based on the fact that they'd left the party together? No, she thought dismally. He knew. He always seemed to know everything. Well the hell with it, she decided, suddenly angry. I'm sick and tired of his cat-and-mouse games.

"You're absolutely right, Arnold," she said evenly. "I find David Bernstein considerably more than just pleasant. Now, what's it to you?"

"Well, that's certainly direct." He sounded slightly taken aback. There was a pause, but when he spoke again his voice was once more smooth and assured. "I forget sometimes how forthright you can be, Erin. It's an interesting quality. It also has the virtue of saving time."

He coughed and paused for another brief moment before continuing. "I am correct, am I not, in assuming David's interest in you is as strong as yours in him?"

"You're correct, Arnold."

"Yes, I rather thought I was. Well, then, we shouldn't have any difficulties here. It's a very simple thing I'm asking. Get David Bernstein to handle Johnny Ryan's Presidential campaign."

"What?"

"Erin, you did hear me, didn't you?"

She stared baffledly into the phone. "Yes, Arnold, I heard you. But I don't understand you. At all! What has Johnny Ryan's campaign got to do with me and David? I mean, David was practically the main attraction at that party. I thought he'd already agreed to handle it. Besides, I don't know anything about these things. What could I do?"

"Please, Erin, no games," he said wearily.

"Arnold, I swear I don't know what you're talking about," she told him bewilderedly.

There was a long pause now on the other end of the phone. When Arnold finally came back on the line, his voice was thoughtful. "I believe you, Erin," he said quietly. "Politics has never been your game, has it? Pictures. Film. That's what turns you on. It never occurred to you that David showed up at that party as a spy, did it? That he was checking out the competition because he'd already secretly pledged himself to another candidate and wanted to find out what they'd be up against."

"Are you serious?" Erin started to laugh. "David a spy? I've never heard anything more ridiculous in my life. He's the most honest, open person I've ever met. If I didn't know better, Arnold, I'd think you were smoking something. Believe me, you're completely wrong about this."

"I certainly hope so," Arnold said calmly. "It would make everything a great deal easier. In the meantime, I can look forward to your call tomorrow morning assuring me that David will be handling Senator Ryan's campaign, can't I?"

The happy, confident laugh suddenly died in her throat. "Arnold, I already told you I don't know anything about these matters. I thought you understood that. If you have any questions, you really should talk to David."

"If I could talk to David, I wouldn't be wasting my time with you," he remarked coldly. "That's apparently something you don't understand. Now, can I expect that call from you tomorrow morning?"

"Arnold, I can't do this!" she exclaimed frantically. "I can't make David's career decisions for him! How can you expect me to do such a thing?"

"How you manage it is of no concern to me," he said, sounding bored. "All that counts is that you do manage it. Because if you don't, you'll never make another motion picture in this town. And that, I assure you, is something I *can* manage." He hung up before she had a chance to say another word.

"You know, if it hadn't been for Johnny Ryan, we would never have met," Erin announced as she carried a tray of hot hors d'oeuvres out of the kitchen and set it down on the coffee table.

"Without question one of his finest achievements." David gave her an amused grin. "Does that mean he's won your vote?"

"Well, first he has to get the nomination. But of course that won't be any problem if you handle his advertising campaign," she remarked as she snuggled up next to him on the couch. "Everybody says that the candidate who has David Bernstein behind him is a shoo-in."

"I didn't know you were so cynical about politics."

"Cynical? I don't know what you mean, darling. I was complimenting you."

"But hardly the system," he said dryly. "Apparently you buy Joe McGinniss's thesis."

"Who?"

He shook his head. "Sorry, love, I guess that was before your time. Joe wrote a book called *The Selling of the President 1968*. He was one of the first to contend that getting a man elected President of this country isn't too much different from selling a new detergent. Both go after the same national market and both, he claimed, succeed or fail based on their advertising efforts, irrespective of their merits. Remember Hubert Humphrey?"

"Hubert Humphrey?" She stared at him blankly. "What does Hubert Humphrey have to do with anything?"

David picked up his glass and absently swirled the contents. "Wait a minute. Let me see if I can remember how he put it. 'I'm fighting packaged politics. It's an abomination for a man to place himself completely in the hands of the technicians, the ghost writers, the experts, the pollsters, and come out only as an attractive package.' Now doesn't that sound just like selling soap?" David asked her with a wry smile.

"But that's your business you're talking about," she exclaimed in shock. "How can you do it if you feel that way about it?"

"Because I don't feel that way about it." He took a swallow of his drink, suddenly looking quite serious. "Erin, politics today is a mare's nest, and media holds a prime responsibility for putting it into that condition. All I try to do is even the score. Give the right people a chance to make it in this crazy arena. Because our country deserves it."

He shrugged and gave her a slightly embarrassed grin.

"Forgive the soap box speech. And no pun intended. Now enough of all this. Where would you like to go to dinner?"

"David." She reached out tentatively and touched him. "David, are you going to handle Johnny Ryan's campaign?"

He looked at her in surprise. "No, of course I'm not. Where did you ever get that idea?"

"But you were at that party! Why did you go to the party if you weren't planning to run his advertising campaign?" she asked desperately.

"Hey, what is all this?"

Erin lit a cigarette and inhaled deeply, trying to regain her composure. "The thing is . . ." She paused. "The thing is I was thinking about giving a fund-raising affair for Johnny after you officially announced you'd be handling his campaign. You see, I've known Johnny for several years and am quite fond of him. So I thought it would be a nice thing to do."

She wet her lips nervously. "I was really looking forward to it. It never occurred to me that you wouldn't be handling his campaign. I mean, you *were* at that party."

"Honey, I don't understand why you keep harping on that," he said with an exasperated laugh. "If a movie producer gives a party to announce a new picture and a well-known director happens to show up at that party, does that mean he's going to direct the picture?"

"Yes," she said flatly. "It usually does."

"Oh." He looked faintly startled. "Well, that proves politics and show biz aren't as much alike as I feared."

"David." Erin leaned forward, her eyes fixed intently on him. "David, I want you to handle the advertising campaign for Johnny Ryan. He's a fine man, and I really want you to do it."

"You don't know what you're talking about," he said impatiently. "Johnny Ryan is a lightweight. Just another pretty face. He'd make a lousy President. Now why don't we make a bargain? I'll let you take care of the movie business and you let me take care of the political business. That way we'll both be fine."

"Aren't you being awfully unfair?" she asked tensely. "Why should Johnny Ryan be penalized just because he's good looking? After all, he's also a senator with an established record. Does being ugly mean you're automatically a better person? I mean, look at the other candidates! That dreadful Thurgood Ralston, for example. I wince every time I see him. Is it someone like that you're going to support?"

"No." David set his drink down on the coffee table and regarded her strangely. "As a matter of fact, the man I'm supporting is Richard Longworth. It's not for publication yet, though."

"Richard Longworth? I never even heard of him!"

"Well, that's a problem I'll be correcting soon," he smiled. "Longworth's one of those unsung heroes, an honest man who gives an honest day's work and has no time to play around and get media hype. He's a congressman from Wisconsin and one of the finest legislators around today. His voting record is outstanding, and his integrity is without question. He'll make a superior President."

"Were you already committed to handling his campaign before you came to Johnny Ryan's party?"

"Yes." David frowned as she continued to stare at him. "Why, what's the problem?"

"Oh God, Arnold was right! You *were* there as a spy."

"What?" He broke into laughter. "Erin, I don't know who Arnold is, but I think you should send him back to one of the studios. Maybe he could become the next Hitchcock."

"It's true, though, isn't it? You did come to that party, knowing you were going to support another candidate, just to check out the competition."

"Of course. That's standard operating procedure." His amused grin started to fade as she kept on staring at him. "What the hell is the matter, Erin?"

"Everything," she said miserably. "Absolutely everything!"

"You want to tell me about it?" he asked, his eyes dark with concern.

"Do you love me, David?"

"You know I do," he said huskily. "I love you more than anything in the whole world."

"Even more than your principles?"

"Jesus Christ, Erin, what is this?" he asked in alarm. His

face whitened as she turned away, refusing to speak. "That stupid little speech you made about wanting to hold a fundraiser for Johnny Ryan was all crap, wasn't it?"

She nodded, unable to answer.

"Then lay it on me," he said heavily. "Tell me what it's really all about."

There was a long, painful silence in the room when Erin finished telling him about Arnold Scorsi.

"Please, David," she begged. "Please help me."

"Erin." He shook his head, not trusting his voice, then reached for his drink and gulped at it. "Jesus, Erin, how could you have let yourself get involved with someone like that? You must have known what kind of a person he is. You've lived in this town long enough to know that!"

"But what else could I have done? I was in jail. I was all alone. There was no one else to turn to. Besides, how was I to know this would happen? I didn't even know you then, David. I thought . . ."

She started to cry. "I thought the worst thing that could happen was that he'd want something from my production company. And I was willing to give him whatever he wanted. Because nothing could be as bad as going to prison. Nothing, David! Can't you understand that?"

"Christ!" He rose and started to pace the room. He stopped and turned to face her, his expression bleak.

"Don't you see what this means, Erin? If Arnold Scorsi wants me to handle Ryan's campaign, it means that your pretty little friend is something more than just a lightweight. Something very frightening. It means he's a pawn for the people behind Arnold Scorsi.

"Do you want me to be responsible for electing a President who has to answer to those kind of people?" he shouted with sudden fury.

"David, I'm not asking you to get him elected. All I'm asking is that you handle his advertising campaign."

"Goddamnit, Erin, don't play the hypocrite to me now!" he turned on her savagely. "Or have my talents abruptly diminished during this past hour? After all, it was just a scant sixty minutes ago you assured me that any candidate who had David Bernstein backing him would be shoo-in."

"I'm sorry, David," she said quietly. "I don't have any of the answers you'd like to hear. I'm not an idealist. I know very little about politics, and I have to admit I don't really care very much. I've never known any politician that really changed this country for the better. Maybe your man Richard Longworth could accomplish that. But if he destroys me in the process, I would not find it a worthwhile accomplishment."

She gazed at him, her eyes steady now. "What we're really talking about is me. Which is the only thing I do know. And I don't want to be destroyed. You can save me, David, if you want to. It's all up to you."

He looked at her helplessly, this beautiful, bewitching, green-eyed woman who'd brought him to heights of ecstasy he'd never dreamed existed and so obsessed him that he could hardly eat or sleep for thinking about her. The thought of losing her was literally unbearable.

"All right," he said in a voice he had trouble recognizing as his own. "I'll take on Johnny Ryan's campaign."

"Oh, darling!" She flew over to him, covering him with kisses. "You've made me so happy, darling. You'll never know how much this means to me. And you mustn't worry. It's all going to work out just fine. Why, in no time at all we'll have forgotten the whole thing."

He knew she was wrong. It would not work out fine, and he would never forget it. But he could live with it, he told himself, as long as he had her. He could live with anything as long as he had her.

Twenty - five

Two months after David took on Johnny Ryan's campaign, Ardis Kendall's first book was published. It was titled *Liberation* and the advance publicity on it created such excitement that bookstores across the country were deluged with requests for it weeks before it came out. It was number one on all the bestseller lists within its first week of publication, and every studio in Hollywood was bidding for the screen rights.

Much of the excitement was generated by the notoriety of the author herself. Fifteen years ago, at the age of twenty-five, Ardis Kendall had made the front page of every major newspaper in the country when she publicly accused twenty of the top U.S. corporations of using women as slave labor, and backed it up with documented wage and salary figures she had managed to obtain, by what means no one ever learned, from the personnel files of those prominent corporations.

She continued to make news as she joined forces with Gloria Steinem in forming the National Women's Political Caucus and Women's Active Alliance, and quickly became one of the most famous and, to many, most feared leaders of the feminist movement in America due to her startling exposés of the power elite in the country. Now, with her first book, she promised to deliver the most sensational revelations of her entire sensational career; for *Liberation* was reputed to rip the lid off some very explosive secrets in the lives of some very well-known public figures.

Erin had never felt such a fierce hunger for a property. David listened with patient indulgence as she paced like a restless tiger back and forth across the living room of her penthouse apartment, telling him in short, staccato sentences what a dynamic opportunity this was, how it could turn her whole career, her whole life, around and bring her back to the top for good. Of course he didn't believe for a moment that she had the faintest chance of getting the screen rights. It was obviously impossible. But then David still had a lot to learn about Erin.

Ardis Kendall's agent was horrified when his prize property announced that she was going to talk to Erin Connolly before she signed any studio contract.

"Have you lost your mind?" he shrieked. "She's poison, Ardis! Everything she touches dies. Please, please listen to me. You know I only want what's best for you."

"Nonsense, Leonard," she replied crisply. "You only want what's best for you. And you exaggerate ridiculously. Poison indeed," she sniffed scornfully. "The lady may have had some problems, but she's hardly poisonous. Besides, her lawyer did get her acquitted of that drug charge on the basis that she was deliberately framed. Which she probably was, considering that Derek Marston, that stupid stud, was involved. His manager undoubtedly set up the whole thing. Pigs, all of them."

Ardis munched pensively on the dry piece of whole wheat toast that, along with a cup of black coffee, comprised her entire breakfast as she sat in her expensive bungalow at the Beverly Hills Hotel watching her agent wolf down scrambled eggs, ham, and bagels thickly slathered with butter, jelly, and cream cheese. And once again she cursed her peasant ancestors who had given her a body and an appetite that would have been perfect for a truck driver but was a disaster for a bestselling female author. Sighing, she forced down the last, tasteless crumb and looked across the table.

"Anyway, Leonard, you're missing the point. Erin Connolly

is the only major woman producer in this male-dominated town, and I think it would be a great mistake for me to ignore her totally. It would be a little hard to explain to the sisters."

"Well, if that's all there is to it." Leonard relaxed visibly, leaning back in his chair and giving her a relieved grin. "Okay then, go ahead and do your good deed, and I'll make sure we get some nice publicity out of it. But don't take too long about it," he warned her. "This town isn't like New York. It cools off as fast as it heats up. Today your book is the hottest property around. Tomorrow it could be forgotten."

"Don't worry, Leonard. I'm just as well aware of that fact as you. Which is why I scheduled a luncheon meeting with the woman today."

She pushed back her chair and stood up. "Now run along and do your publicity thing and let me get dressed."

"My pleasure, sweetheart," he beamed. "And tomorrow we'll get down to serious business." He blew her a kiss as he left the room.

She waved absently in return, then looked down longingly at the two bagels left in the basket next to his plate. "No, Ardis," she said firmly. "Be a good girl, and maybe we can give you a little treat for dinner."

But as she walked into the bedroom and gazed at her reflection in the full-length mirror, she decided glumly that there wouldn't be any treat for dinner either. "I wonder if Erin Connolly is as slim and beautiful as her pictures," she mused. She smiled and gave the finger to her mirror image. "So what if she is?" she announced. "Look where it got her. Nowhere! *I'm* the one with the power. Dumpy forty-year-old body and all."

Considerably cheered by that realization, she bypassed the expensive but dreary black dress designed to slim down her beefy contours and chose instead a bright, colorful pantsuit. While the pantsuit made her look like a balloon, it also made her feel relaxed and comfortable. And as she dressed, she found herself looking forward with interest to the upcoming lunch.

Ardis had been both amused and admiring about Erin Connolly's approach to her. Less than an hour after she'd checked into the Beverly Hills Hotel, the hand-delivered telegram had arrived at her bungalow. Its message was challenging, and its delivery more than a little arrogant. For Erin had blithely ignored all the sacred rules of procedure, going over the heads of publishers, managers, and agents to zero in directly on her quarry, the author of the book. Such things were rarely if ever done, especially when the producer not only had no ties to a major studio but was, in fact, practically ostracized by the entire movie industry.

Ardis had chuckled when she read the telegram and was still chuckling when the phone in her bungalow rang precisely fifteen minutes after the telegram had been delivered.

"All right, Erin Connolly, you've made your point," she'd announced into the receiver. "Let's have lunch tomorrow, and we'll discuss the matter."

"Ms. Kendall?" The voice on the other end of the line had sounded slightly stunned. "You knew it was me calling?"

"Of course, child," she'd laughed. "Whatever your faults might be, I doubt that subtlety is one of them. So when my phone rings fifteen minutes after I get this telegram, who else could it be? You see, I've got you all figured out. So you'd better watch your step with me. You're dealing with a pro here, you know."

"Yes, I know. Which is why I'm making this effort. And if you'll allow me, may I thank you for being exactly that? A pro?"

"Oh, I think so." Ardis smiled, amused again. "Now I hope you don't mind having lunch here at the hotel, because I never go out in this crazy town. I wouldn't even know how to pilot a car down your insane freeways."

"Good Lord, Ms. Kendall, I wouldn't *dream* of asking you to do that," Erin had exclaimed. "I'd planned on our having lunch in the Polo Lounge. If that's all right with you."

"Sounds just fine, my dear. I'll see you there tomorrow at noon."

Ardis turned slowly now back and forth in front of the mirror as she recalled her conversation with Erin Connolly, then frowned unhappily as she saw the way the top of her pantsuit bulged out around her waist. "Oh what the hell!" she told herself in disgust. "Who cares? Certainly that woman won't. The last thing in the world she'll notice is how I look."

Ardis couldn't have been more mistaken.

"Ms. Kendall!" Erin raced forward as Ardis came through the doorway to the Polo Lounge and walked inside, holding out her hands in welcome. "What a pleasure to finally have the opportunity of meeting you."

"And what a pleasure to find you here waiting for me." Ardis cocked her head, a faint smile on her face. "I thought it was against the law in Hollywood to be on time."

Erin laughed. "I'm afraid it must seem that way some times, but it is not a practice I subscribe to. And I most certainly would not have been late for this meeting! I know how very valuable your time is, Ms. Kendall. May I thank you again for your courtesy in seeing me?"

"If you'll drop that Ms. Kendall crap and call me Ardis." The small, shrewd eyes roved over Erin in frank appraisal. "You really are as pretty as your pictures. Maybe even prettier."

Erin's own eyes narrowed slightly in sudden speculative interest as she observed the way the famous feminist author was looking at her. She returned the searching gaze with one equally searching, carefully noting every detail about Ardis as she took in the short cropped hair that was turning gray, the square face with its blunt features and pugnacious jaw, the thick shapeless body in its garish pantsuit.

"Being pretty in Hollywood is more a liability than an asset," she said lightly. "For every girl who's pretty, there are a thousand girls who are beautiful. It's the cheapest and least respected commodity in this town. I don't know a single woman who wouldn't gladly trade it all for what you have."

"Really?" Ardis said dryly.

"Really." Erin gave her a warm, glowing smile. "But of course you know that. It's what makes women everywhere care so much about what you write, and care so much about you as well. I hardly need to belabor the point to you, of all people. Please forgive me, it just happens to be something that's quite important to me. Now let's go on in and get comfortable."

She took hold of Ardis's arm and started to lead her into the restaurant, then stopped abruptly. "Ms. Kendall? I mean, Ardis. I booked a booth for us inside, so we'd have a chance to chat in quiet. But maybe I'm being selfish. It's a beautiful day today. Perhaps you'd rather eat out on the patio?"

"No, you did just fine. To tell you the truth, I hate your California sunshine. It makes me squint, and puts lines on my face. And those rotten little patio chairs put creases on my bottom."

Erin gave a delighted laugh. "Ardis, you're wonderful! Because, you know, that's exactly how every woman in Hollywood feels. We've just never had the courage to come out and admit it. I think you should do a piece about it, and liberate us poor souls."

Ardis found herself laughing along with Erin as the maître d' led them to a large, comfortable booth. "Maybe I will," she chuckled as she settled back in the booth, spreading her thighs to let air circulate between them. "Now, what do you recommend?" she asked as she opened the menu.

"For openers, the seafood salad. And then . . ." Erin's voice dropped to an intimate whisper. "And then . . ." She let the words hang there.

Ardis blinked, feeling a sudden rush of heat as the luminous green eyes gazed knowingly into hers. "And then what?" she demanded hoarsely.

Erin smiled, a slow, teasing smile, as the small, pink tip of her tongue came out and delicately wet her lips. "Well, why don't we wait and see how the seafood salad works out first?" she suggested mischievously.

"I don't believe it!" Leonard screamed in anguish the next day when Ardis brought him the contract from Erin. "Have you completely flipped out?"

"Stop foaming at the mouth, and just read the contract," Ardis instructed him calmly. "I think you'll find it an excellent deal. Erin has offered a higher percentage of the gross than any of the major studios. And, as you well know, that's where the real money is for a writer."

"Oh it's Erin, is it?" Leonard snarled. "A week ago you didn't even know the bitch. Now you're on a cozy first-name basis."

He tore at his thinning hair in frustrated rage. "Christ, if I didn't know better, Ardis, I'd think she got to you in some way. I mean, it's common knowledge she'll do anything to get a picture she wants—lie, cheat, steal, and God knows what else."

"She's a woman trying to make it in a man's world, and her options are limited," Ardis said gently.

She flushed and straightened in her chair as she saw her agent staring at her peculiarly. "And in case you've forgotten, that happens to be what my book is all about," she added with her usual crispness. "Besides, Erin Connolly is a first-class producer. I don't think you can argue with the quality of her work."

What Ardis refrained from mentioning was that Erin Connolly was also the most breathtakingly exciting woman she'd ever met. Her pulse began to race just at the memory of the way Erin had looked at her as she talked in that low, husky voice about how moved she had been by Ardis's book, and how deeply she felt that women owed each other a special commitment.

Ardis could hardly wait to see her again. Because then the promise in those beautiful, tantalizing eyes would turn into fulfillment. And oh what a fulfillment it would be! Ardis had never felt such desire in her whole life.

Erin's gleeful delight in discovering that Ardis Kendall was a lesbian faded rapidly on her second meeting with the famed feminist leader. For Ardis was very different from all the other people that Erin had manipulated, used, and then discarded. Ardis would not settle for vague promises. She not only knew what she wanted, she demanded to have it. Immediately! And when she didn't get it, she became extremely difficult.

Erin had talked rapidly and nervously the night that Ardis had come up to her penthouse apartment with the contract. It had taken her over an hour to convince the angry and now suspicious woman that this was not the right night to consummate their relationship, and all of her considerable powers of persuasion to placate Ardis. But she finally managed it, and Ardis left smiling after signing the contract and handing it to her with a loving kiss.

"Thank God that's over!" Erin muttered as the door closed behind Ardis and she collapsed on the couch with a sigh of relief. But Erin was wrong. It was far from over.

Ardis showed up unannounced the following evening, carrying two large bags of groceries.

"I thought we'd eat in," she announced cheerfully as she barged inside without waiting for an invitation, setting the bags down on the counter in the kitchen, and opening the refrigerator door.

"My God, child!" she exclaimed in horror as she peered inside. "You don't have a single thing in here! I think I got here just in time."

"Ardis. Ardis, I can't have dinner with you tonight. I already have a dinner date."

"Well, then, you'll have to cancel it." Ardis turned around, placing her hands on her hips and giving Erin a long, hard look. "Because you and me, baby, have some unfinished business to take care of. Business that can't wait any longer. You understand?"

Anger flared in Erin's eyes. "I'm afraid you're the one who doesn't understand," she snapped. "I don't take orders from anybody, and frankly I'm appalled that you should try giving them. It goes against everything I thought you stood for, everything that made me believe in you. I am equally appalled," she continued tightly, "by your storming into my home without even the bare courtesy of calling first to see if it's convenient for me to see you. Now I think you'd better leave."

"What the hell are you trying to pull?" Ardis grabbed hold of Erin's arm.

"It's obvious we have a very basic misunderstanding here," Erin replied icily, freeing her arm with a curt gesture. "One we should clear up as soon as possible."

"Oh no you don't!" Ardis said, suddenly grim. "If you think for one moment I'm going to let you get away with making a fool out of me, you've got a lot to learn. Nobody, but nobody, makes a fool out of Ardis Kendall! My agent will have that contract nullified before you're through your first course with your dinner date tonight."

"I don't think so. Not when he finds out what's involved."

She smiled, a cool, confident smile. "After all, my dear Ardis, I'm not the one who has a reputation to protect. They could hardly say anything worse about me than they already have. But you? Well, that's an entirely different matter, isn't it? Imagine the shock and horror when your devoted public finds out that their esteemed leader is not only a lesbian, but a lesbian who used her position of power and influence to try and bully the only real woman producer in Hollywood into bed in exchange for the screen rights to her book."

Ardis withdrew but she didn't retreat. The story broke simultaneously in the Hollywood trade papers and the national newspapers shortly after production started on *Liberation*. "ARDIS KENDALL SAYS 'STAY AWAY FROM MY MOVIE!' " the headlines announced. In the story that followed, Ardis stated that Erin Connolly had totally compromised the integrity of her book. "I don't know what she's afraid of, since she refused to tell me," Ardis was quoted as saying. "All I know is that I was proud of my book, but I can't be proud of the movie she's making out of it. She's killed all the truth in it, and left it without heart or guts."

The three leading actors cast in the movie broke their contracts the day after Ardis's story came out, and the director walked off the set two days later. A week later International Pictures triumphantly announced that they had just acquired the screen rights to Ardis Kendall's new book and would be starting on the picture immediately. Production on *Liberation* was quietly canceled.

Erin's career hit rock bottom after that, and her relationship with David deteriorated right along with it. There was no way she could tell him what had really happened, and his innocent questions and misguided sympathy drove her mad.

"Would you please do me a favor and just shut up about it?" she screamed. "How do I know why the woman planted that insane story? Because she's insane. What else can I tell you?"

Making matters worse was the fact that David was now thoroughly caught up in the campaign for Johnny Ryan, traveling around the country almost three weeks out of every month; and when he came back to Los Angeles he had the demands of his family to meet. Erin, on the other hand, had nothing to do. The forced cancelation of *Liberation* brought her production company close to the edge of bankruptcy again. The New York investor who had put up the money for the picture angrily demanded the full amount of his investment back, plus interest, leaving Erin to absorb all the expenses that had been incurred. As a result, Con-Well Productions found itself completely stripped of its liquid assets.

Max sighed and muttered as he leased out the sound stages at the San Fernando studio and tried to make some financial sense out of the chaos, and Erin cursed and often cried as one long, lonely hour followed another while she paced back and forth in her apartment, staring out the window and waiting for David to come back to her.

Inevitably, she turned on him. "It's obvious you don't have time for me," she shouted one afternoon when he came over. "You have lunch with your business people, you have dinner with your family, and you fit me in between when it's convenient for you. Well, I'm not going to put up with it any longer! I'm going to find someone who has time for me *all* the time." She burst into tears.

"Erin, please," he begged.

"No," she sobbed. "This is it. Get out of my life. Give me a chance to find someone I can count on."

He left, but he couldn't stay away. Three weeks later he showed up at her apartment, pale and exhausted looking. "I can't live without you, Erin. I'm getting a divorce."

"Oh, David!" She threw herself into his arms, hugging and kissing him. "Oh, darling, I love you so much."

For the next few months they were very happy. David started taking her on his business trips with him, and since he had an extremely generous expense account they were able to enjoy the best that places like San Francisco, New York, Miami, and New Orleans had to offer. But it didn't last. Because all the exciting, glamorous, romantic trips in the world couldn't make up for the fact that she wasn't making pictures. So Erin went back to Hollywood to try again.

This time, however, she was stopped cold before she could even start. In the past, she'd been able to overcome all the incredible obstacles in her path because she'd always possessed the one big trump card, a bestselling property. But now, after Ardis Kendall's scathing denunciation of her, she found the world of literary agents and writers had implacably closed ranks against her. There wasn't one decent property in the entire town that she could get her hands on, because the major agents and writers flatly refused to sell to Con-Well Productions.

She fought it like she'd fought everything in her life, but nothing worked. The final humiliation was that all the third-rate agents and hack writers in Hollywood descended on her like vultures. There are no secrets in Hollywood. Everyone knew about the boycott being imposed on her, and they assumed she'd been brought to the point where she was desperate for any material. So they deluged her with their wares: books that had died after a minimal first printing; unsold and unwanted screenplays; shoddy, hastily improvised treatments; even pornography.

At first she haughtily rejected them. But as the months passed, and she became as desperate as they'd originally assumed she was, she swallowed hard and agreed to look at their material. She and Nancy spent hours at their desks in the small, cramped offices of Con-Well Productions in Beverly Hills reading through the huge stacks of submissions in the forlorn hope that one, just one, might have some value. Sometimes she and Nancy broke up at what they were reading, striking dramatic poses and declaiming various passionate purple passages to each other before collapsing into helpless laughter. That was on the good days. But there weren't many of those. Most of the days Erin just buried her head in her hands and tried to keep from crying.

And as the bad days steadily increased in number, Erin

found her fighting rage turning into depression. Nothing was working, and she began to believe that nothing would ever work for her again. She came home one Friday afternoon, crawled into bed, and just stayed there.

When Nancy called anxiously the following Monday to find out why she hadn't shown up at the office and discovered the state Erin was in, her concern and alarm were so great it managed to penetrate through Erin's lethargic fog. Frightened now by the seriousness of the depression that held her in its grip, she realized she had to do something to break out of it before it destroyed her. But what? The only real cure would be getting Con-Well Productions back into the business of producing pictures. But the way things stand now, she reflected dismally, there's no chance of that.

Then an idea came to her. There was another possible cure. It would only be temporary, but if it worked it might boost her spirits enough to bring about the real cure. After all, she told herself, how could she expect to accomplish anything when she was down all the time? And she'd give it up as soon as things started going right again, she promised herself.

Erin went back on cocaine the next week, and her depression vanished in a soft white cloud of pleasure. "Oh God, I'd forgotten how wonderful you are!" she sighed. "What a fool I was to let people scare me off you."

But Erin's ecstasy turned to apprehension the second week when she discovered how much cocaine she was consuming. It had been dangerously easy to slip back into using it, and she found herself wanting more all the time. With grim determination she forced herself to limit her use to evenings and weekends. Never during the day when I'm working, she told herself firmly. And no other drugs. I'm not going to get back into the condition I was in with Derek. I'm going to handle this the right way.

David was horrified when he found out. "My God, Erin, I can't believe you'd do this to yourself!" he cried. "Especially after what you went through with that drug trial. Are you completely crazy?"

"No, I'm sane for the first time in months," she replied

evenly. "And I'm going to stay that way. Believe me, I have this under control. There's no danger at all."

"You really are crazy," he said hoarsely. He bowed his head, ran his hands through his hair, then looked up at her. "And you lied to me too, didn't you? That drug charge wasn't a frame at all. You were guilty as hell. That's why Arnold Scorsi has such a hold on you."

"If it bothers you so much, leave," she told him coldly.

"I can't," he said miserably. "I'm as hooked on you as you are on that filthy stuff."

The issue didn't go away, though. David was unable to accept the fact that Erin continued to use cocaine, and they fought about it constantly. However, by that time they were fighting about so many things, it lost its importance in a long list of growing grievances on both sides. David became increasingly unhappy about his campaign for Johnny Ryan after he discovered the truth about the situation that had forced him into it. And his depression grew as he found out what was happening to Richard Longworth, the only candidate he'd truly believed in and committed himself to; for Longworth was desperately strapped for campaign funds and fighting a hopelessly uphill battle with minimal support from an advertising agency and public relations firm that was, to put the best possible face on it, second-rate.

Compounding David's depression at abandoning his political principles was the terrible guilt he felt at leaving his family. His wife had taken the divorce very badly, and his youngest son had run off from his private school. It took two private detectives almost a month to find him.

David was moody and morose a great deal of the time. And this absolutely infuriated Erin. She had finally managed to break out of her own depression, and she was damned if she'd let David drag her back into it. So they quarreled about that as well, with Erin frequently threatening to leave him.

After one particularly bitter fight, David showed up at the apartment with an armful of flowers and announced with forced gaiety that he was taking her to a party. "It's just what we need to get us out of the doldrums."

"I don't want to go to a party," she said sullenly.

"Come on, honey," he coaxed. "It will do us good to go out and be with people for a change. You'll enjoy it, I promise."

"No I won't. I'll be bored to death. You know how I feel about politics."

"Of course I know how you feel about politics. I also know how you feel about the movie industry."

"What?"

"Surprise!" He grinned at her. "This is a very lavish party, in the best Hollywood tradition. No politics, all entertainment, and a cast of thousands. So what do you say?"

She looked at him uncertainly. "Whose party? And what's the occasion?"

"Harry Kingston, the man who invented the Hollywood party, will be our gracious host. And the occasion, I suspect, is some high-level wooing of Sheldon Avery."

"Sheldon Avery?" Her head snapped up. "You mean the author of *Secret Rites*?"

"The one and only," he agreed smilingly.

"But that doesn't make any sense." She shook her head, frowning. "Why would Kingston bother holding a party for Sheldon at this late date? Everybody knows that Columbia offered a million dollars for his book, and frankly I thought his agent had sewed up the deal."

David shrugged. "I guess hope springs eternal in the hearts of movie producers when an Academy Award-winning property is up for grabs. Especially when there's still no official announcement of the sale. On the other hand, maybe Harry Kingston knows what I do. Although I can't think it would be very useful to him."

Erin straightened suddenly and stared at him. "What do you mean, David? What do you know about Sheldon Avery?"

He looked at her, puzzled. "Well, I didn't realize it was all that big a secret. Avery is practically queer for the actor Keith Ramsey. He's worshiped the man all his life, even though he's never met him, and his dream has always been to get Ramsey in one of his pictures. There's no doubt in my mind that Avery would happily give up a million dollars if some producer could guarantee delivering Keith Ramsey for the lead role in *Secret*

Rites. Of course it's impossible. Ramsey is a very stubborn maverick."

David chuckled. "I must say I admire the hell out of that man Ramsey. He told the industry to fuck off after his last picture. He was retiring for at least a year, and he wouldn't be back until he felt like it. He meant it too. He's completely disappeared. No one knows how to reach him."

"Well in that case, I imagine you're right," Erin said softly. "It certainly doesn't sound like Harry Kingston has much of a chance."

She stood up, walked over to him, and gave him a kiss. "But I guess we don't have to worry about Harry Kingston's problems, do we?" she murmured as the tips of her fingers caressed the back of his neck. "We can still enjoy his party, can't we?"

"You'll go, then?"

"I wouldn't miss it for the world."

Erin closed in on Sheldon Avery forty minutes after she and David arrived at the gala party. "There's something extremely important I have to talk to you about," she whispered in his ear. "Something nobody else can hear. Meet me out on the patio in five minutes."

"Are you sure?" he gasped, hope and disbelief mingling in his wrinkled pixy face. "I mean, everybody told me . . ."

"Everybody told you wrong," she assured him quietly. "Because Keith Ramsey *is* available for the right property. Don't you remember what he said before he took off? That he would come back when the right picture appeared? Well, he told me that *Secret Rites* is that picture."

"He really said that?" Joy blazed out of Sheldon's face.

"He said more than that." Erin smiled warmly. "He said it was the only picture that could bring him back."

Suspicion suddenly shadowed the happy face. "Then why doesn't anybody else know about this?" he demanded accusingly. "Why didn't Harry Kingston tell me about it? Why didn't my agent? Why didn't Columbia Pictures?" he screeched, his voice rising dramatically.

"Why ask me?" Erin spread her hands in a helpless gesture.

"Maybe because they don't have any way of getting in touch with Keith."

"That's true," he muttered to himself. "They don't. They told me that." He looked up at her. "And you do? You can guarantee that?"

"Why else would I be talking to you?"

"Okay. Okay." He started pacing around the patio, then turned back to give her a hard stare. "Can you deliver Keith Ramsey, signed contract and all, one week from tonight?"

"It could take two weeks. Because he really is out of touch." She gave him a light smile. "I might have to take a canoe up river to deliver the contract."

"So start paddling. Because two weeks is all you've got."

"Hey, I was right, wasn't I?" David beamed as they drove away from the party. "You really did enjoy yourself."

"Yes, David, you were right," she said dreamily. "It was indeed a marvelous party."

Erin curled up in the seat, resting her head against the window as she gazed absently at the flashing lights of the passing cars and began to figure out a way to get hold of Keith Ramsey.

"So let's go celebrate tomorrow night. A private party for David and Erin, who've just made it through the doldrums and are coming out just fine!"

"Tomorrow night?" she said vaguely. "No, David, I don't think I can make it tomorrow night. I've got a lot of things to think about."

"What the hell are you talking about?" He braked abruptly and turned around and stared at her. Horns screamed in protest as the line of motorists behind him pushed desperately on their own brakes to avoid hitting him, swerving wildly around him and hurling curses as they passed.

"Jesus Christ, David, what's the matter with you?" Erin shouted. "Are you trying to kill us?"

"It's a thought." His smile appeared strangely twisted in the glare of headlights from approaching traffic.

"That's not funny, David," she said furiously. "And, for that matter, you're not much fun these days either. I think I was right when I suggested last month that we take a rest from each other. And I think now is the time to do it!"

"You can't do that to me, Erin." His voice was low and calm as he pressed down on the accelerator and began moving the big car down the highway once again. "I've given up too much for you. My career, my family, everything I believed in. You're all I have left. So you can't leave me. Ever. Do you understand that?"

"No, I *don't* understand that," she snapped. "If I want to leave you, I'll leave you. And that's all there is to it."

Then she swallowed in fright as his hands tightened so hard on the steering wheel that his knuckles gleamed white, and the car leaped forward in a surge of uncontrolled power.

Twenty - six

IT was three o'clock in the morning, and thirteen days, seven hours, had passed since Harry Kingston's party. Twelve hours had passed since a furious Sheldon Avery had called Erin at her office and delivered his final ultimatum: deliver the signed contract from Keith Ramsey within forty-eight hours or lose the picture. Six hours had passed since she and David had sat in a booth at Chianti's restaurant and the maître d' brought the phone to their table, whereupon she learned from Keith Ramsey's answering service that the actor was backpacking somewhere in the Sierra Mountains and there was absolutely no way of reaching him. Three hours had passed since David had walked into her bedroom and sat down at the foot of her bed, a faint, mocking smile on his face as he idly played with the gun in his hands, pointing it at her for a few heart-stopping moments before turning it around, pulling the trigger, and killing himself instantly.

The police were gone now, and the apartment was very still. Erin huddled on the couch in the living room, unable to face the thought of going back into the bedroom. Convulsive sobs continued to rack her body, although her eyes were dry, for by this time there were no tears left. She rocked back and forth in silent agony, pausing occasionally to drink from the large crystal brandy snifter in her hand. Finally the potent liqueur, combined with the two sleeping pills she'd taken earlier, did its work. Her rocking became slower and slower then stopped altogether as her head fell wearily against the arm of the couch, and she slept.

The phone rang, shrilly and persistently. Erin struggled out of her narcotic fog and groped for it. "Hello?" she mumbled thickly.

"Erin Connolly? Is this Erin Connolly?" The voice was crisp, sharp, and obviously angry.

She blinked, then grimaced at the terrible taste in her mouth, running her tongue around her teeth and trying to swallow. "Yes," she said with an effort. "Who's this?"

"Keith Ramsey," the voice barked. "And I have some questions for you, Miss Connolly. Like what the hell did you think you were doing harassing my answering service that way?"

Still numb with grief and shock, Erin was for once without a cleverly contrived story. She simply blurted out the truth about her outrageous promise to Sheldon Avery and the desperate reason behind it, then began to cry as she told the actor about David's death.

It was, although she didn't realize it at the time, the only way in the whole world she could have gotten Keith Ramsey to consider taking the part in Avery's picture. Because Ramsey was, in addition to being one of the most powerful stars in Hollywood, a genuinely sensitive, compassionate man, and his instinctive reaction to the terrible thing that had just happened to her was to offer whatever comfort and help he could.

An hour after the phone call, a copy of Sheldon Avery's screenplay was on its way by chartered plane to Keith Ramsey's lodge in the Sierra Mountains. The following day a special messenger brought Erin the signed contract from the actor.

Hollywood was rocked by the news of David's suicide and even more stunned to learn that Con-Well Productions had not only obtained the screen rights to Sheldon Avery's smash bestseller but signed Keith Ramsey for the lead.

Executives at the giant studio that had originally optioned the book fumed in impotent rage. They had a legitimate suit against both Sheldon Avery and Con-Well Productions, but what the hell would it look like if they sued and took the picture away from Erin Connolly, who was now being portrayed as a tragic figure gallantly striving, in the best show business tradition, to rise above her personal afflictions, past and present, and make a comeback? They knew exactly what it would look like. Ruthless big business heartlessly crushing one lone, brave human being who was not only a small, independent producer but a woman. Cursing and gritting their teeth, they let the picture go.

Keith Ramsey's agent was equally furious, as was Twentieth Century-Fox. Just three weeks ago the agent had flown up to Ramsey's mountain lodge with a major new property, and the actor had agreed to take the part, subject to certain conditions. Jubilant executives at Twentieth Century-Fox had agreed to every condition and moved immediately to start production, not bothering to wait for the signed contract since it was just a formality. Now they found it was a great deal more than just a formality. They'd lost their star, and without him the picture would never get off the ground.

But there was probably no one, in the long list of stunned and furious people, who was more upset than Arnold Scorsi. A man who prided himself on his ability to remain cool, calm, and totally in control no matter what happened, he found himself suddenly shaking like a terrified child, perspiration soaking through his elegantly hand-tailored silk shirt, as he picked up the private phone in his office and dialed an unlisted number that was known to only five people in the entire country.

"Yes, we heard," a flat voice replied. "Will the suicide seriously hurt Johnny Ryan?"

"No. Not per se. Voters never pay any attention to the ad agency or public relations firm that backs a candidate."

"Any incriminating evidence?"

"I'm sure there isn't."

"How sure?" the voice asked. It was still flat, emotionless, but now there was an undercurrent of threat in it.

"Positive," Arnold said quickly. "Our investigators have already, uh, surveyed David Bernstein's office."

"Good." The voice was approving. "No traces, I assume."

"Oh no! None at all."

"Can you replace Bernstein with somebody as good?"

"I'm working on it." Arnold cleared his throat. "But . . ."

"What?" the voice snapped.

"It looks like we're going to be facing some unexpected opposition," he said unhappily. "A major power in Hollywood has recently come out for Richard Longworth. As long as we had David Bernstein handling Johnny's campaign, I didn't see any real problems from it. But now that David's gone . . ." He trailed off.

"We do not accept that as an explanation," the voice informed him coldly. "Your job is to neutralize the opposition. That's one of the things we pay you for. So you will manage it, won't you?"

"Of course." Arnold forced a smile into his voice. "Haven't I always?"

"So far you have," the voice said distantly. "But you're only as good as today's success." The voice laughed. "Isn't that what they always say in that show biz world of yours?"

"Yes, that's what they always say," Arnold agreed shakily.

"Well, then, we understand each other. We'll expect another report from you within the month. In the meantime, be sure to give our best to your lovely wife."

"I'll certainly do that." Arnold hung up the phone, wiped the perspiration off the receiver, and started thinking very hard.

Erin was oblivious of the rumors, uncertainties, private rages, and public speculations that swirled around Hollywood after the twin announcements of David's suicide and her acquisition of *Secret Rites*. The only thing she knew was that this was truly her last chance, and if she didn't make it with this picture she was finished.

But this time around it looked like she was finally going to get support from the film industry that had so relentlessly shunned and ostracized her. Her phone rang constantly. People extended their sympathies for what had happened to David and wished her luck on the new picture; actors and agents were eager to discuss casting possibilities; directors, cinematographers, even set designers and film editors, offered their services. Many of the calls came from some of the biggest and most respected names in the business, and Erin accepted them gratefully. But the most important call of all didn't come . . . the one from the money men. And without that call, all the support in the world couldn't help her. Because Con-Well Productions was, quite simply, incapable of producing *Secret Rites* on its own. At the most conservative estimate, it would take eight million dollars to bring in the picture. Con-Well Productions' current financial statement showed the company had total liquid assets of $75,000. If she mortgaged the San Fernando studio she might raise another two million dollars, although even that was doubtful. But it didn't matter, because even if she raised double that amount, it wouldn't be enough.

In the first flush of excitement and pleasure generated by all the warm, friendly calls pouring into her office, Erin had failed to notice that no one was offering any financial support for her picture. But as a second week passed, the calls dwindled and both Sheldon Avery and Keith Ramsey's agent began to press her about the start date for production, she realized with sudden shock that she was committed to a picture she couldn't afford to make.

She got on the phone quickly to those few major studio executives who had called her, remembering now that there had been very few of them indeed. Most of the calls had come from the private sector of Hollywood: actors and actresses, directors, film technicians, agents, and press people. Now she discovered that even those few studio executives who had called had suffered a sudden relapse of memory. They were in fact such victims of amnesia, they couldn't even come to the phone.

Erin found herself talking to an endless line of bright young executive assistants who all sounded faintly bewildered by her call but assured her cheerfully that they would pass on her message to their bosses. The message coming back from them

to her was unmistakable. Erin Connolly might have finally won
the sympathy of the film industry, but that's all she'd won.
There wouldn't be a single penny of financial support.

In desperation she went to New York, where she found there
wasn't even sympathy to be had. The money men there hadn't
forgotten the disaster that had occurred the last time one of
them had invested in an Erin Connolly production, when Ardis
Kendall had forced a close-down of her picture *Liberation*.
They turned her down flat.

That left Erin with only one place to go. She put it off as
long as possible, filled with dread at the thought. But eventually she reached the point where she was forced to admit she
had no other choice unless she gave up *Secret Rites*. And that
she couldn't do, because doing that would be tantamount to
giving up her life. So, pale and tense, she picked up the phone
and dialed the number that once again would deliver her into
the hands of the one person in the world who utterly terrified
her.

"This is not an easy thing you're asking. Not easy at all."
Arnold Scorsi peered at her over the top of his glasses. "Things
are considerably different now than they were when you came
to me with *Street Scene*. I'm sure you understand that."

"No, Arnold," she said with difficulty, twisting her hands in
her lap. "I'm afraid I don't understand. It seems to me this is an
even better proposition for your investors. When I came to you
with *Street Scene*, I was virtually an unknown producer. It's
true I had a bestselling novel, and a box-office star in Derek
Marston. But this time I come to your people with a proven
record as an Oscar-winning producer, to say nothing of having
the hottest property in town and the most prestigious actor in
Hollywood. Surely you'll agree that the combination of
Sheldon Avery and Keith Ramsey is something very special. In
terms of money alone, they have to be valued at ten times what
Derek Marston and that now forgotten author of *Street Scene*
were worth."

She swallowed and smiled nervously. "And there's also the
fact that for the first time Hollywood is behind me. I get calls,
Arnold. I get calls all the time from important people, wishing

me luck. I think even the academy will be supporting me this time around. I really believe they'd like to be able to give me another Oscar. That's money in the bank for your investors."

"Somehow I doubt they'd look at it that way," he remarked dryly. He took off his glasses and tapped them reflectively on the desk for a moment, then unexpectedly smiled at her. "However, I suppose there's no harm in trying. After all, we've been friends for a long time, Erin, and I think one should make a special effort for friends. Give me a week or so to see what I can do. I'll be in touch."

"Thank you, Arnold," she said tremulously. "Thank you very much."

"Please, my dear, don't thank me yet," he protested as he stood up to escort her to the door. "I haven't promised you anything, you know. All I can do is try. So save your thanks for if and when I accomplish something. In the meantime, relax and take care of yourself."

There was no question in Erin's mind, as she left Arnold Scorsi's quietly expensive suite in the exclusive Century City high-rise building which only a few short golden years ago had housed the flourishing business offices of Con-Well Productions, that the cold, smiling man could accomplish anything he wanted to. The question was, did he want to? And if so, why?

She'd been prepared to give up virtually everything she owned in order to get the financing for her picture, but not once during their conversation had he asked for anything in return for that financing. There hadn't been even a hint of what terms he would require. The obvious conclusion was that he was giving her a polite brush-off. Except polite brush-offs were not Arnold Scorsi's style. He never bothered with such amenities.

Erin found herself incapable of following Arnold Scorsi's advice to relax and take care of herself while she waited to hear from him. She paced around her apartment, snapped at the few people who continued to call her, and hid behind the oblivion of cocaine when she couldn't stand to think about the problems facing her for one more second.

Exactly one week after she had gone to see Arnold, he called her. "Well, I think we may have something possible here," he announced cheerfully. "Can you come down to the office today? At two?"

Erin arrived promptly just as the exquisitely fashioned miniature grandfather clock on the wall in the reception room chimed the hour. Then she chain-smoked three cigarettes before Arnold finally opened the door of his office and smilingly beckoned her inside.

"Sorry if I kept you waiting, my dear."

"That's all right, Arnold. I know how busy you are." She sat down in the chair he indicated, then waited tensely as he settled himself behind the desk and extracted a sheaf of papers from a folder.

"Are you familiar with the Marchison brothers, Erin?"

"The Marchison brothers?" she repeated nervously. "No, I can't say that I am."

"Hm. Well, I suppose that's understandable. They're not exactly a household name in Hollywood. But they're very smart men. Built a billion-dollar empire by taking over small quality retail clothing stores across the country. Continued to operate them under their own names, of course, but by putting them under the Marchison corporate umbrella they were able to achieve extraordinary discounts from the major fashion houses through volume buying.

"And they're interested in backing my picture?"

"Ah, as usual you come directly to the point." He beamed at her. "Most refreshing, I might add, for a lawyer who is forced to spend the majority of his time with clients who tiptoe around every issue, waiting for someone else to speak the first word."

"Will they put up ten million dollars? Arnold, I must have at least ten million dollars. I know the prospectus I gave you showed eight million, but that was bare bones. To do it right, I need that cushion."

"Erin, they're not cheap people," he chided her gently. "If they decide to come in on the picture, they'll come in with style. After all, they want a winner just as much as you do."

"Well, they sound like the kind of backers every producer dreams of," she said with a shaky laugh. "Now what do I have to do to get these Marchison brothers?"

"Very little, actually. Outside of the usual, normal terms, they've made only one condition."

He paused, and Erin took a deep breath. Here it comes, she told herself. "Okay, Arnold," she said, managing somehow to keep her voice steady. "What's the condition?"

"That you bring in a co-producer."

"A *what?*" It was absolutely the last thing in the world she'd expected, and the worst thing she could ever have imagined. A co-producer on *her* picture?

"Please, my dear, try to calm yourself," he said reprovingly. "If you'll just stop and think for a moment, I'm sure you'll be able to understand why they're requesting this. Investors need to feel a sense of security when they entrust their money to someone, and your profit-and-loss statement these past few years has been . . . well erratic, to say the least. Naturally this troubles them. However, they are still willing to take a chance on you. And all they're asking in return is a little simple insurance on their money; the security of having a responsible co-producer with a good solid track record. Frankly, I think they're being more than generous."

He squared the edges of the papers on his desk. "Their choice is Mike Sobel. He has a number of advantages to offer, including the fact that he can operate both as co-producer and director. I think it's an excellent choice. Do you agree?"

Erin wanted to stand up and shout that she not only didn't agree, she absolutely refused to even consider it. This picture was hers! She'd fought for it all alone, won it all alone, and nobody else had the right to come in and take over production on it. But as she looked at Arnold Scorsi's coldly appraising eyes, she knew she wouldn't say anything at all. Because if she didn't accept his terms, she'd lose the picture altogether. Numbly, she took the contract he handed her and signed where he indicated.

It wasn't until she'd left his office that Erin allowed the bitter tears of rage and misery to fill her eyes. Mike Sobel! Oh God, why of all people did they have to choose him? The thought of having any co-producer on her picture was practically unbearable, but with someone else she would have found a way to manage. There were all kinds of ways to take care of co-producers. You flattered them, then worked around them so they never knew what was really happening; you gave them impossible assignments; you shunted them off into dreary administrative duties; if nothing else worked, you bought them off. But you couldn't do that with Mike Sobel. He'd been around the track, there was nothing that ever escaped him, and he was the most demanding bastard in the whole world.

"He's going to take my picture away from me," she sobbed as she drove out of the Century City parking lot.

By this time the anguished tears were running down her cheeks in such a steady stream she could barely see. There was a sudden terrifying screech of brakes as she headed blindly onto Santa Monica Boulevard, and a car making a right turn smashed full force into her. Her radiator exploded, sending up a furious spout of steam, and she stared at it in horror as the driver of the other car shouted, "You crazy bitch! You could have killed both of us!"

Unexpectedly, she started to laugh. "Well, I'll be damned if I'm going to make it this easy for you, Mike Sobel. Nobody's going to hand you my picture on a silver platter. You'll have to fight for it. And I warn you right now it won't be an easy fight. When it's over, there'll only be one of us still alive in this business."

xxx

Twenty - seven

xxxxxxxxxxxxxxxxxxxxxxxxxxxxxxxxxxxxxxxxxxxxxxxxxxxxxxxxxxxxxxxxxxx

MIKE Sobel was only eighteen when a Broadway producer spotted him in a summer-stock production of *Oklahoma* and promptly signed him for the juvenile lead in his upcoming play.

The play opened to lackadaisical reviews and closed after a short, disappointing ten-week run, but critics and audiences alike were wildly enthusiastic about the young, unknown actor who appeared in it. *"An exciting new presence has arrived on Broadway,"* one critic raved. *"A brilliant newcomer redeems mediocre play,"* another announced. *"Mike Sobel is unquestionably the big find of this season,"* a third critic proclaimed.

The audiences, mostly female as the play drifted into matinee performances, couldn't have cared less what the critics said. They came to see the young actor who gave them back their youthful dreams, gazing raptly at him as he gently introduced the fragile-looking ingenue to the mysteries and delights of making love.

"Oh God, isn't he beautiful!" they sighed rapturously to each other as the curtain fell for the intermission.

He wasn't beautiful, of course. He wasn't even handsome. Only five feet nine inches tall, with sandy hair, a thin, angular face, and a tight, wiry body, he would have been completely undistinguished looking if it weren't for his eyes, which were an extraordinarily clear, penetrating blue. But the way he looked was totally unimportant, because Mike Sobel possessed a magnetic vitality that drew people like a light draws moths, and he completely mesmerized audiences.

During the next five years he became one of the most sought-after young actors on Broadway, but he grew increasingly dissatisfied with the narrow, restricted world of acting. What he really wanted, he finally realized, was the freedom to create his own world through directing and producing.

He made it big on his first production, *Ducktail*, a wildly energetic musical parody of the fifties; and after that he could pretty much call his own shots. Musical comedies, though, left him with a curiously empty feeling. He needed to create something that made people think and feel, and maybe even weep. But serious dramas just weren't making it on Broadway at that time. So, despite the pleading of his friends, he packed his bags, and took off for the West Coast to accept an almost impossible assignment offered him by a major studio.

Hollywood was not only skeptical but downright hostile when the twenty-nine-year-old Mike Sobel was brought out to replace the beloved veteran director who had lost his last battle with the bottle and had to be literally carried off the set of *Amnesty*. But less than two weeks after he'd taken over, the word was out that a new genius had arrived. And when *Amnesty* walked off with eight Academy Awards, the entire audience stood up and cheered. Mike Sobel had proved himself a professional in every sense of the word.

But in spite of the unqualified success of his first picture, the next six months turned out to be the most frustrating and unhappy period of Mike Sobel's entire life. At first he was deluged with offers from studio executives eager to cash in on the reputation of Hollywood's new reigning genius. However, those executives quickly became dismayed and then infuriated by the attitude of the young director. For Mike Sobel was a perfectionist. And the only thing Hollywood dislikes more than a failure is a perfectionist. Because perfectionists are stubborn and argumentative. Perfectionists make impossible demands. Worst of all, perfectionists cost money.

They warned him, then they threatened him. When the warnings and threats failed to bring him around and make him accept their way of doing things, they used their ultimate weapon. They refused to let him make pictures.

He almost starved to death, but he never gave in. He was saved by a struggling young independent producer who took a chance on him. It was the smartest thing that producer ever did. Mike gave him an Oscar-winning picture that same year, and after that Mike Sobel never had any problems with Hollywood again.

Ten years later he'd established his own production company, and he was the most respected director/producer in Hollywood. He was smart, he was knowledgeable and, above all, he possessed that most unusual attribute, integrity. It became a mark of honor for the money men in the business to claim they'd backed a Mike Sobel production. Which was unusual in itself. Generally, money men only go where there are big profits to be realized, and Mike Sobel rarely produced big moneymakers. He waited for the right pictures to come along, the ones he really believed in, and he never went into television. Sometimes two years went by before he came out with a new film. But his films always won awards, and the industry revered him as someone who had set a new standard of excellence in their often tawdry world.

They were also more than a little afraid of him. He never socialized with them, living alone on his huge ranch in the San Fernando Valley after his wife of three years was tragically killed in an automobile accident. Not that he became a recluse. Just the opposite, in fact. He was extremely active in civic affairs and worked closely with a number of important community leaders. But he never went to the parties Hollywood gave or showed up at the chic "in" restaurants. So they rarely saw him, and what little they knew about him came from occasional stories in the newspapers about his activities. Recently there'd been quite a number of those stories, for Mike Sobel had come out with the announcement that he was actively supporting the Presidential candidate Richard Longworth.

• • •

"We have a problem," Arnold Scorsi said abruptly as Erin picked up the phone. "Mike Sobel has refused our offer to act as director and co-producer on *Secret Rites*."

"Well." Erin leaned back in her chair, and lit a cigarette. "To you, Arnold, it may be a problem. To me, it's the best piece of news I've had in days. I never wanted the stubborn bastard in the first place."

"I repeat, *we* have a problem. Because without Mike Sobel you don't have a picture. Now, does that clarify the situation for you?" he asked coldly.

"Arnold, you can't be serious," she protested. "To tell you the truth, I never understood why you wanted him to begin with. I mean, he's hardly the biggest moneymaker in Hollywood. I can think of at least ten other people who would be a better risk."

"What you think is of no importance at all," he snapped. "It's what the Marchison brothers think that counts."

"Are you saying they won't settle for anybody but Mike Sobel? But, Arnold, that doesn't make any sense at all. From what you tell me, they're just a couple of shrewd businessmen who want a maximum return on their investment. Can't you make them understand that they'd be much better off with someone else?"

"No," he said flatly. "This is their first venture into the movie business and, as I told you earlier, they like to go in style. To them, Mike Sobel is style."

"Oh for God's sakes, Arnold, that's a bunch of crap and you know it. Now explain the facts of life to them."

"For some reason, Erin, you seem particularly obtuse today. That's not like you. I certainly hope I'm mistaken, but it almost sounds like you've gone back on drugs. I trust I am wrong about that," he added softly. "Because that would be a most unfortunate development. It would force me to withdraw all financial support from your picture, for obvious reasons."

"You are wrong, Arnold," she choked, her hand gripping the receiver so tightly that her wrist began to ache. "Believe me, you're wrong."

"I'm glad to hear that," he said, now sounding quite

cheerful. "So we understand each other then, don't we? You'll get in touch with Mike Sobel and convince him to come in as co-producer, we'll make ourselves a fine Oscar-winning picture, and everybody will be happy. May I suggest you drive out to his ranch to discuss this with him, instead of calling him on the phone? It's so easy to turn someone down over the phone, but if you show up on his doorstep he'll have to talk to you. He's much too much of a gentleman to close the door in your face."

"*What?*" she gasped when she was finally able to find her voice. "Arnold, I don't even know the man. How in the world can you possibly expect me to talk him into doing the picture when your own investors couldn't manage it? I'm the *last* person in the world he'd listen to!"

"For your sake, I hope that isn't true," he remarked quietly. "Because you either get Mike Sobel or lose the picture." There was a click, then a faint, empty buzz.

"Oh shit! Oh shit, why does it always have to be this way? Why can't I be free to make pictures like everybody else?"

"Are you okay?" Nancy asked nervously when she walked into the office and saw Erin slumped over the desk, staring dismally into space.

"No, I'm *not* okay!" she screamed in sudden rage as she looked up at her secretary. "I'm absolutely rotten! Any more questions?"

"Sorry I asked." Nancy started to back out of the office.

"Hey, forget it. It's not your fault."

Nancy paused, a frown on her face. "Is there anything I can do to help?"

"I guess so." Erin sighed. "I need the home address of Mike Sobel. That ranch. And you'd better get me a road map along with it, because I understand it's a million miles out in the boondocks."

"Are you serious?" Nancy asked incredulously.

"Unfortunately, I am."

"Well . . ."

"No, Nancy, don't ask me any questions. Just get me the information." Erin swiveled around in her desk chair and stared at the blank wall behind her, leaving her secretary standing there.

When it became obvious that Erin wasn't going to say anything else, Nancy walked out of the office and began calling her contacts. It took an hour to find out Mike Sobel's home address. The road map was easier. It was a standard California Auto Club map, detailing little known access roads leading into the ranch spreads of the original San Fernando Valley settlers. Most of those original settlers and their families had long since disappeared, but the roads remained the same.

The huge brass door knocker that still bore the marks of the artisan who had hammered it into shape made echoes throughout the old Spanish ranch house as Erin lifted it by the handle and then let it fall against the massive oak door.

Mike Sobel opened the door and gazed in surprise at the slim young woman with the luminous green eyes who stood there smiling uncertainly at him.

"May I help you?" he inquired politely.

"Mr. Sobel, I'm Erin Connolly, and I'd very much like to talk to you."

The pleasant expression on his face vanished abruptly as he recognized her. "I'm afraid we have nothing to talk about, Miss Connolly," he announced with cold formality. "I have no interest in working as a co-producer on your picture, and I assure you there's nothing you could say that would change my mind. Now, if you'll excuse me, I'm rather busy."

"Please, would it be all right if I just came in for a moment?" Erin swayed, then reached out for the door jamb to steady herself. "It was a terribly hot, long drive up here, and I'm not feeling . . . quite well."

"Good Lord, of course!" Concern momentarily darkening his clear blue eyes, he put his arm around her shoulders and quickly led her inside. "Here, sit down and let me get you something. Lemonade? I just made a fresh pitcher."

"No, a glass of water would be fine," she said faintly. "You're most kind."

As he hurried off to the kitchen, Erin curled up on the long, low, comfortable couch, reached inside her purse for a cigarette, decided that was the wrong image and instead let her head fall wearily back against the cushions.

"Now drink it slowly," he ordered as he came back into the living room and handed her the glass.

"Tastes marvelous," she murmured, sipping it as he'd instructed.

"Genuine well water." He grinned at her, an engaging grin that gave his thin, angular face a puckish charm. "Can't get that in Los Angeles."

"Seems like I can't get anything in Los Angeles," she said ruefully. "Maybe you had the right idea moving out here."

The friendly grin disappeared as his eyes thoughtfully surveyed her. "That's the way life works, Miss Connolly. You give up some things to get other things. For me, it was this ranch and a certain way of living. But somehow I don't get the feeling that you'd give up the Los Angeles life-style even if you were guaranteed all the fresh well water in the world."

"Somehow I have the feeling you're right," she admitted with a reluctant smile, realizing that it was going to be impossible to con this man.

She sat up and lit a cigarette, staring at him through the smoke. "I want you on this picture very much, Mike Sobel, and I'd appreciate it if you'd tell me why you're refusing. It's your kind of picture, a fine, quality film. Everyone agrees it could well be the next Academy Award winner.

"So is it just ego that's making you turn it down?" she challenged him. "Because you'd only be a co-producer and have to share the glory with someone else?"

He laughed with undisguised amusement. "That's quite a speech coming from you, Miss Connolly." His eyes narrowed and he gazed at her speculatively. "But since you've brought up the subject, I confess to a certain amount of curiosity. Why do *you* want me on this picture? It seems to me that if anyone would object to the thought of co-producing, it would be you. Especially since this was your project from the beginning."

"That's true," she said calmly. "Personally, I don't want a co-producer. Personally, I hate the very thought of it."

He blinked in surprise, clearly taken aback by the frank statement. "Then why in the world . . ."

"Because I don't have any choice. The investors insist on a co-producer before they'll put up any money. And it can't be just any co-producer. It has to be you. Those are their terms, and they won't budge."

She leaned forward, her eyes fixed entreatingly on him. "This picture is my last chance. If I lose it, I lose everything. So please, please won't you reconsider? Believe me, I wouldn't dream of asking you if I thought it would compromise your standards in any way. But surely you can see that isn't the case here. We're talking about a film anybody would be proud to produce. A film that would do credit even to your distinguished career. And I promise I'll give you a free hand in directing it. I'll never get in your way."

"Look, Miss Connolly, I wish I could help you." He stopped and shrugged uncomfortably. "But the fact is I have a number of commitments now, and I simply don't have the time available to get involved in a new picture."

"Then forget about the directing. I'm sure the Marchison brothers will agree to getting another director. All they want is your name as co-producer. So this way you won't have to spend any time at all on the production. You can just come in on the set when you want and I'll handle everything else."

He looked at her quizzically. "Maybe the Marchison brothers would agree to that, but do you really believe I would?"

"No," she said miserably, bowing her head. "You're the kind of stubborn son-of-a-bitch who'd insist on supervising every single step of the picture."

He chuckled in spite of himself. "Well, apparently you know more about me than I realized. So you also must know that the whole thing is impossible."

"Would you do me one favor? Would you read the screenplay before you say no?"

"I'm sorry," he replied gently. "I'm afraid I can't do that."

"Then will you do me this favor?" She stood up, collected her purse, and walked toward him, her hand resting for a moment on his arm. "Will you please not say no today? Will you let me walk out of your house without having to hear that?"

"Why?" He regarded her with genuine puzzlement. "It's not going to change anything."

"If I told you it would make it easier for me to leave, would that be a good enough reason?"

Embarrassed by her intensity, he nodded. "All right, Miss Connolly. But the answer will still be the same tomorrow as it is today," he warned her as he walked her to the door.

"Well, I'll deal with that tomorrow."

There was no doubt in Erin's mind as she drove away from the big old Spanish ranch house that Mike Sobel meant what he'd said. He was not going to do the picture.

If only I could get him to read the screenplay, she thought despairingly. It was truly a superb script. She couldn't imagine any director turning it down once he'd seen it. But how was she to get him to see it? He'd been polite but absolutely firm in refusing to look at it, and she could hardly stand over him with a gun and force him to read it.

What if she sent it up to his house tonight by special messenger with a pleading note attached? Erin shook her head. No, that sort of trick wouldn't work with Mike Sobel. He'd simply return it unopened. Then, just as she was about to give up hopelessly on the whole thing, the idea came to her.

It was shortly after eight that evening when Mike opened the door of his house in response to the heavy knock, and gazed in disbelief at the tall, impressive figure standing there.

"Oh my God, not you too!" he groaned. "What is this? A conspiracy?"

Keith Ramsey gave him a faint, apologetic smile. "Sorry, old buddy. But you know how it goes. They always send in the marines when everything else has failed."

"Jesus Christ!" Mike muttered feelingly. "And I didn't even know I was in a war."

"It's a very friendly war," Keith assured him with a grin. "Even though you don't know it, we're both on the same side."

"Yeah? You couldn't prove it by me."

"So how about giving me a chance?"

"Okay. You can come in and do your number as long as you promise to leave me in peace once you're finished."

"Would I leave any other way?" he protested, laughing. "A peace-loving fella like myself?"

"Very funny," Mike replied sourly. "All right, let's go. What's *your* pitch?"

"This." Keith walked into the living room, laid the screenplay down on the coffee table, and opened it to a well-creased page. "Just read, my friend. Just read."

Reluctantly, Mike approached the script and looked down at it. The words leaped out at him, and he bent closer. Then, without conscious volition, he turned the page. An hour later he was still reading.

Mike Sobel and Erin Connolly circled warily around each other during the first few weeks of production on *Secret Rites*. It was at best an armed truce, their relationship limited to short, clipped, impersonal discussions about budgets and shooting schedules, set designs and location sites. But by the second month Erin's guarded hostility toward the man who had been forced on her as a co-producer began to relax. And by the third month it had disappeared completely. Because Mike Sobel was just as good as his reputation, and she found herself excited and stimulated by his genius. For his part, Mike was genuinely impressed with Erin's crisply competent professionalism and fierce, hard-working dedication to quality.

They soon got into the habit of going out for dinner together after the daily rushes, and one night Mike didn't leave Erin's apartment after he took her home.

They were both a little stunned by the incredible chemistry that leaped between them in that first lovemaking, and they both wore similarly dazed expressions when they showed up on the set the next day. Which didn't escape the sharp eyes of the cast and crew, who guessed immediately what had happened. There was a lot of sly kidding around the set that day, but it was basically good-natured. Everybody respected Erin and Mike as top-flight professionals, and they couldn't have been more pleased that the feud between them had been settled in such a rewarding way.

As it turned out, they had every right to be pleased, for the picture flourished right along with Erin's and Mike's love affair. Even the most difficult scenes went smoothly. Cameras and lights worked perfectly. Nobody forgot lines, stepped on the wrong marks, or tripped over cables. And everyone involved in the production looked forward each morning to coming to work. It was that rarity, a "happy set."

Secret Rites came in under budget, finished shooting a full two weeks ahead of schedule, and showed such brilliant clarity and power even in rough cut that the cast and crew were already congratulating each other on an Oscar winner.

"I think we deserve a little time off for a private celebration," Mike told Erin as they left the jubilant wrap party. "I've already postponed final editing until next week. Hope you don't mind."

"Well." She grinned at him mischievously. "That depends on whether or not you're going to make me an offer I can't refuse."

"How about coming with me to paradise? A beautiful place with fields of flowers and sparkling mountain streams, warm golden days, and star-filled nights. The ones from the sky, not Hollywood."

"I think I just got that offer I can't refuse," she said a little breathlessly. "Do you really know a place like that?"

"Just pack your bags, lady, and I'll show you."

They left Los Angeles early the next morning and arrived in the glorious wine country of California, located just north of San Francisco, shortly after dusk. Mike had booked a room for them in a charming, rustic inn situated in the center of the lush Napa Valley vineyards. Erin fell in love with it immediately.

"Everything smells so clean and fresh!" she exclaimed.

"That's because it is. Now go out on the balcony, take a deep breath, and look around. It might even convert you permanently to the natural life."

By the third day of their stay, Erin was coming close to being converted. Everything was just the way Mike had promised it would be. Their mornings and afternoons were spent in explorations of the idyllic countryside, and their nights were filled with slow, sweet lovemaking. On their last evening they had a quiet dinner at the inn, eating by the glow of slender tapers and drinking an exquisite chardonnay produced by a fine local winery. They were so obviously in love that everyone in the room smiled on them.

After dinner they went into the lounge, where Erin curled up in a dark leather chair and slipped off her shoes. Mike moved his chair closer to her, reaching over and caressing one slender foot as they gazed into the cracking flames in the fireplace. They had Courvoisier in large crystal brandy snifters, and kissed between sips. When the flames finally died down and the logs had settled with a comfortable groan into embers, Mike gently pulled her to her feet and handed her the shoes she'd tucked under her chair. Then they walked outside-and strolled along the path that led from the main building of the inn to their snug little cottage. The moon was very bright, and there was no sound at all except for the whisper of their feet on the fragrant pine needles.

Once inside their room Erin unzipped her dress and carelessly tossed it into the closet, then smiled as she climbed into bed and watched Mike undress. He was so neat and careful, she loved observing him. First he removed his jacket, making sure it was perfectly aligned as he hung it on the clothes hanger. Then came the shirt and tie. A brief pause to light a cigarette before taking off the shoes and pants. As always, he brought the cigarette over to her at that time.

There were two puffs left when he slid into bed next to her. They finished it together, then he turned out the light and pulled her close to him. They fell asleep in the middle of a kiss.

The phone woke them the next morning. The voice on the other end informed them they had only thirty minutes left to make breakfast before the dining room closed, and then apologetically reminded them that check-out time was noon.

"Well, I guess it's time to pack up and leave," Mike told her with a regretful smile as he hung up.

"I wish we didn't have to," Erin said sadly. "It's been so special here."

"Hey, honey, don't look so unhappy," he protested, leaning over to give her a hug. "Don't you know we have lots and lots of special times ahead of us?"

● ● ●

The message from Arnold Scorsi was waiting for Erin when she walked into her office the following morning.

"Did he say what he wanted?" she asked Nancy, puzzled.

"Just that it was important, and you should call him the minute you came in."

"Strange." Erin shook her head, frowning, then shrugged. "Oh well, I guess there's only one way to find out." She picked up the phone and dialed his number.

"We have to talk," Arnold announced preemptorily as he came on the line. "Can you come over to my office now?"

"Now?" she repeated, stunned. "You mean right this very minute?"

"Yes, that's what I mean."

"But, but why? What's happened?"

"We'll discuss it when you get here." He hung up.

As Erin drove the short distance to Arnold Scorsi's office in Century City, she kept telling herself there was nothing to worry about. How could there be, when everything had gone so well? The Marchison brothers had received more than they could possibly have dreamed of in their first motion picture venture, and they should be among the happiest investors in the world at this moment.

But despite her efforts to reassure herself she had absolutely nothing to be concerned about, Erin found her throat dry and her hands clammy with fear as she stepped off the elevator and opened the door that led into Arnold's coldly elegant reception room.

Arnold came out from his inner office a bare three seconds after she'd shakily given her name to the plain, middle-aged receptionist.

"You made excellent time," he said approvingly. "Come in, Erin."

She followed him jumping nervously as he closed the door behind him with a resounding thunk.

"Good heavens, my dear, you seem a bit on edge," he observed with a faint smile. "That surprises me. I thought you'd just returned from a most relaxing vacation."

"Please, Arnold," she said tensely, clutching her purse to her. "Please tell me what this is all about."

"Right to the point as always," he nodded as he walked

behind the desk and sat down, leaning back in his chair and regarding her thoughtfully. "Unfortunately, we're facing a rather unpleasant problem with our picture. It appears our esteemed co-producer, Mike Sobel, has embezzled a million dollars from the production company, which he has turned over to Richard Longworth's presidential campaign in return for certain favors to be granted once Longworth comes into power. As you know, the election is only two weeks away. The story will appear in tomorrow's papers."

"Have you lost your mind, Arnold?" Erin exclaimed incredulously. "That's the most insane thing I've ever heard! Mike Sobel wouldn't steal a penny from anybody, and I can assure you he hasn't touched any of the production company's funds, because I've personally handled all the disbursements.

"Who is this idiot anyway, that's planting this ridiculous story?" she demanded in sudden fury. "Just give me his name, and I'll take care of him!"

"It's not a him," Arnold said softly. "It's a her. And the name is Erin Connolly."

"Oh no," she whispered, sinking into the chair opposite him. "Oh no, Arnold. I beg you, don't do this to me."

"It's really a very simple matter," he smiled. "All the details have already been taken care of. You won't be involved in any way. Just follow my instructions and you'll have your Oscar-winning picture all to yourself."

"You don't understand," she said desperately. "I don't care any longer about having it to myself. I love Mike Sobel. I *want* to share it with him. I want to share my whole life with him!"

"Well that's too bad, because I'm afraid you'll find that a little difficult to accomplish after you break this story. However, you mustn't brood about it. I'm confident you'll get over it and go on to someone else. After all, you always have. That's one of the things I admire most about you, Erin. The way you put the past behind you and go on to new ventures unburdened by any regrets."

"I'm not going to do this for you, Arnold," she said grimly. "If you want to destroy Richard Longworth, that's your business. I don't want to know anything about it, and I promise you I'll never say anything about it. But I'm not going to let you use Mike Sobel to accomplish it, and there's no way you can force me to!"

"Do you really believe that?" he asked mildly.

"I not only believe it, I know it!" she replied fiercely. "And you know it too. Every penny of that ten million dollars the Marchison brothers invested in *Secret Rites* is fully accounted for, and I will be more than happy to allow a public auditing of our books. There's no way in the world you can prove Mike Sobel siphoned off a million dollars of it unless I agree to fix those books. And I am *not* going to fix those books. I flatly, totally refuse!"

She stood up. "Good bye, Arnold."

"You really disappoint me, my dear," he said quietly. "How could you possibly imagine I would leave such an important matter up to the vagaries of your emotions? I thought you knew me better than that."

She had already started to march out of his office. At his words she froze awkwardly in mid-step, then turned back and looked at him, swallowing hard to get rid of the lump of terror in her throat.

"Don't try to bluff me, Arnold. I won't buy it."

"I never bluff," he replied coldly. "That's something else I thought you knew."

He swiveled slowly in the big, leather chair, idly contemplating his templed fingers. "The fact of the matter is that the Marchison brothers didn't invest ten million dollars in your picture. They invested eleven million dollars." He looked up at her. "So even you can see that leaves one million unaccounted for."

"That's impossible!" she cried. "My records clearly show ten million dollars is all they invested."

"Really?" he murmured. "Then I wonder why the Marchisons' corporate records clearly show that eleven million dollars was paid to Con-Well Productions. To say nothing of a contract signed by you acknowledging a loan from them in that amount?"

"I don't care what your phony documents say, Arnold," she declared, white-faced. "You'll never get away with this, because no one in this town will ever believe Mike Sobel embezzled that money. Especially when I swear he never had access to the company's funds."

"You have an interesting point there, Erin. I wouldn't be surprised if you were right."

He tilted forward in his chair, startling her with a sudden, cheerful smile. "So it looks like you're worrying needlessly about this whole thing, doesn't it? The odds are good that Mike Sobel will be acquitted by the jury when he comes to trial. At the very worst, he'll be sentenced to a few short years, and even that sentence will probably be suspended. In no time at all he'll be back in Hollywood, making bigger and better pictures than ever, and the whole unpleasant matter will have been buried and forgotten.

"Of course it wouldn't work quite that way in your case," he added softly, his eyes narrowing as he studied her.

"What?" she said bewilderedly.

"The embezzlement charge, my dear. You see, there *is* a deficit of a million dollars, and naturally it causes the Marchison brothers considerable anxiety.

"Now suppose *you* should be the one charged with that embezzlement?" he inquired politely. "After all, if it isn't Mike Sobel, it has to be you. Those are the only two choices available. And somehow I don't think this town would find it too difficult to believe you'd embezzle funds. Actually, I believe you'd be tried and found guilty. You might serve as long as ten years in prison. Even if you should get off with a lighter sentence, it seems highly unlikely that you'll ever be allowed to make another picture.

"Well, the choice is yours," he concluded quietly. "What's your answer?"

Her entire life since she'd been three years old had been spent fighting for survival, no matter the cost. And so now there was only one answer Erin Connolly was capable of giving.

The story broke in newspapers across the country the next day, and Mike Sobel was indicted on charges of grand larceny.

Twenty - eight

GIANT searchlights stabbed at the sky as the long line of gleaming black limousines glided up to the entrance of the Dorothy Chandler Pavilion and let off their distinguished passengers, who emerged with uniformly smiling faces that concealed the desperate hopes and even more desperate fears that raged inside them on this most important of all nights, the Academy Awards presentations.

Gary Morrison, a popular local TV talk show host, bounded forward eagerly each time another limousine pulled up, a camera crew hot on his heels as he thrust his microphone into the faces of the arriving celebrities with such force they barely refrained from cringing back in sheer self-defense.

"And here's Keith Ramsey!" he panted deliriously as the tall, commanding figure stepped out of a limousine, then turned around and gently held out his hand for the small, shy middle-aged woman with gray-streaked hair who had been his wife for twenty-five years.

"Well, what do you think, Mr. Ramsey?" Gary cried. "They're saying you've got it locked up for Best Actor. You feel that way too?"

"I feel I'm going to have to wait, just like everybody else, to find out," he smiled politely.

"But what about the scandal?" Gary's voice dropped to a conspiratorial whisper. "You think that could affect your chances?"

Keith Ramsey's expression turned suddenly cold. "Actually, what I think is that you exhibit extremely bad taste, Mr. Morrison. Now, if you'll excuse me." He took hold of his wife's hand and curtly walked away.

"Well," Gary babbled, embarrassed. "There we have a very loyal man. Now let's see who else . . . oh wait a minute!" he shouted happily. "Here's someone we really want to talk to. It's Erin Connolly herself, the controversial producer of *Secret Rites*."

With the camera crew racing after him, Gary rushed up to the next limousine as Erin stepped out. "Miss Connolly, I must say we've all been waiting rather breathlessly for your arrival," he announced, shoving the microphone at her. "Keith Ramsey has already told us that the scandal won't affect the picture's chances of winning. What do you say?"

"In my opinion, Gary, the only scandal will be if Keith Ramsey doesn't win," she informed him with a pleasant smile. "Because he certainly deserves to, don't you think?" And with that she walked quickly away, leaving him with his mouth open and a slightly foolish expression on his face.

But Erin's smile faded as she entered the lobby of the Dorothy Chandler Pavilion, and her hands clenched involuntarily as she felt the sharp cramping pain in her stomach that occurred every time someone mentioned the embezzlement.

Put it out of your mind, she told herself fiercely. Forget it, and concentrate on what's ahead of you tonight. Your picture's been nominated for six Academy Awards. Just think about that, and nothing else.

The immense theater was filled almost to capacity as Erin walked inside. Voices rose and fell in short, explosive bursts of nervous energy, occasionally punctuated by shouts of laughter; a myriad of lights cast a soft glow over the luxurious pelts of several thousand sacrificial minks, and then sparkled brilliantly as they caught the reflections from a million dollars worth of diamonds; frantic television crews rushed up and down in response to the barked commands from their directors;

and the air was almost oppressively sweet with the mingled scents of several dozen expensive perfumes.

As Erin made her way down the long, red-carpeted aisle toward the front of the theater where her reserved seat was located, people stopped abruptly in the midst of their conversations to stare at her. No one called out a greeting. Head held high, looking straight ahead and ignoring the buzz of comments as she passed, Erin refused to give them the satisfaction of breaking and running. She walked slowly, with dignity and pride. Tears blurred her eyes, though, when she finally reached her seat and looked over at the empty place next to her. The place where Mike Sobel should have been.

As usual, the ceremonies started with the presentations of relatively minor awards. First came Special Effects, followed by Best Sound Score, Best Feature-Length Documentary, Best Short Subjects in a Documentary Film, and Best Achievement in Sound. The presentations halted briefly before the awarding of the Irving Thalberg Lifetime Achievement Award to give the millions of television viewers at home a little entertainment.

"Oh God, enough already!" Erin moaned as she watched the chorus line of Hollywood's current hit musical dance out on the stage, and then looked at her watch. Two hours had passed since she'd sat down and nervously clutched at the arms of her chair, waiting for her verdict. Two hours that seemed like a lifetime.

But finally, as the chorus line finished its number and danced off the stage to enthusiastic applause, the real Academy Awards began.

Erin bowed her head as the names of the nominees for Outstanding Achievement in Directing were read off. Mike Sobel had requested that his name be withdrawn after his indictment, and the academy had honored his request. Now Leon Aronson, a talented young director with a wild mop of black curly hair and a reputation for exuberant risk-taking, seemed curiously subdued as he stepped up to accept his award. The audience stirred expectantly as he fingered the Oscar placed in his hands and looked out at them. But the moment of potential drama passed as he simply muttered his thanks and walked away.

The next award was for Best Screenplay adapted from another work, and Sheldon Avery won it. His wrinkled pixy face beamed out at the audience as he gushed his thanks to Keith Ramsey for making this possible. No one missed the fact that he refrained from making any mention at all of the producer of the picture.

There was a hush in the audience when the nominees for Best Actor were announced, then a wild screaming as the envelope was opened and the presenter cried out, "Keith Ramsey!"

Erin leaped up along with everyone else, clapping delightedly as she moved toward the distinguished actor who was just now getting to his feet. He turned around as she approached, his face a mask of icy contempt. Her cheeks burning in humiliation, she stumbled back and allowed him to cross in front of her as he made his way up to the stage.

"And now it's time for that big one," the emcee said, "the one everyone here tonight has been waiting for—Best Picture." He glanced over at the two famous movie personalities who'd just appeared on the stage. "Are we ready?"

"We're ready," they smiled back.

Erin swallowed hard as they read off the names of the nominated pictures, and the TV monitors flashed scenes from each of the films.

"And the winner is . . ." The presenter was overcome by a sudden coughing fit, and Erin stared at the palms of her hands where tiny flecks of blood had appeared as she'd dug her fingernails into them.

"And the winner is *Secret Rites!*" he shouted. "A Con-Well Productions production. Producer, Erin Connolly. Co-producer . . ." He broke off awkwardly. "Erin Connolly, producer," he finished lamely.

For one brief awful moment there was no sound at all in the huge theater. Then someone started to clap, others joined in raggedly, and soon there was a respectable if not overwhelming level of applause.

Erin jumped up with a wild cry, ran onto the stage, and

clutched the Oscar to her with both hands. "I want to thank . . ." she began, flushed and breathless. Her eyes traveled over the faces of the crowd, then came to rest on the empty seat next to hers in the theater row. Except it wasn't empty! Blinking in disbelief, she found herself looking at Andi Steiner.

"I got it, kid!" Andi announced, her face delirious with joy. "Production assistant to Leland Devereaux!" Then the joyful face suddenly contorted into raging hatred. "Bitch! Filthy, lying, cheating bitch! You stole it from me! The one thing I wanted more than anything else in the world. And I trusted you. I trusted you so much."

"My God, I must be losing my mind," Erin muttered to herself. She blinked again, and Andi disappeared. Nervously she cleared her throat. "I want to thank . . ." she repeated.

But once more her eyes were inexorably drawn back to that empty seat. And now it was James Lee sitting there, smiling at her. "All right," he said softly. "All right, Erin, if you want to be a producer that much, I'll find a way to help you."

His features blurred, dissolved, and it was Anthony Wellington looking up at her, his gentle homely face alight with excitement. "If you could have anything in the world you wanted for your birthday, what would it be? How about a studio? I built it for you, darling! Con-Well Productions now has its very own studio! Hurry and get dressed, darling. I'm so eager for you to see it."

Oh please, Anthony, she begged silently. Please go away.

Obedient even in fantasy life, he promptly vanished, and Lynn Powers took his place. "Well, here he is!" she announced with breathless pride. "The most exciting new director to hit Hollywood in over a decade. Garth darling, meet Erin Connolly, the best friend I've ever had in my whole life."

Erin felt a sharp stab of pain as she gazed at the lean handsome man with the crisp black hair and intense blue eyes that blazed out of his face like a beacon. "I loved you so much," she said forlornly. "Why did you leave? Why didn't you give me a chance to make it up to you? I would have, Garth. I swear I would have!"

It was almost as though he were rejecting her again, for at

her words he abruptly disappeared and it was David sitting there, staring at her with dark, troubled eyes.

"Don't cry," David said softly. "I'll take on Johnny Ryan's campaign. I'll do it for you. I'll do anything for you." He leaned forward as though he were about to tell her something confidential. But then she saw he wasn't leaning, he was falling. And there was blood everywhere, pouring out of him and flooding the seat, spilling onto the floor.

Stop! she screamed silently. *Stop it*! *Stop it*! She closed her eyes to blot out the terrible scene.

When she opened them, he was gone and so was the blood. And she saw with heart-pounding relief that it was Mike sitting there. It had been Mike all along, she thought wonderingly. The rest had all been some strange, twisted figment of her imagination.

He looked so good, so normal, she almost wept with happiness. He sprawled comfortably in the seat, the way he always did, one arm draped across the back of her chair and a faint, quizzical grin on his face as he looked at her. But there was something wrong, she thought puzzledly. His clothes, that was it! He was wearing the same sports jacket he'd worn at their last dinner in that charming rustic inn in Napa Valley where they'd gone for their vacation, while every other man in the theater was formally dressed in a tux.

Well of course he wouldn't be wearing a tux, she scolded herself. He'd never owned one, and as he'd told her on numerous occasions, he never planned to. So obviously he'd had no time to rent one when he'd been suddenly released to attend tonight's ceremonies. But why hadn't he called her to tell her that he was free and all the trouble was over?

Because, naturally, he wanted to surprise her, she acknowledged with a happy smile. And what a wonderful surprise it would be for everyone in the audience.

She raised her hand and waved at him, then bent over the microphone to announce the marvelous news that the brilliant co-producer of *Secret Rites* was here, in person, to accept his well-deserved award.

But just as she started to mentally rehearse her speech, the one that would give all the credit to him, he disappeared as abruptly as all the others. The seat was empty, as empty as it had been when she'd walked into the theater over two hours ago. There was no one beside her at all. She was alone, as she'd always been.

Erin looked down at the small statuette still clutched in her hand. It was as cold and leaden as the feeling in her heart as she realized, too late, that she'd given up everything to get . . . nothing.

Carefully, she set it down on the podium. Then, as the audience gasped in astonishment, she turned around and walked off the stage.

About the Author

Jodie Rhodes grew up in Detroit, Michigan. She graduated from Ohio Wesleyan University with a B.A. in English, and went on to graduate studies in English at Ohio State University. She began her advertising career in a small Columbus, Ohio, agency, and later migrated to California where she worked with several major agencies in San Francisco and Los Angeles.

At the age of forty, Ms. Rhodes took a two-year sabbatical to see if she could really write a book. *American Beauties*, her first book, was published in 1980. Ms. Rhodes now resides in Malibu, California, where she is working on another book.